MW01592929

MURDER AND HORROR IN THE HAUNTED JERSEY PINE BARRENS SEND A YOUNG SCHOLAR ON A DEADLY QUEST TO DISCOVER AN UGLY TRUTH.

Archaeology Professor Rebecca Glass is murdered hours before delivering a paper proving that a fire that killed eight Cloistered nuns in the nearly uninhabited New Jersey Pine Barrens was purposely set. But the proof — and the paper — are missing.

His university assigns Assistant Professor of English Dominic Rossi the task of locating the missing paper. Unbeknownst to him, its grisly revelations would be devastating to a network of powerful people who are determined to stop him — at all costs.

"Well plotted and deftly paced, *A Darkness in the Pines* blends mystery and suspense with a rich academic environment that keeps the reader fully involved throughout. Excellent fiction."— *John Vance, author of Awake the Southern Wind, (forthcoming), Echoes of November, Death by Mournful Numbers, and Convergences.*

i

"Mr. Luce expertly explores greed, arrogance, and family dynamics — and pathologies — using exciting storytelling as his vehicle. A gem."—*Dr. Pat Pope, Clinical Psychologist.*

What connection does the brutal murder of Rebecca Glass, an archaeologist from Mount St. Benedict University have with a fire decades ago that killed a dozen nuns in the remote New Jersey Pine Barrens? Dominic Rossi a young English professor at the university who shared an office with the dead woman is surprised when the college provost concerned about the reputation of the college asks him to investigate the murder. Rossi quickly learns no one is quite who or what they seem to be as he navigates a web of deceit and danger to find the answer. Before he finishes the investigation, he suddenly realizes the truth has put his own life in jeopardy. The characters are engaging, the dialogue flows and the action moves. Hank Luce has crafted a complex, well-written mystery with enough twists and turns to keep you guessing and turning the pages.—*Preston Holtry, author of the Morgan Westphal mystery series.*

A DARKNESS IN THE PINES

HANK LUCE

Moonshine Cove Publishing, LLC
Abbeville, South Carolina U.S.A.

FIRST MOONSHINE COVE EDITION DECEMBER 2016

ISBN: 978-1-945181-03-0
Library of Congress PCN: 2016919337

iii

About The Author

Hank Luce has had a successful career in global pharmaceutical advertising as a copywriter, creative director, and creative strategist. He has undergraduate and graduate degrees in English and taught on the college and university level for a number of years earlier in his career. His published work embraces both non-fiction and fiction and has appeared in academic journals and general interest magazines.

Hank's first novel, *Crown of Thorns,* was published in 2011 by Salvo Press. Midwest Book Review called it "A must read for fans of religious thrillers." It was recently published in Brazil where Jornal O Tempo said it, "Combines skill and knowledge to create a powerful and deeply engaging thriller."

His second novel, *Brainways*, was published in 2013 by Moonshine Cove Publishing. The *Star Ledger*, New Jersey's most widely circulated and influential newspaper, said, "It's a thriller and a mystery. History and philosophy are deftly woven into a love story. Above all, it's captivating...intellectually demanding and frightening."

Hank's most recent novel, *Secret of the Nightingale Madonna*, also from Moonshine Cove, was published in 2015. The *Star Ledger* wrote, "A stunning work of fiction, it expertly melds intrigue, backstabbing, art and church history, feminism and journalism. The most important label of this book is that it is profound."

A Vietnam veteran, Hank served in the infantry with the 82nd Airborne Division, the 1st Infantry Division and the 101st Airborne Division. Hank and his wife, Karen, live in Flanders, NJ. They have two sons.

http://www.amazon.com/Hank-Luce/e/B00N7JTKB6

For Paul and Stephen, who inspire my stories — and always, always for Karen, who inspires my life.

Author's Note

This is a work of fiction. While readers familiar with New Jersey will recognize a number of actual places, establishments and locales, the incidents, characters, and events associated with these places, establishments and locales are strictly fictional and intended solely to advance and enhance the verisimilitude of the story.

ACKNOWLEDGMENT

Much of the inspiration, as well as the information, for this story derived from John McPhee's wonderful book, *The Pine Barrens.* In addition to my own firsthand explorations of the area, I visited a number of very helpful websites; included among them were pineypower.com, njpinebarrens.com, and pinelandsalliance.com.

A special note of thanks goes to canoeist/kayaker extraordinaire Ron Phillips for sharing with me his insights and expertise related to traveling the fascinating and always intriguing Pine Barrens' rivers. For those readers interested in exploring the rivers for themselves, Micks Canoe and Kayak Rentals in Chatsworth is a great place to start.

Finally, my thanks to Gene Robinson and his wonderful team at Moonshine Cove Publishing. You guys are the best.

"Vision is the art of seeing what is invisible to others."

—Jonathan Swift

A DARKNESS IN THE PINES

Prologue
Somewhere in the New Jersey Pine Barrens
June, 1958

Darkness, stillness, and silence filled the old house, a house that had never known plumbing, or electricity or heating, not in one hundred years. It was a cold, forbidding and hateful place, deserving of its fate, as were the bitch devils that inhabited it.

It had to be now, while her tormentors slept, while they were vulnerable — as she had been vulnerable, for five painful, brutal months. But tonight it would end. She would take her sweet, beautiful bundle — beautiful but for the mark on her cheek — and escape into the night. Then she would deliver her sweet bundle into a new life.

She left her cold sterile space in the rear of the house and walked silently down the long narrow hall to what they called "the infirmary," for they could not bring themselves to say what it really was — a charnel house. She saw a faint light spilling out from under the door then quietly opened it. As she hoped, the one guardian was asleep at her table. The carpenter's hammer that she stole and now carried seemed so heavy at first. Now it felt light, it felt perfect.

She smashed the skull of the sleeping bitch devil then smashed it again. She dropped the hammer and quickly hurried to the small crib with its filthy stained sheets and picked up her bundle. She wrapped her bundle in the cleanest cloth she could find then fastened the cloth with the silver brooch she stole from the man who'd done this to her — the brooch designed like a horse with a horn in front of a castle.

Then she took the kerosene lantern from the guardian's table and poured its contents across the floor and lit it. She hurried into the parlor and did the same with the kerosene lamp there, and the kitchen, and the chapel.

Then, her bundle clasped tightly to her chest, she ran out of the now burning house — and into the darkness of the pines.

Leaving her tormentors to burn in the hell they so richly deserved.

Chapter 1
Thursday, May 9, 2015
Long Branch, New Jersey

The annual three-day meeting of the Archaeological Association of New Jersey was being held this year at the Ocean Place Resort and Spa in the popular shore town of Long Branch. Over the years, the meeting had never been known for generating controversy or excitement. Decorum was *de rigueur.* Its members were, after all, scholars. Papers were always delivered, presentations made, and business conducted efficiently and harmoniously. Still, there was always plenty of time left for socializing, networking, and gossiping. This arrangement suited the members perfectly. Once in a while, though, they did enjoy — even hoped for — a good academic dust up.

This hope was the reason for the unusually animated conversation taking place around the busy lobby bar at seven-thirty on the evening before the meeting's final morning session. It was centered on the rumored contents of a paper to be delivered at the concluding presentation.

Entitled, "A Darkness in the Pines," the paper supposedly had something to do with an old legend — and a new discovery — in New Jersey's mysterious Pine Barrens, a vast wilderness area only ninety miles from Manhattan. Attendees knew only that the presenter, Professor Rebecca Glass, Associate Professor of Archaeology at Mount St. Benedict University in Morristown, was a well-known maverick whose work could always be counted upon to raise an eyebrow or two. Leave it to Rebecca to generate some buzz.

Tragically and ironically, it was later learned that as these conversations were taking place, Professor Glass was having her skull bashed in at a remote section of the sand dunes at Seven Presidents Park, one mile to the south.

Earlier that evening, wearing a purple velour warm up suit and sneakers, and having fastened a fanny pack around her waist

13

containing her room key card, smart phone and wallet, Professor Glass had left the beachfront hotel and headed out along the water's edge, jogging south towards her previously scheduled meeting at the park. The early evening air was chilly, the sky beginning to darken and cloud over. In early May, Seven Presidents Park was open from 8:00 a.m. until dusk. There was no charge for admission, but there were also no services. Lifeguards and full use of the facilities would not be available until Memorial Day Weekend. The snack bar and changing pavilion were closed, but visitors were allowed to walk along the beach and among the dunes. At this time of day, the park was virtually deserted.

Professor Glass had reached the tall dunes on the north end of the park when a voice among the dunes said, "I'm over here."

Professor Glass paused then followed a narrow path into the dunes where the meeting evidently would take place. She said to her contact, "Christ, I said be discrete but this is a bit much. Okay, what did they say?"

"They will ensure that you get as many and whatever research grants you request and a promotion to full professor."

"And Father Jack is going along with this?"

"Father Jack has no say in it. It's up to the Board of Trustees and the Provost. Father Jack will have to go along."

"What about the cash?"

"The offer is fifty thousand dollars. In return, you don't reveal anything you've learned. You delete all the potentially damaging details from the presentation and never mention or refer to them in the future. And you turn over to us whatever notes, data, and supportive material you have assembled."

"*Fifty thousand?* I can get ten times that much as an advance on a book about this. Christ, producers will be fighting over the film rights. These fucking people spend more than that on their weekly bar bill!"

"They feel it is a fair and generous offer. Do you accept?"

"No, I don't accept! You have to do better or you are totally fucked. I have the proof! Go tell your buddies what I said. You have one hour."

She turned to go, but her contact said, "Wait."

14

Professor Glass stopped and turned back, saying, "Don't even bother — "

The contact swung a short, heavy lead pipe and viciously hit Professor Glass on the left front part of her skull, above the left eye. She dropped to the sand as if shot. It was immediately apparent that the blow was fatal. But the contact bent over and smashed her again in the head.

"Bitch," the contact said then quickly went through Professor Glass's fanny pack, removing her wallet and smart phone. The contact noticed a slim gold chain around her neck and ripped it off, then removed her watch and a gold bracelet.

After making certain there were no traces, the contact hurried off down the beach, turned away from the water and walked quickly back to Ocean Avenue, got into a car and drove north towards Monmouth Beach. Along the way, the contact threw the pipe, along with the phone, wallet and jewelry into the Navesink River. They would eventually be carried out into the Atlantic.

The contact then made a quick call. "It's done."

The voice on the phone asked, "Were you able to get into her room?"

"No problem. I found the hard copy and the flash drive with the Power Point version on it. I destroyed them. Your asset at the university had already checked her office computer. Everything's clean."

The voice on the other end said, "Good work. There's one other thing. We know what she learned, but we don't know how she learned it. If she found out, others can too. We'll need to trace her research so we can tie up any loose ends."

"Not in my skill set. Is there a plan?"

"Yes. We'll be using a colleague of hers, a young English professor named Rossi. Smart but has no idea what he'll be involved in. I'll keep you in the loop. By the way, good job. I'm proud of you."

"It was my pleasure, as always. We make a good team."

"We always have."

The next morning, after the discovery of Professor Glass's body, a stunned and horrified Archaeological Association cancelled the remainder of its program. At that point, the contents of Professor Glass's presentation didn't seem to matter.

Chapter 2
Friday, May 10
Mount St. Benedict University

"The thing is, Doc, Iago is an asshole, but Othello can't see it. He can't see who's on his side and who's not. So he keeps getting in deeper and deeper until he's totally screwed and everything goes all to hell. It's like Othello brings all that crap down on himself."

Dominic Rossi, newly minted Ph.D. and recent appointee to the tenure track position of Assistant Professor of English at Mount St. Benedict University, smiled at the young African American man and said, above the chuckles coming from the other students, "Well, that's not quite how most Shakespearean scholars phrase it, Dontay. But you're exactly right. In much of Shakespearean tragedy, blindness — not seeing things as they really are — is the great tragic flaw. It's all over the place in *King Lear,* but it's also the case with Othello."

As Dom Rossi headed to the blackboard, Dontay Robinson smiled at the young African American woman seated next to him. "I told you. I'm all over this stuff now." She patted him on the knee.

Dom said, "Okay, in the *Poetics,* Aristotle referred to the tragic flaw as *hamartia* — something in the hero's personality that leads to his destruction. Remember early in the semester when we read Sophocles? We said Oedipus was guilty of *hubris,* overweening pride. That was his tragic flaw. Othello's is similar but slightly different — blindness, as Dontay pointed out. They may be thought of as two sides of the same dramatic coin. But in all tragedy, not seeing things as they really are inevitably turns out to be catastrophic. And it's not just true in literature. It's true in life."

Dom glanced at the wall clock. One minute left. He said to the class. "Okay, guys, that does it for today. Remember, check the English department website for the final exam schedule."

This was met with a degree of grumbling and several good natured 'boos.' He went on, "Next week, I'll spend the first two classes doing a pre-exam review of what we covered during the semester here in World Lit 1 — Antiquity, the Middle Ages, and up to the Renaissance. We'll save the final class of the semester for specific questions or issues you guys want to go over. Your only assignment is to have a good, and safe, weekend."

As Dom was packing up his notes and placing them in his backpack, Dontay and the young African American woman approached his desk.

The young woman said, "Doctor Rossi, while you have a minute, I just want to say thank you for hanging in there and working so much with Dontay. He's all caught up and will graduate right on time. This English course was the one he was most scared of."

Dom smiled. "Sharelle, I think you worked as hard on this as Dontay. He's in great shape going into the final. Keep doing what you're doing and it'll be just fine." Dontay Robinson stood six feet five inches tall and weighed in at two hundred fifty pounds, with practically zero body fat. An All-American Tight End, he'd been timed in the forty-yard dash at 4.40 seconds, usual wide receiver speed.

Dom said, referring to the NFL Draft the following April, "Dontay, I'm predicting late to mid first round. What are you hearing?"

"You may be a bit optimistic, Doc. But once the combines start next February, I think my stock will go up. Sharelle will keep me on the straight and narrow until then. And Coach Pierce has fixed it so I can still work out here. He's hired me to be an assistant to the assistants." He then said, "Say, Doc, did you ever think about declaring for the draft back in the day?"

Dom laughed. "Jeez, Dontay, you make seven years ago sound like the leather helmet days. But no, no one was interested in a five foot ten inch, one hundred seventy pound cover corner. Imagine me trying to tackle a guy like you. Plus, I was looking at a three year Army ROTC obligation."

"Well, Coach Pierce still says you're one of the toughest guys he ever coached. And no one studied more film or got more out of it than you. He said it was your edge. You knew what the receiver would do before the receiver did."

"I always figured it was a kind of survival strategy. Anyway, have a good weekend guys."

As Dom exited the classroom, a man and a woman whom he did not recognize, but who reeked of some sort of official capacity, approached him. The man was stocky and fit and looked to be about fifty. The woman was slender with dark hair and dark eyes and was striking. She was perhaps in her mid-thirties and radiated a compelling intensity.

The man held up a gold detective's badge. "Professor Rossi, I'm Detective Sergeant Mulroney, this is Detective Craig. We're with the Monmouth County Prosecutor's office. Is there somewhere we can talk?"

"I guess my office. It's tight, but my colleague, Professor Glass, is at a conference for a few days, so there will be chairs for all of us."

The School of Humanities and Social Sciences, of which the English Department was part, was located in a large, multi-winged, four floor building known as Trinity Hall. Faculty offices were arranged by academic discipline, and most members of the full-time faculty had their own individual offices. Sometimes, however, office assignments were made according to the ancient academic tradition of reinforcing pecking orders and doling out favors and slights.

As the most junior and most recently appointed full-time faculty member, Dom was low man on the totem pole and ended up sharing an office with a controversial professor in the archaeology department, Rebecca Glass. The office was tiny, remote, and at the end of a long corridor. On the day Dom moved in, Rebecca Glass said, "Welcome to the land of outcasts, misfits, and rebels. You want coffee?"

Dom and the two detectives arrived at Dom's office and the difference between his side of the small room and that occupied by Rebecca Glass was striking. Dom's was neat and orderly; stacks of papers waiting to be graded were piled neatly, and those already marked were stacked on the windowsill. Two bookcases stood behind Dom's desk in which volumes were arranged by subject, then alphabetically by author. His desk held only a

18

laptop, a spotlessly clean coffee mug with the college's logo, and a silver-framed photograph of a lovely young woman.

Rebecca's side was a mess. Her desk was covered by journals, pages of notes, dead plants, a stained, chipped coffee mug and the remains of her mid-morning bagel from three days ago. The bookcase behind her desk was a random collection of archaeology books and journals in no discernible order. On top of it were several more dead plants and a small ebony statue of an African fertility goddess.

Dom slid a chair from Rebecca's side next to the one fronting his desk. Detective Mulroney sat; Detective Craig chose to remain standing. Dom said, "Okay, Detectives, how may I help you?"

Detective Mulroney, looking at the photograph, said, "Pretty girl, Dominic. Who is she?"

"My late fiancée."

A smirking Mulroney asked, "Oh, you mean 'late' like you broke up?"

"No. She passed away two years ago. Ovarian cancer."

"Sorry," Mulroney said, displaying no sincerity. "Tell us, Dominic, what's your relationship with your officemate, Professor Rebecca Glass?"

Dom was startled at the question. "Why do you ask? Is Rebecca okay?"

"Just answer the question, Dominic."

"We're colleagues and casual friends. I've known her just under a year, since I joined the faculty here at Mount St. Ben's. She wasn't a faculty member when I was an undergraduate here, and when I was working on my Ph.D. in English I had no occasion to run into her. We have coffee or a drink together now and then, but our work and interests mostly take us in different directions. Why are you asking?"

Ignoring his question, Detective Craig asked, "Do those different interests clash in any way, Professor?"

"I'm not sure what you mean, Detective Craig. Frankly, if you people would just tell me what you're seeking to learn, perhaps I can be more helpful."

19

Detective Mulroney said, "Let's get back to these different interests. Tell me, Dominic, does it bother you that she's a dyke?"

After a moment, Dom said, "What bothers me, Detective Mulroney, is that she's a Red Sox fan."

Mulroney just sat there, looking at Dom, again with a smirk. He said, "You're kind of young to be a professor, aren't you, Dominic? What are you, in your twenties? You look like a student. You must be pretty smart. How old are you?"

"I'm twenty-eight."

Mulroney went on, "You even had a book published." He referred to his small notebook. "*Patterns and Purpose: Close Reading and the Function of Imagery.* Hell, I bet they're just lining up to buy that one. Tell me, Dominic, does any of this shit you people do here have any relevance at all to real life?"

Dom looked at him directly for a moment. Then he said, "Relevance to real life? Well, two things, Detective. First, close reading and the attention to imagery helps readers, especially scholars, to understand and appreciate literary works in a much deeper way. It gives them richer insights into character, plot, mood, setting, and theme. That's the scholarly part.

"Second, close observation can be very revealing with respect to what you refer to as 'real life.' So let's talk real life. You, Detective Mulroney, affect an aggressive, no nonsense cop demeanor. You purposely come on as a bullying hard ass, and you clearly enjoy it. Your tie is pulled away from your open collar, and you let your suit jacket hang open so I can see your service weapon. You act dismissively towards me, demean my work, and call me by my first name all as a means of intimidation. You are trying to put me on the defensive, so you can control the situation.

"But let's take a closer look. Your tie is silk and very expensive. Your suit probably costs as much as my monthly rent. Your fingernails are professionally manicured and you obviously dye both your mustache and your expensively cut hair. Though not well. Your shoes are Italian. You wear an inordinate amount of jewelry, and your cologne is heavily applied and cloyingly floral.

"All of that indicates excessive vanity and a certain psychological ambivalence, despite the tough guy act. It compromises your credibility as a hard ass, Detective. You might want to tone it down a bit. But that's just a suggestion.

"Detective Craig dresses well but with attention to function and practicality. Her shoes are strictly for comfort. Although, when she shifts her weight from one leg to another it suggests the shoes don't fit that well or she has back issues — probably her back. Her fingernails are raw and bitten quite closely. It is called onychophagia and indicates anxiety or a tendency towards obsessive-compulsive behavior. I suspect other identity issues may be operant as well.

"Detective Craig's hair is cut in a short, casually functional style probably done by a barber rather than a hair stylist. That she eschews make-up suggests that she does not wish to draw attention to the fact that she is remarkably pretty — not something one necessarily wants to emphasize when one is a female detective.

"So, Detectives, my point is that close observation is more than merely academic bullshit. In any case, how else can I help you?"

Detective Craig flushed but remained silent. Detective Mulroney said, "All right, you fucking smartass, Professor Rebecca Glass was found dead this morning, lying in the dunes at Seven Presidents Park down in Long Branch with her skull bashed in."

Dom closed his eyes briefly. "Oh God, oh Rebecca. What the hell happened?"

"Some guy walking his dog came across her body. Well, the dog actually came across her body and the guy called 911. A patrol car unit secured the area and Long Branch PD detectives found her room key card and traced her to the Ocean Place Resort. The assistant manager made the identification. The LBPD also found evidence of what was probably a missing necklace, no watch and no phone or wallet. Then they called us. Preliminary report figures time of death between seven and nine the previous evening. It has all the hallmarks of a mugging, plain and simple. But Detective Craig and I need to make sure.

21

"My question for you, smart guy, has to do with whether there was anything going on in Glass's life that would suggest a motive beyond a run-of-the-mill mugging."

A shaken Dom said, "Not that I know or can imagine."

Detective Craig spoke up. "Professor Rossi, we've been interviewing people on campus — faculty, administrators, students — for about two hours now. We've just come from the office of Professor Martin O'Bannon, who was especially helpful."

Dom was surprised. "Martin O'Bannon in Criminal Justice? I'm surprised he was even aware of Rebecca. Why would you speak with him? Their academic disciplines have nothing to do with each other."

Detective Craig brushed the question aside. "Be that as it may, Professor, we've learned that Professor Glass was a controversial figure — opinionated, combative, and an aggressive feminist. That she was a lesbian, albeit discrete and private, on a Catholic college campus speaks volumes about her alienation."

Dom said, "It also speaks volumes about her honesty and courage."

Mulroney said, "Yeah, sure. Have it your way, Rossi. But what about things like lifestyle shit or enemies, anything like that?"

"Not that I am aware."

Mulroney shrugged and looked at Detective Craig, who handed one of her cards to Dom. "Okay, Professor Rossi. If you think of anything, please let us know."

After they left, Dom sat there for a while looking over at Rebecca's empty chair. Though certainly friends, they had not really shared intimate life experiences or deeply personal thoughts. Although once or twice Rebecca had alluded to her "partner," Diana, and Dom had explained about losing Gina. Rebecca was always helpful and good-natured towards Dom, despite her reputation in the college community as a troublemaker and firebrand.

She was, nevertheless, decidedly quirky and given to offering him odd bits of advice and insights.

Once, when commenting on the general duplicitousness of university administrators, she advised Dom, "Be careful out among them, English."

After returning from faculty meetings, which she usually somehow managed to disrupt, she would say, "Remember, Dom, life is like archaeology — it's not just what you *find*, it's what you *learn*."

And perhaps most cryptic of all, on one occasion in the previous few weeks, during which she seemed preoccupied and furtive, she told him, "Dom, if you ever wonder — I keep my secrets in my heart." Then she laughed heartily and long.

Rebecca's idiosyncrasies aside, what was most important to Dom was the fact that when he was a newcomer to the complex, competitive world of the Mount St. Ben's faculty, Rebecca had been warm and welcoming. He did not know what, but he felt he owed her something.

Chapter 3

Mount St. Benedict University was located in the green, hilly country of northwestern New Jersey, about two miles west of the historic town of Morristown. The campus occupied some four hundred acres among the priciest land values in the state. Originally a Benedictine monastery that later started a small, highly selective prep school, the university had grown over the years into one of the most prestigious co-educational Catholic colleges in the country, on a par with such schools as Boston College, Fordham, Georgetown, and Notre Dame. The school's eight thousand undergraduates and two thousand graduate students were taught by a highly skilled and qualified cadre of professors, eighty percent of whom were laypeople and the remainder clergy.

The current President, just over a year into his tenure, was Monsignor John Whalen, OSB. He had previously been Dean of the Business School at St. Ambrose College in Great Barrington, Massachusetts. His selection had been something of a surprise. Most interested parties had been betting on Felix Delaney, Mount St. Ben's current Provost and Chief Academic Officer. Foremost among them was Delaney himself, who was bitterly disappointed at having been passed over.

President Whalen was charming, gregarious, a terrific PR man and a proven fundraiser. Indeed, it was his stated goal to increase the Mount St. Benedict endowment from $1.6 billion to $2.6 billion during his tenure. He was significantly less interested in faculty and academic matters, which he left to Felix Delaney. It was Delaney's executive assistant who called Dom the following Monday morning.

"Professor Rossi, Provost Delaney wishes to see you on an urgent matter. He's in his office. May I tell the Provost you'll be right there?"

"Certainly, Ms. Conklin."

Ten minutes later, Dom entered Felix Delaney's expansive office.

"Professor Rossi," Delaney said, "I'm sorry to see you under such tragic circumstances. I understand you were quite friendly with Professor Glass. My condolences." There was not a shred of sincerity in his voice or manner.

He indicated the other person in the office, saying, "I'm not sure if you've met Brian Shaughnessy. Brian is President of our Board of Trustees. He's also President of the Loyal Sons of Cu Chulainn (he pronounced it 'coo cullen'), North Jersey Chapter, whose wonderful charitable work I'm sure you know."

Dom shook hands with a robust, sixtyish-looking man with a shock of vivid white hair, bushy eyebrows of which he seemed particularly proud, and tiny blue eyes devoid of warmth. He wore an expensively tailored navy blue suit with a chalk stripe, crisp white shirt, and a deep maroon tie. His cufflinks were large, silver and fashioned in the shape of a unicorn in front of what appeared to be a castle.

Shaughnessy was a third generation principal in Shaughnessy and Partners, a hugely successful and powerful law firm founded by his grandfather which had made untold millions in aspects of the law as diverse as corporate and securities law, criminal law, intellectual property law, and family and juvenile law. He was semi-retired and did not litigate anymore, but he remained deeply involved with the firm and never missed senior management meetings, where his opinion carried tremendous weight.

The Loyal Sons of Cu Chulainn was a fraternal organization founded in 1881 that was made up of wealthy, religiously and politically conservative Irish-American men who, ostensibly, were dedicated to supporting the Catholic Church and to performing charitable works and civic service.

More accurately, though more surreptitiously, they primarily existed to advance to the power and influence of their Irish-American membership. The secrecy of the organization's inner workings rivaled those of the Masons and Shriners. It had chapters in cities up and down the east coast. Brian Shaughnessy was a fourth generation Loyal Son; his forebears had been the organization's founding fathers.

With respect to Shaughnessy's role at Mount St. Ben's as President of the Board of Trustees, Shaughnessy had more clout than even the university president. He was the heaviest of heavy hitters as far as the university was concerned. Dom knew he was in some serious company.

Shaughnessy said to Dom, "I'm hopeful you can help us, Professor Rossi. Though that remains to be seen. And I remain to be convinced."

At this, Dom looked questioningly at Provost Delaney, who said, "Professor, as you will learn, the matter is awkward."

Felix Delaney was a tall, gaunt, fair-skinned man with gray eyes and faint wisps of gray hair compensated for by a carefully tended beard, who bore an unfortunate resemblance to an aardvark. He was given to wearing mock turtleneck sweaters in dark colors all year round.

Delaney said, "Professor Rossi, we are, of course, shocked and saddened by Rebecca's tragic death. However, she was, as you know, a controversial and provocative figure here on campus. But here is the main point of this meeting.

"I spoke over the weekend with Norman Hamilton, Chair of the Archaeology Department. He was at the Archaeological Association meeting, too. Norman said that there was considerable buzz about a paper that Rebecca was scheduled to deliver. He knew, of course, that she had been working quite diligently on something for several months, but she was being very secretive about it.

"The specific contents remain unknown and there is no sign of the paper itself. But Norman had the feeling that, given Professor Glass's radical proclivities, it might turn out to be embarrassing for the university if it ever came to light. The Board of Trustees wants to ensure that there is nothing in Rebecca's work that might reflect badly on the university."

Dom saw Delaney make eye contact with Shaughnessy. The eye contact told Dom that Shaughnessy was the driver here. The direction was coming from him.

Delaney went on, "That's where you come in, Professor Rossi. We want you to look into this mysterious research that Professor Glass was doing and determine whether there was anything that might compromise the university in any way. Go where you need to go, talk to anyone and everyone who might be helpful, find out what there is to know and report back to us. We will take it from there."

Dom was thoroughly disconcerted. "Provost Delaney, I have final exams to administer and grades to prepare for four classes. And summer sessions start soon. I have all kinds of preparation to do."

"I'll see to all of the academic considerations. I've already spoken to your Department Chair, Sister Patricia. We'll have someone administer your exams. As for the summer classes, don't worry about them. You'll still receive your stipend and we can spread the classes around the department, if this project goes on that long. This is critically important to the university, Professor."

"Evidently. But why me? I'm certainly no archaeologist."

"First of all, you are a highly skilled researcher yourself. You notice everything and you see things that others do not. You were in the military and served in Afghanistan. Most important, you are the closest thing on this campus that Rebecca Glass had to a best friend.

"Professor Rossi, there may be nothing to this at all. But left as it is, rumors and innuendo will inevitably besmirch Professor Glass's reputation — and ultimately that would reflect poorly on the university. If her reputation can be saved, you are the one to do it."

Impatient with the soft sell and not caring at all about Rebecca Glass's reputation, Brian Shaughnessy said, "Let's cut to the chase, here. I have a tee time at Spring Brook Country Club in half an hour, and I want this damn thing settled.

"Rossi, this mission is vital to the good name of this university. I want to know if that matters to you and if you're up to the task. Frankly, I have my doubts."

Dom looked at him. "Ever since I set foot on this campus eleven years ago as a seventeen year-old freshman, I've felt a powerful affinity towards Mount St. Ben's. For four years it was virtually my home. Now it's the foundation of my career."

Dom's eyes became cold. "But if you have any doubts about my commitment or capabilities, you can feel free to get someone else. I'll try to live with the disappointment. And frankly, Mr. Shaughnessy, I feel under no obligation to convince you of anything, Board of Trustees or not."

27

Seeking to head off further unpleasantness between the two, Delaney quickly interjected, "It is crucial to the university, Professor Rossi. May I have your answer?"

Turning his back on Brian Shaughnessy, Dom said, "Okay."

Felix Delaney said, "Good. Now then, you are encouraged to utilize any and all resources of the university, but you are expected to be totally discrete in your inquiries. Report to us regularly on your progress."

Dom asked, "What about Father Jack? Do I report to him, too?"

Delaney looked at Shaughnessy then said, "We will keep Father Jack apprised of your progress.

"Now, I want you to keep track of whatever expenses you may incur. I suggest you speak to Norman Hamilton so he can give you a sense of the Archaeological Association meeting. Also, I want you to be absolutely sure to seek out Martin O'Bannon in the Criminal Justice Department and see if he has any additional insights into what happened to Rebecca."

Dom thought, *O'Bannon again. Why?*

Delaney concluded, "After that, you should go wherever the trail leads you. Do you have any questions?"

"None."

Following Dom's departure, Brian Shaughnessy said, "What a remarkably arrogant little bastard."

"I'll keep an eye on him," Delaney said.

Shaughnessy replied, "So will O'Bannon."

***

After leaving the President's office, Dom immediately headed to the English Department to report what was going on to the Department Chair, Sister Patricia Schaedel. As soon as he entered the department offices, Fran Purcell, the officious administrative assistant who for some reason had no use for Dom, said, "She's already waiting for you, Professor Rossi. You may go right in, this time."

Sister Pat was a very attractive middle-aged woman with blond-going-to-gray hair who chose to eschew the traditional nun's habit in favor of sedate business suits worn with a crisp white shirt and a silver crucifix. Her area of scholarly interest was Medieval Literature, but she was very hip to the here and now.

28

She gave him a rueful smile. "Dom, ever since you were an undergraduate, there's never been a dull moment with you. You wrote research papers on the most arcane topics. And God knew what you were going to come up with in class. The Provost told me enough so that I could rearrange your schedule, and that's all taken care of. But what exactly have you gotten yourself into?"

Dom did not hold back. "Sister Pat, the past few years have been no picnic. I went through a war, I lost a fiancée, and I worked my tail off to get my Ph.D.. Mount St. Ben's has become a kind of refuge for me — a place of tranquility and peace where I can just be free to teach English and try to make students love it. This Rebecca Glass business is getting in the way of that. Plus, something about it stinks. And Delaney and that guy Shaughnessy are at the heart of it. I don't trust either of them."

Dom explained about the meeting in Felix Delaney's office — the assignment, the sense of urgency, the pressure he felt from all sides.

Sister Pat shook her head. "Poor Rebecca. Even after her death people are giving her a hard time. She was an unrepentant troublemaker, undoubtedly. But she was a good teacher and a good scholar. As for her private life, well, as Pope Francis says, 'Who am I to judge.' Frankly, most people would look at my religious vows — celibacy, poverty, and obedience — and say *my* life is bizarre. But you're right Dom, something else is going on here."

She paused a moment then said, "You're a colleague now, Dom. And, frankly, you've always been one of my favorites, so I'm going to give you a political heads up — and be very un-Christian about it. Felix Delaney is a snake. He is ambitious in the worst sense of the word; all he cares about is getting a presidency some day, which he'll do anything to achieve.

"Brian Shaughnessy is motivated solely by the acquisition and maintenance of power. With respect to the University, he does not like or trust faculty; he would prefer to do away with the notion of academic freedom and bring back the Spanish Inquisition. He has Delaney in his pocket. I sense in Shaughnessy a kind of ugly darkness that I can't quite identify, but I am convinced is there. And neither Delaney nor Shaughnessy had any use for Rebecca Glass. Do what you have to do, Dom. But

29

remember, this can impact your career. I'll provide whatever cover I can — help, advice, whatever. Don't hesitate to ask."

"Thank you, Sister Pat. I suspect I'm going to need it."

Back in his office, Dom sat for a while thinking about Sister Pat's question. What had he gotten himself into? He knew nothing about university politics. He'd had one archaeology class as an undergrad, but knew very little about the discipline itself or the people who chose to pursue it.

Still, research was research and it began with asking the right questions. Just for grounding, he went online and read again the news coverage of Rebecca's death.

Dom was not a crime buff and certainly no expert, but the incident sure seemed like a mugging — marks on her neck and wrists where jewelry had been roughly removed, smart phone and wallet with credit cards missing.

Then Dom read that she had been struck twice on the head, though the first blow had been the fatal one. Why twice? He needed to better understand the context of the crime, but news reports alone were not going to do it. He recalled Provost Delaney's direction — "Seek out Martin O'Bannon." He headed out of his office and walked across campus to the Criminal Justice Department.

Chapter 4

Martin O'Bannon was forty-seven years old and had spent three years as a police officer in the northern Monmouth County town of Keansburg, population, 10,115, a somewhat forlorn beachfront community with a trashy amusement park and a drug problem. He then was accepted into the New Jersey State Police, where he spent eighteen years, rising to the rank of Captain and Commander of the Casino Investigations Unit within the Special Investigations Section. His career was successful, but not without serious controversy.

He ended up taking an early retirement following some problems regarding his closeness to the casino industry and to some of its shadier characters. The suspicion was that he did special favors for them — a lot of favors. But there never was conclusive proof. His lawyers were able to work out a deal whereby any possible investigation of that closeness would be foregone if he would accept the early retirement. He did, with his pension fully intact. It was a great deal. His lawyers happened to be from the firm of Shaughnessy and Partners.

But the incident that most impacted his life occurred just before he left the police force in Keansburg. He was twenty-three years old and had responded to a 911 call involving an abusive father, a drug-addled girlfriend and a remarkably pretty fifteen year-old girl. The repercussions of that night followed him still.

Upon his retirement, O'Bannon had been invited to join the Criminal Justice faculty at Mount St. Ben's, based upon the recommendation of Brian Shaughnessy. It essentially meant that O'Bannon owed him favors in return. He was perfectly fine with that. He'd been there before. He'd also become a member of the Loyal Sons of Cu Chulainn and held the position of Sergeant-at-Arms. Although it is usually an honorary and symbolic position in fraternal organizations, Brian Shaughnessy used O'Bannon in more practical ways, as well.

31

Dom had met O'Bannon at the faculty orientation he'd attended the previous summer, but had had little contact with him since. Now, once in the CJ Department, Dom located O'Bannon's office. He was in. Dom knocked on the door. "Hello, Professor O'Bannon, I'm Dom Rossi, from English. We met last August during orientation."

"Oh, yeah, sure. Come on in."

O'Bannon's office was neat and orderly, with a large window affording a nice view of the college grounds. Dom saw that the walls behind his desk and to the right were covered with photographs showing O'Bannon shaking hands with assorted politicians, dignitaries and celebrities, as well as numerous awards and citations. There were photos of O'Bannon in uniform as a young patrolman with the Keansburg PD, others showing him receiving an award from the New Jersey State Police, a citation from the Department of Homeland Security, an award from the Diocese of Trenton and, displayed prominently behind his desk, an award from the Loyal Sons of Cu Chulainn proclaiming him Loyal Son of the Year for 2012.

O'Bannon stood to shake hands with Dom. He was a big man, thick through the neck and shoulders with thinning red hair and wary blue eyes. He must have been an intimidating sight in his uniform.

He said, "Call me Martin. Have a seat, Dom. So how's it been working out for you here at Mount St. Ben's?"

"So far, it's been all I'd hoped. At least up until what happened to Rebecca Glass. I share...shared an office with her. How well did you know her, Martin?"

O'Bannon replied, "Mostly from faculty meetings. She was a lightning rod and a hot head. But word is she was a first-rate teacher. How can I help you?"

"I'm trying to understand more about the circumstances of her death, so maybe I can make some sense of it. Provost Delaney suggested I touch base with you, given your experience and expertise, to see if you could give me any insights. It just seems so random and accidental to me."

O'Bannon nodded and replied, "Muggings often seem like that. But the mugger usually knows his location, knows when to set up, and knows who is likely to enter his target zone. Like that

32

beachfront park at that time of early evening, it's not busy, but there would be some targets. If they're staying at one of the nearby hotels, they're probably well heeled.

"Long Branch has built up tremendously over the last decade or so, but back away from beach in the north end especially, there are some rough areas. The mugger was probably from there. Or he might have come up from Asbury Park or Neptune City. He heads to the beach, waits for his prey, probably walks towards her along the sand, and then pulls a knife or a gun and forces her into the dunes."

Dom nodded in understanding. He said, "I also read that she'd been hit twice with a heavy, blunt instrument, probably a lead pipe. Does that make sense, Martin?"

"Sure. A knife attack is too prolonged and leaves the possibility of the victim screaming for help. Plus, it would leave traces of blood on the mugger. A gun is simply too noisy. As for the second blow, it's for insurance, or it can be pure adrenaline or anger. Sometimes it's even vindictiveness."

"That's interesting. Vindictiveness suggests revenge or getting back at someone. That would indicate prior knowledge of the victim, wouldn't it?"

As Dom said this, he noticed that O'Bannon flushed slightly. It was an odd reaction. Then, O'Bannon waived his hand in the air as if to dismiss the issue. "Well, maybe vindictiveness is the wrong word. In any case, muggings very often go wrong and this was one of those times."

Figuring there was no more to be learned, Dom stood up to go. "Thanks very much for your time and help, Martin. I really appreciate it."

Dom headed back across campus thinking about why Provost Delaney told him to make a special point of checking with Martin O'Bannon. Yes, he was former law enforcement, and yes, Dom had learned important information about muggings. And it all certainly seemed relevant to the circumstances of Rebecca's death. But it seemed to Dom that as a law enforcement guy, O'Bannon should be more concerned with the physical evidence. That 'vindictiveness' observation struck Dom as more emotional, almost kind of interpretive. Why?

After Dom left, O'Bannon picked up the phone. "He's started."

Dom next headed back to the Humanities and Social Sciences building and the office of Norman Hamilton, Rebecca's department chair. He too, was available, though apparently not thrilled to be meeting with Dom.

"Professor Rossi, the Provost told me what this was all about and that I should expect you. I might as well be frank. I find it inconvenient. I have a very busy schedule and many responsibilities. Please be brief."

Hamilton was an older, florid, man with lank brown hair going to gray, rheumy eyes, and tobacco stained teeth. Dom noticed that he made very little eye contact and tended to fidget. The fact that he was proving himself to be an asshole did not require Dom's skill at close observation. Hamilton indicated a chair across from his desk and Dom sat.

Dom said, "Thank you for taking the time, Professor Hamilton. I'd like to understand more about the annual Archaeological Association meeting and Rebecca's role in it."

Hamilton said, "It is quite typical as these things go. Though you, Rossi, are likely too inexperienced to know such things. Association meetings are intended to be collegial gatherings of like-minded scholars in pursuit of knowledge.

"Outsiders might find the proceedings arcane, even a bit stuffy. To my way of thinking, frankly, Rebecca Glass did not fit in. She provoked and exulted in controversy. The Association was tolerant of her antics because they considered her lively and provocative. Some members found her charismatic. I found her to be insolent, combative and disrespectful."

"How was she as a scholar?" Dom asked.

Hamilton looked out of his office window and answered begrudgingly, "She was brilliant, insightful, and tenacious."

"Can you tell me about her current work, Professor, especially about the paper she was to deliver at the Archaeological Association meeting?"

"I actually don't know very much, only that she seemed obsessed with her preparation for the meeting and was being very secretive. But also during that time she became even more assertive and aggressive than usual. She began to talk about wanting a promotion, she insisted on receiving research grant approval, and even demanded a lengthy sabbatical. I don't know where these demands came from. She was not yet in line for them. I told her that it was totally inappropriate."

Dom asked, "How did she react?"

A clearly uncomfortable, fidgeting Hamilton looked again out of the window. "She laughed at me. It was insulting. Now, if that's all, Professor Rossi, I have matters that demand my attention."

"Thank you for your time, Professor. Enjoy your day."

Back in his office, Dom brooded for a while on the foibles and egos of academics and on what a pain in the ass this assignment was already turning out to be. Then he turned his attention to Rebecca's side of the room.

Over the weekend, the buildings and grounds people had come in and removed the leftover bagel, the dead plants and her coffee mug. But Rebecca's papers and journals and assorted texts were still strewn around her side of the office. Delaney and Hamilton would decide what to do with them. There wasn't much of a personal nature. And it was still a mess. Dom sighed and went to work.

First he went on the university's website to learn what classes Rebecca had been teaching during the semester, so that he could sort her debris into what was relevant to class preparation and what was not. Her course load consisted of Principles of Archaeology, Origins of Civilization, Archaeology Field Methods, and Archaeology Laboratory Methods.

Next, he went through the assorted notes and papers on and in her desk and checked her bookcase for any additional active materials. As far as her desktop was concerned, he would have to wait for IT to come in and give him access. But it was unlikely that she would have kept anything confidential on it. There was no telling what was on her laptop or iPad or what she had at home.

After an hour or so, having set the class preparation materials aside, Dom was left with three remaining piles. They were a strange mix. There were notes and articles about the New Jersey Pine Barrens, including printouts of online articles and notes about relevant websites. There was also a copy of the seminal

John McPhee book, *The Pine Barrens*, with a number of well dog-eared pages. Dom flipped through the book, stopping to read sections where it looked like Rebecca had a particular interest.

All Dom knew about the area was that it was a forgotten wilderness comprising forests, ponds, rivers and streams, and scattered trails in the nearly uninhabited south central part of the state. The sections he read seemed to have little relevance to anything he was currently involved in.

A second pile included a brochure from the San Giacomo Engineering Company in Freehold that listed some of their capabilities — site development, concept and feasibility studies, traffic engineering, land surveying, etc. Dom added to the pile several pages of scribbled notes that Rebecca had made referring to something called "rescue archaeology," and its methodologies and practices.

Finally, Dom found other notes referring to something called the Cloister of St. Keira, which was located near the town of Trappe, Maryland. The Cloister had apparently been named after a 7th century Irish abbess and saint from County Tipperary. The notes suggested that Rebecca had been particularly interested in how and why the Cloister had come to America.

Dom could see no connection at all between the three.

Tired, but feeling the stirrings of a challenge, he loaded the material into his backpack, closed up his laptop and headed home.

Chapter 5

Home for Dom was a one hundred and ten year-old Victorian house on Wetmore Avenue in Morristown between Colles Avenue and Ogden Place in what was called the "historic district," about three blocks from the Morristown Green.

Dom's second floor apartment had two small bedrooms, one of which served as a study, a living room with a fireplace, a decent-sized kitchen, modest bathroom, and a narrow closet-like space that held a vertical washer and dryer unit. A small balcony overlooking Wetmore Avenue was accessed through the living room; it was just large enough to hold a couple of chairs, a butcher-block table and a tiny hibachi. The balcony was a great spot to read, relax with a drink, or brood on life's mysteries. He'd lived here since returning from Afghanistan and beginning his Ph.D. studies nearly four years earlier.

His landlady, Mrs. Bonvini, had lived in the house for over fifty years and had raised her three sons in it. When her husband, Augusto, passed away five years ago, she decided to convert the upstairs rooms into an apartment. The third floor remained storage. Her sons were all married, had families of their own and were partners in a very successful local business, Bonvini Brothers Heating and Air Conditioning. Although they and their families visited regularly, Mrs. Bonvini had for some reason decided to take a deep and abiding interest in Dom's life shortly after he moved in. She would often spot him coming and going and stop to make conversation, as she did this day. She was sitting on the front porch in a rocker crocheting as Dom walked up the steps.

"Dominic, you look sad. It's that poor lady professor, I know. A shame. But life goes on. Like when Augie passed, bless his soul. You have to look forward, Dominic."

"Right now, I'm looking forward to a scotch and soda, Mrs. B."

"Gina's gone how long now, God rest her beautiful soul, two years?"

"Two years and three months. And I know, Mrs. B., I should start to see other people."

She nodded her head. "You're such a smart, handsome Italian boy. You're a good catch. But I don't know where those green eyes come from. Not from Anthony and Theresa," she said, referring to Dom's parents. "Maybe you got a little Abbruzzese or Piedmontese in there with the Napolitano."

Dom laughed. She was right, almost. Anthony and Theresa were Dom's adoptive parents. While both were third generation Italian Americans, his birth mother, as little as he knew about her, evidently was fair-haired and light-eyed. As for what he inherited genetically from his birth father, he had no idea.

She went on, "You have to get out more. You can't just do your hifalutin university stuff then sit around like a dreck watching old movies."

"I love old movies."

"Listen to me, Dommy, better you should go out and meet a nice, light-hearted girl. With all those pretty girls at that college, you could have your pick."

"That's not usually a good idea, Mrs. B. I think it's called 'fouling your own nest.' And they're awfully young."

"Don't get all intellectual on me. So pick a graduate student, Dommy. You're too young to start drying up. Anyway, I've got a pot of pasta fagioli on the stove. Stop in my kitchen and take some upstairs with you. At least you can eat good."

Once up in his apartment, Dom placed the bowl of pasta and beans in his refrigerator, deposited his stuff in his den then made himself a tall scotch and soda. He brought it and his laptop out onto his little balcony. He took a long sip then started to create a research protocol, a kind of logical process he could follow as he tried to make sense of Rebecca's eclectic notes and materials.

He'd noticed in the newspaper coverage that there was to be a memorial service for her at the Unitarian Fellowship in Morristown the following afternoon. He'd certainly attend.

Next, he figured he'd talk to Diana, Rebecca's partner and see if she had any insights as to what Rebecca had been up to. Third, he'd research what was meant by "rescue archaeology" then

38

drive to Freehold and talk to the folks at San Giacomo Engineering. Fourth, he would need to read up on the Pine Barrens and, if necessary, go see the area for himself.

Finally, he'd have to figure out the significance of the Cloister of St. Keira. It seemed to have no place in this at all.

***

The Morristown Unitarian Fellowship was on the east side of town, just on the border with the town of Florham Park. It was housed in a beautiful brick mansion once known as "Thorne Oaks" that was listed on the National Register of Historic Places. It had been built in 1912 by the noted architects Delano and Aldrich for a wealthy New York City family who wished to have a country home. From what Dom could see, the Fellowship was evidently a thriving community — well kept building and grounds, blooming gardens, people coming and going. He entered the front door, passed through what was known as the Great Hall and noticed a small, discrete sign saying, 'Rebecca Glass Memorial Service' directing him further on into the Meeting Room.

In the front of the Meeting Room stood a lectern; next to it was a pedestal on which rested a pale green ceramic urn whose sides were decorated in a somewhat oriental-looking leaf pattern. It contained the ashes of Rebecca Glass. The familiar sound of Pachelbel's Canon in D played softly in the background. There were rows of chairs on either side of an aisle facing the urn.

Seated in the front row to the left was a family of four. It included a woman bearing a strong resemblance to Rebecca but who appeared a bit older, perhaps in her late forties; she would glance occasionally at the urn and shake her head, her expression reflecting more disapproval than sadness. Next to her was a dignified looking, expensively dressed gray-haired man, obviously her husband, who kept checking his watch and tapping his foot. Finally, there were two teenage girls who were busily texting and reading messages, and who seemed to have no idea or concern about the propriety of such behavior in these particular circumstances. None of the family appeared to be in mourning.

Behind them in the next few rows, Dom recognized several faculty colleagues and about a dozen students from the university several of whom were weeping. Father Jack was not present;

neither were any of the Deans, the Archaeology Department Chairperson, nor any members of the Board of Trustees.

On the other side of the center aisle, alone in the front row, sat an attractive, athletic-looking woman with short, brush cut blonde hair and brown eyes now red from crying. She was dressed all in black — blouse, slacks, and scarf. Dom guessed that it was Diana, Rebecca's partner. A lone man about forty or so, stood just outside the entrance to the room, observing the proceedings.

The Unitarian Minister, a robust woman with long brown hair parted in the middle and warm, accepting eyes, was delivering something between a eulogy and a blessing. Dom recognized the remarks as having been gathered from a rich variety of philosophical, theological, and literary sources spanning both Eastern and Western traditions; they essentially acknowledged a "larger purpose" and an "eternal presence" in the universe of which we were all a part. These insights were linked to Rebecca's life and career, though not to family.

Following the minister's remarks there was a moment of silence in which each person was asked to recall his or her favorite memories of Rebecca. Then the minister concluded the service and invited everyone into the library for refreshments. As people filed out, Dom went up to the woman who he assumed was Rebecca's sister.

"Pardon me, I'm Dominic Rossi. I was a colleague of Rebecca's at Mount St. Ben's. I am very sorry for your loss."

She seemed surprised — and uncomfortable — that anyone would approach her. "Oh, yes, I'm Barbara Glass Carmody, Rebecca's sister. Thank you, Professor..." She searched a moment for his name, "Rossi. "

She turned to her husband, who said, "We didn't have much to do with Rebecca's life, Professor Rossi. We are here simply as a matter of propriety, an obligation is an obligation."

Dom looked at him. "What an interesting and revealing insight, Mr. Carmody. Thank you for sharing it with me. Enjoy your refreshments."

Carmody glared at Dom then took his wife by the arm and moved her toward the library. Dom moved on to Diana.

"Diana, I'm Dom Rossi from Mount St. Ben's. I was –"

"Her friend. You were her friend." She gave him a brief, awkward hug.

Dom said, "Diana, I'm so sorry for your loss. I know right now is a bad time, but when it's appropriate and convenient for you, perhaps we can talk. I'm following through on some things relevant to Rebecca's work."

She looked around. "Now is a good time, Dom. I want to get the hell out of here. Let's go get a drink. Do you know Rod's over in Convent Station?"

"Sure, of course."

"Meet me there, in GK's Red Dog Tavern."

Rod's Steak and Seafood Grille, a Morris County and New Jersey landmark, was ten minutes from the Unitarian Fellowship. With great food, warm atmosphere, family ownership and an attentive staff, the place had been welcoming old friends and newcomers for several generations. Dom arrived and found Diana already seated at a table for two in the cozy tavern area. He sat down across from her.

A waiter came over and Diana quickly said, "Scotch on the rocks."

Dom said, "Make it two."

After the waiter left, Diana said, "That goddamn Barbara never even looked at me. You'd think she might express some kind of condolence. But no, her sister was a pervert and I'm the co-conspirator. Screw her. At least I got to make the arrangements and pick the site. Reverend Sally helped select the readings. Anyway, Dom, it's nice to meet you. Becca always spoke very highly of you. Thanks for coming." She suddenly sobbed, "Oh God, what a shitty thing."

Dom placed his hand over hers. In an attempt to have Diana reflect on happier times, he asked, "Diana, tell me, how did you and Rebecca meet?"

"I own and operate a yoga studio down the road in Madison, near Drew University." She smiled at the memory. "Becca signed up when she moved here from upstate New York, from SUNY Albany. She wasn't very good at first, but she sure was intense and committed as hell. I started to help her and, well, one thing led to another." She paused, as if remembering, then said, "We were very good to each other, Dom, and very good together."

41

"Did you live together?"

"Almost. I kept my condo in Madison, but several nights during the week and most weekends I stayed at Becca's little house in Morristown. It worked out nicely. The big issue between us was marriage. Same sex marriage has been legal in New Jersey for a number of years, now. I really wanted us to do it. I even talked to Reverend Sally about performing the service. But if we had, it would have been the end of Becca's career at Mount St. Ben's. Father Jack never gave her any grief about being the way she was and he treated her fairly. But the rest of the administration and the religious faculty treated her like a pariah. And the Board of Trustees wouldn't have tolerated it. They'd have fired her in a heartbeat for moral turpitude or some such shit. So we just kept it like it was."

Their drinks arrived, and Diana hungrily took a sip. Dom said, "It's my understanding that Rebecca had been working pretty intensely on a research project for the past several months. Do you have any idea what her focus was?"

Diana shook her head. "I usually didn't pay a whole lot of attention to her work. She was the intellectual one; I'm more emotional and intuitive." She added, "But she really did seem all worked up the past few months. And she traveled more than usual, like to some of those South Jersey counties — Monmouth, Ocean, and Burlington. She'd be down there overnight sometimes."

Another thought seemed to strike her and she said, "You know, it was funny. Becca was pretty tight with a buck. But during this time she began talking about how we should go on a fancy vacation and both move into a bigger house. I have no idea where that came from, so I just let her rant. As I think about it now, maybe it had to do with whatever she was working on, like maybe it would be profitable. But I have no idea how."

Dom recalled what Norman Hamilton had said about Rebecca being even more assertive and demanding. Was there a connection, a pattern?

"Did she have an office at home, Diana? The reason I ask is that if you don't mind, I'd like to see if there's anything laying around that might give me a clue as to what she was up to."

42

"Yeah, she did have an office. And it's funny you mention it. Last week, when she was down in Long Branch for the Association meeting, I dropped by the house to check on a few things. I stuck my head into the office, and I got a very strange vibe. You must know how Becca was — stuff all over the place. But this time her office didn't seem as messy as it usually was. And I all of a sudden got a very weird feeling, like someone else had been in there."

"Were there any concrete indications or evidence of that?"

"No. None. But like I said, I'm very intuitive."

"Diana, do me a favor. Take a closer look at Rebecca's office. And if you see anything that seems out of place or not consistent with how she worked, please give me a call. Then, if it's okay with you, I'll come over and take a look, too."

"Sure, Dom. I'd look forward to your visit. I feel kind of alone now. A good friend of Becca would be very welcome."

They exchanged phone numbers; then Dom said, "Diana, are you going to be all right? Is there anything I can do?"

"You already have, Dom," Diana said, her eyes welling up. "You've been a friend." She reached across the table and held his hand. "Now, I've got to get back to the studio. I have a yoga class later this afternoon. I'm just hoping I can keep it together long enough to get through the damn thing. Maybe it'll keep my mind off the fact the my heart is broken and my life has been shattered."

Outside in the parking lot, the man who'd been in the back of the Meeting Room watched as Dom and Diana drove away. He picked up his cell phone. "He's made contact with the partner."

Martin O'Bannon said, "He's moving quickly. That's good. But that contact with the partner may turn out to be a problem. We'll keep an eye on it."

Chapter 6

It was an august group seated around the small peat fire in Brian Shaughnessy's study at his New Vernon estate known as Ballyporeen, in honor of the small Irish village in County Tipperary his ancestors emigrated from in the mid nineteenth century. They were sipping Black Bush Irish whisky and discussing recent auspicious events. Shaughnessy's wife, Margaret, a pleasant, plump woman in her early sixties, had welcomed the guests, served the first round of drinks and then had discretely disappeared. Brian Shaughnessy barely took notice of her.

In addition to Shaughnessy himself, also present were Fiona Shane, CEO of an enormously profitable specialty pharmaceutical company and mother of the soon-to-be Republican gubernatorial candidate William Shane, who was present as well. Bill Shane was currently the DA for heavily Republican Morris County and a political rising star who, if elected at age thirty-six, would be New Jersey's youngest ever Governor; beyond that, politically speaking, the sky was the limit. Seated across from Shane was Bishop Francis X. Regan, of the Diocese of Trenton, and Felix Delaney from Mount St. Benedict University. A red-faced, outraged Bishop Regan had the floor.

"I'm still appalled. The woman directly threatened me! She demanded money! Had she gone ahead and actually made public these accusations, the press would have gone into a feeding frenzy. The Church would have faced unimaginable derision. It would have been a scandal unlike any seen before." He took a healthy swallow of his Black Bush.

Fiona Shane said, "She was a perverted and twisted woman, Bishop. It may seem cruel to say, but her untimely end was not undeserved. I am sure that the fate of her evil, tortured soul is not in doubt."

Fiona Shane might have been Hollywood's idea of Irish royalty. At age fifty-eight, she was tall and slender, fair-skinned with gray-blue eyes; her make-up was carefully applied, especially to her right cheek; her silver hair was piled into a bun and secured with a jeweled pin.

Though a highly successful and very prominent business woman, she grew up in poverty, raised by parents who were barely literate. She won a full scholarship to Mount St. Benedict University, where she excelled at economics and marketing. Upon graduation at age twenty-one she married Michael Shane (long deceased), an associate at Shaughnessy and Partners. She bore a child, William, at age twenty-two. Then went on to graduate school.

Brian Shaughnessy said, "Just to be safe, Bishop, I'm in the process of making sure that Professor Glass's libelous research cannot be duplicated, that all links to us remain hidden. That includes, of course, any references to the Diocese of Trenton."

"I am most grateful, Brian. Even arrangements made more than a hundred years ago can return to haunt us — and the Church."

Shaughnessy turned back to Fiona Shane. "We have dispatched a very bright — if disagreeably arrogant — junior faculty member from the English department to trace Professor Glass's research protocol, if it can even be done. He was a friend of hers, evidently."

William Shane looked dubious. "An *English* professor? Is he at all qualified to handle such an investigation?" He looked to Fiona. "What do you think, Mother?"

"Just who is this young English professor?" Fiona wanted to know.

Provost Delaney answered, "His name is Dominic Rossi. I have to admit that he is extraordinarily promising both as a teacher and a scholar. He was a gifted student athlete at Mount St. Benedict's as an undergraduate, fulfilled his Army ROTC obligation and served in Afghanistan, then he returned and completed his Ph.D. requirements in three years."

"He sounds quite formidable, Provost Delaney," Fiona said. "Is that wise?"

45

"Not to worry, Mrs. Shane. Junior faculty members are very vulnerable to administration pressure and easily manipulated."

Shaughnessy added, "We'll keep an eye on him. If he gets too close to actually uncovering something awkward, we are prepared to act. I have someone watching."

Fiona Shane smiled. "That's very reassuring, Brian. After all, we don't want anything to mar William's candidacy. And I know I can rely on the enthusiastic support — and considerable influence — of the Loyal Sons of Cu Chulainn. Certainly, the upcoming announcement of William's selection as Loyal Son of the Year will do much to help ensure his election."

William Shane said, "The announcement on Memorial Day will be a wonderful kick-off to the campaign. Preliminary polls already show me in a virtual dead heat with Richardson. And I haven't even formally announced. Plus, he's old and tired. My entry will bring a burst of energy and enthusiasm into the race that Richardson cannot hope to match. At any rate, Brian, I am in your debt and that of the Loyal Sons. And I will remember that, you may be sure."

***

Dom climbed into his twelve year-old, but still serviceable and loyal Honda CRV and headed south on Interstate 287 out of Morristown. He planned to pick up the Garden State Parkway and then take the old Route 9 South to Freehold. He guessed the drive at about an hour. The previous day he had called San Giacomo Engineering and arranged for an appointment with one of their senior staff.

He'd also gone online and learned that "rescue archaeology" was a very common activity. The term referred to an archaeological survey, excavation, or assessment of an area carried out in advance of construction or other kinds of land development. Dom figured that's what Rebecca must have been doing for the San Giacomo folks on a consulting basis, a kind of academic moonlighting to earn some extra money. But he was clueless as to what the connection might be to her mysterious research or the phantom paper she had supposedly written.

Freehold is the county seat of Monmouth County, though miles inland from the Shore. Dom found San Giacomo Engineering about three miles from the center of town. It was housed in an attractive steel and stone two story building set back from Route 9 on what appeared to be almost two acres of well-kept grounds. Behind the building Dom could see assorted vehicles — vans, pick-up trucks, SUVs, etc. — all bearing the San Giacomo logo.

He entered the revolving doors and in the lobby was greeted by a very attractive, smiling young woman whose nametag read, Carol Ann D'Agostino.

"Hello, welcome to San Giacomo Engineering. How may I help you?" She actually sounded like she meant it.

"Hi, Carol Ann, I'm Dominic Rossi from Mount St. Benedict University. I called recently about an appointment."

"Oh sure, Professor Rossi. We've been expecting you." She pushed a button on the console in front of her and about a minute later, an equally attractive and personable middle-aged woman entered the lobby through sliding glass doors, walked up to Dom and extended her hand.

"Professor Rossi, I'm Kathryn Lombardy, Vice President of Operations. Mr. San Giacomo is waiting for you in his office."

She escorted Dom to a comfortable though not at all pretentious office with walls full of diagrams, blueprints and maps, several laptops on different tables and desks, and a huge coffee machine that looked like it got a lot of activity. A tall, smiling man in khaki trousers and a dark blue open collared shirt greeted Dom as he walked in.

"Dr. Rossi, it's a pleasure. I'm Duffy San Giacomo. " As he shook Dom's hand he asked, "Would you care for some coffee? We live on it around here."

"Please, call me Dom. And coffee would be great, thanks, Duffy."

As Duffy poured their coffees he said, "Kathryn told me you were a colleague of Rebecca's. Jesus, what a shame. How can I help you?"

Duffy indicated a table across from his desk and he and Dom sat. Dom said, "I'm trying to track down the nature of some research Rebecca was doing before she was killed, research that may impact the university but is now lost. Some of her notes indicated she was doing some work for you. What kind of work was it?"

"Archaeological consulting, several months ago. She did a great job. She was quirky as hell, of course, but our folks loved her. She was smart, thorough, and fast. Here, let me show you what she was up to."

He walked to a file cabinet and pulled out a large, very detailed map of New Jersey. He spread it out on the table.

"Let me give you some context, Dom. New Jersey on average has over twelve hundred people per square mile. It's the most densely populated state in the Union. In some parts of northern New Jersey, there are as many as forty thousand people per square mile. Union City alone has over fifty thousand people per square mile."

Then he ran his finger over a large section of the south central part of the state. "But in this area, the Pine Barrens, there are only fifteen people per square mile. We're talking about 1.4 million acres. Dom, that's an area almost as big as Yosemite National Park and about the same size as Grand Canyon National Park. The people who live in the Pines, and there are really only a few hundred of them in the deepest parts, live simply and primitively, by choice. It's acres and acres of pine, white oak, and cedar forests, and bogs, ponds and sand; pretty much all wilderness.

"But back in the eighteenth and nineteenth centuries, there was tremendous industrial activity in the Pine Barrens — iron foundries, logging, thousands of people making things like tile, bricks, glass, paper, and even munitions. Most of the travel and traffic was via horse-drawn vehicles at that time, along a series of sand roads weaving throughout the area. One especially significant route ran from Philadelphia right through the heart of the area to Tuckerton, a major port on the coast.

"Now, here's the thing, Dom. For fifty years the state of New Jersey has been talking about building another major highway along that same route — even including a major airport. It never went anywhere. But that talk has heated up recently. They cite the principle of eminent domain in order to acquire the land.

"The idea is to open up the shore area around Tuckerton, Mystic Island, and as far south as Leeds Point to more tourism and real estate development. If the state legislature can get its act together and vote on it, they'll eventually open the project to bidding from various contractors. We decided to do a feasibility study at our own expense to get a head start, just in case."

"Where did Rebecca come in?"

"Engineers and construction people can't just go bulldozing our way through the area. Prospective routes have to be approved in advance and potentially important archaeological and historical sites have to be avoided, so they're not lost or destroyed. Dom, there are sites from Colonial and even aboriginal times in the Pine Barrens. Rebecca was in there on our behalf exploring along our projected route, trying to see if there were any important or notable sites, like old ghost towns and such, that would have to be avoided or would necessitate altering the route."

"Ghost towns?" Dom asked, skeptically.

"Sure. When all those industries failed in the nineteenth century, most people moved elsewhere, but a few stayed and their descendants are still there. The forest eventually and inevitably began to overgrow what remained, so that today there are only a few ruins, maybe the skeleton of a building or two; sometimes it's just a mound of earth where everything else is flat. But beneath the mounds, underground, are the remnants of a town, ruins of buildings, like old brick factories, even houses, and God knows what else. That's what Rebecca was researching."

"Duffy, you seem very familiar with the area, have you done work in the Pine Barrens before?"

"Most of our work is done south of the Raritan River and across to central Pennsylvania and down to Delaware and Maryland, even as far as Virginia. We have a very nice business. But we haven't done much in this particular geographic area, no one has. And much of what I know about the Pine Barrens, I learned from Rebecca." He pointed to a bookcase against the far wall. "That dark blue binder on the top shelf is her report."

Dom asked, "Do you think I might get a look at it? It could be really helpful."

Duffy picked up his desk phone. "I can do better than that." He said into the phone, "Kathryn, do you still have your copy of Rebecca Glass's report? I'd like to lend it to Dom. Thanks."

A minute later, Kathryn Lombardy entered with the report. She said, "Here you go. We still have Duff's hard copy and the whole thing backed up on our computers. But two things — first, it's very preliminary and written in the context of an engineering impact study, not a scholarly study. But it should give you some idea of what she was up to and what she found. You can take it from there. Second, it's confidential. We don't want any potential competitors getting a look at it."

Dom said, "Got it. I'll be very careful. I do have one other question. How did you guys find Rebecca to begin with?"

Duffy pointed at Kathryn. "My ever-efficient colleague went online to the Archaeology Association of New Jersey and found a list of people available for consulting. Kathryn's daughter, Maria, is a nursing major at Mount St. Ben's."

Kathryn added, "When I saw Rebecca was affiliated with Mount St. Ben's, I decided to keep it in the family."

Dom stood up. "You guys have been terrific. Thank you so much for all the time and help."

As Dom shook hands with Duffy and Kathryn, Duffy said, "If you end up heading into the Pine Barrens, Dom, don't forget your GPS. It's like a maze in there — woods, ponds, streams and trails leading nowhere and everywhere. You could wander around in there forever and never be found. Good luck."

Chapter 7

Dom drove away from San Giacomo Engineering in good spirits; the information was helpful and Duffy and Kathryn had been great. Feeling like he was on a roll, he removed Detective Craig's card from his wallet and noted the address. He pulled over and entered the address into his smart phone and learned that the Office of the Monmouth County Prosecutor was only about two miles away, so he figured what the hell. Maybe detectives Craig and Mulroney had learned something more about Rebecca's death.

The prosecutor's office was in a sprawling two-story brick building on Jerseyville Avenue in Freehold. Dom asked at the reception desk for Detective Craig of the Homicide Unit. He was told to have a seat and ten minutes later Detective Craig appeared, dressed functionally but attractively in a brown corduroy blazer, black turtleneck and black slacks. Glossy dark hair, intense dark eyes, still no make-up, and still remarkably attractive.

She said, in lieu of a greeting, "In my line of work, Professor, there's no such thing as a social call, so how can I help you."

"I was in the area and wondering if you'd learned anything more about the circumstances of Rebecca's death. Plus, I've found out a few things, nothing earth shattering, but maybe they might help you in some way. But if this is a bad time, I'll just head back to campus."

She looked at her watch. "To save time, meet me at Federici's on Main Street. You can buy lunch. But don't think of it as a bribe."

At Federici's, Dom and Detective Craig got a table outside facing the street. Detective Craig ordered a club soda with lemon and a personal-sized white pizza. She said to Dom, "I'll eat the rest of it throughout the afternoon." Dom went with fresh mozzarella and roasted red peppers and a glass of the house Chianti.

Detective Craig said, "First, I have to know — that little show you put on in your office, all that close observation stuff, it was pretty impressive. How did you do it?"

"*A Study in Scarlet.*"

"What's that, some kind of methodology or something?"

Dom smiled. "No, it's the first Sherlock Holmes novel. There were four novels and fifty-six short stories. This one is where Holmes and Watson first meet and Arthur Conan Doyle uses the occasion to introduce Holmes's powers of observation and deduction. I read it when I was a kid, and I loved it. So I read all the Sherlock Holmes stories. I loved the idea of observing and analyzing."

"Did you want to grow up to be a detective?"

Dom shook his head. "Not at all. It was the reading that I loved. But I did try to refine my observational skills."

"Well you certainly pegged Mulroney."

Dom shrugged. "I'm not usually like that, but he was behaving like an ass. That tough guy act was unnecessary. He just should have told me what it was you were trying to learn, instead of trying to give me a bunch of crap."

"He's not a bad partner, but sometimes he can come on too strong with witnesses and interviewees. With you, it was one of those times. I noticed, though, that you didn't hesitate to give him crap right back."

"How did I do with you?"

She looked at her fingernails. "I started to bite my nails when I was eleven. It was a rough time, growing up in Keansburg. I was just hitting puberty and family wise it was kind of ugly. My father was...well, rough. And my back does act up from time to time."

"What about the avoidance of make-up and your being remarkably pretty?"

She looked at him for several seconds. "Professor, you're not attempting to hit on me, are you?"

"I'm merely being curious, Detective."

She nodded, as if satisfied. "Okay. Let's move on. Now, it's not protocol, but I'll go first. Mulroney is convinced it was a mugging all the way. I agree. That's what we gave to the DA. He also agrees. We spoke to the partner, Diana Bennington, and she confirmed that Glass was wearing a gold necklace, gold bracelet and an expensive watch. Bennington bought her the necklace and bracelet as gifts and figures together they were worth about $800. She said Glass bought herself the watch, a Patek Phillipe, years ago after she was awarded her Ph.D.. It cost about $1,500 new. Not a big haul, but enough to keep someone in crank and smack for a while.

"I also talked to a lieutenant at the Long Branch PD, Guy Mistretta. He's got a great rep; he's smart and he's been around, knows everyone and everything that's going on down there. Guy said they keep a pretty close eye on the park and that muggings there are unusual. But sometimes they do happen.

"We're watching all known fences and tapping into our informants throughout Monmouth and Ocean counties. The phone company and the credit card companies are on alert for any surge in activity, and we told Homeland Security about the loss of the wallet with Glass's IDs, college and DMV both. Frankly, unless we catch a break — the jewelry or the IDs show up, or some asshole starts bragging — we might never catch the perp. That's just the way it is. Plus, Mulroney and I have an active and growing caseload in a very big county. So, what do you have?"

Having finished her briefing, Detective Craig started on her white pizza, using a knife and fork and cutting very small, very precise pieces, which she ate with great delicacy. After every two bites, she took a small sip of her club soda.

Dom said, "I found out that Rebecca had been working pretty intensely on a paper she was going to deliver at the annual Archaeological Association meeting. The paper was rumored to be quite controversial."

"A 'controversial' archaeology paper?" Detective Craig looked dubious.

"That's what the word is. Anyway, the university wants me to look into it and see if I can learn any more about it, just in case the research is problematic or awkward in some way for Mount St. Ben's."

"So, you really are playing Sherlock Holmes after all."

Dom ignored the dig. "I found out that Rebecca had done some consulting work for a local engineering firm that took her into the Pine Barrens and that she had spent quite a bit of time exploring the area. Also, her mood seemed to have changed; she was both more furtive and more energized, and she talked about buying a bigger house and going on an expensive vacation. She was also busting her department chair's chops about a promotion and access to research grants, and she was being very pushy about it. I'm wondering if all that may be tied in some way to this phantom paper. Maybe she learned something important or found something valuable in the Pine Barrens."

"Oh, you mean like the Jersey Devil or something?"

Dom looked at her blankly. "What's the Jersey Devil?"

Detective Craig laughed, which made her seem much younger and not quite so formidable. "Professor, you really need to do your homework. It's the Pine Barrens' most famous legend. Anyway, I can't see where any of this leads, but keep me in the loop if you do learn anything."

"Can I expect to hear from you if you learn anything?"

"That's not how it usually works. But yes, maybe you will hear from me. I've got to head back now. Thank you for lunch, Professor."

"My pleasure, Detective."

When Detective Craig got back to her office, she ran a check on Dominic Rossi. She of course had known about the Ph.D., but it was his Army record that surprised her — Afghanistan service, reconnaissance platoon leader, Bronze Star for Valor, Purple Heart, several other commendations. And he had compiled impressive academic achievements for someone so young — publications, a book; he was evidently making a name for himself in the academic community. It was becoming clear to her that Dominic Rossi was significantly more formidable than she had thought. And more interesting. Maybe this called for some follow-up.

***

Back at Mount St. Ben's, Dom headed to the English Department to talk to Sister Pat. He explained, "My knowledge of New Jersey is severely limited. I need to catch up."

Sister Pat looked at him, surprised. "I thought you were born and raised here."

54

"I was. But my family spent summers at our cabin in the Adirondacks. Plus, I was never much of a beach guy, so I didn't spend much time at the Jersey Shore. Since my folks retired to Naples, Florida, I tend to spend holidays with them. My familiarity with New Jersey ends at the Raritan River. And this Pine Barrens stuff is totally new to me."

"Dominic, you have this big reputation as a whiz kid. Go do your homework."

"That's what somebody else just told me."

"Here's another suggestion. Go touch base with Ray Alexander — he's Chair of Anthropology. He's in the process of creating a new Folklore Studies program. It's a cross-disciplinary curriculum that's beginning with a focus on New Jersey, including the Pine Barrens. We're involved, as are a number of other disciplines. Give him a call and see if he can help. I'll tell him to expect you. Let me know how it goes."

That evening, Dom decided to do his homework over a bowl of Mrs. B's pasta fagioli — ditalini pasta and cannellini beans in a rich tomato broth with bits of celery, carrot, onion, and chopped pancetta, and flavored with garlic, rosemary and thyme. While it was heating on the stove, he grated some fresh Parmesan cheese to sprinkle over it and poured himself a glass of Chianti. Then he settled down to read.

Kathryn was right; Rebecca's report was essentially concerned with the engineering implications of her archaeological findings, and less with a full explanation of the scholarly ones. Still, by giving the report a close reading, Dom noticed certain subtle shifts in tone and style — use of the passive voice and subjunctive mood — that suggested something else was going on. Rebecca seemed to be trying to avoid revealing too much of what she really thought or had discovered. It was as if she'd been intrigued by something she'd found and would revisit it at another time and for her own purposes. Dom did find a few intriguing and helpful nuggets, however, and the story of a very sad, very tragic incident.

He learned that even now, in the twenty-first century, there were only a few paved roads in the Pine Barrens. The projected San Giacomo route could be accessed only by means of winding, unpaved, largely sand roads and sand trails. Local residents,

55

known as "Pineys," called the sand "sugar sand," because it was so fine and so treacherous to try to navigate in anything other than a four-wheel drive vehicle. The terrain, mostly flat, was eerily similar from one location to another, with few significant terrain features, making land navigation by dead reckoning nearly impossible for anyone not a Piney.

The second interesting finding was that the area was exceptionally susceptible to fire — over four hundred per year. In addition to the high flammability of pitch pine, the dominant species of tree, and the other lush vegetation, the sandy soil has a very low water holding capacity, so vegetation is nearly always dry — all of which can feed the growth and extraordinarily rapid spread of a fire. In earlier years, not only in the eighteenth and nineteenth centuries, but as recently as sixty years ago — that is, in years prior to advances in modern firefighting equipment, techniques, and practices — fires encompassing thousands of acres of forest were not uncommon. Some were of natural causes; many were arson. In those days, by the time help arrived, any buildings, houses or other structures in the fire's path were doomed, so rapidly did the fires spread. Eventually, the forest would reclaim what little remained, as Duffy had explained.

And that led to the story of the tragic incident. As an example of the horrible consequences of fires in the Pine Barrens, Rebecca had cited the death of eight people — all nuns — in a 1958 blaze that utterly destroyed a chapter house of the Cloister of St. Keira, evidently located somewhere south of the community of Friendship and north of the town of Jenkins, not far from the West Branch of the Wading River — virtually in the middle of nowhere.

Rebecca had noted that the fire had reduced the one hundred year old wooden building to a pile of smoldering ashes by the time help arrived, which took several hours because of the remoteness of the location and the unpaved, sandy roads. Moreover, the help consisted largely of men with water tanks on their backs and others with axes, shovels and rakes. The physical remains of the nuns were not only unidentifiable; they were nearly unrecognizable as human, due to the ferocity of the blaze.

After citing the story, Rebecca's report moved on to other matters. It was an interesting albeit grim story, but why did she cite it at length and with such passion? Yes, there were engineering implications with respect to the fire and the terrain, but why go into such detail?

Dom felt a sudden rush — could she have discovered something more about the causes and consequences of the fire? Could that discovery have been the source of her paper? Maybe that was why Rebecca had made reference to the Cloister's Mother House in Trappe, Maryland; maybe she'd wanted to learn to learn why the cloister had opened a chapter house in the remote and barely accessible Jersey Pine Barrens to begin with. Dom figured he would have to head to Maryland for the answer.

After finishing Rebecca's analysis, Dom decided it was time to give a preliminary report to Provost Delaney. The following day, he entered the Provost's office. Delaney said, "Good morning, Professor Rossi. What have you learned?"

Remembering Sister Pat's warning about Delaney, Dom decided there was no way he was going to share all of his insights and suspicions with the guy.

"Rebecca was doing some consulting work for an engineering company in Freehold. It took her into the Pine Barrens. Whether the company acts on Rebecca's findings depends on whether the state goes forward with a highway construction project. For now, it's moot. There are one or two other leads that I have yet to track down. But so far I can't find anything about her research that seems in any way controversial or threatening to the university."

The Provost said, "Keep at it. We have to be absolutely certain about this. And it will be to your credit if you come through. However, it is best that you understand that if you fail and something damaging to the university emerges, it will be very unfortunate — especially for you. Report in as soon as you learn something new."

Chapter 8

Dom had read online that the Cloister of St. Keira in Trappe, Maryland, was actually within the Diocese of Wilmington, Delaware. His first stop then would be the diocese's Chancery Office, the source of official information about the diocese's activities and history, hopefully to include information about St. Keira's.

Next, knowing he couldn't simply drive around looking for the Cloister itself and, if he found it, just walk up and ask for an interview, he'd decided to visit St. Gregory the Great Parish in Easton, the largest parish close to Trappe, and see if the pastor might know what it would take to get permission to visit. Finally, if all went well, he'd pay a visit to the Cloister.

It took about two hours from Morristown to Wilmington, south on I 95, always a grim, boring ride, with heavy traffic inevitably building up and slowing down around Philadelphia. Once in Wilmington, Dom found the Chancery Office on Delaware Avenue and was actually able to park right out front. It was a three-story brick building with two front entrances leading to a vestibule that seemed to be an architectural afterthought. In the lobby he walked up to a frowning, late middle-aged woman with steel gray hair and reading glasses hanging from a silver chain around her neck. She was seated at the information desk.

"Good morning, I'm Professor Dominic Rossi from Mount St. Benedict University. I'm hoping to speak with someone about the Cloister of St. Keira in Trappe, Maryland."

"You might have called ahead and asked for an appointment, young man. This is a very large diocese and we are very busy."

"I did call ahead."

Her frown became even more pronounced. "Well no one told me. And you can't just barge in here, seeking to speak to heaven knows whom for God knows why. This is all very irregular and inconvenient."

Dom immediately thought of Cerberus, the three-headed dog in Greek mythology who guards the gates of hell. "Yes, Ma'am. And I'm sure you have grave responsibilities. But I'm hoping you will find it in your heart to help me out."

She looked at Dom suspiciously, uncertain as to whether he was being sarcastic, but nevertheless picked up a phone on her desk. "Muriel, there's a young man here, he says he's a professor. He needs to talk to someone about St. Keira's. He'll wait."

Twenty minutes later, an officious-looking man about thirty years old came out to see Dom. He was dressed like an undertaker — black blazer, dark gray shirt, black tie and gray slacks — though his demeanor was much less courteous than that of an undertaker.

"I'm Philip Dolan, Assistant Director of Public Affairs for the Diocese. You are inquiring about St. Keira's, I believe."

"Yes, I'm hoping to learn a bit about the Cloister. For example, can you tell me when it was founded and anything about its history?"

The man sighed, a gesture obviously intended to indicate to Dom that he had more important things to do. "Follow me, please."

He led Dom down a corridor and into what seemed to be a library. Along one wall were four computer stations. Dolan pointed to a rectangular table in the middle of the room and said, "Please have a seat. I'll just be a minute."

He went into the stacks and two minutes later emerged with a cloth bound volume which he flipped through and, finding the page he wanted, explained to Dom, "In 1891, a group of Irish nuns, the Sisters of St. Keira, whose namesake was a 7th century Irish Abbess from County Tipperary, petitioned the then Bishop of Wilmington, John J. Monaghan, to let them open a cloister in Maryland. It was to be built on a piece of land donated to the Sisters by a former merchant sea captain who had retired to the Eastern Shore. Bishop Monaghan gave his approval and the cloister was built. It has been there ever since. Is there anything else?" He closed the book and looked at Dom.

"Do you happen to know, or can you help me find any record of how the Cloister spun off a chapter that was built in the Jersey Pine Barrens?"

"No."

Dom looked at the guy for several moments. "Thank you for your time, Mr. Dolan. By the way, Cerberus out there doesn't happen to be your mother, does she? If so, what does that make you? Have a nice day." The man was too ignorant to feel insulted.

Dom's next stop was St. Gregory the Great parish in Easton, about an hour and a half south. Twenty minutes into his drive, his cell phone rang.

"Dom, this is Diana. I'm here at Becca's going through her office again, like you said. Nothing out of the ordinary jumps out at me. But I did find a weird note. You know how you jot something down to remind yourself to do something? It's like that, but I don't understand it."

"What does it say?"

"It says, 'Find the Caretaker.' And it has a couple of exclamation points after it."

"Who's the caretaker? Some guy who weeds the garden or does the lawn or something?"

"That's what I'm saying. I don't know. Becca and I did all the stuff around the yard — mowing and planting and raking leaves and stuff. We enjoyed it. I just thought this was weird cause it seems so, what's the word, incongruous."

Dom couldn't see where this was going or what it would lead to, but he said, "Okay, thanks for the heads up, Diana. I'll add it to our list of things to think about. I'll call you when I get back to Morristown."

An hour later, Dom pulled up to St. Gregory's. The church and the grounds around it were well kept and gave the impression of being the center of a very active and prosperous parish. Off to the left of the main church was an attached annex, which evidently held the parish's administrative offices, classrooms and common rooms. He pulled up in front of the building, parked and headed inside.

Three women were very busily attaching photographs to a large bulletin board in what most likely was the parish's main common room. One of them, a stout, smiling African American woman, turned and saw Dom.

"Well, hi there! We're putting together a collage of Father Tom's twentieth anniversary celebration last Sunday. It sure was fun. Folks brought all kinds of food — Lord, you wouldn't believe all the crabs! And the Bishop was here and there was music and singing and we were all making a joyful noise unto the Lord. You should have joined us! You'd have loved it! But how may I help you today?"

"I'm Professor Dominic Rossi from Mount St. Benedict University. I called and spoke with someone about gathering some information about the Cloister of St. Keira."

The woman said, "Oh, that was me! I'm Letitia Franklin, the parish secretary, bookkeeper, and director of communications. Father Tom gave me the title of director of communications cause I love to talk to everybody. How y'all doing, Professor? I'll head down the hall and get Father Tom. He's been looking forward to meeting you."

Two minutes later she returned with Father Tom Marino, who turned out to be a tall, lanky, dark-haired man with thick, black-framed glasses and a ready smile. "Professor Rossi, it's a pleasure. Mount St. Ben's is a great school. Come on back to my office. I'm eager to know why a professor of English from such a prestigious university is interested in a group of cloistered nuns."

As Dom followed him down the hallway, he noticed that Father Tom had a pronounced limp.

Father Tom's office was modest and neat and mostly as expected — religious texts, missals, hymnals, a closet for vestments. The only unusual elements were half a dozen photographs dated 1988 of a tall young man in the uniform of the Rochester Red Wings who, at the time, were the Triple-A affiliate of the Baltimore Orioles. In one prominent photo, the young man, a first baseman, was making a diving stab at a line drive between first and second. It was like a first baseman's version of the famous Ozzie Smith photograph. Several others showed him at bat, trotting around the bases, or diving into the stands for a foul pop-up.

Dom was impressed. "Wow, Father Tom, is that you?"

"Yeah. Those were good days." He patted his knee. "Prior to ripping up my knee in a skiing accident of all things. That was the end of my baseball career. At the time, I was sure my life was over. But you know, Professor, it was the best thing that ever happened to me. In my despair, I turned to Jesus — and He came through in the clutch. I found my vocation and it's been wonderful. Now, tell me, what are you doing down here on the Eastern Shore?" He began to set out coffee.

Dom explained about Rebecca's mugging and his being asked by the university to determine if she was engaged in any research that might reflect badly on the school.

Father Tom shook his head. "I'm sure no expert, Dom, but this smells very political to me. Especially given poor Ms. Glass's situation with the school, as you explained. My guess is that somebody has decided this is cover their ass time."

"That's what my department Chair, Sister Pat, thinks, too."

"She's got good instincts. So, where does the Cloister of St. Keira fit in?"

"Rebecca discovered that in 1958, a cloister affiliated with St. Keira, which was located in the New Jersey Pine Barrens, was totally destroyed by a fire, resulting in the death of eight nuns. I'm beginning to suspect she might have found the remains. But I'm trying to understand why cloistered nuns would be in the Pine Barrens in the first place."

"Dom, the cloistered life is an ancient and honored tradition in the Church. But it is not for the faint of heart."

"How do you mean?"

Father Tom explained that cloistered nuns choose to live entirely removed from the world, that they have almost no contact with people outside the walls of their cloister.

"To most people, that kind of life seems bizarre. But to the nuns, it allows them the space and the silence to have a deeper, richer, unobstructed and more personal relationship with God. They're not like other orders, whose ministry is out in the world. Benedictines, as you of course know, follow the Rule of St. Benedict, a life of prayer and work. At Mount St. Ben's that work is teaching and administering the university. Dominicans are also very involved in teaching, as are the Franciscans. Other orders minister to the poor and the sick and the dying. But cloistered orders, like Trappist monks or the Poor Clare nuns, dedicate themselves exclusively to prayer and contemplation."

"Do the nuns ever leave the cloister?"

"Only for circumstances such as illness. They rely on volunteers or what are called 'extern sisters' to do their shopping or drive them to doctors' appointments. Some orders are totally cloistered. But others allow the exchange of letters with families, or even visits once a month inside the cloister in a special area. And, too, many cloisters conduct religious retreats for women. Another important activity is allowing, even encouraging, women who are considering a vocation to spend various lengths of time in the cloister, so they may experience what that life is like."

"I see. So living in a remote area that is barely accessible to outsiders would make a certain sense, then."

"Absolutely. And a place like the Pine Barrens, in the heart of nature and far removed from worldly matters, would be very appropriate for a cloister."

He added, "But you have to understand, Dom, the cloistered life is not all sweetness and light. That kind of isolation can also have seriously detrimental spiritual and psychological effects. Instead of turning outward towards God more fully, the isolation can turn people inward, towards the darkest impulses of the self. It can make them rigid and narrow, crippling both their spirituality and their humanity. Church history is rife with examples of monasteries and cloisters gone rogue, so to speak."

"I guess then it's not possible for me to visit St. Keira's. So, Father Tom, how can I learn more about their history down here?"

"There's a guy named Stanley Bartkowski, he's a docent at the Rural Life Museum of Trappe. He's in his late sixties and he knows more about this area and its history than anyone. I've got his number. You can give him a call right now."

Dom made the call and Stanley said, "Oh, yeah, Father Tom's a terrific guy. Listen, Dom, the museum is open to the public tomorrow, Saturday, from one until four. But I'm usually there puttering around early. Stop by tomorrow, say around noon."

The arrangements made, Dom bid good-bye to Father Tom and drove south on Route 50 towards Trappe and found an inexpensive chain motel. As he was checking in, he asked the desk clerk, a young Indian man, where he could get some dinner and a drink.

"State Bank of Trappe on Main Street."

63

"No, no, I mean something to eat, you know, dinner and a glass of wine."

The man smiled and repeated, "State Bank of Trappe Pizza Company. Great food, good prices, and very friendly folks. It's in a restored 19th century bank that was robbed by Bonnie and Clyde in 1932. They keep up the gangster theme, as you'll see. Be sure to tell them Arun sent you; I'll get a free slice and a glass of wine next time I show up."

The place turned out to be great.

Chapter 9

The Rural Life Museum of Trappe was small but charming. It was made up of four restored buildings, Defender House, Scale House, Carriage House, and the Slaughter Smokehouse. Dom found Stan Bartkowski standing on the steps of Defender House, the museum's headquarters and anchor building, as they referred to it.

"Hi, Dom. I'm Stan Bartkowski. Welcome." Stan was a big, barrel-chested guy with merry blue eyes and not a hair on his head. He wore clean and pressed overalls over a white collarless shirt. After vigorously shaking Dom's hand he led him inside. Dom saw that the main room held a number exhibits and a collection of local artifacts, memorabilia and assorted antiques all relating to life, commerce, and culture in the area. What caught Dom's eye was the "Home Run" Baker exhibit.

"Hey, Stan, 'Home Run' Baker was a local guy? Didn't he hit a big World Series home run off Christy Mathewson?"

"And another off Rube Marquard, same game, 1911. That's where he got the nickname. That's Father Tom's favorite exhibit, as you might imagine."

Stan led Dom to a small room off the main exhibit space that turned out to be a tiny office holding only a desk, two chairs and a bookcase. He gestured Dom to a chair in front of the desk and then sat down.

"First things first," he said. He reached into a drawer and extracted a bottle about three-quarters filled with a clear liquid and two eight-ounce blue enameled metal coffee mugs. "Stuff eats through paper or plastic." The bottle had an obviously self-designed label with a picture of a plum and the words "Bartkowski's Best."

Stan explained, "Homemade slivovitz. I can only get Father Tom to take a few sips. He says with his bum knee he has enough trouble walking as it is. Well, the sun's over the yardarm somewhere." He poured them each about three fingers. *"Na zdrowie!"*

Dom took a small sip. It tasted like rocket fuel with only a vague suggestion of plum somewhere in the background. Dom's eyes watered. An obviously delighted Stan took a healthy swallow of his.

When he felt able to speak, Dom asked, "Were you born and raised along the Eastern Shore, Stan?"

"Nah, Wyoming. But I hated all that dumb cowboy shit. Soon as I graduated high school I left and joined the Navy, thirty years. After a few years I got stationed over to Patuxent Naval Air Station. Loved it, loved the area. When I retired, I bought a little place on the water, got a little boat, did some charter business. Nothing big, mind you, just took visitors out crabbing, sightseeing, swimming and picnics. My wife's a local girl, used to work at the base commissary. A wonderful woman, I'm blessed. My kids and their families are nearby. My son is in DC, a lawyer for the Interior Department. Daughter is the senior occupational therapist over to Bethesda Naval Hospital. See them regular. But tell me, Dom, what are you seeking to know about the Cloister?"

"I'm trying to learn how nuns from that order ended up in New Jersey."

Stan nodded. "Well I don't know much about the religious part, but let me tell you what I do know.

"The land for the cloister was donated by a guy named Sean McNulty in 1889. He was a former merchant sea captain who made a pile of money, a little shady, most likely smuggling. Anyway, I know that area well, Dom. It's remote, but it's a nice piece of land, a bit southeast of here. A little finger of the Chesapeake Bay extends up in there and the property has a nice view of the water. After McNulty donated it, construction started in 1890, a bunch of local people worked on it. An architect from Baltimore came out and designed the place in the late Federal style, some brick, mostly timber, ten rooms, and a small outbuilding. The nuns, who'd come from Ireland, moved in several months later. Been there ever since."

66

"Okay, I understand that McNulty donated the land. But where did the nuns get the money to bring in an architect and build the place?"

Stan took another sip of the fiery plum brandy. "Charitable donation from an organization out of Baltimore, the Loyal Sons of Cu Chulainn, named after the famous warrior in Irish mythology. He's like the Irish version of Achilles in Greek mythology. They started in Boston back in the late nineteenth century, late 1870s or so. The Baltimore chapter started around 1880. The Loyal Sons have chapters up and down the east coast. A big one near you in North Jersey, smaller one down the Jersey Shore."

Holy shit, Dom thought. A connection he had never dreamed of. But where did it lead? "Do the Loyal Sons still have any connection with the Cloister?"

"So far as I know, they make a hefty donation each year. Beyond that nobody has any connection with the Cloister at all. Which, I guess, is the whole point."

***

Diana Bennington jogged regularly and religiously every evening. On this Friday evening, she left her condo on Ardsleigh Drive in Madison, crossed Madison Avenue and jogged south along Loantaka Way, a small, quiet side road that ran between the outskirts of the Drew University campus and the corporate park known as Giralda Farms. Since it was evening, she was wearing her reflective clothing, although there usually was not much traffic on her preferred route.

It was about 8:30, and she was jogging at a very respectable clip when she saw headlights coming up the road in the opposite direction. The asshole had his high beams on and was obviously traveling way too fast for the small road. She moved slightly more to the side of the road and couldn't help but look away, since the lights were so bright.

It was then that the vehicle swerved directly towards her and hit her straight on, knocking her into the air for some thirty feet and leaving her in a smashed, crumpled, bloody heap some twenty feet into the corporate park. The vehicle kept right on going. The driver smiled.

***

Mrs. Bonvini was sitting in her rocking chair on the front porch, crocheting as usual when Dom arrived home from Maryland about 6:00 p.m.

"Dommy, good for you. It's a start. I don't get the impression she's all that light hearted, but she's very pretty. And certainly no teenager, thank God."

"I'm sorry, Mrs. B., but who's very pretty and no teenager?"

"Sarah, upstairs in your place. She's been there about a half hour."

Dom was completely befuddled. "Who's Sarah and what is she doing upstairs in my place?"

"Waiting for you with her heart all aflutter, I'm sure. I let her in. Sarah Craig. She told me she's from Freehold. It's a little far away, but hey, Dommy, at this point Chicago would be okay."

A thoroughly confused Dom went upstairs and opened his front door to see Detective Craig standing there, wearing jeans, a burgundy V-neck sweater, and an uncertain smile.

"*Sarah?* What's going on?"

"I was in the neighborhood. I guess it's a social call."

Dom shook his head in confusion. "Excuse me, but I thought that in your line of work there was no such thing as a social call. Also, as I remember quite clearly, you and I were going nowhere."

"I've been thinking about that. I think you and I can go somewhere, at least for a little while."

"How little?"

"How about tonight and tomorrow? If that's all right and not presumptuous or anything."

"It's perfectly all right. Though it is presumptuous. Suppose I had company?"

Sarah smiled. "Mrs. Bonvini told me it would be okay. She keeps pretty close tabs on you."

"So what now?"

"Now I go down to my car and get my overnight bag. Then we go to bed, have free wheeling, uninhibited sex, and later we can open a bottle of wine and get some Chinese take-out. How's that sound?"

And that's exactly what they did.

***

68

While they were devouring their Chinese take-out and a bottle of Alsatian Gewurztraminer, Sarah said, "Any more thoughts on this Rebecca Glass thing, or are you too busy getting ready for exams these days?"

"Nothing definite, but it's beginning to seem more involved than I first thought. There are more things connected to it than I realized. But I'm still wandering around in a haze."

Sarah paused in mid-bite. "You going to keep at it?"

"Yeah, it's become like an itch I have to scratch."

"You sure you want to do that?"

"Yeah, I'm very sure. Something stinks here."

She looked at him a few seconds then said, "If anything reveals itself, give me a heads up. Maybe I can help."

"Will do."

The following morning, after greeting the day with another round of energetic sex, Dom staggered out of bed and pulled on his jeans and an old sweatshirt. He put on some coffee then went out and bought the Sunday *New York Times* and a copy of the local paper, the *Daily Record.*

Next he stopped at Morristown Bagel & Deli and picked up a half dozen assorted bagels. unsure what kind Sarah would prefer, three different flavors of cream cheese and some lox. By the time he returned, Sarah was showered and dressed and had poured herself some coffee. Her overnight bag was on the table in the vestibule by the front door.

Dom said, "Oh, okay. Do you at least have time for breakfast or are you on your way out the door?"

She smiled. "I do have time for breakfast. But first I want to thank you for this wonderful..." She searched awkwardly for the word.

"Interlude?"

"Yes, this wonderful interlude."

She looked at him curiously, as if he were from another planet. "You're an unusual man, Dom. You're not at all like other men I've known. You're a little... disconcerting I guess is the word. You're funny, kind, and smarter than anyone I've ever met. Now, may I please have an everything bagel with cream cheese and lox?"

Following Sarah's departure, Dom poured himself some more coffee and went out and sat on his little balcony, thinking. He had just experienced perhaps the oddest romantic encounter of his life. Though as he thought about it, romance had little to do with it. He didn't feel guilt; Gina was gone too long for that. And it had certainly been physically satisfying. But it had been nearly emotionless.

He felt more like a participant than a lover. It was as if Sarah had been both engaged and distant. There had been no pillow talk, no sharing of background or life story, no suggestion of any kind of future. Only a question about Rebecca Glass. Dom felt almost a sense of relief that it would go no further. He figured he was not meant for one-night stands.

He cleaned up the breakfast debris, showered and shaved and started in on the papers. Usually, he just skimmed the *Daily Record* and settled in with the *Times* for several hours. Today was different.

In the local section of the *Daily Record* he noticed a headline, "Madison woman killed in hit and run." The article identified the woman as Diana Bennington, 37, owner and operator of a successful yoga studio. She had been pronounced dead at Morristown Memorial Hospital at 10:00 p.m. Friday. Evidently, she had been struck while jogging on Loantaka Way near Drew University and Giralda Farms some time between 8:30 and 9:00, after her last yoga class. The vehicle and driver had not been found.

Jesus Christ, what the hell is going on?

Dom immediately called Sarah on her cell phone. She said, "Dom, I just got in. Look, if this is some kind of guilt or regret or..."

Dom had neither the time nor the patience for small talk. "Put a lid on it, Sarah. This is serious. Someone ran down Diana Bennington in the street Friday night. She's dead. What the hell is going on here?"

"I'll get back to you."

70

Chapter 10

The headquarters of the North Jersey Chapter of the Loyal Sons of Cu Chulainn was located in a large, impressive Tudor-style mansion on MacCulloch Avenue in Morristown, across the street from the Thomas Nast Museum and, coincidentally, just four blocks from Dom's apartment. The offices were quite expensively furnished, which President Brian Shaughnessy felt was entirely appropriate for an organization with as much power and influence as that wielded by the Loyal Sons — influence that extended to business, politics and the Church.

With respect to business, the awarding of lucrative contracts throughout northern New Jersey, leverage with unions, the granting of clearances, approvals and licenses — all fell under the influence of the Loyal Sons or people connected to them, as did political nominees for local, statewide, and regional offices. And their power did not end there.

More than one priest in the archdioceses of Patterson, Newark and Trenton who were considered too liberal or whose views were inconsistent with those of the Loyal Sons found their ecclesiastical career stalled — courtesy of the Loyal Sons. Indeed, the current Bishop of Trenton owed his appointment to the Loyal Sons; and the priest who had been thought of as his chief rival, Father Lawrence Mancini, a liberal, was ultimately banished to an abjectly poor parish in Camden. Such was the power of Loyal Sons of Cu Chulainn.

While much of the organization's business was conducted on the first two floors of the mansion, the heart of the headquarters was its large "ceremonial chamber," located in what used to be an immense basement which had been redesigned and rebuilt to house the Loyal Sons' secret ceremonies. This was where the members of the governing body met, in robes and gowns appropriate to their position and with candle-lit solemnity, to take care of the organization's business. The walls were draped with banners and tapestries bearing a variety of Irish heraldic images representing families of the members, including the Shaughnessy clan, whose symbol was a unicorn in front of a castle.

On this day, in addition to Shaughnessy, gathered in the chamber were all of the senior members of the organization's governing body — Vice President Aidan Cavanaugh, Secretary George Brennan, Treasurer Patrick Kenney, and Historian Edward Manning. All were third or fourth generation Loyal Sons; all of them knew the stakes — for the organization, as well as for each of them as individuals — should Rebecca Glass's research become public knowledge.

The organization's chaplain, Father Sean Gilhooley, had begun the meeting with a prayer asking the Lord for wisdom, guidance, and success in their holy endeavors. Immediately following this, Father Gilhooley left, not wanting to know any more than necessary about the organization's private affairs.

Also present was the Sergeant-at-Arms, Martin O'Bannon. Shaughnessy said to O'Bannon, "So that little bastard Rossi lives practically right down the street. That should make things easy when the time comes."

"My guy has been on him for several days now. Rossi has done a lot of running around, but it doesn't seem he's come up with anything. The way it looks, we're in the clear."

Cavanaugh said, "Perhaps. But we know what is out there. What if this Rossi turns out to be more tenacious than expected,?"

Shaughnessy said, "It's unlikely, Aidan. From what I can see, he's just another effete, obnoxious academic. Nevertheless, Martin, how good is your man?"

"Very good, and very tough. Frank Burns, a former investigator for the Morris County Prosecutor's Office, now private. He's also a Loyal Son."

"How much does Burns know about our business?" Kenney wanted to know.

"Only that the kid could be a threat and that he's smart."

Shaughnessy nodded in approval. He asked, "What about the University, Martin? What's our status there?"

"You know as well as I, Brian. The Chair of the English Department, Sister Patricia Schaedel, is a key Rossi ally — very savvy and very independent. She could be a problem we may have to resolve, depending on how things go. But for now, I have someone inside the department. Father Jack is being kept out of the loop by Delaney, who of course expects to be rewarded for his efforts."

Shaughnessy said, "And he shall be. Becoming president of such a prestigious university is certainly a significant reward. And knowing Felix as I do, he'll do anything to achieve it."

He paused then asked, "How about the incident the other night?"

At this question, they all focused intensely on O'Bannon. Each of them knew what had been called for; each had approved the decision.

O'Bannon, looking each man in the eye, said, "My outside resource pulled it off flawlessly. I'm comfortable that we're covered all around."

Most of the men around the conference table nodded and smiled, pleased and reassured at how things were playing out. Except, Shaughnessy noticed, for the Historian, Edward Manning, who had said nothing during the meeting.

Shaughnessy said, "Edward, do you have any questions or problems as to how we are proceeding? If so, please feel free to express them. After all, we are all in this together."

Manning was a fussy, middle-aged man who much preferred studying documents and cataloguing old photographs and correspondence to attending meetings such as this. A former lecturer in History at the College of St. Elizabeth, he had been denied tenure and released a number of years earlier — the result of an ill-conceived dalliance with a female freshman history major. He felt his career had been destroyed. Then, the Loyal Sons threw him a lifeline and appointed him as Historian, the only paid position in the organization. He owed them. Manning now looked at Shaughnessy then quickly glanced away.

"No, Brian. I have no problems I wish to raise, at this time."

Shaughnessy said mildly, "Are you suggesting, Edward that you might at a later time? That would not be very helpful — or appropriate, given what we have to do. So I ask again, are you totally with us in this endeavor?"

Still not making eye contact, Manning said, "Yes, Brian. I'm with you."

Shaughnessy smiled. "Splendid. That's how I like it. Let's keep it that way."

Some time later, after resolving the immediate matters at hand, Brian Shaughnessy adjourned the meeting. While the others left, he asked Edward Manning to remain for a moment.

"Edward, it is clear you're feeling some distress. What's troubling you?"

Manning, obviously uncomfortable, said, "Brian, I knew — and accepted the fact — that we would have to be aggressive in protecting the good name of the Loyal Sons, indeed protect its very existence. But what I did not foresee was that we would be so...so final in our actions. It deeply troubles me, frankly. I feel torn, in a way, between the tremendous good we are doing and the...the means we sometimes employ. It seems so antithetical to what we truly stand for. Perhaps we should have a general meeting to discuss these issues with our full membership."

"You know that is impossible, Edward. Such matters are for the leadership only. After all, that is what leaders do — make the hard decisions. "

Manning nodded his head. "Yes, yes, I understand, Brian. Still, I have grave concerns."

Shaughnessy then made an executive decision. He patted Manning on the shoulder and, smiling, told him, "Not to worry, Edward. I'll take care of you."

After Manning left, Shaughnessy poured himself a tumbler of Black Bush Irish whisky and lit up a cigar. Things were becoming messy, a state of affairs that offended him. It called for action, bold action. It was his legacy. And he relished it.

He fondly recalled a conversation between his father and grandfather when he was fourteen or so, having to do with their legacy. He had been thrilled that he was allowed to be present at the consideration of such grave matters.

They were in his grandfather's mansion in Spring Lake. Dennis Shaughnessy had said to his son Liam, "We are vigorous men, Liam. Virile men. Men such as we have certain...needs and requirements that must be fulfilled so that we may go about our larger business. Women are part of those requirements, those needs. But they must never influence our business. Mistakes, 'indiscretions,' if you will, will inevitably occur. But that is why we have the Pines, always the Pines. That is where the 'indiscretions' go. Do you understand, Liam? Are you willing to carry on, do you have the strength?"

Liam answered, "Absolutely, sir. You may be assured."

The old man, Dennis, had then turned and looked at the boy, Brian. "And you, lad. Can you fulfill the trust when it is your turn?"

Brian Shaughnessy had replied, "I can, grandfather. I will. "

***

Monday morning arrived with a chilly, heavy, wind-driven spring rain, causing Dom to sprint from the Mount St. Ben's faculty parking lot into the Humanities and Social Sciences Building to meet with Professor Ray Alexander, a smiling, gray-haired, avuncular middle-age man who had been with the University for over twenty years. To look at him was to immediately think, 'professor.'

Dom explained about his looking into Rebecca Glass's research and how Sister Pat thought Ray might be able to help.

"My knowledge of New Jersey extends mostly to writers — James Fennimore Cooper, Walt Whitman, Joyce Kilmer, Stephen Crane, William Carlos Williams, Amiri Baraka, Ntozake Shange. Beyond the literature, though, I'm hurting."

Ray laughed and said, "Dom, we'll help you and educate you, both. Let get's coffee and I'll tell you what we've got going on with this folklore stuff."

They settled in Ray's office. "Dom, as you of course know, folklore is essentially a community's traditional stories and legends which are transmitted orally from generation to generation. Some universities and scholars use the term 'folkloristics,' to distinguish the study of folklore from the actual folklore itself. Frankly, that sounds a bit pretentious to me. We keep it simple.

"But the program as it is developing is quite sophisticated. Initially, our principal focus will be on the folklore of New Jersey. Then we'll expand our area of inquiry regionally, heading up and down the east coast and then, well, we'll see what happens."

Ray explained how the program was tapping into scholars and disciplines all across the University — Arts and Humanities,

75

Social and Behavioral Sciences, and Education and Human Ecology.

"The idea is to prepare young scholars and students for working in a whole variety of settings — libraries and archives, museums, historical associations, arts councils, publishing, funding agencies, the federal government, and of course various academic departments in colleges and universities."

"How's the enrollment going?"

Ray smiled wryly. "We're never going to rival the Business School, but it's moving along well. I've even recruited a hotshot graduate teaching assistant, whom I want you to meet. She's a Monmouth University honors grad, dual major, Sociology and Anthropology. Fred Berkowitz down there sent her to me. She's a piece of work. We've had her to the house for dinner several times and Peggy, my wife, is ready to adopt her. She's brilliant, eager, and she has more energy than any twelve people."

He checked his watch. "She should be down in the lab about now. She's been researching the Ramapo Lenape Nation up in the Ramapo Mountains for a couple of weeks — doing interviews, recording stories, filming, and living right there with the Nation. She's got a real talent for getting folks to open up and talk freely. That's a vital skill in an anthropologist and especially in a folklorist."

"Didn't the Ramapo Lenape used to be referred to as 'Jackson Whites' — Native Americans with a smattering of African American, German Hessians, British Loyalists, and even some Dutch?"

"That's correct, and it was a pejorative and demeaning term. And some very ugly and false things were written about them. They finally were awarded Native American status by the State of New Jersey in 1980, but the damn feds haven't gotten around to recognizing them yet. In any case, that culture is a fascinating one from both an anthropological and an historical perspective. And it no doubt will be rich in folklore. That's what we're trying to learn. Let's head downstairs and see if she's there."

The Folklore Studies program borrowed space in the anthropology lab on the first floor of the building. Dom and Ray entered from the rear of the lab just in time to see a disheveled, rain-soaked young woman come barging in the front door.

"Shit! What a freaking mess!"

The wind had blown back the hood of her rain slicker and her hair and face were dripping wet. She was carrying two plastic garbage bags filled with God knew what and had a backpack slung across her shoulders. All of which she dropped on the floor, rain slicker included, still muttering and dripping. She wiped off her face then looked up and saw Dom and Ray. And gave them a sunburst smile.

"I make a great entrance, don't I? Hello, Dr. Ray." She went to him and gave him a hug. Then she extended her hand to Dom. "Hi. I'm Caroline Allyson Bridget Lacey. But everyone calls me Lacey."

Her hair was the color of autumn leaves, a wild mixture of various shades of red and gold; it was cut very short and plastered to her face, accentuating her fine, delicate bone structure. Her large, expressive eyes were a startling blue. She was about an inch or two shorter than Dom's five ten. From what little Dom could tell from the flannel shirt and faded jeans she wore, she was very slender but with obvious female attributes — and legs that seemed to go on forever. All things considered and even in her disheveled state, she was stunning.

"I...I'm Professor...I'm Dom Rossi from English. I mean, I'm in the English Department here. I'm very pleased to meet you, Lacey. And, well, Ray was just singing your praises..."

She laughed. "Hey, I've heard of you — 'Dr. Dom.' So, what's up, guys?"

"Lacey, Dom is involved in a kind of special project for the university. He's looking into some research the late Professor Rebecca Glass was doing. Some of it may fall within your areas of expertise."

Dom said, "I think a key part of it has to do with the folklore of the Pine Barrens, about which I'm almost totally ignorant. I'm hoping maybe you could point me in the right direction"

She nodded. "Sounds interesting. Tell you what, Dr. Dom, let me put this stuff away and get cleaned up. How about I meet you in the Lair in a half hour?"

Ray said, "Thank you, Lacey. It'll be the two of you. I have a class to get to."

77

The Lair was Mount St. Ben's Student Center, formally named the Reverend Gerard Lair, OSB, Student Center, after the University's longest serving and greatest president. The building housed the Office of Student Life, offices of the campus newspaper, yearbook, and literary magazine, as well as dining halls, a food court, game rooms and the campus Pub, known as the Falcons' Lair.

One half hour later, right on the button, Lacey walked into the Lair. Now wearing a red turtleneck and tight jeans tucked into calf high brown leather boots, she was even more striking. Heads turned as she walked in. Dom saw her look around the student lounge and, seeing him, give him a big smile and a wave; then she walked over to his table.

"Hi, Dr. Dom. Let's get a coffee and talk." They walked over Java Jane's Koffee Klatsch and each ordered a large Columbian roast with milk and sugar. Lacey said, "Want to split a blueberry scone?" They did.

Dom said, "This is on me. Can't have a highly promising graduate teaching assistant going broke."

Once seated, Lacey divided the scone, gave Dom half and took a healthy bite of her own piece. She said, "So please explain more about this mission you're on having to do with the Pine Barrens. It sounds very mysterious."

"I have to warn you, this whole deal is a little strange. How familiar were you with Rebecca Glass?"

"Not very. I only met her once, but gossip on a university campus is worse than at the hairdresser's, and she sounds like a pisser. I wish I could have known her better. How well did you know her?"

"We shared an office. And she was a friend. That's why the university asked me to look into this."

He hesitated, trying to think how best to proceed. He didn't want to scare off this young woman or jeopardize her burgeoning career in any way. "Look, some of what I'm about to explain is what I've learned; a lot of it is pure conjecture. Here is how I think it goes.

"Several months ago, Professor Glass got a consulting job from San Giacomo Engineering down in Freehold to assess their proposed highway route through the Pine Barrens, roughly from

78

Philadelphia to Tuckerton. Her job was to look for any archaeological or historical sites that the proposed route would have to avoid. Her report included mention of a devastating fire in that area almost sixty years ago in which eight nuns from the Cloister of St. Keira died.

"Here comes some conjecture — I think Rebecca may have found something significant connected to the fire. I also learned that the Cloister had a Mother House in Maryland that was sponsored and supported by the Baltimore Chapter of the Loyal Sons of Cu Chulainn.

"I'm beginning to suspect that whatever she found resulted in her writing a very provocative paper that she was scheduled to present at the annual meeting of the Archaeological Association of New Jersey. Then, before she was able present it, she was mugged and killed. But whatever controversy she found is still out there and, the University fears, is potentially embarrassing or damaging."

Lacey was about to take a bite of her scone then stopped. "Wait a second. Are you suggesting there's some kind of connection between the fire and the Loyal Sons of Cu Chulainn here in New Jersey? Excuse me, Doc, but that sounds a little nuts."

"There is a connection, albeit a tenuous one. The President of the Mount St. Ben's Board of Trustees is President of the North Jersey Chapter of the Loyal Sons. I'm pretty sure he's the driving force behind my assignment."

"So what? My Dad was a member of the Loyal Sons, Jersey Shore Chapter."

"You're from the Shore area?"

"Yeah. We lived in Rumson, in Monmouth County. My Dad was a pharmacist. He had a store in Red Bank, Lacey's Apothecary. We use to spend summers at our little bungalow on Mystic Island, just below Tuckerton on the eastern edge of the Pine Barrens. It's right on a lagoon with easy access to the bay. My parents retired to Florida, but we kept the place. I still go there when I can."

"Where in Florida did they retire?"

"Naples. They love it."

"Hey, my folks are in Naples, too. My father was an architect and my mother was a graphic designer. Maybe my folks and yours are neighbors."

Lacey smiled at him. "Well, Dr. Dom, in that case, maybe we should take a road trip together sometime and visit them."

Dom felt himself blush. He had been thinking the same thing. "Okay, let's get back to Rebecca. I have to tell you something else before you volunteer to get into this — if you do. Rebecca's partner, Diana Bennington, was struck and killed by a hit and run driver several nights ago. I don't know if it's at all related, but you should know that bad things are happening around this little quest."

"Jesus. Her partner got killed only a few days after Professor Glass got killed? Is anybody looking into this?"

"A very smart detective from the Monmouth County Prosecutor's Office. She's checking on the hit and run for me."

"What exactly do you want from me?"

"Well, first off, I need to know more about the Loyal Sons of Cu Chulainn's connection to the Cloister. But I'm reluctant to go marching into the offices of the North Jersey Chapter and start digging into their archives. So I've decided to go to the founding chapter in Boston and see if I can find anything helpful. Then, assuming it's warranted, I'll head down to the Pine Barrens. That's where you come in.

"If you're willing, I'd like you to accompany me and use both your knowledge of folklore and your familiarity with the area to help me learn what Rebecca may have uncovered — if anything. What do you say?"

"Boy, no one told me a graduate teaching assistantship could be so rife with intrigue." She thought for several minutes, a slight frown appearing on her face, which did nothing, Dom noticed, to mar her extraordinary beauty.

She said, "Okay, how about this? I'm scheduled to teach an Introduction to Folklore class during the third summer session. It's a six-week course that begins July 8th and goes to August 18th, so I have to have time to prepare well before then. Also, I have my own work to do. So, here's my idea — what if we make this quest of yours into an Independent Study for me; we'll call it Folklore of the Jersey Pines. Everything I do and learn I then turn

80

into a research paper for credit. You're my mentor, to make it official. I'll get the approval from Dr. Ray. What do you say?"

"It's a deal. So, how do I contact you? Where do you live?"

"I have a little apartment above a Latino restaurant at the corner of Speedwell Avenue and Early Street, El Chicharron. It's a BYO and it's wonderful. All kinds of people, from the folks who live in the Hollow to the Courthouse crowd come in for lunch or takeout nearly every day. Even the DA himself is in there several times a week. I'll take you there sometime. Here are both my cell phone and my home phone numbers."

Dom in turn gave her his numbers and the address of his apartment on Wetmore Avenue. That settled, they looked at each other, somewhat awkwardly.

"Well," Lacey said, "I'll see you when you return from Boston, Dr. Dom."

Her blue eyes seemed to sparkle. Or maybe it was wishful thinking on Dom's part. He said, "Okay, then. I'm really looking forward to seeing you again, Lacey — I mean, you know, when I get back from Boston. So I can tell you what's going on. And it's just plain Dom."

She smiled and said, "Okay, just plain Dom. I'll be seeing you."

Dom thought her smile was a glorious sight.

Chapter 11

On Tuesday, Dom did some work at his office on campus then headed north at noon. He arrived in Boston just before 4:00. He had always liked Boston, its literary history, its look, its location. He smiled as he remembered the Mark Twain quote, "In New York, they ask how much a man is worth. In Boston, they ask how much does he know." If it weren't for the Red Sox, it would be a great town.

About mid way through his drive he called the Mount St. Ben's English Department and left a message with Fran Purcell. "Fran, please let Sister Pat know that I had to go to the Loyal Sons of Cu Chulainn chapter in Boston on some university business. I'll touch base with her tomorrow and fill her in when she's available."

"I'll be sure she gets the message, Professor." Following which, Fran called the Provost's office. "He's on his way to Boston, Provost Delaney. He says he's on some kind of university business having to do with the Loyal Sons."

Dom found the headquarters of the Loyal Sons of Cu Chulainn on the block between Beacon Street and Chestnut Street, just a few steps away from Boston Common. This was, Dom knew, very pricey territory. He found a parking garage three blocks away and set out on foot to the offices. Spring in Boston was in full bloom, bright sun, streets crowded with affluent, attractive people, the feel of a smart, vibrant, dynamic city.

The Loyal Sons building was an impressive four-story brownstone with a large bronze plaque next to the entrance. Inside, Dom found himself in an expansive lobby that was more like a museum than an office building. The directory on the wall indicated that the first floor held exhibit rooms, a library and a gift shop; the second and third floors were given over to various administrative offices, and the fourth floor held conference rooms and private offices of the organization's senior officials. After signing in at the front desk, Dom headed for the exhibit rooms.

He found that the exhibits, mostly photographs, framed documents, and old newspaper articles, were essentially a history of the founding and the activities through the years of the Loyal Sons. In addition to Boston, several of the other major Chapters were featured — Philadelphia, Baltimore, Washington DC, and the North Jersey Chapter.

As he perused the exhibits, it struck Dom as odd that despite the proud, sometimes painful, and always interesting history of Irish immigration to America (a story which was certainly worth significant exhibit space), the exhibits focused almost exclusively on the Loyal Sons of Cu Chulainn as an Irish success story. Moreover, the exhibits were not just assertive in their presentation of the organization's growth, influence, and activities; they were aggressive and bordered on the self-aggrandizing.

As he moved through the exhibits, one in particular caught Dom's eye and struck him very personally. It was a history of the Loyal Sons' involvement with orphanages and foundling homes. The term "foundling home," long out of use, sounded to Dom like something out of Charles Dickens, like the baby farm where Oliver Twist grew up.

He learned that foundlings were not just orphans; they were infants who had been purposely "exposed and abandoned," usually by unwed mothers, left either to somehow be salvaged, or to die. Some of the photographs reinforced this notion — nuns and nurses in grim, Victorian-looking hospitals holding sick, damaged, blank eyed infants and toddlers of various races and ethnicities.

It occurred to Dom that had he been born in an earlier time, one of these infants might have been him. He considered how fortunate he had been. Anthony and Theresa Rossi had adopted Dom through a private adoption agency just a matter of hours after his birth, the arrangements having been made well in advance. He had been wanted right from the moment he drew his first breath — obviously not by his birth parents, but certainly by Anthony and Theresa. And they had raised him that way.

Dom then saw other photographs that were strikingly different. In them, the infants were obviously well cared for and healthy — and all were Caucasian. *What accounted for the difference?*

As he read further, he learned that these infants had benefitted from the support of the Loyal Sons of Cu Chulainn, North Jersey Chapter. In one prominent photograph dated 1908, a beautiful baby girl was being held by a large, smiling, prosperous-looking man with white hair, whom the caption explained was President of the North Jersey Chapter of the Loyal Sons — Dennis Shaughnessy. Dom thought, *it must be Brian Shaughnessy's grandfather.*

But then, for reasons unexplained, the support of the Loyal Sons North Jersey chapter apparently ended in 1958. There were no more entries or mentions after that.

"Good morning, is there anything I can help you with today?" Dom turned to see standing there a red-haired woman who looked like a forty year-old version of Maureen O'Hara in *The Quiet Man*, which, given the surroundings, was probably the whole idea.

Dom said, "Gee, you don't look like a Loyal Son."

Her smile was instantaneous. "You know, I've always wanted someone to say that! I'm Megan Feeney. I'm the curator."

Dom returned the smile. "It's a pleasure to meet you, Ms. Feeney. I'm Dom Rossi. I teach English at Mount St. Benedict's University in New Jersey."

"Oh, that's a great school. Please call me Megan. How can I help you, Dom?"

"Megan, I was wondering how closely the founding chapter here in Boston stays in touch with the other chapters around the Northeast. I'm especially interested in who determines the recipients of the organization's charitable activities. Would it be the Boston headquarters or the North Jersey chapter itself, for example?"

She looked at him for a moment "Each chapter has a great deal of autonomy. As long as they adhere to our Mission Statement and obey the by-laws, chapters can determine for themselves where to direct their largesse. Sometimes those activities overlap, simply as a matter of shared values and interests. The specific determination is made by each chapter's Benevolence Committee."

"Benevolence Committee?"

She laughed. "It is obviously an old term, dating from the organization's founding. It's a committee that reviews and evaluates worthy causes, people, or institutions and makes recommendations. Each chapter has one. It's in the by-laws."

"Would beneficiaries of the largesse include religious orders, monasteries, convents, or cloisters?"

"Oh sure. As you probably know, most of those kinds of places and institutions receive support from the Church. But many of them require additional assistance to maintain their ministries. The Loyal Sons of Cu Chulainn has been providing such support for religious orders emanating from Ireland or connected to Ireland since the organization's founding."

After a moment, she added, "But you know, each Chapter has an Historian, you could easily speak with the one in the North Jersey Chapter. His name, I believe, is Edward Manning."

"Yes, that's a good idea. I have one more question. Are you familiar with the story of the Cloister of St. Keira in New Jersey?"

"I am, and it's both a tragic and fascinating story. I'd love to tell you about it, but, frankly, I'm kind of in a rush now. I have a staff meeting to get to." She smiled at him, a little provocatively he thought. "Maybe we can talk later. Are you available, say, after five o'clock?"

"I certainly can be."

"How about we meet for a drink after I get off, say five-fifteen at the Avery Bar in the Ritz Carlton. That way we don't have to rush."

"Sounds great. I'll see you then."

The Ritz Carlton was just across Boston Common from the headquarters of the Loyal Sons. Dom used the time to stroll the area, trying to piece together the assorted elements of the puzzle that seemed to be developing right before his eyes — St. Keira's, orphanages, fires, assorted Shaughnessys. He could not connect the dots, but he believed that the connection had to be there.

The Avery Bar was decorated in a retro-1950s modern design, lots of leather and fabric furniture and a gorgeous raised fireplace. At five-fifteen precisely, Megan Feeney walked in at waved at him. It struck Dom that all of a sudden all kinds of interesting women were showing up in his life. His guard went up. No one's luck is that good.

He and Megan found a table near the fireplace and a waitress immediately came over to take their order.

"Cosmo," Megan said.

Dom ordered a scotch and soda. He asked, "Megan, about the Cloister of St. Keira in New Jersey, do you have any idea how the Cloister supported itself?"

"That particular group of nuns came to New Jersey directly from Ireland in 1891. But there was barely any contact with the Mother House in Maryland. It was the Loyal Sons North Jersey Chapter who made the initial contact with the order when they were still in County Tipperary, near the village of Ballyporeen, and arranged for them to come to America. The North Jersey Chapter was given approval by the Bishop of Trenton.

"As far as I know, the New Jersey cloister was quite active sewing various types of vestments for priests in the dioceses of both Trenton and Camden — albs, chasubles, cassocks and the like. They also offered retreats, and a young woman could stay there for a time to determine if her vocation was in fact authentic."

Dom said, "A priest in Maryland told me the cloistered life is not for the faint of heart. It sure sounds like it. Was there anything that distinguished St. Keira's from other cloistered orders?"

A suddenly uncomfortable Megan took a healthy sip of her Cosmo and said, "Well, they were quite strict, and kept themselves very isolated. After they left Ireland, the order died out, except for the two houses in America."

"Do you know why they left Ireland? And why did they die out? How did the Loyal Sons North Jersey Chapter even get involved with them to begin with?"

Dom noticed her break eye contact as she said, "There evidently was some kind of problem in County Tipperary that moving the order to America somehow solved. I was never able to learn exactly what it was. As for the involvement with the Loyal Sons of Cu Chulainn, my understanding is that the relationship had its roots in County Tipperary. Beyond that, no one really knows."

She took another healthy pull at her Cosmo. As Dom observed her facial expressions and body movements, he got the very strong feeling that she was dissembling, very likely withholding what she really knew.

Unnoticed by Dom, the man who had been at Rebecca's memorial service and who had followed Dom and Diana to Rod's entered the Avery and sat unobtrusively at the main bar. Frank Burns hadn't been thrilled with having to drive all the way to fucking Boston, but at least the money was good. Still, Burns would have liked a little more action. Tails and stakeouts, like this job with the kid, were boring as hell. But they paid the bills. Burns wondered where the kid would head after Boston. All he seemed to be doing was talking to people. He said as much when he called O'Bannon.

"I can't see he's got much of anything, only that he's picked up some history on the Loyal Sons. He's having a drink with the woman I got to earlier, who said she'd go along with us and give me feedback on what he was up to.

"She's no kid, but she's a real looker. But it's obvious now that she's not suited to this kind of work and Rossi doesn't seem to be going for it. Looks like a waste of time — and a hundred bucks."

"Okay," O'Bannon told him, "forget her. Let's see what Rossi reports to Delaney. Then we'll decide what's next for Professor Rossi. In the meantime, keep on it."

Dom, oblivious to this conversation, asked Megan, "In the exhibit about orphanages, I noticed a photograph of beautiful, well-cared for infants. Where was that picture taken?"

"Holy Innocents Orphanage in Mt. Holly, New Jersey. They did wonderful work, until it closed. In 1958."

Dom thought, *Jesus, 1958 was a hell of a year.* He asked, "Where did the babies come from?"

She hesitated before answering, "Well since it was a Catholic orphanage, I'm sure the Diocese of Trenton helped people in the process." She signaled the waitress for another Cosmo.

Dom again noted her discomfort. "Beyond your own research, does a history of the Cloister of St. Keira exist anywhere, if I want to learn more?"

"I can't imagine that one does exist. I certainly would be aware of it. And why ever would you want to know more? That's old news."

She quickly attacked her second Cosmo. Then, in an abrupt and bizarre change of topic, she asked, "Are you spending the night in Boston, Dom? Do you have any plans? Dinner together would be lovely. And perhaps later..."

Dom suddenly thought of what Lacey might think of him if he did so. Where the hell did that come from?

"Megan, you've been very gracious and helpful. But I have to get back."

Megan took hold of his hand and said, "Maybe next time you're in Boston..."

Chapter 12

Dom located his car but then sat in it for several minutes, thinking. He had originally planned to head back to Morristown, but there was something Megan said that was bothering him — her remark about there having been some kind of trouble for the Order in County Tipperary that caused them to abandon Ireland for America. He needed to learn why and then determine if it was relevant.

What he needed was an expert on Irish history. He was optimistic about finding one — this was Boston, after all. Using his smart phone, he went online and after ten minutes, he hit pay dirt. He discovered that Boston College, just over six miles away in Chestnut Hill, had a highly regarded, multidisciplinary program in Irish Studies. It offered undergraduate and graduate courses addressing social, political, and economic history, as well as Irish literature, medieval arts, sociology, music and Irish language.

It was closing in on 7 p.m. and even though Dom knew that universities had people around at all kinds of hours, he decided to find a place to sleep and check out BC early the next morning. He located a Super 8 Motel in Waltham, less than two miles from the BC campus, and made a reservation online. On the way, he picked up a quart of beer and a roast beef sub (known as a "grinder" in New England) to eat in his room.

Once ensconced in his room at the Super 8, he called Lacey.

She asked, "How are you doing? Anything helpful?"

"I'm learning all kinds of things, but the connections still elude me. I'm heading over to BC tomorrow to the Irish Studies department. There's something weird about the Sisters of St. Keira."

"Well give me a heads up as soon as you get back. I...I'm really looking forward to seeing you."

A very pleased Dom answered, "Me, too. See you, partner."

The Center for Irish Studies at BC is located in the Connolly House on Hammond Street in Chestnut Hill. Dom had learned that the Director was a Jesuit named Father Theodore Kerry. Dom arrived at the building promptly at eight-thirty. It was a stately former residence and boasted an elegant curved portico supported by four columns, set back on an expanse of green, well-tended lawn. Dom parked around the corner and headed into the front entrance.

In the large lobby he saw a sign to his left directing him to an administrative office farther down the hall. He entered and, typical of most colleges, the place was already bustling with students and faculty all going about their business. An older woman smiled at him as he entered.

"Good morning, how may I help you?"

"I'm Professor Dominic Rossi from Mount St. Benedict University in New Jersey. I apologize for showing up without an appointment, but I'm hoping to speak with someone about an order of cloistered nuns who moved from County Tipperary to America in the late nineteenth century. I was wondering whether there's someone available who might be able to help."

"You're in luck, Professor. Father Ted is already here and back in the kitchen having breakfast. Please wait a moment and I'll see if he can speak with you."

She exited the room then returned a minute later and smiled. "Please go right on back, Professor Rossi. The kitchen is straight ahead then make a right."

When Dom entered the kitchen, he saw a stocky, middle-aged man in a Roman collar standing by the stove making coffee. The man looked at Dom and said, "I know. This is the Irish studies program — I should be having Irish breakfast tea, fried eggs, bacon, blood sausage, grilled tomatoes, and baked beans."

There was a box of Dunkin' Donuts on the table. Father Ted said, "If you promise not to tell, I'll share." He smiled and shook Dom's hand. "Welcome Professor Rossi. What brings you to BC?"

As Father Ted poured them both coffee and opened the box of donuts, Dom explained about Rebecca and her interest in the Cloister of St. Keira. "I get the impression they left Ireland under some kind of a cloud."

Father Ted reached for a Boston cream donut. "It's not a pretty story, Dominic, at least as far as what's been learned. As you know, the order was based in County Tipperary, just outside of the village of Ballyporeen, and was founded in 1849. They took in unwed mothers, prostitutes, and what was generally described as 'fallen women.' While the women stayed there, they helped sew altar vestments for surrounding parishes and monasteries."

Dom helped himself to a crumb cake donut. Father Ted nodded, "Good choice."

After a satisfying bite, Dom said, "Sounds pretty innocuous so far, Father Ted. What went wrong?"

"Dominic, the history of the Church in Ireland is checkered — it has been a tremendous force for good and an appalling source of suffering. As repressed as it was by Protestants, it has been equally repressive towards its own people, women especially.

"Pope Francis's call for mercy in the contemporary Church is about one hundred eighty degrees from what the Irish Church was up to in the old days — even into the twentieth century. Witness the excesses and brutalities in what were known as 'mother and baby homes,' perpetrated by the likes of the Magdalene Sisters and the Bon Secours Sisters. The Bon Secours had a convent in the village of Tuam in County Galway. Hundreds of babies of 'fallen women,' perhaps even more, died there under controversial, but clearly brutal circumstances. Their remains were found in septic tanks.

"From what I know, the Sisters of St. Keira fell into that pattern, perhaps worse, if one can believe it. They treated 'fallen women' horribly in their Cloister outside of Ballyporeen — to the extent that the local bishop chastised the convent and later chose to withhold the Church's support. With no consistent means of support, the convent moved to America — with the assistance of several wealthy American Irish Catholic foundations and families. You probably know of whom I speak. What it amounts to is that the Cloister was thrown out of Ireland."

"How familiar are you with the activities of the St. Keira's sisters in America?"

"I know they became established in Maryland and New Jersey, continued to sew vestments, and that the New Jersey Cloister suffered a terrible tragedy in the late-fifties. Beyond that, it's been silent; I suspect on purpose — but that's just conjecture on my part. If you're looking into their activities, you may find some painful aspects. And there are some people who won't be happy with you. But I'd be very interested in what you learn in your research. Go with God."

***

Hunterdon County is the wealthiest county in New Jersey and the fourth wealthiest in the United States. Somerset and Morris counties in New Jersey rank as the eighth and tenth wealthiest. The twenty-five or so people gathered in the 12,000 square foot palatial home of Fiona Shane in the charming Hunterdon County town of Oldwick, all resided in one or another of these counties.

Liveried servers passed among the crowd, bearing platters of smoked salmon, imported caviar (Beluga and Ossetra), chilled shrimp and crabmeat, goose liver pate, assorted cheeses and canapés. Two bartenders were quite busy serving various kinds of cocktails made with premium brand spirits; the wines were all vintage. A violinist and a cellist provided gentle background music (a lot of Mozart). Presiding over all of this was Fiona Shane, who mixed among her guests like a dowager empress, smiling, nodding, pausing to charm, flatter and cajole as appropriate.

All of the guests were involved in New Jersey's gigantic bio-pharmaceutical industry, an industry which included not only such giants as Johnson & Johnson, Pfizer, Merck, Bristol Myers-Squibb, Sanofi-Aventis, and Novartis, but scores of smaller firms — all of which led to the industry being called the "crown jewel of the New Jersey economy," and to New Jersey's being known as the "medicine chest of the world."

Brian Shaughnessy knew most of the people present, his law firm having represented one or another of their companies over the years. (Bio-pharmaceutical companies were perpetually involved in litigation of one sort or another.) If all went well over the next few months, Shaughnessy and Partners would become the official, exclusive legal counsel of the New Jersey Pharmaceutical Manufacturers' Association. It would be worth

92

hundreds of millions of dollars annually. And given Shaughnessy's connections to soon-to-be Governor William Shane, it would be a sure thing.

On this particular evening, Shaughnessy and the others were all there to hear Bill Shane make his case for their support for his gubernatorial run.

New Jersey gubernatorial campaigns typically begin on Labor Day, in the belief that no one is paying attention before then, since everyone is on vacation. Moreover, since campaigns are so costly, monies are usually husbanded until they can be unleashed in a narrowly focused period of time in order to have maximum impact.

Fiona Shane, not only the mother of the candidate but also his campaign manager, had decided to break precedent and go all out early, kicking off the campaign on Memorial Day with William's being honored as Loyal Son of the Year — an honor arranged by Brian Shaughnessy.

They would campaign in all twenty-one New Jersey counties, and spend big and consistently. The idea was to completely overwhelm the competition and dominate the media coverage. This strategy, typically bold on Fiona's part, called for massive amounts of cash. Hence, the current gathering intended to garner big time support for her son.

Bill Shane was fair-haired and blue-eyed, handsome in a boy-next-door kind of way, with an engaging smile. He'd been the poster boy for the Republican Party in northern New Jersey for the last several years. His future was one of endless possibilities, and a lot of people wanted to go along for the ride. His mother was driving the bus.

Speaking now to the assembled guests, Bill Shane concluded his remarks by saying, "Not many candidates would stand here and dare to quote Calvin Coolidge" (this brought appreciative laughter from the audience), "but Coolidge was right when he said 'the business of America is business.'"

There was much head nodding and agreement. Bill Shane continued, "But let me take that a step further and say that the business of New Jersey is primarily the bio-pharmaceutical business. As you know better than I, the pharmaceutical industry is a $30 billion industry our state, providing nearly 125,000 jobs.

But we are feeling competition from other states, such as California and Massachusetts.

"But when I am elected governor, the industry can count on a loosening of restrictions on research and clinical testing, tax incentives to fund them, as well as an extension on the patent life of your most profitable drugs. To be totally candid — the further growth, success, and profitability of the pharmaceutical industry in New Jersey will be my foremost priority. I stand with you and for you. And you can count on it."

This was met with tremendous applause and an appreciative smile from Fiona. New Jersey Pharma obviously had a big stake in the election of Bill Shane — and Fiona would continue to make sure they knew it.

Arnold Fisher, CEO of Perseus Pharmaceuticals and President of the New Jersey Pharmaceutical Manufacturers Association, sought out Fiona.

He said, "Fiona, I admire you. Your company out-markets my brands with a third of the budget; you cause me all kinds of headaches. Yet you have no reluctance to ask me for a generous donation to support Bill's campaign. You are a woman of brains, beauty, and more than your share of chutzpah."

Fiona smiled and said, "I merely compete where I must and collaborate where I should. Thank you for coming tonight."

"It is my pleasure. I must say, however, I do not envy you the going over the damn press will give you and Bill once the campaign begins in earnest. They'll be scouring your past for the slightest transgression."

Fiona laughed. "My past is too boring to have transgressions, Arnold."

"That's most comforting. We don't want anything to stop Bill. It's too promising, too big — for all of us."

Fiona patted him on the arm. "Rest assured, Arnold. Rest assured."

Fisher nodded and smiled; then he said, "I do have a question, though. When Bill becomes governor of New Jersey, what will be your status at Shane Bio-Pharma?"

"I'll very likely sell the company. It would be a conflict of interest not to do so, given what William's priorities will be. I intend to remain very close to him and continue to advise him, unofficially. Why do you ask, Arnold?"

"When you go ahead and decide to sell, I hope you will keep me in mind. An offer from Perseus would be very generous, Fiona, very generous."

"As I'm sure your donation to William's campaign will be. When the time comes, Arnold, we will certainly talk. Enjoy the rest of the evening."

As she watched her son bask in the respect and approval of these powerful and wealthy people, she felt confident that his election was assured — as long as nothing from the past intruded. Like that damn Caretaker issue. After all these years...*the Caretaker.*

Following the guests' and her son's departure, Fiona Shane headed upstairs to her bedroom suite. She closed the door behind her, undressed, and then, naked, admired herself in the full-length mirror, proud of her still-youthful body. She removed her rings, earrings, bracelets — and the silver brooch that was the source of her power.

It was a brooch with the design of a unicorn in front of a castle. Her mother, Emma Jean, when explaining to Fiona the circumstances of her birth when Fiona was fourteen, had told her how the brooch had been holding together the blanket she was wrapped in. But Emma Jean, uneducated and barely literate, had no idea of the story behind it. Only that it had been her birth mother's and that it was believed to be an old Irish symbol of some sort. Fiona had been intrigued.

Years later, as a freshman at Mount St. Ben's, Fiona had researched Irish heraldry and was astonished to find the unicorn brooch and the name of the family for whom it served as a coat of arms. She had heard of the family — and immediately formulated a plan as to how to exploit this knowledge.

She now replaced the brooch in the jewelry box and went to the small refrigerator in the sitting area part of the suite and poured herself a glass of chilled Pouligny Montrachet. She sat naked on the small loveseat and said to Brian Shaughnessy, "I thought that went very well, don't you?"

Clad only in a black silk robe and sipping Black Bush, Shaughnessy answered, "Very well Fiona. As I have no doubt the remainder of the evening will, too."

She smiled and glanced at the front of his robe. "From the look of you, Brian dear, I have no doubt either."

***

Detective Ed Mulroney sat at his desk in the detectives' squad room at the Monmouth County Prosecutor's Office and said to his partner, "Sarah, don't you think it's awfully damn coincidental that first Glass gets killed, and then Bennington gets smashed all to hell on some dark road three blocks from her condo? Don't we always tell each other not to believe in coincidences? This is too fucking coincidental for me."

"Come on, Eddie, you know as well as I do that sometimes shit just happens. And this is one of those times." She pointed to the pile of folders on both their desks. "We have a lot other shit to cover and I for one want to get to it."

Mulroney sat at his desk, looking over at Craig. The Madison PD had told him that yes, it was a straightforward hit and run. He asked Sergeant Harrison if there was anything at all unusual about the injuries to Ms. Bennington.

"Not really. But the woman was really clobbered, Detective Mulroney. She was hit straight on. That poor woman never had a chance."

"How about the vehicle? Any clues?"

"A big SUV reported stolen in Dover then later dropped off in the parking lot of a shopping center in Whippany. Wiped clean. Someone was very smart and very careful. Beyond that, it's a big zero."

The Bennington hit and run did seem pretty straightforward, except for the vehicle being wiped clean. Mulroney didn't like it. And Craig's acceptance of coincidence was troubling. That was not the way they worked; it was very un-cop-like. He was still brooding on this when Craig called Dominic Rossi.

"Dom, the Madison PD says it was a hit and run. But there are no leads. It's just one of those things."

Mulroney couldn't argue. But he didn't like it. He hated fucking coincidences.

Chapter 13

Dom and Lacey were in Dom's CRV driving south on the Garden State Parkway. They were about an hour from their destination — Lacey's parents' bungalow in the Mystic Island neighborhood of Little Egg Harbor, just south of Tuckerton and a few miles east of the heart of the Pine Barrens. It would serve as their base of operations.

As he drove, Dom told her about his experiences at the Loyal Sons in Boston (excluding his awkward personal experience with Megan Feeney), and his meeting with Father Ted.

Lacey said, "So Father Ted believes there's something fishy about the Cloister of St. Keira and their treatment of unwed mothers? Wow. They sound like a tough and unpleasant bunch. I wonder what they were up to in New Jersey."

"He wasn't entirely sure. But based on what he intimated, it could be ugly. That's one of things we have to find out. Maybe we'll find it in the Pine Barrens."

"Okay, here's my plan," Lacey said between bites of croissant and sips of coffee.

"Wait a minute, wait a minute. I thought *you* were the student and *I* was the mentor. Shouldn't it be my plan?"

"Eventually, sure. But for now, you know zip about the Pine Barrens and it's my area of expertise. Just relax and let me explain, Dr. Dom."

"Why do you persist in calling me Dr. Dom? We're colleagues now."

"That conversation comes later. But first we have to get you oriented, give you some context for your investigations. I don't think we need to go wandering through the Pine Barrens trying to follow Rebecca Glass's footsteps, at least not yet. Who knows how far off the San Giacomo route she went? She could have explored a mile in each direction. That's typical of that kind of archaeological evaluation. After you get a feel for the area and we learn more about her activities, then we'll go exploring."

97

"So what do you suggest?"

"We'll give you a sense of the geography and the terrain by driving around a bit, we'll talk to some old timers, and I'll regale you with bits of folklore and tall tales of the Jersey Pines. Maybe we'll even see the Jersey Devil."

"Just who is this Jersey Devil everyone knows about except me?"

She laughed and said, "Well, as the story goes, in 1735 a woman named Mrs. Leeds, over in Estellville, learned that she was pregnant with her thirteenth child. She was not thrilled with this realization and in her dismay and disgust she supposedly screamed out, 'Let it be the devil!' And sure enough, when she gave birth, it was to a baby devil. Whereupon, the baby devil gave a horrifying screech, unfolded its wings and flew out the window, or up the chimney depending on the version of the tale, and into the Pine Barrens, where, as the stories go, he is spotted or otherwise makes his presence felt from time to time, as the mood suits him. He's got fan clubs and websites and in 1938 was officially proclaimed the State Demon. For marketers, he's become a kind of brand."

Dom shook his head. "I thought it was just a hockey team."

"Stick with me. I'll make you into a Piney yet."

They turned off the Parkway at Exit 58 and headed into Tuckerton. Lacey said, "We need to stop and pick up some groceries and stuff. And here's another nugget — Tuckerton was an important port of entry into the United States around the time of the Revolutionary War. But it really wasn't the third official port of entry, as residents like to claim. In any case, the Tuckerton Seaport Museum is very cool."

After picking up some groceries, they arrived at Lacey's parents' house and Dom saw that it was a charming, well-kept bungalow right on the lagoon. Instead of a front lawn, it had the yellow-pebbled gravel typical of Jersey shore houses. The backyard was the same, but included a deck with a gas grill, assorted lounge furniture, and an outdoor shower; below that was a small floating dock.

Dom said, "This is really nice, Lacey. Did you get much damage during Hurricane Sandy?"

"We lost the floating dock and a little tool shed in the back yard, and a few shingles from the roof. They all ended up in the bay somewhere. But as you can see I had them replaced. Overall, though, we were very lucky. Some houses around here really got pounded. Over on the next street a guy's boat ended up on a neighbor's roof. It was nuts."

Dom saw that the inside of the house had an open floor plan with the kitchen opening onto a family room area, an informal dining area, and sliding doors opening out onto the deck. It was light and airy and decorated in the easy-going beach house style typical of the Jersey Shore — wicker, nautical artwork, fishing or seafaring motifs and paraphernalia hung on the walls.

Lacey said, "The bedrooms are down the hallway to the left. You can drop your stuff in the second one and then we'll put the groceries away."

Their chores completed, Dom said, "You mentioned talking to some old timers. Where's the best place to start?"

"The Lower Bank Tavern. It's about fifteen minutes away. My folks and I used to go there all the time when we came down here. Practically everyone in there is a Piney."

During the ride to the LBT, Dom asked, "So, in terms of Pine Barrens folklore, what else is there besides the Jersey Devil?"

"It's really very rich and it spans a long time, from the late 1600s through the American Revolution, even to modern times. It's a folklorist's treasure trove — stories about the Black Dog, a ghost hound who roams the beaches and forests; the Golden Haired Girl, another ghost who forever mourns her drowned lover; the White Stag, who supposedly appears to help people lost in the Pine Barrens; the Caretaker — "

Dom nearly drove off the road. "The *who*? What did you say?"

She looked at him. "The Caretaker — it's a legend of relatively recent origin, maybe sixty years or so. Why are you reacting like that?"

"Just tell me more, please, Lacey."

"Well, the Caretaker is another ghost, a woman who always appears off in the distance in Wharton State Forest, usually around Jenkins and Friendship and Speedwell — really remote, isolated areas. She's always seen wearing tattered clothes and is described as haggard and scruffy looking. All the sightings say she carries garden tools in a bucket — stuff like pruning shears, a hand trowel, a hand weeder, stuff like that."

"Do the stories say what the source of the legend is? How it got started?"

"Not really. There are conflicting accounts — some say she was an escapee from a mental hospital in Philadelphia who died in the Pines, another says that she was a servant for a wealthy industrialist from Baltimore who got her pregnant and abandoned her, and she committed suicide. But the really weird thing, especially for a ghost, is that when you go back and read the stories of the sightings, from the earliest sightings to the most recent, she ages."

"She *ages*? In your experience, have you ever heard that before?"

"No, never. What's going on? What aren't you telling me?"

"I think we may be on to something. But for now, let's just get lunch. I'll explain later."

The Lower Bank Tavern looked pretty much like what it was, a one-story, cabin- type roadhouse bar in the middle of nowhere. But once they entered, Dom saw that it was warm, friendly and welcoming. Everyone in the place seemed delighted to be there and were thoroughly enjoying themselves — shooting pool, playing darts or pinball, watching sports on the widescreen TV or simply having a few drinks and chowing down.

He said to Lacey, "What a great place. Let's sit at the bar. It'll be easier to get into conversations with people."

As soon as they were seated, the bartender, a smiling man probably in his late fifties came over to them, a bar towel thrown over his shoulder.

"Hello, folks, welcome to the LBT. What can I get you?" Then he took a second look at Lacey. "You've been here before, Miss. Didn't you used to come in pretty regular with your folks when you were a kid? Welcome back. I'm Vern."

"That's why you're so successful, Vern. You remember everyone. My name's Lacey and this character is Dr. Dom."

"Doctor of what, Dom?"

"I teach English at Mount St. Benedict University up in Morristown. Lunch is our first priority, but I'm also trying to learn more about the Pine Barrens and its folklore. Lacey here is my tutor."

Vern said, "Let me bring you folks some menus, then give me a couple of minutes and we'll talk."

As Dom perused the menu, Lacey, not having glanced at the menu, said, "I'm going with the LBT Burger, a house salad, and a beer."

The LBT burger was a half-pound burger with chipotle aioli and Monterey Jack cheese; it also came with a generous portion of fries. Dom looked at her.

She said, "It's my metabolism. I never gain an ounce — ever. I could eat a walrus for lunch and a moose for dinner and I'd still be a hundred and twenty-eight pounds. And my cholesterol is lower than the President's approval ratings. I'm not skinny, but I'm certainly on the lean side. As you may have noticed."

Dom was about to respond that she looked absolutely perfect to him but then thought better of it and refrained from comment. Still, he could not help but think of the old Spencer Tracy line about Katherine Hepburn in the movie *Pat and Mike* — "Not much meat on her, but what's there is cherce."

Dom went with the chef's salad and a glass of red wine and Lacey ordered her burger, salad, and beer. After they placed their order, Vern returned and said, "Doc, there's so much to know about this area, you could study it forever — history, fauna, flora. There are all kinds of things out there. We got ghost towns, cranberry bogs, hidden rivers, weird trees and shrubs, exotic mosses, herbaceous plants, even Venus flytraps. Why there's even forty or fifty species of wild orchids growing in the Pine Barrens, all by themselves. What in particular are you interested in?"

"About sixty years ago, there was a fire in which eight nuns perished. A colleague of mine at Mount St. Ben's was researching it, but passed away before she could present her findings. I'm trying to figure out what she learned."

"Oh, yeah, that's the St. Keira's fire. People still talk about that. It was awful. I remember my folks talking about it when I was a kid. It really spooked everybody."

"Why was it spooky?"

"There was a suspicion...no, it was more a feeling that folks around here had that the fire was set. There never was any proof, and the poor cloister was just a pile of smoldering ashes when help got there. Anyway, the best the authorities came up with was that a kerosene lamp spilled and started the whole thing while the nuns were asleep.

"The building was over a hundred years old and never had electricity. Some rich European guy built it then abandoned it. The nuns arrived from Ireland and just moved into it. Damn fire went on for three days and burned over four thousand acres, though that's not unusual here. As for what really happened, who the hell knows."

Their food came and Vern left them to tend to other customers. Dom watched Lacey enjoying her burger, smiling contentedly between generous bites. His chef's salad was surprisingly good — fresh, crisp greens, ripe tomato and generous portions of turkey, ham, roast beef, and both Swiss and American cheese in a tangy house dressing.

Vern returned after a bit and said, "You know, Doc, now as I think on it, you should try and talk with Abner Stroud."

"Who's he?"

"He's an old timer and something of an odd duck, I guess in his seventies, Piney born and bred. Family's lived here for over two hundred years. I don't think old Abner's been out of the Pines for more than a day or two in his life. He drops by two, three times a month, has a few beers, eats a large bucket of our hottest wings, then personally says good-bye to everyone in the place and heads home. They say he lives over in Shamong Township, somewhere around Atsion."

Lacey explained to Dom, "Atsion was an important iron works in the 18th and 19th centuries. Also a village. Now it's mostly ruins and a few preserved buildings, but there is a Ranger station. Maybe the Ranger knows where Mr. Stroud lives. "

Dom said, "Thank you, Vern. We'll give it a try."

"Good luck, folks. Come on back and let me know how it goes."

The drive from Lower Bank to the Atsion Ranger station took about twenty minutes, west along an old county road then north on the larger State Highway 206, through Wharton State Forest. It was Dom's first extended look at the area.

"It really is beautiful in a unique sort of way, but I can understand how someone might easily get lost. And despite all the green, even now in the spring it looks like a tinderbox. No wonder fires here travel so quickly."

They found the Ranger Station on Route 206 near Quaker Bridge Road. It was housed in what used to be Etheridge's General Store, back when Atsion was an industrial town, instead of a ghost town.

Lacey said, "That place behind the Ranger Station is the old Richards Mansion. The family ran a bog iron empire in the Pine Barrens for decades. Eventually, the financier Joseph Wharton, for whom this forest is named, bought the place. They've restored it to the way it was in 1826, when it was originally built."

"Wharton like the School of Business at Penn?"

"That's him."

They pulled into the dirt and gravel lot, parked and entered the ranger station. Like many similar facilities, it had a number of kiosks filled with assorted pamphlets and brochures, a wall of photographs of various sections of the State Forest, topographical maps and trail maps, a couple of chairs and, behind the counter, an American flag and the New Jersey State flag, and a tall, smiling State Forest Ranger.

"Afternoon, folks. Welcome to Atsion. I'm Ranger Paul Larsen. How may I help you today?"

Dom introduced himself and Lacey, identifying them as scholars from Mount St. Benedict University. "I'm following up on some research done in the Pine Barrens by a late colleague. Someone in Lower Bank suggested we try to talk to a man named Abner Stroud. Might you have any idea where we can find him?"

Ranger Larsen chuckled. "Well, at any given moment there's no telling where to find old Abner. He could be anywhere in the whole of Wharton State Forest, and usually is. But I can tell you where he lives. Whether he's there or willing to talk with you, I can't really say. But if he is, you're in for an experience."

"That would be great, thank you."

"Head south on 206 for just over two miles. On the east side of the highway, the left hand side, you'll see a dirt road with a

103

large boulder at the entrance. Abner's place is about three miles down the dirt road. But you have to take care. That's sugar sand back there in some places, and it's easy to get stuck. What are you driving?"

"A twelve year-old Honda CRV."

"Not bad. But be real careful. You'd do best parking alongside the road where it's firm and going the last half mile or so on foot."

Following Ranger Larsen's directions, they turned off the highway and on to the unpaved road leading to Abner Stroud's place. It was narrow and rutted and curved along the edge of a wild cranberry bog. Dom could see smaller, even more narrow paths and trails heading off into the pinewoods, leading heaven knew where. He pulled to the side of the road and they continued on foot. The day was sunny and cool, a slight pine-scented breeze whispered through the trees.

After a while they came upon an old, two-story shack made of pine and white cedar and covered with tarpaper. A pump was in the front yard along with assorted debris; an ancient pick-up truck with dents, scrapes and cracked windows was parked randomly in the yard, the driver's side door hanging open. An aluminum canoe rested on two sawhorses along the side of the house. A wooden outhouse was visible in back.

Dom shouted at the front door, "Hello, Mr. Stroud? Are you available?"

The outhouse door opened a crack and a gravelly voice called out, "Hell no, I ain't available! I'm doing my damn business. Whoever you are go wait in the house. I'll be in when I'm done. Don't steal nothing. Have a drink you want it. In the cupboard."

Lacey put her hand over her mouth to stifle her laughter. The inside of the house was just as ramshackle as the outside — dirt floor covered with several layers of ancient, frayed rugs, mismatched chairs, a scarred wooden picnic table, two sofas with stuffing spilling out and pillows and cushions randomly thrown on top of them; in one corner was a wood-burning stove, an ancient ice box, and next to it a sink with a hand pump for water. Several kerosene lamps, a smaller propane stove and assorted flashlights were scattered around randomly. A hallway off the main room seemed to lead to perhaps two other rooms, a rickety-looking stairway to the second floor, and a back door.

After a few minutes, a short, wiry, leathery man entered the living room from the rear of the house. He wore rubber soled boots, tan canvas pants held up by a rope belt, and a worn, frayed sweatshirt with the sleeves cut off at the elbows and bearing the wildly incongruous name and logo of Princeton University.

"Howdy, folks, howdy, howdy. You sure caught me with my pants down didn't you?" He laughed merrily. "Have a seat anywheres."

While Dom and Lacey settled themselves, he went to a cupboard near the sink and extracted an earthenware jug and two surprisingly clean glasses. He poured several ounces of a pale blue liquid into the glasses and handed one each to Dom and Lacey. It occurred to Dom that he'd had more homemade hooch in the last week than he'd had in the previous twenty-seven years.

"Here's to ya," Abner said. Then he put the jug to his lips and took a long, obviously satisfying swallow. Dom and Lacey each took a tentative sip of their drinks. Whatever it was tasted faintly of blueberries and was surprisingly smooth, though with a noticeable kick.

The man sat down on one of the old sofas and said, "My name's Abner. Call me Abner. Abner. Now, who the hell are you and what do want with me?"

Dom and Lacey introduced themselves and they all shook hands. Abner patted Lacey's hand and said, "Damn, Miss Lacey, you're the prettiest girl ever visited me since Miss Audrey Hepburn last stopped by."

Lacey smiled and said, "Why thank you, Abner. That's very sweet of you. But when exactly was the last time Audrey Hepburn stopped by?"

"Never! That makes you the prettiest ever!" He laughed delightedly, took another swallow from his jug and said, "Now, then, what can I do you for?"

Dom gave his by now usual explanation of what they were up to, mentioning Rebecca, St. Keira's, and the fire.

Abner shook his head, "Damn shame, a shame. No figuring things sometimes. But yup, yup, Miss Rebecca — a sturdy, handsome woman. Better suited to trousers than dresses, if you

105

get my drift. But real pleasant, pleasant, good company, liked a drink. She came to visit and I showed her these woods. Real interested in that old fire. Sad, sad, thing. I was a boy about fourteen, went along with the Rangers and firefighters try to help. Nothing left, everybody dead. Couldn't hardly tell they was people."

Dom asked, "Mr. Stroud, did anyone ever learn how that fire started?"

"Abner, call me Abner. Weren't no 'how,' son. Were a 'who.' Fire like that don't just start. Was set. One kerosene lamp gets knocked over, it's a accident. Three or four ain't no accident."

"Any idea who? Did the authorities investigate it?"

"No telling the who, Doc. But it was strange, strange — one day the Fire Marshall is combing through the ruins, looking for clues, next day he ain't. Like he was told to stop. Never could figure it. Never could."

Lacey asked, "Abner, did the Cloister have any contact with the outside world?"

"Oh they was a cloister, for sure, you bet, Miss Lacey. But folks came and went. Tough going back there, though — sugar sand, puzzle trails, fingerboards, curve arounds. Get lost easy, get stuck easier. But deliveries of food and supplies was made. Mostly by a fella from over in Jenkins. He'd also come by to pick up those priest clothes they made, what do you call them? Vestments? What would happen was he'd drop off the supplies maybe a half mile or so from the cloister house. Them vestments got picked up same way. The ladies, nuns that is, would carry stuff back after the delivery guy left."

"Where would he deliver the vestments, Abner?"

"I believe over to the bishop's place, over in Trenton, Bishop of Trenton."

Dom asked, "Abner, do you know if Rebecca Glass ever found the ruins?"

"Well sure, Doc. Sure she did. Yup, she did. Them ruins ain't no big deal. I been by there lots a times. I showed her. And later on she went back by herself. Was real interested. It's just a few old burnt beams and charred bricks. Forest about swallowed everything up. No mystery about the where. Mystery is about the who."

Dom thought out loud. "Jesus, I wonder if Rebecca figured out the 'who.'"

Abner nodded. "Might could be, son. Might could be. She's a smart one."

"I have one last question," Lacey said. "Are you familiar with the old story about a ghost known as 'the Caretaker'?"

After taking another hearty pull at his jug, Abner said, "Ain't no ghost, Miss Lacey. It's a lost woman. I seen her three, maybe four times over all these years. Never could catch her or find her, not so much as a trace. And I know these woods. Sure do, yup, I do. Born and raised here. But she's out there. Just no telling where she is, probably never will be. These woods is like that."

Abner took another swallow then gave them a big smile. "You folks about done asking? I got a couple squirrels to cook — real long and slow, long and slow or they tough, damn tough them old squirrels. They ain't all that big but we could share. Roast some turnips with them, you want."

Dom looked at Lacey, who smiled broadly and said, "Abner, thank you so much for all your help today. But more than that, it was wonderful spending time with you. Dom and I will be back here in the Pines again. Is it okay if we look you up?"

Abner laughed. "Sure thing, Missy. Be a pleasure. I look forward to it, be nice, look forward to it."

Apropos of nothing, Abner asked, "You two together? You look good together, look easy together."

"We're...we're colleagues, Abner. We work together," Dom said.

"You oughta work on making babies together. They'd be handsome, happy babies for sure, damn sure. You both got the look. Yup, you do. Bring them babies around when you have them. I'll teach them these woods. Be seein' ya."

107

Chapter 14

Back in the CRV heading towards Tuckerton, Dom said, "Well, that was certainly informative and enjoyable. It looks like you've stolen another heart, Lace."

She looked over at him and smiled. "Another?"

"It's just a figure of speech. Like 'water under the bridge.'"

She laughed and said, "And 'never the 'twain shall meet.'"

"Lacey! You know *Hold That Ghost?* You're too young for Abbott and Costello."

"I love A&C! I watch them on Turner Classic Movies. I can ask for directions to the Susquehanna Hat Company on Bagel Street and even tell you Who's on First."

"I'm impressed! You're a girl after my own heart. A&C, who knew?"

Her smile was mischievous. "But I have to ask, what do you think about Abner's comment about babies?"

Dom blushed. "It was...a little awkward."

She reached over and patted his arm. "It's okay, Dr. Dom. We'll talk later about the babies. But in the meantime, where does all that lead us?"

Dom turned serious. "I'm betting Rebecca discovered the cause of the fire, or as Abner says, the 'who.' But even if she did, I don't understand yet what ties the fire to the Loyal Sons, if anything. But I can't help but feel they're very deep into this thing."

"Dom, that angle really bothers me. I mean, what with my Dad and all."

"Don't worry. I'm not damning the whole organization. But you have to admit, they are all over the place in this. Especially the North Jersey Chapter."

She nodded then asked, "How about the Caretaker? Could Abner be right? Do you think she really exists?"

"I don't know. But Abner knows his territory and its history probably better than anyone. And Rebecca knew about her, or at least the story." Dom told her about the note Diana found in Rebecca's home office.

"My God, Dom! Why didn't you tell me? That means the Caretaker really does exist! Did Rebecca try to find her? *Did* she find her? But then, there's no telling when Rebecca may have written the note or whether she acted on it."

"That's exactly right. But sooner or later, we're going to have to find out. It probably means visiting Abner again and heading out into the woods. But for now, I want to hit this from another angle."

Dom explained about the significance of 1958. "It was the year of the fire at the Cloister, the year that the Loyal Sons North Jersey Chapter ceased donating to the orphanage, and the year the orphanage shut its doors."

"What was the orphanage?"

"Holy Innocents in Mt. Holly, the county seat of Burlington County."

"Okay, that's just northeast of Wharton State Forest, on the edge of the Pine Barrens. I know from my sociology studies that orphanages as institutions began to be phased out after World War II. Group homes, foster care and other facilities began to replace them. So the closure is not necessarily nefarious.

"But given the other things you mentioned, we absolutely have to look into it. Holy Innocents would have been within the Diocese of Trenton. We could visit the Chancery Office to learn more about it.

"Let's get back to Mount St. Ben's first and sit on it for a few days. Commencement is Saturday; I need to attend and you'd probably like to. I also need to give some kind of briefing to Delaney and Shaughnessy."

"What are you going to tell them? If the Loyal Sons, at least the North Jersey Chapter, are involved in this somehow, you can't tell them what you know — or suspect."

"I'll try to reassure them that I've found nothing to harm the University. With any luck, they'll tell me to drop the whole thing."

"But there's no way in hell you're going to drop it, is there."

"Not a chance. Something about this stinks. I'm going to keep at it."

She shook her head. "Jesus, Dr. Dom, you certainly know how to create a unique independent study. Is life with you always going to be this interesting?"

Dom had no answer for that — on several levels.

As they drove south on Route 206 heading towards county road 542, they passed a car pulled over to the side of the road, a black Honda Pilot. Dom glanced at the man behind the wheel; he felt sure he'd seen him somewhere before but couldn't place it. It gave him a bad feeling and he mentally filed it away for future reference.

They traveled on in comfortable silence for a while. Then, as they neared Tuckerton, Dom asked, "Is there a good seafood store in town?"

"Sure, Parson's. Why?"

"Let's pick up some fresh clams. I'll make you some linguini with white clam sauce for dinner. How does that sound?"

"You are a man of surprising talents. That sounds perfect. We can stop at Tuckerton Liquors and pick up a jug of wine."

Back at the bungalow, Dom scrubbed the clams while Lacey chopped the garlic, shallots and parsley. He put some water on to boil and added a handful of salt. Next, he heated some olive oil in a pot, sautéed the garlic and shallots until translucent then added the clams, a pinch of red pepper flakes and a generous pour of the white wine.

"Okay," he said, "these bad boys will be ready in a few minutes and the pasta will be al dente. I'll swirl in some butter and sprinkle on some fresh parsley. Then we feast."

In the meantime, Lacey had set the table, added a couple of candles and put on some soft jazz. She said, "You know, we make a pretty good team. In a lot of ways."

Dom looked at her. "Is that one of the conversations for later tonight?"

"Yeah, it is. But after dinner."

The meal having been devoured and pronounced delicious, they were seated out on the back deck, overlooking the lagoon, each with a glass of wine.

Lacey took a healthy sip and said, "Okay, here goes. We haven't known each other very long, Dom, just a few days. But it is very apparent to me that you are falling in love with me."

Dom nearly jumped out of his chair. "Wait a second, hold on, who said — where did you get the idea — I never — "

Lacey laughed at his discomfort. "Calm down, Dom. It's okay! In fact it's more than okay. I'm feeling the same way. I have right from the very first. And as we spend more time together, I have to admit that the feeling even grows."

Her laughter gone, her face serious, Lacey said, "But here's the thing. You and I both carry some serious emotional baggage. That 'Dr. Dom' thing — you have a reputation, sort of. I heard about you shortly after I arrived on campus. There are about five thousand women at Mount St. Ben's, and the open secret is that about two-thirds of them would love to get involved, on any basis, with 'Dr. Dom.'"

"Jesus Christ, Lacey, that's crazy."

"Not at all. You are quite the romantic and tragic figure. You're brilliant, handsome — and every young woman on campus knows the story of how you stuck by your fiancée through her illness. You were always right by her side, administering her medications, bathing her, and even giving her injections. You stayed with her and comforted her, all while finishing your Ph.D.. Not many men would do all that. And you've been practically oblivious to women ever since."

Dom did not respond and Lacey went on. "But there's a price to pay. When you love someone that much, and then you lose that person, it's very damn hard to love deeply ever again."

She took a swallow of wine then said, "I know about that. I went to Red Bank Catholic High School. On the first day of freshman year I developed a huge crush on a guy named Kenny Miller. We dated all through high school, neither of us even looked at anyone else. When we graduated, I went on to Monmouth, and Kenny decided to join the Marines. His family was not very well off and he didn't want to burden them with trying to help pay for his education. So he figured he'd enlist, do a three-year hitch, then go to college on the GI Bill.

"The idea was he'd join me at Monmouth. They have terrific services for veterans; they really appreciate them and take care of them. Anyway, we saw each other when we could. After his training in the States he did a tour of duty in Afghanistan. And then had to go back for a second one.

"One day during my junior year, I was heading back to my dorm after class and I saw my Mom and Dad standing in front of the dorm. My Mom was crying. I didn't need to be told why. Kenny had been killed in a firefight somewhere near the Pakistan border. I wanted to die, too.

"Since then, I haven't been open to relationships...of any kind. Not even temporary ones. But now, with you, maybe I'll try again. I'm very scared. And I don't promise anything. But maybe I can love again — and to an extent I didn't think possible. I'm sorry this is so heavy, so soon. But I had to be honest. We've both experienced loss. Maybe we can experience love, together. But I'm really scared about rushing into it."

Dom put down his wine glass and went over to her and knelt beside her chair. He took her hand, kissed her palm then gently touched her face. "We'll take our time, Lace. And when it's right, we'll both know. For now, just being with you is a joy."

***

Frank Burns met Martin O'Bannon at the Dublin Pub in Morristown. Burns said, "He just seems to be riding around talking to people. I lost him in the damn woods down there for about two hours. I just sat in my car off Route 206 and waited for him to show up. I got no idea what the kid was doing back in there. The fucking place is impossible, it all looks the same, thick woods, crazy sand roads and trails that lead all over the place. It's a fucking mess.

"Anyway, he and the girl stayed the night at her place and came back to Morristown the next morning. I don't know if he's fucking her or not, but I could find out if you want. He'd be stupid not to. The girl is amazing. On the lanky side, but a face like a model, killer long legs and an ass to die for."

O'Bannon had no interest in Rossi's sex life, but maybe his relationship with the girl would come in handy later on. It made him vulnerable.

"What Rossi is doing might look random, but he's very smart. He very likely is putting things together and making connections we don't know about. I want you to stay on him. Where he goes next and who he decides to talk to could give us a hint as to what he's thinking and how far he's gotten."

112

Burns shrugged. "Your call. As long as I get paid, I'll keep on it."

After leaving Burns, O'Bannon returned to Mount St. Ben's and sat in his office. He was getting a bad feeling. Rossi was doing exactly what they'd wanted him to do — determine if Glass's findings could ever be duplicated. But he was moving surprisingly quickly. It could end up biting them in the ass. It would be critical to learn what Rossi chose to report — and what he chose to leave out.

But then another thought struck O'Bannon. It was unlikely that anyone else could trace Glass's activities as effectively. That meant that when the time came to get rid of Rossi, they could feel secure in the knowledge that what he'd learned would die with him. O'Bannon made a phone call.

"I think Rossi may be getting close — already. He's touching all the bases. But he's a special case. No one else could pull it off. Bottom line, when you give the word, we can get rid of him. And the girl he's started to pal around with."

Brian Shaughnessy said, "Let's give it a bit longer. I want to see how close Rossi actually comes. While we are discussing such matters, Martin, you told me that your resource said Glass mentioned 'proof' of her claims. Is there any sign that such proof actually exists or that Glass really had it?"

"None."

"Excellent. We're nearing the finish line. Let's stay on top of things — and you can be sure you'll have approval to act, when the time comes. In that regard, Martin, there is another issue we need to address — Edward Manning. He's getting weak in the knees. With what he knows, he can be a mortal threat. The situation, I believe, calls for some housekeeping."

"I understand, Brian. I fully agree. I'll be happy to take care of it myself."

***

As soon as Dom walked into the English Department the following morning, a smirking Fran Purcell told him he was wanted in Provost Delaney's office. "You're to go there immediately, Professor Rossi. The Provost was quite adamant."

When he arrived at the Provost's office, Brian Shaughnessy was there, and so was Martin O'Bannon. They were all seated at

113

a rectangular conference table, Delaney at the head. He said, "As you can see, Professor Rossi, we've asked Martin to join us. Since this is an investigation of sorts, his expertise is welcome. Now then, what have you learned about Glass's activities?"

Dom figured he had to stay close to the truth, but without giving away what he was really thinking. He started at the beginning; he explained about San Giacomo Engineering and his trip to Maryland, where he learned about the Loyal Sons support of the Cloister, and then his follow-up trip to Boston.

"Given Mr. Shaughnessy's association with the Loyal Sons, I assumed you'd want to know any possible connection to the Cloister of St. Keira. I went to Boston simply because records at the founding chapter figured to be the most extensive. They were. It was very much like a museum, interesting, informative and enjoyable."

Dom watched each man carefully to determine each one's level of acceptance or skepticism. Delaney appeared to be buying it; Shaughnessy kept a poker face and O'Bannon was even harder to read. Dom sensed that both exuded suspicion.

"Now, as for what I've learned — other than the Loyal Sons North Jersey Chapter being very supportive of the Cloister for a number of years, as well as their generous contributions to many other deserving organizations and institutions, I don't see any relevant connection between the Loyal Sons' activities and Rebecca's research."

He added, "I did see a photograph of an early president of the North Jersey Chapter. Am I correct in assuming that Dennis Shaughnessy was your grandfather, Mr. Shaughnessy?"

Shaughnessy answered proudly, "He was indeed. My father was also a past president. The Shaughnessy clan has been at the heart of the Loyal Sons and its driving force since the organization's founding."

Martin O'Bannon said, "Let's get specific here. Professor Rossi, was there anything about Glass's research about the Cloister that could be controversial?"

Dom answered, "Her interest in the Cloister mainly had to do with the fire that destroyed it. As far as the fire itself is concerned, its cause remains a mystery, though a spilled kerosene lantern seems to be the most likely explanation. Fierce fires rage in the Pine Barrens all the time."

At this point, Dom decided to obfuscate. "It's possible that Rebecca's research may have uncovered flaws in the firefighting methods used sixty years ago or issues with the response times of the firefighters. That could be considered controversial, and the firefighting authorities would not be thrilled about any lapses or failures becoming public knowledge, were it actually the case. But nothing I've learned suggests anything potentially damaging to the University."

Delaney looked at Shaughnessy. "Well, Brian, are you satisfied that the University has nothing to fear from Rebecca Glass's phantom research?"

Shaughnessy said nothing for several moments; he just looked at Dom. "Perhaps. In any case, Felix, with respect to Rossi's academic activities, it's your call."

Delaney said, "Professor Rossi, as far as the university is concerned, you may return to your normal duties. Thank you for your efforts."

After Dom left the room, Shaughnessy said, "I don't trust that little bastard. I think our Professor Rossi knows more than he's let on. Martin, I want you to stay on it."

"You got it."

Dom headed back across campus to the English Department, where the officious Fran Purcell told him that Sister Pat was available. "She has an exam to administer in fifteen minutes, Professor Rossi, so that gives you five."

Dom knocked on Sister Pat's office door and entered. He said, "I'm supposedly off the hook, at least as far as Delaney is concerned. But O'Bannon and Shaughnessy clearly don't trust me and I still think something stinks in the Pine Barrens."

Sister Pat said, "Knowing you as I do, that means you'll continue to pursue this on your own. Okay, Dom, here's what we'll do. I'll schedule you for classes during the summer session beginning June 17th. You'll teach Critical Reading and Composition, and two sections of American Lit 2. That will give you a bit more time to investigate."

115

"Thank you, Sister Pat. Oh, by the way, Ray Alexander was very helpful. And his graduate teaching assistant, Caroline Lacey, is...well, she's really special."

Sister Pat gave him a knowing smile. "I'm acquainted with her, Dom. I also find her to be a very special young woman. I had a feeling you two would get along."

Back in his own office, Dom called Lacey in the Anthropology Department. "I had the meeting. When can you meet me for coffee in the Lair?"

"Give me an hour. I have to finish grading some exams for Dr. Ray. And I have a nugget for you, sort of."

Lacey arrived a few minutes after Dom, and just as before, heads turned when she entered. Dom felt a kind of possessive pride, but tried not to show it. They got coffees and sat at a table for two at the far end of the cafeteria. Lacey also got a blueberry muffin.

He said, "I told them I didn't find anything damaging to the University. I'm pretty sure Delaney bought it, since he told me to pull the plug. But they had Martin O'Bannon from Criminal Justice there. He's a former Keansburg cop, later a State Trooper and a recipient of the Loyal Son of the Year award. I'm sure he thinks I was holding back, Shaughnessy too.

"Lace, I didn't mention it at the time, but when we were heading back to Tuckerton from Abner's place, I saw a guy in a car parked along the side of 206. He looked familiar, but I don't know from where. It will come to me, though. But I'm beginning to think that some people are looking more closely at this — and at us — than we thought. I don't know the stakes, at least not yet. But they have to be big."

"Well, just to make things more complicated and even more weird, I did some more research into the Caretaker legend, working from what Abner told us. Here's the nugget. Remember how I said it started about sixty years ago? It turns out that the first reported sighting of her — as a young woman — was during July of 1958. The St. Keira's fire took place in June of that year. What the hell is going on?"

"Jesus, could she be connected somehow to the fire? If so, how?"

"That's what I'm wondering. So, what do we do next?"

116

"Let's learn more about this Holy Innocents orphanage, if only to rule it out. What struck me as odd was that the pictures I saw in Boston show very healthy and attractive babies. They did not at all look like babies who came from impoverished backgrounds or who got left in a doorway or a garbage can or something. What would account for that?"

"It must have to do with where they got the babies. I never heard of an orphanage being selective, but I guess they could have been, especially a private one. For a Catholic orphanage, though, it seems contradictory. I mean the whole idea is to help babies who are helpless, not to pick and choose. When should we check it out?"

"As soon as we can after Commencement. We'll go to the Diocese of Trenton Chancery Office and see if we can get a look at their archives. How's that sound?"

She gave him her megawatt smile. "Sounds like a plan, Doc."

Chapter 15

Commencement ceremonies are the highlight of the academic year. Dom had always enjoyed the pageantry, the sense of optimism and accomplishment, even the speeches. But this one, he had to admit to himself, was even more pleasurable. It was the first time he would be attending as a faculty member and wearing his full academic regalia. His gown was black, with three velvet stripes on the sleeves signifying his Ph.D. status and the white velvet hood signifying his field, the liberal arts. He fought off the temptation to take a selfie and send it to Anthony and Theresa in Naples.

Mount St. Benedict commencements began at noon, lasted some three hours and were typically held in the Richard Iverson Field House, which could hold several thousand people. Following the commencement ceremonies were numerous receptions and parties hosted by different schools and departments all across the campus.

As the ceremony began, Dom was part of the procession of faculty, administrators, Board of Trustees members and other dignitaries. Accompanied by appropriately celebratory music by Handel, they marched into the main auditorium, which was packed with joyous students, beaming parents, proud relatives, and assorted members of the Mount St. Ben's community.

During the entrance procession, Dom spotted Lacey in the audience; she had managed to snag an aisle seat and was waving and smiling at him as he entered and walked past her. She was even taking pictures of him with her smart phone. He took his place to the left of the main stage along with faculty from the School of Humanities and Social Sciences. Other schools and faculty were seated together as well, all facing the stage on which the Board, Father Jack, Provost Delaney, the Deans and other dignitaries arranged themselves facing the audience.

The ceremony began with an invocation by Abbot Marc Scoles, OSB, from St. Paul's Abbey in Glastonbury, Connecticut, and then moved on to a warm and gracious welcome from Father

Jack. Normally, this would be followed by some brief, generally innocuous remarks from the President of the Board of Trustees, a speech by the Provost, and then the awarding of degrees. This year was a little different.

Like most other universities, Mount St. Ben's included in its Commencement ceremony the awarding of honorary degrees, usually a Ph.D. *honoris causa* ("for the sake of the honor"), as a way of honoring a distinguished individual's contributions to a specific field or to society.

As announced by Provost Delaney, among this year's honorees was a woman named Fiona Cramer Shane, CEO of Shane BioPharma, a Mount St. Ben's alumna who was being honored for her contributions to New Jersey commerce and industry. But instead of the award being presented by the Provost, as Chief Academic Officer, it was Brian Shaughnessy who cited her accomplishments, contributions, and achievements, all of which Shaughnessy put into near heroic perspective by describing the abject circumstances of her childhood.

"That she has risen to such heights is a testament to her courage, intelligence and tenacity. Fiona Shane was born into poverty fifty-eight years ago. Her parents were poor and uneducated; her father drove a truck and they managed to augment a meager living by picking blueberries in the summer, cranberries in the fall, chopping cordwood and gathering holly, laurel and mistletoe in the winter, then collecting sphagnum moss in the spring. My friends, life in the tiny town of Jenkins was difficult. But Fiona Cramer Shane not only survived; she triumphed. She graduated *cum laude* from this university, then as a widowed single mother, earned her MBA in Pharmaceutical Marketing from our neighbor, Fairleigh Dickinson University. She is truly a Mount St. Ben's and an American success story."

Dom's phone vibrated in his pocket. He removed it as surreptitiously as he could and read the text message. It was from Lacey. *"She's a Piney! Jenkins is near the Cloister! She was born in 1958. How many freaking coincidences can there be?"*

Dom texted back, *"Meet me after this. We have to talk."*

Following the Commencement ceremony, Dom caught up with Lacey outside the field house.

"The English Department is hosting a reception for graduating majors and their families. I need to be there. I also want to make a quick stop over at the Business School reception. Give me a couple of hours. Then, can you meet me at my apartment? We have to put this in perspective."

"Sure," Lacey said. "I'll go home and change then walk over to your place. It's less than a mile."

At the English Department reception, Dom nursed a glass of wine and made a point of personally congratulating and chatting with each English major and his or her proud family members. Then, he walked across campus to the Business School and found Dontay and Sharelle. Both were still in cap and gown. With them was a handsome, middle-aged black couple.

Seeing Dom walk in, a delighted Dontay said, "Hey! Dr. Dom! Thank you for coming by, man. Meet my folks."

He introduced Dom to a tall broad shouldered man and said, "Doc, this is my Dad, Earl Robinson," and then to a slender, vibrant woman, "and my Mom, Marion Mason Robinson. Mom and Dad, this is the professor I told you about."

They all shook hands and Dom offered his congratulations to Dontay's parents. Then he said to Marion, "Excuse me, but I'm thinking 1988 Seoul Olympics. Didn't you run that amazing anchor leg on the fifteen hundred meter relay? That was one of the greatest comebacks in all of track and field."

She laughed. "Dr. Rossi, I'm surprised you're even aware of that! You had to be only a newborn back then. These days I take it pretty easy, but I can still outrun Dontay."

Dom turned to Dontay's father. "And you, sir, that Chicago Bears defense you were part of in the mid and late eighties was one of the greatest. It's a pleasure."

"Dr. Rossi, the pleasure is ours. Marion and I want to thank you for giving so much time and help to Dontay. It means a lot to us for him to graduate. And I know it means a lot to Sharelle." He chuckled and said, "Check out her finger."

Sharelle held up her left hand and flashed a huge smile and an engagement ring at Dom. "I told Dontay he'd have to graduate before I said yes. We're counting on you to make the wedding next year, Dr. Dom."

"I wouldn't miss it for anything, Sharelle."

After leaving Dontay and his family, Dom, on impulse, made a stop at the nearby Whole Foods and picked up a few things — baby lamb chops, some salad greens, radishes, a cucumber, mixed olives, pita bread, and a chunk of feta cheese. His spur of the moment plan was to invite Lacey to stay for dinner. He arrived at Wetmore Avenue and was surprised and pleased to find a parking spot close by his apartment. As he walked up the front steps, he was greeted with an astounding sight.

Mrs. Bonvini was seated in her rocking chair crocheting, as usual. But seated in a chair next to her also crocheting was Lacey. She was wearing tight jeans, a blue polo shirt that matched the color of her eyes and a pink cotton sweater vest; she looked amazing.

Lacey called out, "Dom, look! Mrs. B. is teaching me the hourglass cable stitch! How cool is that! I know the basic stitches my Gram taught me, but the hourglass cable is really tricky. Look how well I'm doing!"

She held up several inches of yarn in an elaborate pattern, hanging from a crochet hook. Dom was totally ignorant of the crocheting process, but it looked like Lacey actually had something pretty sophisticated going.

Mrs. Bonvini said, "Dominic, after you drop off your groceries, go in my dining room. On the credenza there's a decanter of sherry. Please bring it out with two glasses. Lacey and I are talking so much we're getting a thirst."

Dom did as directed and when he returned with the sherry, Lacey beamed up at him. Mrs. Bonvini said, "Dommy, now *this* is a lighthearted girl. This one's a keeper. Go have your scotch and let Lacey and me do our work and talk. She'll see you later."

Upstairs in his apartment, a bemused Dom changed into jeans and a Mount St. Ben's sweatshirt then made himself a scotch and soda. He took it out on the balcony, sat, sipped, and marveled at the turns life takes so quickly and unexpectedly. In just a matter of a few days, Lacey had entered his life and become a significant part of his world.

An hour later there was a tap on his front door and Lacey came in, walked right up to him and planted a resounding kiss on his mouth. It was a splendid kiss.

"To what do I owe this pleasure?" Dom asked.

121

"Two things. First, that was for future reference — and the reference was terrific. Second, it's a gorgeous day, hope springs eternal, you looked very impressive in your academic regalia, and Mrs. B. is a gem. She told me she likes me way better than the last woman you had here — which I won't get into. And she said I should visit anytime I want, and not only to see you. These things have to be celebrated. It's called life. And you and I are right smack in the middle of it — together. Do you have some wine?"

"Always."

"So please pour me a glass and let's go solve this freaking Pine Barrens mystery we're involved in."

Dom led her into his study. On the way she checked out the kitchen, living room and his bedroom. "You just passed a big test. You're a very neat housekeeper, especially for a guy. I can relax and enjoy myself."

"No relaxing yet, my girl. We have problems to resolve. "

Dom booted up his computer and opened a file labeled "Pines." Lacey pulled up a chair next to him. Dom pointed to the screen. "Let's stay with the basic premise — Rebecca Glass found something in the Pine Barrens during her work for the San Giacomo folks that is a big problem for someone. And it's very likely still out there."

"And it has ramifications we haven't come close to figuring out yet."

Dom pulled up a diagram listing the assorted people and issues he'd come across. All the elements were connected by lines showing their relationship to each other, various patterns and connections, and accompanied by brief notes.

Lacey asked, "Why did you do all this?"

"It helps me see things more clearly and understand better. It's like tracing image patterns in literature. For example, in Shakespeare's Henry IV Part 1, there are all kinds of verbal references — images — to thieves, stealing, and to clothes that don't fit. Shakespeare does that so audiences get the point that Henry usurped or 'stole' the crown, and that the crown doesn't 'fit' because he doesn't deserve it. Elizabethan audiences, even the groundlings, would have picked up on that. I'm just tracing patterns and connections between the elements in our puzzle.

"Here are the active elements in our puzzle — Rebecca herself, the Pine Barrens, the Cloisters, the Loyal Sons, the fire, the orphanage, the year 1958."

"And now we should add one Fiona Cramer Shane, Mount St. Ben's alumna, business woman, and mother of the soon-to-announce Republican gubernatorial candidate. Our girl Fiona seems to be at the convergence of location and time."

"Exactly. And also Brian Shaughnessy. He's the one who sent me on this quest. Plus, in any commencement I've ever attended, the Provost as Chief Academic Officer usually bestows the honorary degree and gives the *honoris causa* speech. But Shaughnessy did it for Fiona Shane. Why? There has to be something else going on."

"Okay, so there are all kinds of connections, but I don't see where they lead."

Dom smiled at her. *"The world is full of obvious connections which no one ever observes."*

"Who said that?"

"Sherlock Holmes, in *The Hound of the Baskervilles.* The point is that the significance of the connections is there. We just have to add more data and observe it carefully then follow it to its conclusion."

Then he pointed to the lines between the elements. "Let's hit it from another direction. What seems to be the outlier, the 'least connected connection' back to Rebecca?"

Lacey looked at the chart. "The orphanage."

Dom nodded. "So that's where we head next, in order to rule it out — or find more connections. You said it the other day, the Diocese of Trenton Chancery Office. Since it was a Catholic orphanage, it had to be registered with them. But then you mentioned it was unusually selective. We need to find out why."

"Agreed. When do we go there?"

"What's your schedule? I'm really flexible, but you still have duties."

"On Monday morning Dr. Ray is going to look over my draft syllabus for the Introduction to Folklore class I'll be teaching. When I get his input and approval, I'll finalize it and send it to the Registrar to be formally included in the Summer Session 3 course catalog. Then I'm good for a couple of days."

"Okay, let's figure on Tuesday. We'll check the records at the Chancery and do some cross-referencing as we go. Do you have an iPad?"

"The department has one I can borrow. I'll bring it along."

"Great, that's settled." He hesitated then asked, "For now, for tonight I mean, can you...Lacey, would you like to stay for dinner? I can grill some baby lamb chops and mix up a salad. Then I'll drive you home. How does that sound?"

Her smile was glorious. "I'll marinate the chops."

Chapter 16

A Chancery is the administrative center of a diocese. It handles all the written, printed and electronic materials used in the diocese's operation. Among these are the diocesan archives, which normally hold ledgers, correspondence, documents noting the appointment of bishops and pastors, parish histories, birth certificates, marriage records, priests' personnel files, financial records, and sacramental records.

The Chancery of the Diocese of Trenton was located in Lawrence Township, about an hour south of Morristown. Dom picked up Lacey at nine, and at her insistence stopped briefly to get coffee and corn muffins. It occurred to Dom that stopping for food with Lacey was now becoming part of their modus operandi.

They headed south on Interstate 287, on their way to pick up Route 206. They were passing through Bridgewater, about three miles north of the exit for 206 when Dom spotted the black Honda Pilot in his rear view mirror.

"Oh shit. The black Pilot, center lane, about two hundred yards back, it's the guy I saw down near Abner's."

Dom called up the scene in his mind's eye, seeing the man behind the wheel of the parked Pilot. Then he remembered. "Jesus, Rebecca's memorial service! That guy was standing in the back of the Meeting Room."

Lacey turned to look. "You mean he's been following you since then? How could that be? Who sent him?"

Dom swerved from the left lane into the center lane. "It has to be O'Bannon and Shaughnessy. Delaney told me to hang it up, but it must mean that O'Bannon and Shaughnessy don't believe I did. The black Pilot must be their man."

"Shit, what now?"

Dom glanced again in the rear view mirror, swerved into the right lane and said, "We go to the Mall."

Without signaling, he abruptly took the exit for Bridgewater Commons, a huge mall near the intersections of highways 287,

202, 22, and 206. He swung on to a feeder road and headed into the Mall proper, zipping past high-end retailers — Bloomingdale's, Lord & Taylor, and Macy's — and in and out of various parking lots and parking garages, speeding by appealing restaurants and scores of retail shops.

As Dom sped through the Mall, cutting off cars left and right, Lacey tightened her seatbelt. Dom took a back way out of the Mall and briefly picked up Route 28 then hung a quick left onto county road 567 heading south. "It looks like we lost him," he said.

"Lost *him?* I almost lost my breakfast. So what do we do now? Is the guy going to be around forever?"

"For now, since we're in the clear, we'll continue on to the Chancery. But sooner or later I'm going to have to deal with the guy."

"I liked it better when we were in the Pine Barrens."

Dom kept looking in the rearview mirror, but there was no sight of the black Pilot. They eventually got back to Route 206 and arrived at the Chancery, a two story building next door to Notre Dame High School; they parked around the back.

Arriving at the information desk, Dom asked to speak with the archivist. Several minutes later a sixtyish looking man with sparse gray hair and glasses walked up to them and introduced himself. "Good morning, I'm Francis Fitzgerald. I am the Chancery archivist, how may I help you?"

Dom said, "Mr. Fitzgerald, I'm trying to learn more about my parentage. I grew up in a single parent household, just my mother, and I wish to learn more about my late father, whom I never knew. My mother, who is also deceased, told me that as an infant he was in a Catholic orphanage in New Jersey and later adopted. I have reason to believe that it was Holy Innocents. I'm hoping that there are some records I might look at."

Lacey looked wide-eyed at Dom, knowing that both of his folks were alive, well, and living the good life in Naples, Florida.

The man said, "Well, there are a few records, but of course much of that information is confidential. Still, we may be able to help. Please follow me."

He led them down a corridor, past various offices and meeting rooms and into a large room housing the diocesan archives, which were arranged on rows of metal shelves, some stacked, some in boxes and crates.

He said, "Holy Innocents opened in 1871 and closed in 1958, but I'm afraid the records are rather sketchy and limited. What is your name, please? And your father's name and the year you believe he might have been at Holy Innocents."

"My name is Dominic Rossi. My father was Anthony Rossi. I think he was there in 1957."

Fitzgerald looked at Dom, slightly flustered. "Rossi? Rossi? I don't...I mean it is very unlikely that he was at Holy Innocents, Mr. Rossi."

"Could you please check, sir? My fianceé and I have come all the way from upstate New York."

Fitzgerald, still flustered, walked down one of the aisles, paused, then withdrew a clothbound volume from one of the shelves.

"Please have a seat. This contains the records of admissions and adoptions for Holy Innocents from 1950 to 1958. Please be careful with it. I will return shortly."

Dom and Lacey sat at the table. When Fitzgerald was gone, Lacey said, "*Fianceé*? Aren't you getting a little ahead of yourself after one kiss — as terrific as it was?"

"It was the first thing that popped into my mind."

"I'll refrain from playing psychologist. And that stuff about your 'late' parents. Right now, your folks are probably on the third hole of the Naples Country Club, playing five-dollar Nassau. But I have to admit, it was very creative on such short notice."

Dom opened the ledger and flipped through the pages, looking at the names and dates of infants who came to Holy Innocents and were later adopted. "I was adopted, but the arrangements were made even before I was born. Anthony and Theresa told me the story and how careful and formal the process was — lawyers with a specialty in adoption services, medical histories, professional counseling, interaction with the State of New Jersey — all kinds of checks and balances. The Holy Innocents process seems to be way less formal."

She was surprised. "When did you learn that you were adopted? Was it troubling or anything?"

127

"Anthony and Theresa were very open and loving, and they talked about it one way or another very early on. The extent and detail they went into always depended on how old I was and how much I could understand. I always heard about the day they met me, and how thrilled they were when I came to live with them. They used the word 'adoption' freely, never making it a big secret or a strange thing to happen. I always felt loved and cherished.

"But then things changed. When I got to middle school, Our Lady of Mercy, the other kids treated me differently, like being adopted was some kind of disgrace. It was as if I was a bastard or something. I got into a lot of fights. I began to call my folks Anthony and Theresa instead of Mom and Dad."

"How did they respond to that?"

"With love and patience and kindness. But I still call them Anthony and Theresa. Sometimes I feel..." He didn't finish sentence.

Lacey sensed in him embarrassment and perhaps regret. She said nothing and Dom kept reading.

After a few moments Dom said, "Holy shit, Lace! Look at this! No wonder Fitzgerald was flustered."

He handed Lacey the journal. She flipped back several years, then ahead.

"Dom, the names of all the people who adopted the babies, they're all Irish! *Monahan, Kelly, Curry, McCarthy*...that's why Fitzgerald was so flustered. He knew *Rossi* would never be in there. But he didn't say anything."

Dom continued to flip through the ledger. "Jesus, Lace, look at these legal authorizations. The babies' adoptions were all facilitated by Shaughnessy and Partners. That's why Dennis Shaughnessy was holding the baby in the old photo I saw in Boston. His law firm was arranging the adoptions. And donations from the Loyal Sons were financing it."

Lacey kept reading the ledger, looking at the entries, which were arranged by the date the baby came to the orphanage, the date of birth, and the date of adoption. But another startling thing jumped out at her.

"Dom, all the babies were adopted. All of them." She turned the page and looked at earlier entries. "And there were only

128

between five and eight per year. And according to the dates, they do not appear to have stayed at the orphanage more than a few weeks."

"No one bats a thousand. Let's get out of here and go talk somewhere."

While Dom and Lacey were looking at the ledger, Francis Fitzgerald was making a phone call. "I must speak with Bishop Regan's personal secretary. It is most urgent."

Shortly thereafter, Martin O'Bannon received a phone call from the Bishop's secretary. "I'll take care of it," O'Bannon told him. He also heard from Frank Burns.

"I've been made."

"Switch cars and stay on him."

O'Bannon then made a phone call to Brian Shaughnessy and explained the situation. Shaughnessy told him, "It is now time to dissuade our Professor Rossi from continuing his investigation."

***

Heading north on 206, Dom said, "We'll stop at the Yankee Doodle Tap Room at the old Nassau Inn in Princeton. It's on the way, about ten minutes from here. We'll grab a drink and try to figure this out."

"And get a snack. My stomach's growling. Plus, I need to do a little research. There's something bothering me. It has to do with what you said about connections. We know that Shaughnessy is connected to the orphanage and to the Loyal Sons. But how the hell is he connected to Fiona Cramer? Where does she fit in with him?"

She pulled out her iPad and went online.

Ten minutes later, they entered the famous old tavern, with its beamed ceilings, oak furniture, Norman Rockwell painting, photos of famous Princeton alumni, and giant hearth over which read the inscription, "Rest Traveler, Rest and Banish Thoughts of Care; Drink to Thy Friends and Recommend Them Here."

They seated themselves at one of the old oak tables with years of students' names carved into the wood. Dom asked Lacey, "What would you like?"

"A glass of sauvignon blanc and the hummus, grilled flatbread and olive platter."

Dom raised an eyebrow. "What? No walrus?"

She grinned at him. "Maybe for dessert."

Dom ordered a glass of Chianti. Lacey said, "The trendy wine world currently revolves around Cabernet, Pinot Noir, and Malbec, and you're drinking Chianti?"

"I'm just an old fashioned Italian peasant boy."

"Hardly."

Their order arrived shortly and they got down to work.

Dom said, "Okay, on the surface, it seems straightforward — we have a private Catholic orphanage catering to Irish Catholic families seeking to adopt. A prestigious and powerful law firm, Shaughnessy and Partners, arranges and facilitates the adoptions, and an Irish fraternal organization, the Loyal Sons of Cu Chulainn, is footing the bill — until the closure of the orphanage. All that's perfectly legitimate. But it also raises the question you asked at the Chancery."

Lacey, working on her iPad, nodded and said, "Where did the babies come from?"

"It had to somehow be the Loyal Sons and the Shaughnessy clan; they've been the baby suppliers, from several generations back."

Lacey, still looking at the screen of her iPad said, "Oh boy. Here we go. I had a feeling something was weird was going on.

"I'm looking at a biographical profile of Fiona Shane that was published in the trade journal *Pharmaceutical Executive* in 2005, the year she became CEO of Shane BioPharma. We already know about her graduating from Mount St. Ben's and going on to FDU. But it explains here how she then went into marketing at Schering-Plough Pharmaceuticals and later at Pfizer where she took off like a rocket. Now, here's the nugget — while on scholarship at Mount St. Ben's, she got an internship at a prestigious New Jersey law firm. Guess which one, Dom."

"Oh shit, you're telling me it was Shaughnessy and Partners."

"Bingo. And that's where she met her future husband, Thomas Shane. But Dom, she was a business major with a concentration in marketing, right? So how did she end up interning at a law office? Especially that law office."

"Something stinks. See if you can find out more about Thomas Shane."

After several minutes she said, "Okay, got something — the

Star Ledger. It's a 1980 press release announcing the promotion of Thomas W. Shane, 29, to associate partner at Shaughnessy and Partners."

Dom looked at her. "The guy made associate partner in one of the Northeast's most prestigious and powerful law firms when he was only three or four years out of law school? Jesus, who did he know? What else do you have?"

"Hold on, hold on. Ah, okay, here's his obituary, also in the *Star Ledger.* Let's see, born 1951, died 1981. Princeton University '73, Rutgers Law '76, then accepted a position with Shaughnessy and Partners. Married Fiona Cramer in 1979, son William born in 1980. They evidently wasted no time getting pregnant."

"So Thomas Shane was significantly older than Fiona, seven years."

Lacey looked up and smiled at him. "You're nearly seven years older than I am."

"Just over six. And you're very mature for your tender age. Keep searching, kid."

She laughed and kept searching. "Okay, here's an article in the *Asbury Park Press* about his death — a boating accident off Manasquan Inlet while fishing. He fell overboard and drowned. He was not wearing a life vest. His wife, Fiona, was below deck, asleep. She'd taken a lot of Dramamine to fight off seasickness. She never heard anything — a splash, calls for help, nothing. She finally awoke when the boat smacked up against the rocks in the inlet. And when she called out for Shane, he was gone. The Coast Guard came and towed her into the marina.

"Dom, Manasquan Inlet can be very tricky. I'm no boatnik, but I know the Jersey Shore. Most boaters are very careful. Not wearing a life vest is more than unusual. In any event, this particular hotshot young lawyer didn't exactly have a long career."

"To borrow from a Hemingway short story, it sounds like 'the short happy life' of Thomas Shane. Okay, so Fiona's rise to stardom is very impressive, especially for a single Mom. But she had to have help, certainly financial help."

Lacey looked at him questioningly. "And you're thinking the help came from...?"

131

"Shaughnessy and Partners. But why would they be so supportive of our girl Fiona? There must be something besides her relationship with Thomas Shane."

Dom thought a moment while Lacey spread some hummus and olives on a piece of flatbread. Then he said, "Fiona was raised in the middle of the Pine Barrens, correct?"

After swallowing a bite Lacey said, "Yup, Jenkins. But it's more like a crossroads than a town."

"Didn't Abner say that Jenkins was where the Cloister's delivery guy was from?"

Lacey stopped in mid bite. "You think there's a connection, Sherlock?"

"It's like you said. How many freaking coincidences can there be? Let's try to learn more about Fiona's upbringing in Jenkins. Also, we need to understand how she became so tight with the Shaughnessy clan. How's that sound?"

Lacey gave him one of her sunburst smiles. "Like a plan, partner."

Chapter 18

Fiona Cramer Shane was in her study, along with her son William and his press aide, Marcy Washington, a striking young African American woman. Brian Shaughnessy was also present. Fiona was assessing samples of logos and graphic designs that would appear on William's campaign materials — letterhead, bumper stickers, posters, etc. The designs reflected patterns of stars and stripes, rising suns, or waves in predictable colors of red, white and blue. The name Shane lent itself well to graphic design.

Fiona said, "These are acceptable. We'll do some focus group testing and see which ones generate the best response. Marcy, please arrange that, quickly. My personal assistant, Jeremy, will provide help, when you require it." If Marcy picked up on the subtle jab, she didn't deign to show it.

Fiona watched closely as Marcy quickly and efficiently made notes on her iPad. She watched closely, too, as her son gazed upon Marcy. The young woman was indeed striking — exotic, full-figured, and obviously intelligent. The sexual chemistry between them was palpable. This, Fiona thought, will never do. Especially given the new direction for the campaign.

Fiona said, "William, in terms of your campaign positions, you are firmly established with the business community, for which I must take significant credit. And certainly you have the support of the law enforcement community, given your position in the County Prosecutor's Office. But now it is time to begin to appeal to other constituencies, traditionalist Catholics, Evangelicals, staunch conservatives. And the way to do that is through a message espousing traditional values, family values."

Brian Shaughnessy glanced at Fiona, a slightly ironic smile on his lips. William Shane, eager to hear and follow his mother's directions, as always, asked, "How exactly are you defining that, Mother?"

"You will acknowledge that although the traditional family

structure has, unfortunately, changed dramatically as society has changed, traditional values endure. You will epitomize those traditional values.

"I am referring to values such as responsible sexual mores, respect for the family, a diligent work ethic, respect for authority, and patriotism. And certainly having faith in God. I realize that such a stance will lose you voters in geographic areas such as Newark, Patterson, and Camden, and among such groups as the LGBT community, people of color, many academics, and the damn Progressives. But we would never have their support anyway. The plan is to force Alan Richardson to be aligned with the breakdown of traditional values. In other words, we make Richardson have to defend the godless and the perverted."

"When and how do you see this emphasis taking place, Mother?"

"You will do it in dramatic fashion in your acceptance speech when you receive the Loyal Son of the Year Award at the annual Loyal Sons of Cu Chulainn dinner on Memorial Day. Following Brian's announcement of you as the award's recipient, there will be a several minute video presentation highlighting your background and achievements. Then, you will accept the award and give a speech — a powerful, ringing speech that will arouse and sustain the passion of everyone who believes in tradition and values. I, of course, will write it for you. The audience is a supportive one and the media coverage will be extensive. It is the perfect setting. Don't you agree, Brian?"

"I think it's a brilliant idea. But it makes certain demands on both of you, does it not?"

William asked, "What kinds of demands?"

His mother said, "Your personal conduct must be beyond reproach." She looked at Marcy and back at William. "Certain matters in your personal life will come under intense scrutiny — who your friends are, elements of your early life, elements of my life. And most assuredly, anyone with whom you are suspected of having any kind of romantic or sexual relationship.

"In that context, if — just for example — you were having a relationship with Ms. Washington here, it would be seen as totally inappropriate by this particular audience." She smiled with no sincerity and Marcy. "No offense."

Marcy Washington maintained her poise and simply nodded. "None taken, Ms. Shane." But inside, she knew that if the opportunity ever presented itself to fuck over this racist white bitch, she would jump on it.

William Shane, blushing, said, "It's an awkward example, mother, but I get the point." This was the closest he had ever come to challenging Fiona. It wasn't much.

Changing the subject, Brian Shaughnessy said, "Speaking of the dinner, as each of you know, in earlier years, it was predominately a male affair. However, in recent years many highly accomplished women of Irish descent and others have been welcomed. Some have even been invited to sit on the dais. Most recently invited was the distinguished publisher-editor of *New Jersey Countryside Magazine*. I have suggested to the members of the Board of Trustees of the Loyal Sons — and everyone wholeheartedly agrees — that given the occasion, it would be most appropriate to invite you, Fiona, to join us on the dais. It is a significant honor."

Fiona smiled. "Of course, Brian. I'd be delighted. It will be a glorious evening."

***

After dropping off Lacey at her place, Dom returned to his campus office to put in several hours preparing for the classes Sister Pat had assigned him to teach during the summer session — selecting texts, developing assignments, making notes on topics for classroom discussion.

Critical Reading and Composition taught students how to do close readings of literary texts (poems, plays, novels, essays, etc.), then to write critically about them, refining skills such as summary, analysis, and evaluation.

American Lit 2 covered the country's rich literary history from 1865 to the present. In addition to the usual authors, (e.g., Mark Twain, Walt Whitman, Edith Wharton, Scott Fitzgerald, Ernest Hemingway, William Faulkner, Robert Frost, Langston Hughes, J.D. Salinger, John Updike, etc.), Dom included examples of Native American oral traditions, selections from the famous Harlem Literary Renaissance of the 1920s and 30s, as well as contemporary writers working in various online media. It was an ambitious syllabus, especially for a summer session. By the time he'd finished, it was after 9:00 p.m. and he was ready to call it a night.

Parking on Wetmore Avenue was always a little dicey, and this night Dom found he had to go nearly to the end of the street to find a space. After living here for almost four years, Dom was familiar with many of the residents' vehicles, but people were always coming and going and unfamiliar cars were not unusual.

What was unusual was two men sitting in a white Ford van in front of Dom's place and a single individual in a burgundy Toyota Camry across the street watching Dom as he headed up the street. Dom glanced at the license plates of the two vehicles.

He was about a block from his apartment, when the two men exited the van; the guy in the Toyota climbed out of his car as well. The two men stood to his front, blocking the sidewalk. The third stood to his rear. Both of the men to his front were over six feet tall and weighed well over two hundred pounds each. They seemed very pleased with themselves and very sure of what they were doing.

One of the men said, "Okay, asshole, here's the message. Stay the fuck away from anything related to Rebecca Glass."

"Why do you give a shit about Rebecca Glass? Who are you?"

Dom felt what was obviously the barrel of a gun jab into his back. The man behind him said, "You don't ask questions. You do as you're told. You and that hot girlfriend of yours with her long legs and gorgeous ass and perky tits. Maybe I'll go visit her later. Either way, both of you are in more shit than you ever dreamed."

"You're not about to shoot me in the middle of Wetmore Avenue, so go fuck yourself."

"You're right. I'm not going to shoot you."

Then the right side of Dom's head seemed to explode as the man smashed him with the butt end of his pistol. He collapsed to the sidewalk. Frank Burns told the other two men, "Throw him in the van."

Dom was barely conscious and completely helpless as the two men threw him into the van. He was aware of duct tape being slapped across his mouth and his wrists being taped together in front of him. Blood flowed freely down the side of his face from the gash above his right ear. The inside of the van was empty and smelled of exhaust fumes and gasoline. His face was pressed against the corrugated metal floor.

Slowly becoming more conscious, he tried to ignore the pain and get some sense of the directions the van was taking, first a right, then a left, another left, another right then what felt like moving down a hill. He figured he must be somewhere beyond Speedwell Avenue, a part of Morristown he was unfamiliar with.

After a few minutes the van stopped and Dom was dragged out and thrown to the ground. He was in a small park in a low to moderate-income housing project called Manahan Village in an older section of Morristown formerly known as The Hollow. As the two men proceeded to kick and punch him, Dom tried to roll away and protect his head and groin and block as many blows as he could with his arms and legs. Then they hauled him to his feet to try and do more damage when suddenly Dom heard voices from across the street.

"The fuck you doing there? Get the fuck out our neighborhood, motherfuckers."

In previous years, the housing project had experienced significant drug and crime problems. Residents had then formed a Neighborhood Watch where volunteers patrolled the area, breaking up muggings, fights, drug sales, and other criminal activities. As a result, the project was significantly more crime free, but residents had no tolerance for strangers. The Neighborhood Watch put up with no shit.

Three young black men stood across the street. "We coming to kick your ass you don't get the fuck out of here." They started walking towards the park.

The two guys beating on Dom saw them coming and ran back to the van and took off; the guy who had been driving the burgundy Toyota was right behind them. The young black men came over to Dom.

One of them, wearing a do-rag, said, "Shit, man, they liked to kill your ass. Here, let me get that shit off your mouth and hands."

He removed the duct tape with surprising care and gentleness. "You need 911, man? We tight with the EMTs. They be here quick."

Dom was still bleeding from the head wound, but it was just

137

seeping now. He had been successful fending off the blows to his face and groin, though his nose was bloodied, and the rest of his body was battered and bruised. There was no way he could make it all the way home. But there was refuge close by, maybe.

"No, I'm okay. But thank you, guys. Jesus, I'm glad you came along."

"It what we do, man, we take care of the 'hood. No fucking strangers mess around here no more. Where you from?"

"Across town. But look, I have to get to Speedwell Avenue, El Chicharron. Can you point me in the right direction?"

"Shit, man, you in no shape to go the Cheech! You all bleeding and shit."

"I've got a friend who lives over the place. She'll take care of me."

"Your call, man."

The men walked a limping, staggering Dom through the project until they arrived at the principal street going in and out. The man with the do-rag said, "Go up a block and turn right will get you out to Speedwell. The Cheech be two more blocks down, across the street. Try not to get mugged."

"Thank you again, guys. I really mean it."

Do-rag said, "Yeah, well maybe some day you bring us a few bags of take-out from the Cheech. Beyond that, man, you best stay the fuck out of here."

Dom limped his way up the street, crossed Speedwell then entered a doorway next to El Chicharron. There were three mailboxes on the wall in the small vestibule, each with a buzzer over the top. He found the name 'Lacey' and pressed the buzzer.

After several moments he heard Lacey's voice. "Who's there, please?"

"It's Dom. I need your help."

"*Dom*? What — Take the stairs to the second floor, first door on the right." She pressed the buzzer to let him in.

By the time Dom made it upstairs, Lacey was already waiting for him. She was wearing a white terry cloth bathrobe and her short red-gold hair was still damp. He'd obviously pulled her out of the shower. She smelled like soap and fresh lemons.

"Dear Jesus, Dom! Get in here and let me take care of you."

She led him inside her little apartment. It had a small living room area, a kitchen alcove and a tiny bedroom down the hall. And it was spotless. She quickly led Dom into the bathroom.

"It was three guys, that guy in the car following us and two others. I'm going to — "

"Don't talk. Just let me clean you up."

She helped him take off his shirt then wet a washcloth in warm, soapy water and gently wiped the blood from the cut over his ear.

"God, Dom, you're back and arms and chest are all bruised and there's a lump the size of Cleveland on your head." She gently probed the gash over his ear. "Okay, it's stopped bleeding. It doesn't look like you need stitches." She wiped the blood from his nose and face. "Take off the rest of your clothes and get into a hot shower. I'll get some Advil. Toss your clothes outside the bathroom. I'll wash off the mud and blood in the kitchen sink. Tomorrow morning I'll take them down to the Laundromat next door. There are clean towels in that little wicker hamper." She returned quickly with the Advil.

Dom gingerly climbed into the shower in the tiny bathroom and stood under a spray as hot as he could stand it. He was aware of every one of his bruises, and tried to expose each part of his battered body to the hot spray. By the time he had dried off, the Advil had kicked in. He wrapped a towel around his waist and went out to Lacey.

She had made up the living room sofa with sheets, blankets and a pillow. She was sitting in one of the chairs, oblivious to the fact that her bathrobe had separated and partially exposed one long, elegantly slender leg and a glimpse of smooth, white thigh.

"How are you feeling? Any better?"

"I'm pretty sure I'm going to survive. Thank you."

"I asked you a few days ago if life with you was always going to be so interesting. I guess I got my answer."

"I'm sorry to have dragged you into this. You can quit any time, no hard feelings. Anyway, thank you for making up the sofa. It looks really inviting."

"I don't quit. And I won't quit on you. The sofa is for me. You're the wounded warrior. You get the bedroom."

He shook his head. "Absolutely not. I'm feeling much better. And there's no way I'm chasing you out of your bed."

She was silent for several moments, just looking at him. Then, her blue eyes wide and a faint blush coloring her face, she said softly, "If you want, Dom, we could share."

There was no mistaking her meaning. "Yes, Lacey. Let's share."

Chapter 19

The following morning, Dom and Lacey sat in a booth in a small cafe on Speedwell Avenue, shoveling food into their mouths as fast as their hands could move. Lacey was attacking the Lumberjack Special — three eggs over easy with biscuits, sausage, country ham, bacon, and home fries. Dom was having the huevos rancheros with chorizo and a side of jalapeno corn bread.

Lacey paused briefly to look up from her plate and glance furtively around the room. "Dom, do you think they can tell? I mean, you know, what we've been up to?"

"Lace, we've been making love — one way or another — for ten hours. You are glowing. And there should be a racing stripe on your fork. I have circles under my eyes, my hands are twitching, and I limped my way in the door. They know exactly what we've been up to. And everyone in the place is either benignly amused or insanely jealous."

She beamed at him. "Oh God, Dom, I'm so happy and I love you so much, and every time I think of last night and this morning I get all tingly. But what now? What are you going to do about those guys?"

"I'm going to make a couple of phone calls. After which I'm pretty sure they won't bother either of us. Later, we're going on a picnic down in the Hollow. But the real problem is, what are Shaughnessy and O'Bannon covering up? It has to be devastating. It has to be about St. Keira's and the Pine Barrens. And I have to be getting close."

"So, we should pay another visit to Abner."

He nodded. "He's our secret weapon. We'll talk to him and then try to retrace Rebecca's steps somehow. If we get real lucky, maybe we can learn more about the identity of the Caretaker. I think she's the key."

Lacey gave him one of her best smiles. "We can use my folks' bungalow as a base of operations again. But this time, we'll 'share'."

Dom took her hand. "Sharing with you is my new favorite thing."

After their breakfast, Lacey dropped off Dom at his place on Wetmore Avenue. They agreed that Lacey would come over to Dom's that night for dinner and, given their new relationship, spend the rest of the night sharing. Then he got to work making his phone calls.

"Sarah, it's Dom. I need a favor. I need you to run a couple of license plates for me and give me the names and addresses of the vehicles' owners." Dom had memorized the plates from the previous night.

"Does this have to do with that Rebecca Glass thing?"

"Big time. And the guys who are connected to these two vehicles tried to beat the shit out of me last night and get me to stop looking into it."

He heard her sigh. "And, of course, you're not going to stop."

"Not a chance."

"Okay, give me a couple of hours. I'll call you back."

Next, Dom turned on his computer and pulled up a file containing contact information for each of his students. Then he made his next call.

"Dontay, it's Dom Rossi."

"Hey, Doc, it's great to hear from you! What up?"

"Dontay, I need a favor."

"Hell, Doc, name it."

Dom explained what had happened and what he had in mind. Dontay said, "Shit, Doc, it'll be my pleasure. And I know just the guy. Just give me a heads up on the location and the time."

An hour later, Dom heard back from Sarah. "Okay, the white van was a rental. Renter's name is Frederick Carnahan. Second driver was listed as Charles Eagan. I followed up on both. They're small time hoods. Both have records — mostly stuff like assault, extortion, possession of small amounts of cocaine, that kind of thing. But Carnahan was also convicted four years ago of felonious assault and battery and did three years in the joint. And two years ago Eagan did eighteen months on a sexual assault charge. They tend to work as bouncers in low-end clubs and strip joints." She gave Dom the name of the club where the two were usually found. "My question to you, Dom, is what are you going to do with this information?"

"Discourage them. How about the Toyota guy?"

"This gets more interesting. His name is Frank Burns, former investigator for the Morris County prosecutor's office, now a licensed PI." She gave Dom the address. Then she told him, "I called a contact in Morris County. Burns evidently considers himself a tough guy. He's known to be mean, highly aggressive, and was suspected of being dirty, though no charges were ever brought against him. What does all of this have to do with Rebecca Glass's mugging?"

"When I find out, Sarah, you'll be the first to know."

***

The Bahia Club was located in a single story brick building on East Blackwell Street in the town of Dover, about twenty minutes northwest of Morristown. Compared to the restaurants and clubs in Morristown, it might as well have been on the dark side of the moon. Morristown would never be in the running for the pole dancing capital of New Jersey; Dover would.

The Club was the current place of employment for Frederick Carnahan and Charles Eagan. Both men thought it was a pretty good gig. They worked as bouncers, or as they preferred to call it, security consultants. This position permitted them to extort sex from the dancers, bully the customers, and eat and drink for free. They usually worked from about 7 until 2 a.m., after which they had a few more drinks and headed home. Since they both lived in the same rooming house in Dover, they rode together back and forth from the club.

On this night, following their usual schedule, they exited the club about 2:30 and were heading towards their car in the dimly lit parking lot when they saw a very tall, impressively built young black man leaning against their car.

Carnahan, the more aggressive of the two, said, "What the fuck you doing on my car, midnight?"

It was then that a section of the building's wall seemed to come to life and Carnahan and Eagan looked to see a very large figure step out of the shadows and move towards them.

Walter "Pinky" Plucinski was one of only three males in the Mount St. Ben's Bachelor of Science in Nursing program. He was also a three year starter on the school's football team; he was the nose tackle. Mount St. Ben's played a 3-4 defense. Nose tackles in a 3-4 tend to have big, wide bodies and tremendous strength. This is because they are responsible for holding the point of attack and forcing the offensive guard and center to double team them. Pinky, though still a junior, was considered among the best collegiate nose tackles in the Northeast.

Pinky looked from the two men to Dontay Robinson. He asked, "'Tay, what's he mean 'midnight'?"

"It's a racial slur, Pink. He's disparaging my being black."

Pinky thought a moment then said, "Well, that's not very polite."

Then, with astonishing speed, he grabbed Frederick Carnahan by the neck and the crotch and lifted him over his head, carried him to Carnahan's Pontiac, and body slammed him onto the hood. Then he picked up Carnahan again and threw him through the windshield. Simultaneously, Dontay buried his left fist deep into Eagan's solar plexus then followed it up with a right cross to the jaw, rendering Eagan immediately unconscious. Pinky walked around to the passenger side of the Pontiac and opened the door, grabbed Carnahan by the hair, and slammed his face into the dashboard.

Dontay leaned in the door and told Carnahan, "Blindness is not seeing things the way they really are. You and your pal here saw yourselves as real tough guys. Well, you're not tough guys. You're softer than shit. That's your tragic flaw. And unless you want your life to turn into shit, you better stay the fuck away from Dom Rossi. And don't you even say Caroline Lacey's name."

Pinky smashed Carnahan's face again. "Nod if you understand him," Pinky said. Carnahan nodded.

Dontay said, "Cross me, and we're coming back. And we're coming back mad."

As Dontay and Pinky walked away, Pinky said, "'Tay, you think maybe I should give up this nursing thing and try out for World Wrestling Entertainment?"

"I don't think the WWE is violent enough for you, Pinkster. And you're too honest for that fake shit. Besides, you got the perfect disposition for nursing. You could be in charge of the psychiatric floor."

Pinky thought about it for a few seconds. "I'd like that." Then he said, "'Tay, you think we could get something to eat now? I'm a little hungry."

"Sure thing, Pink. Be my treat."

Pinky told him, "That's very generous of you, Dontay."

Given Pinky's prodigious appetite, it was very generous indeed.

***

Earlier that evening, Frank Burns was in the study of his comfortable two-story, three bedroom house on Diane Road in Morris Plains. He had been doing a little bookkeeping. Thanks to his work for Martin O'Bannon, it was looking to be an exceptionally profitable month. So profitable, in fact, that he thought about getting a larger place. Maybe one with an in-ground pool.

Then the doorbell rang and a voice called out, "Pizza delivery. One large pepperoni with extra cheese."

Burns partially opened the door, leaving the chain in place. He saw a young man standing there holding a pizza box whose open lid obscured his face. He was wearing sunglasses and a Yankees cap. The delivery guy said, "We're supposed to show off the pie like this. Looks great, doesn't it? That'll be $14.95, no charge for the delivery."

Burns said, "I didn't order pizza. Beat it."

"Isn't this 8 Diane Road, Morris Plains?"

"Yeah, but I didn't order any fucking pizza. Now hit the road."

The delivery guy said, "Well shit, you might as well take the goddam thing. I'm going to have to pay for it anyway, and I don't want to look like an asshole in front my boss by bringing it back."

Burns figured it was a good deal. He would get a free pizza and the kid would have to pay for it. He removed the chain and opened the door. That was when Dom Rossi shoved the pizza into Burns' face and planted a vicious kick squarely between his legs.

Burns screamed and dropped to the floor, holding his crotch and writhing in agony. Wearing his work boots for this express purpose, Dom kicked Burns in the side of the head. Then kicked him again. Burns lost consciousness. Dom waited patiently for him to recover. After several minutes, Burns groaned and opened his eyes; seeing Dom he started to crawl away. Dom blocked his way and kicked him in the ribs.

"Jesus, no more! No more!"

"I keep remembering what you said about my girlfriend's long legs and gorgeous ass and perky tits. And what you said about visiting her — especially about visiting her. That was very disrespectful to her. And very disturbing to me." Dom stomped on Burns' ankle, fracturing it. Burns screamed.

"Ankle fractures are a bitch, Burns. They often don't heal correctly. You may very well have a limp for the rest of your life. If I fracture the other one, which I'm seriously considering, you'll be on crutches. But you can prevent that. Just tell me who is behind all this shit. And what was your part in it?"

"O'Bannon hired me. He takes orders from Brian Shaughnessy. It all has to do with the Loyal Sons. I was supposed to follow you and report on your activities. I don't know why. I was just supposed to do it. Then they told me to warn you off."

"I'm taking aim at your other ankle, Burns. What else?"

"Nothing else! I don't know anything else! Only that the Loyal Sons of Cu Chulainn see you as some kind of threat. That's all I know. I swear to God."

"What did you have to do with Rebecca Glass? Tell me the truth, Burns, or it's your fucking spine I stomp next. You'll never feel your dick again and you'll have to hire someone to come in and wipe your ass, because you won't know if you've shit yourself until you start to smell it."

"Oh God, please. O'Bannon had me break into her house in Morristown and look for anything that resembled a report or a presentation on a disc or a flash drive. I didn't find shit, honest to God. All I know is that the next night she got mugged. I don't know anything about what actually went down or who did it. I wasn't there. I swear to God."

Dom looked at him for several seconds then said, "Enjoy your pizza."

***

The following afternoon, Dom picked up Lacey and they stopped

146

at El Chicharron. The owners, Elena and Javier, greeted Lacey with much hugging and kissing. When they learned what Dom and Lacey had in mind, they suggested and prepared an array of their best delicacies. Armed with bags of takeout — chicharrones, empanadas, pork carnitas, black beans and rice, along with several cellophane wrapped packages of plastic cutlery and paper plates — Dom and Lacey headed down to the small park in Manahan Village. They unloaded their stuff and sat at one of the metal picnic tables bolted onto a concrete slab. It took only about five minutes before Do-rag and the two other large young black men walked over to them.

Do-rag said to Dom, "You either dumb as shit, man, or you got some brass." Then he laughed and reached out his fist. "Name's Stick. This is Lamar and Montego."

Dom gave Stick a fist bump. "I'm Dom. This is Lacey. You guys care to join us?"

Stick said, "That stuff from the Cheech? Hell yes."

Dom pulled out a six-pack of Colt 45 in sixteen-ounce cans.

Stick smiled and nodded at the cans. "This a cliché?"

"No, it's the most brew I could get for the least amount of money."

They dug in and ate for a while, enjoying the food. As Stick reached for an empanada he asked, "How you end up in that shit the other night? What you do?"

"I teach English over at Mount St. Ben's University."

"Shit, those guys don't like their grades so they decide to kick your ass?"

Dom explained about Rebecca, the mugging, and how the university was worried both about her reputation and its own, how he was supposed to discover what Rebecca had been working on, and that the guys the other night were warning him off.

"But Lacey and I think there's a whole lot more going on here."

Stick turned to Lamar. "What you think, Lamar?" He said to Dom, "Lamar have experience in these matters."

Lamar put down his Colt 45 and shook his head. "Don't sound like no mugging. Sound like she offed on purpose. Somebody messing with you big time."

147

Lacey, wide-eyed, asked, "Wouldn't that mean they knew what Rebecca had on them? So why even involve Dom? Why not just leave it with Rebecca?"

"They using Dom. See if he find out what Rebecca found out. He don't, they in the clear. He get too close, they warn him off. He find out, they off Dom, too."

"My God, that's diabolical."

Montego shrugged and said, "Way it be. Means they cold and they got some big time shit going down. You and Dom best figure out what, else they keep coming after you. "

Stick asked, "Who you think behind this shit, Dom?"

"A guy who's the President of the Mount St. Ben's Board of Trustees. He's also a big time lawyer. Name's Brian Shaughnessy."

Stick thought a minute then said, "Burly white guy, maybe early sixties, head of white hair, bushy eyebrows and little beady blue eyes?"

Dom was stunned. "Jesus, Stick. That's him! How the hell do you know him?"

Stick's smile was rueful. "I don't just kick ass down here in the hood, Dom. I do some DJ shit and rap in some of the local hip-hop clubs, drive some truck. I also work part time as a locker room attendant over at the Spring Brook Country Club. Done it since I was a kid.

"This Shaughnessy a longtime member, come to the club regular, play some golf, showers and shaves, and him and his boys play some big time gin rummy and drink a mess of Scotch. Cheap-ass tipper and a smug son of a bitch, if it the same dude."

"Same dude, no question. Look, let me give you my cell number in case you see or hear something we can use."

Dom and Stick exchanged contact information. Then they all ate and drank and kicked it around for a while, each of them contributing to the discussion. Finally, Stick said, "What you think, Dom?"

"I think you guys are right. It had to be on purpose. And that really pisses me off."

"You figure to stay on this?"

"Yeah, I stay on it. I owe it to Rebecca."

Stick shook his head. "Hell, Dom, I right the first time. You either dumb as shit, or you sure do got some brass."

Lacey took a swig of her Colt 45 and patted her mouth with a paper napkin; then she smiled and winked at them. "Trust me, gentlemen. I'll vouch for the brass."

Everyone howled with laughter.

Chapter 20

Martin O'Bannon figured he had to deliver the bad news to Brian Shaughnessy in person, not that he relished the idea. O'Bannon had earlier received a call from Frank Burns explaining that they had not at all intimidated Dom Rossi. It was a disturbing call.

"The guy is an animal, O'Bannon. A fucking English professor! I've got a cast on my ankle that's going to be part of me for ten weeks. You can consider me off the damn case. And you'd better watch your own ass, too."

Now, O'Bannon sat across from Shaughnessy in the latter's office in Morristown. Shaughnessy said, "You told me everything was covered, that your man was a pro. Now you tell me this. It's most troubling, Martin. What do you plan to do about Rossi now?"

"I have another resource, tougher and more efficient than Burns — as Glass and Bennington are evidence."

"I do not need the particulars. You are certain this resource will deliver again?"

"Yes. And I will be personally involved. I'm looking forward to it."

"And Rossi will finally be dissuaded?"

"One way or another. It's merely a matter of time."

"Good. We need this resolved before the Loyal Sons Dinner on Memorial Day."

"I assure you, Brian. It will be a memorable dinner."

***

Following Dom's suggestion about developing a plan of action, Lacey decided to start with learning more about Thomas Shane. There was something about his relationship with Fiona Cramer that was nagging at her; it seemed to have progressed way too rapidly, from the courtship (whatever it had been), to the marriage, to the pregnancy. Lacey was unable to nail down the source of her discomfort, but she had the distinct feeling it was somehow relevant to all the craziness they were uncovering.

150

She went back over Shane's obituary and noticed again that he'd graduated from Princeton University in 1973. It occurred to her that Professor Julian Haines, her favorite sociology professor at Monmouth University, also graduated from Princeton that same year. She gave him a call.

"Lacey! It's wonderful to hear from you, dear. To what do I owe the pleasure?"

"Professor J, a friend and I are working on a project, a kind of combination of folklore and historical research, that has led us to a man by the name of Thomas Shane. I've noticed that he was at Princeton the same time you were. If you remember him and it's convenient for you, we'd like to drop by for a bit and pick your brains about him. But I have to tell you, it's a little complicated."

"Thomas Shane! I remember him well, dear girl. Meet me at Ron's West End Pub at noon tomorrow. You can buy my memories for the price of several martinis."

Ron's was located in the section of Long Branch known as West End, about a mile and a half from the Monmouth University campus. A generation earlier, the area had been a kind of hippie enclave with head shops, used clothing stores, espresso joints, galleries, bars, and an elegant, albeit incongruous Italian specialty food store, Primavera's. Now, although still a thriving area, it was decidedly less interesting.

Ron's, however, retained a kind of funky chic that was uniquely appealing. It sported rocking chairs on the front porch, antiques, photos of the old days, and an eclectic and convivial assortment of patrons — college students and locals, straight and gay, newcomers and regulars — who all tended to return again and again. It was here that Dom and Lacey met Professor Julian Haines.

He was seated at a table next to the front window and waved them over. He was a tall, slender man in his mid-sixties with light blue eyes and elaborately coiffed and sprayed blond hair. He wore crisp white slacks, a blue blazer over a pink, open collar button down shirt, and a yellow paisley ascot.

He kissed Lacey on both cheeks in the European manner and said, "Darling girl, you are clearly thriving. You're positively glowing! And who is this dashing young fellow with you, whom I suspect is the source of your glow?"

Lacey introduced Dom as an assistant professor of English at Mount St. Benedict University and as her "very good friend."

Shaking Dom's hand, Professor Haines said, "Ha! Dominic, you'll excuse me, but judging by Lacey's glow, 'very good friend' does not at all do you justice."

Lacey blushed noticeably.

Professor Haines went on, "Mount St. Ben's is a wonderful institution. Is Sister Patricia Schaedel still chairing the English department? She is a first-rate scholar. We worked together on several committees for the Association of Independent Colleges and Universities of New Jersey. She is a delight. And she takes no shit from anyone."

Dom laughed and said, "Yes, sir, she still is — and she still doesn't. She's been a wonderful friend to me."

"I'm delighted to hear it. Now then, if we don't order immediately, I'll absolutely perish from thirst."

An attractive young waitress came over, gave them a wide smile and said, "Hi, Professor J. Extra dry Grey Goose martini, straight up, three olives?"

"Dina, you are a saint and you are performing a corporal work of mercy. God will bless you for it. And my friends will have?"

Lacey asked for a glass of sauvignon blanc; Dom went with a glass of Merlot.

As their drinks arrived, Lacey and Dom filled in Professor Haines on what they were engaged in. Lacey said, "Here's what bothers me, Professor J — Thomas Shane gets this plum job with Shaughnessy and Partners right out of law school. He's there only a few years, marries a young woman from an impoverished background who was working as an intern, gets a big promotion, and he and the young woman have a son almost immediately. Then he drowns. And she, although a young widow and a single mother, manages to finish college, go to grad school and then carve out an amazing career in the pharmaceutical industry with some big time corporations. And then she becomes Chair and CEO of her own company. It just strikes me as improbable."

Professor Haines took a hefty pull at his martini and said, "My dear, it is more improbable than you even imagine. The late, dare I say it, unlamented Thomas Shane did make an extraordinary rise at that prestigious firm, but I've always suspected it was for

152

reasons other than his legal prowess."

"What are you suggesting, sir?" Dom asked.

"Dominic, I do not believe for one moment that Thomas Shane is the biological father of William Shane. I knew Thomas at Princeton. We were not particularly close, but we did share some, how shall I put it, 'common interests.'"

Dom shook his head. "I'm still not following you, Professor."

Professor Haines smiled, knowing he was about to drop a bomb. "Thomas Shane was gay. He was certainly closeted, as nearly all gays were in those days, but gay he surely was."

A shocked Dom said, "Gay? Are you sure, Professor J?"

"Dear boy, look at me. Do I look as if I would not know such things?"

Lacey asked, "Then why would he ever marry Fiona Cramer, Professor J?"

Professor Haines patted her hand. "You are such an innocent, my dear. He married her because she was his beard — a disguise for his sexual orientation. Consider this, if you will; Shane attains an enviable position at a prestigious Irish Catholic law firm and has a promising future. But he has certain 'proclivities.' Should those proclivities become known, he would immediately lose his job and be disgraced. So to hide his orientation, he marries. Such occurrences were quite common at the time, usually with sad and often tragic consequences. They were known as 'lavender marriages.'"

Dom took a hefty swallow of wine and said, "Oh, shit."

Professor Haines said, "Dominic, you're having an insight. What is it?"

"Professor J, this is going to sound crazy. But what if someone else at the firm — someone important, someone who was already married — impregnated Fiona? It's potentially a scandal of gargantuan proportions. And since the firm is basically Irish Catholic, abortion is not even considered. To avoid disaster, the firm pressures Shane into marrying her because he's an available single guy and junior enough to be pressured.

"Why does Shane go along with it? It's a kind of quid pro quo. He gets a beard; he gets promoted to associate partner — and they owe him. On the other side, the firm itself is spared any scandal or embarrassment. A sexual scandal at such a prestigious firm would have cost them millions. They might never have recovered."

Lacey picked it up. "I get it! Then Shane conveniently drowns but the firm continues to support Fiona, because of the importance of the real father. And the connection exists to this day. My God, Professor J, could that have actually happened?"

Professor Haines nodded. "It may be conjecture, my dears, but it is consistent with what we know, and it has its own internal logic. But questions remain. Who was the real father? And, not to be paranoid, it raises the question, was Thomas Shane's drowning truly accidental? It was, as you say, certainly 'convenient.' There's your mystery. Go solve it. In the meantime, I'll have another martini."

Lacey looked at Dom. "Jesus, what do you think?"

"I'm sorry to keep repeating myself, Lace. But oh, shit."

Chapter 21

Once back at Dom's place on Wetmore Avenue, Dom booted his computer and said, "Okay, we need to find out who exactly was employed at Shaughnessy and Partners back in 1980, the year Fiona interned there and became pregnant."

"Because why?"

"Because we need to talk to someone who can give us a feel for the place and for what the internal dynamics were like. You use the iPad and I'll use the desktop, and we'll come at it from different directions."

They had been working for about a half hour when Lacey said, "Got something! Take a look. It's a group photograph of members of the firm taken at the New Jersey State Bar Association Annual Meeting in Cape May, September, 1980."

Dom slid over next to her and looked at the photo. "That's a young Brian Shaughnessy. He looks like a smug bastard even there. And the older, white haired guy on the left must be his father, Liam. Who's the woman on the right?"

Dom was referring to a smiling, sturdy, fair-haired woman who, even in a photo, seemed to exude the personality of a mischievous but intelligent cheerleader.

"The caption says she's Kathleen Culhane; she was then a staff lawyer."

"How old do you think she is in that photo?"

Lacey looked at the picture a few seconds. "Maybe thirty or so."

"Okay, so now she'd be in her late sixties. Lawyers go on forever. Maybe she's still practicing."

He Googled the New Jersey State Bar Association, then followed a link to the Morris County Bar Association, and found a list of members. "Aha!"

Lacey looked at him. "'Aha'? Is that a specialized Ph.D. research term?"

"Only for the most astute of us. Here, look. Kathleen Culhane

155

is now the principal partner with Culhane, Cilo & Destefanis, PLC. It looks like they're a big time firm headquartered in Chatham, about twenty minutes away."

"So let's take a ride and see if we can get to talk with her. If nothing else, you can buy me dinner."

"Dinner sounds great. But if I'm paying, I'll expect something in return." He winked at her.

Lacey nudged him. "Oh, that. That was on the menu anyway."

Chatham is just a few miles east of Morristown, past university row — the College of St. Elizabeth, Fairleigh Dickinson University, and Drew University, and beyond the town of Madison. As they drove through Madison and past Loantaka Way, Dom could not help but think of the death of Diana Bennington. There was an ugliness underlying this whole thing that he did not yet understand, but that he was sure was there. And he was determined to find out exactly what it was.

Downtown Chatham has a tree-lined Main Street with assorted Mom & Pop shops, gracious Victorian houses, and a drugstore that boasts an actual old-fashioned ice cream counter. The offices of Culhane, Cilo & Destefanis were located in one of the larger old Victorian houses. Dom and Lacey parked in the small lot and entered through the front door. A smiling, fresh-faced young man sat at a desk in the lobby and asked, "How may we help you?"

"I'm Dr. Dominic Rossi from Mount St. Benedict University, and this is my colleague, Ms. Caroline Lacey. I know this is most irregular, but my colleague and I need to see Ms. Culhane. We do not have an appointment."

The guy appeared horrified; he looked as if Dom had asked to see Pope Francis without an appointment.

"I'm very sorry, sir. She is unavailable — and certainly not without an appointment. I can put you in touch with her executive assistant so that you may determine a more opportune and convenient time."

Dom smiled what he hoped was an engaging smile and said, "Perhaps you can just give her a quick message. Tell we're here about her former colleague, Thomas Shane. We'll wait."

The guy, still horrified, picked up a desk phone as Dom and Lacey took seats in the waiting area. There were a number of magazines available, the most appealing of which was *New*

156

Jersey Countryside — it was intelligent, attractive, and informative. Dom read an article about the old Moravian village of Hope, New Jersey, while Lacey checked out an issue featuring the best BYO restaurants in the state. She pulled out her smart phone and started making a list.

Fifteen minutes later, much to the shock of the young man at the desk, an attractive, chunky, older woman came out and stood before them, obviously sizing them up, looking first at Dom and then at Lacey.

She said, "You should know that I am an attorney of some note. Actually, I'm a big deal. Clients and potential clients usually wait weeks, even months to see me. And everyone knows it. So I just had to see who was either ignorant enough or ballsy enough to march in here without an appointment and ask me about the late, obnoxious Thomas Shane. But you two actually look kind of interesting. I'm Kate Culhane. You might as well come on back to my office. I'm between client meetings, so we have a few minutes. I'll have coffee brought in."

She led them to a well-appointed office decorated with antiques, a small library of assorted law books and legal tomes, and selections of original art by the late-19th-mid-20th century American illustrator, graphic artist and painter, A. B. Frost.

She indicated they all sit at a highly polished, antique cherry wood table. It was covered with a lace doily and held a small bowl of fresh apples and pears. Dom and Lacey sat across from her. They introduced themselves.

Kate Culhane smiled and said, "Okay, Dr. Rossi, what are you two characters up to that got you to track me down? It's been over thirty years since I was at Shaughnessy. And what does all this have to do with that twerp Thomas Shane?"

Dom immediately liked her. She was smart, direct, and would obviously tolerate no bullshit.

"I think something stinks at Shaughnessy and Partners, and I suspect that Thomas Shane was part of it. I think it goes back four generations, and it involves the Cloister of St. Keira, the Loyal Sons of Cu Chulainn, the Diocese of Trenton, and may even have enormous implications for the State of New Jersey."

Kate smiled wryly. "Just for the record, Professor, is there anyone else in the Western Hemisphere you want to implicate?

Still, this is most intriguing, assuming you're not drugged up or completely delusional. Please go on."

Dom explained about Rebecca, her research, her death, and how the more they looked at it, the more involved Shaughnessy and Partners seemed to be. "Rebecca very likely discovered something threatening to them and she ended up dead. Bottom line, Ms. Culhane, I think they're dirty, big time."

Kate was silent, looking from one to the other. She said, "Give me a dollar."

Dom reached into the pocket of his jeans and handed her a crumpled dollar bill.

Kate said, "Okay, by this payment I am accepting you as my clients. That means you have the benefit of attorney-client privilege. All further communication between us is privileged and confidential. It can be open and candid and I can never reveal it. Now, keep talking and let it all hang out — knowledge, speculation, conjecture."

Dom said, "If we're correct that Rebecca's death was more than a mugging, it must in some way touch Shaughnessy and Partners. We cannot say with any certainty that they were involved in her actual death, but they're clearly within the sphere of activity and could have had a compelling interest.

"Added to that is the suspicion that Thomas Shane was not the biological father of William Shane. His background and behavior suggest that he is not, nor could he have been. But frankly, the more we learn, the more convoluted it gets. It's like Lacey and I are trying to untie what is beginning to look like the Gordian knot."

The coffee service arrived — bone china cups and saucers, cream, both sugar and Splenda, and a platter of fresh baked gingerbread cookies. Kate poured them each a cup. She said, "Dr. Rossi, I spent five years at Shaughnessy and Partners; not entirely pleasant years, especially for a woman. But they were certainly worthwhile from a learning and experiential perspective."

"Please, call me Dom. And this is Lacey. How many lawyers were there at the time?"

"And I am Kate. There were six; I was the only woman. There were, however, a number of young women employed in other capacities — administrative assistants, paralegals, interns and the like."

Lacey said, "I'll bet it was no treat for those women. Not in those days."

Kate nodded and said, "True indeed. The old man, Liam, was courtly and gracious, in a patriarchal, nineteenth century sort of way. But I got the feeling that he was always staring at my ass or my chest and would grab either one, if the opportunity ever presented itself. I made it a point to never be alone with him. He had a stroke shortly after I left and lived for a while, but never returned to the firm.

"As for the other attorneys, most of them were married, but they all behaved like it was some kind of fraternity house and open season on any female."

Dom asked, "Did you have much to do with adoption services when you were with Shaughnessy and Partners, Kate?"

"No, that was strictly handled by Liam himself and also by Brian Shaughnessy when he joined the firm."

Dom was intrigued. "Brian Shaughnessy must have been, what, twenty-six or so back then and just out of law school. How did he behave, what was he like?"

Kate looked at Lacey, "Do you have particularly delicate sensibilities, Lacey?"

"Fuck no," Lacey said.

Kate laughed heartily. "Very good. The expression, I believe, is cock hound. He was a notorious lecher and wildly promiscuous. He was also smug, arrogant, and even though just out of law school, he acted as if he were the heir apparent — and I guess, he was. He even tried to hit on me. He was married at the time, about two years. I actually met his wife at a Christmas party one year. She seemed to be a very pleasant and gracious woman, though Brian paid little attention to her.

"Anyway, because the atmosphere at the firm was so uncomfortable for women, I decided to go out on my own. The firm was shocked and outraged that anyone would dare to leave them by choice. They went out their way to make professional life tough for me for a number of years. But it was the best decision I ever made."

"How about Thomas Shane," Dom asked. "How did he fit in at the firm?"

"Not well at all. He was even more ambitious than everyone else, and we were a very ambitious bunch. But he wasn't like the others, didn't socialize with them or play their stupid male chauvinist pig games. Frankly, I always suspected he was gay.

"That's why I was shocked when he married that very attractive young college intern. But I must say, the idea that he was not the biological father of William Shane has merit. I can believe it. The question of course is, absent DNA testing, which provides positive proof, how can you prove it."

Kate's remark about DNA testing struck Dom as interesting — but how the hell did someone go about getting DNA, especially on the sneak?

Lacey said to Kate, "The intern's name was Fiona Cramer. Did you know her?"

"I didn't know her well and left shortly after she arrived. As I recall, she was a very hot number but in a kind of cool and distant way. And she knew it. It was clear from the outset that she had most of the men in the firm salivating. She went on to have a very significant career in pharmaceuticals, as you of course are aware."

Dom said, "I have one last question. What was the relationship between Shaughnessy and Partners and the Loyal Sons of Cu Chulainn?"

"Oh, hell, they're practically one and the same. Shaughnessys have always been the driving force behind the whole organization. They were the founders, back in the nineteenth century, shortly after the clan arrived from County Tipperary, from the village of Ballyporeen.

"Things were very difficult for the Irish back then, very difficult. So, the original idea was to form an organization of successful, prominent Irish men and then exert whatever influence and power they could to help other people of Irish descent, as well as individuals and organizations in need, including the Catholic Church, while increasing their own power and influence. My Dad was a Loyal Son, Philadelphia Chapter."

"Mine, too," Lacey said. "Jersey Shore Chapter."

Kate nodded and went on, "I've been invited to a number of the annual dinners over the years — after they got over the fact of my leaving the firm on my own volition and they started to allow

160

women. The Loyal Sons of Cu Chulainn do wonderful work on behalf of all kinds of deserving causes and, frankly, those connections have helped my career. But the organization over the years has morphed into one largely seeking to increase its own power and that of its members. It might as well be called the Loyal Sons of Shaughnessy."

Kate then asked Dom and Lacey, "So, given their power and influence, how are you two going to proceed? If you're thinking that Shaughnessy and Partners or anyone associated with them is somehow involved in the death of this Rebecca Glass you told me about, you have a hell of a big challenge. And you certainly cannot leak any of your suspicions. You'd be sued for libel in a heartbeat — or worse."

Dom said, "We're pretty much just going to keep pushing and asking questions. If we actually come up with anything, is it okay if we run it by you?"

"Absolutely. You're my clients, now. And you are an interesting pair, with an intriguing story. But be aware of this — Shaughnessy and Partners is incredibly powerful and, I know from experience, utterly ruthless. Be careful what rock you turn over. Something very ugly can come crawling out."

Dom and Lacey stood to go and shook hands with Kate. "Thank you for all your time and insights, Kate. Lacey and I really appreciate it."

"My pleasure, Dom. Please keep in touch. I'll be most interested your progress."

Dom and Lacey headed back to Morristown, picked up a bottle of Chianti and stopped for dinner at a little BYO Italian restaurant on South Street called Provesi. They sat at a table next to the front window and shared a platter of calamari fritti then split a sausage pizza.

Lacey said, "I really liked Kate. I'm glad she's on our side, especially if this little quest of ours gets ugly and we need some help. So where do we go from here?"

"I'd go into combat with her in a heartbeat. As for where we go, it's back to the Pine Barrens. We need to know what Rebecca found down there."

Lacey helped herself to a second slice of pizza. "What about those gorillas who came after you, or the person who sent them?

161

It was O'Bannon under Shaughnessy's orders, right? Do you think O'Bannon will try something else to stop you?"

Dom nodded. "Yeah, he will. So we have to be alert for anything."

***

Before he and Lacey headed back down to the Pine Barrens, Dom again went through Rebecca's report for San Giacomo Engineering. He'd purchased a detailed map of the area, so he could match Rebecca's geographic references with locations on the map. His plan was to get a rough idea of where to focus the search and then run it by Abner. Then they could determine the best way to explore the target areas in the hope that they'd come across what Rebecca had discovered — and what was causing all the trouble. In addition, they would try to learn more about Fiona Shane's upbringing.

After doing his research, Dom called the English Department at Mount St. Ben's. He said to Fran Purcell, "Fran, please let Sister Pat know that I'm heading down to the Pine Barrens for a few days on university business. I'll be in the area around Speedwell and Jenkins, but I'll be headquartered at Caroline Lacey's place near Tuckerton. If Sister Pat needs to contact me, my cell phone is probably best."

Immediately following Dom's call, Fran Purcell contacted Provost Delaney. "Rossi is going to the Pine Barrens day after tomorrow. Near places called Speedwell and Jenkins. He'll be staying at the home of that graduate teaching assistant, Caroline Lacey."

Delaney then called O'Bannon, who said, "Thank you, Felix. I'll get right on it."

O'Bannon smiled. He loved being back in the game.

Chapter 22

Dom and Lacey arrived at the bungalow in Mystic Island later that afternoon. They put their overnight bags in the same bedroom. Lacey looked at the bags sitting next to each other on the bed and smiled. "This makes me very happy."

"It's only the beginning." He kissed her gently. She responded enthusiastically. He laughed and said, "Before this goes too far, Lace — and it will in a heartbeat — we'd better go see if we can find Abner. I promise you, we'll be sharing all night."

She gave him an affectionate nudge. "Show off."

It was about a half hour drive from Mystic Island to Abner's place. They were heading west on county road 542 towards the intersection with Route 206, then north to Shamong. The day was sparkling clear and the air redolent of pine and lush vegetation.

Dom said, "One of these days, Lacey, I'd just like to wander around this area at our leisure and not be on some kind of mission. It's really fascinating."

"I have a great idea! Let's pack a picnic basket and some wine — and find a very, very secluded spot." She winked lasciviously at him.

"That's why you're such a hotshot graduate teaching assistant — you're just filled with creative ideas."

They parked along the dirt road as before and Dom grabbed his notes and map, and they walked the last half-mile to Abner's place. Abner's battered old 4-wheel drive pick up truck was parked randomly in a different section of the front yard, again with the driver's side door open. Evidently, Abner saw no need to bother closing it.

Dom called out, "Abner, it's Dom and Lacey! I hope this isn't a bad time."

The front door opened and a smiling Abner, this time wearing a Monmouth University sweatshirt and old jeans held up by a rope belt, stood in the doorway and gestured them inside. He was limping, using an old fashioned cane and wearing only one boot.

The other foot was bare, and his big toe seemed red and swollen.

"Well, howdy, folks, howdy. It's a pleasure to see you, a pleasure, yup it is."

Lacey said, "Oh, my goodness, Abner, what happened? Are you alright?"

He pointed to his toe. "It's the gout, Missy. I got me a touch of the gout, damn gout. Can't hardly walk. But come on in, we'll have a drink. That'll help, it surely will."

When Dom and Lacey entered, Abner shook Dom's hand and kissed Lacey's. Smiling and beaming, he said, "Miss Lacey, you're looking even prettier, yup, even prettier. If I had neighbors they'd be gossiping all to hell seeing you show up here. Let's get our drinks. We'll have a drink."

He ushered Dom and Lacey to the old wooden picnic table in what might charitably be called the kitchen and went to fetch the drinks. He poured them generous measures of the same blueberry flavored moonshine from their first visit. After taking a long pull from the jug for himself, Abner looked from Lacey to Dom and back to Lacey. His weathered face lit up in a huge smile.

"Well, hell, you're damn sure together now! Sure you're together, you look good together. Hah! Knew you'd be together."

Lacey and Dom both blushed.

Abner laughed, slapped his thigh and took another sip. He said, "Start working on making them babies and bring them around. They'll be smart, handsome babies and good in the woods. I'll teach them real good. Now then, babies aside, what can I do you for?"

Dom explained how they were intending to try to retrace Rebecca's route through the area in order to learn what it was she had found that was causing so much trouble. Dom spread out his map on the table and they all gathered around.

"Abner, I'm pretty sure that whatever Rebecca discovered that's at the heart of all this was near the St. Keira's ruins, and I think she discovered it after she saw the ruins."

Abner nodded, "After the ruins...yup, I get you, Doc. I get you. If she found it before, it wouldn't make no difference to her. But after she seen the ruins and knew the story, she had a...what do you call it, Miss Lacey? A context for what she found?"

"Exactly! Abner, you're all over this."

164

Abner pointed to the map. "Okay, now, look here. You see this here kind of box-looking area of Wharton State Forest bounded west by Route 206, south by 542, east by 563 and north by 532? It's big, big, some hundred thousand acres. But only about twenty or so folks live in the whole damn area. I know most of them. Shy, real shy folks.

"Now look closer still. That little river there's the West Branch of the Wading River, a little river, slow flowing mostly, but it's sneaky, sneaky. It's pretty, real pretty back there. Anyways, in that small space between the river and route 563 a couple miles down from Speedwell and a little ways north of Jenkins is where you want to be looking. That's where Miss Rebecca went looking. That's where the old Cloister was, where them ruins is. I'd take you myself but for this damn gout.

"But you got to know it's thick back there, plenty thick, thick. And you got to take care from the Timber rattlesnakes, now, too. Usually quiet, they are, quiet, and real shy. Mind their business. Won't bother you. But now they're mating, springtime mating, it gets them all cranky and nervous and mean, real mean they get disturbed. Come right at you. Guess it's understandable, though, when you think about it.

"And it's a firetrap back there, cause of all the layers — leaves and pine needles, sheep laurel, blueberries, huckleberries, scrub oaks, white oaks, cedars, and pitch pines — what us Pineys call Jersey Bull Pines. They burn fiercest of all cause of the oils and resins. And the layers is always dry back there, always dry, dry. But if Miss Rebecca found something near them ruins, it's back in there."

Dom nodded. "Okay, Abner, then what Lacey and I will do is explore the area west of the road and east of the river, that little strip you pointed to. We'll move steadily south until we reach Jenkins. What do you think?"

"Sounds good, son, real good. That's the area, all right. But the best way to do it is by canoe, canoeing the Wading River. You can go slow, stop, get out and look yourselves around and then keep going. The river is slow, slow, but it speeds up real sudden and sneaky in places. No white water, but if you ain't careful, it'll take you right into a tree or overhang or flip you right over. Got to take care, take care."

Abner continued, "You can take my canoe outside. Old but sturdy, sturdy. Drive on back here and we'll strap it to your car. River won't be busy yet. Busy comes in about three, four weeks. Have the river all to yourselves now. Next month it'll be a damn traffic jam, full of outsiders. Can't hardly see the water for all the damn canoes. It's quiet now, though, real quiet."

Abner pointed to a place on the map. "Now look here, son, this here's the put-in spot, where you want to put the canoe in the river, right here. Best thing is to start in the morning, early morning, tomorrow morning. You're going want to head over to Speedwell and go a mile and a quarter or so south past Speedwell on Route 563, and look for a fallen white cedar next to a sand road on the west side of 563. Back in there, maybe two hundred yards is the put-in.

"Figure five, maybe six miles down the river, exploring as you go. After the first mile, look for a sandy bank and pull over, beach your canoe. Follow a sand trail east then it turns a little north, just a little north. Back there's the ruins. Say maybe five, six hours for the whole trip, depends on how much you explore."

He reached into the pocket of his overalls and Dom and Lacey were astonished to see him pull out a smart phone. "Then you call me and I'll come with the truck, load the canoe and bring you back to your car. How's that sound, sound good?"

Lacey said, "Abner, you're a treasure. There's one other thing. You told us last time that there was a man from Jenkins who used to deliver goods to the nuns at the Cloister and pick up the vestments. Do you recall his name?"

"Sure do, yup I do, Missy, I do. It was Ethan Cramer."

Dom and Lacey looked at each other. Lacey asked, "Did he have a family, Abner?"

"He did, Missy, they was a strange family, though, strange. My Momma and Daddy knew Ethan and his wife, Emma Jean, not close, mind you, not visiting close, but to say hello. Them Cramers was a hard working, God-fearing couple, went to church regular. But they was private, real private, private. Folks in these woods are, but they was even more so.

"I remember my Momma saying how she didn't even know Emma Jean was expecting, and then one day Emma Jean has a baby, baby girl, little girl. They was a bit older, too, as I recall,

Ethan and Emma Jean. My Momma never could figure that out. I guess I was fifteen or so, back in '58, so I wasn't paying much attention. But I do remember thinking it was passing strange."

"Abner, whatever happened to Ethan and Emma Jean?"

"Passed on, Missy, passed on. Didn't have no other family, nope, just that little girl. Child grew up and went on to college, so I hear tell. Got herself a scholarship. I didn't have no cause to keep track, not my business. Strange family, though, strange."

Lacey asked, "Abner, as far as you know, once the girl left for college did she ever come back again?"

"No, Missy. Never came back. Except for once, when Ethan and Emma Jean died. Died in a fire of all things, house fire, was no explanation. They was asleep. Propane, electric, it's still a mystery. Kind of like the old Cloister fire. Girl came back from college for the church service over in Jenkins then was never seen again here in the Pines."

Dom shook his head. "Fires, foundlings, orphanages, adoptions, unknown fathers, surprise births — there are strange families all over this. I have a bad feeling."

Abner took a pull at his jug and said, "Strange ain't no stranger in the Pine Barrens, son. Just the way it is."

Chapter 23

Immediately upon learning Rossi's itinerary, Martin O'Bannon called the Association of New Jersey Fire Chiefs and spoke with the president, Norman Carter, with whom he'd had dealings over the years.

"Norm, it's Martin O'Bannon. You just pushing papers or are you getting out into the action once in a while?"

"You know me, Marty, I like to keep my hand in and savor the action. How about you? You getting bored giving exams and correcting papers? I bet you miss busting the occasional head, as you were known to do."

"I surely do miss it, Norm. There's a big part of me misses the hunt. And I try to give as few exams as I can get away with. Listen, I need a favor."

O'Bannon told Carter about the folklore studies program and its interest in the Pine Barrens. "Our work led us to the story of the St. Keira's fire, and we're seeking to learn more about it. Maybe even explore the ruins. I'm wondering if your society has any information about the actual location of the Cloister and if you'd be willing to share it."

"Hell, Marty, that was a long time ago. But let me check our archives. We should have something. In fact, we may have records of the route that the first responders took to the blaze. That would include actual map coordinates for the location of the Cloister. Would it be helpful if I copied them and faxed them to you?"

"More than you know, Norm. Thank you."

The following day, O'Bannon received a fax that pinpointed the location of the St. Keira's Cloister and a map of the route that the firefighters had followed all those years ago. Some of it was along sand roads that had existed since before the Revolution, but it showed O'Bannon exactly where the ruins were. This was where Rossi and the girl were headed. It was now time for Martin O'Bannon to resolve the problem of that fucking pain in the ass

Dominic Rossi. He headed south towards Atlantic City. But he had to pass some familiar territory along the way.

O'Bannon's route took him south on I 287 then south on the Garden State Parkway. Once over the Driscoll Bridge, which spans the Raritan River and essentially divides northern New Jersey from southern New Jersey, he entered old familiar territory. He passed Exit 117 for Keyport/Hazlet. It was also the exit for the shoddy beach town of Keansburg, where O'Bannon had begun his law enforcement career — and where it had taken a most unexpected turn.

On a hot, humid summer night twenty years earlier, O'Bannon, then a patrolman with the Keansburg PD, had answered a domestic disturbance call in one of the trashier areas of Keansburg. Neighbors called in complaining of hearing screams and shouting from a run down two bedroom ranch on Seeley Avenue, several blocks from the beach. Upon arriving, O'Bannon approached the house slowly, but could hear no shouting. Before entering he looked in the front window — and saw a body lying on the floor in a pool of blood.

O'Bannon burst through the front door and saw that the body had multiple stab wounds on the chest, neck and groin. He rushed over and checked for a pulse. The man was clearly dead. A woman lay comatose on the sofa. On the coffee table in front of her was a pile of crack cocaine, obviously heavily dipped into, and two well-used pipes.

A strikingly attractive dark-haired, dark-eyed young girl, perhaps fifteen, was standing near the body, a bloodied kitchen knife in her hand. She was wearing only a sleeveless t-shirt that ended well above her midriff and bikini underpants. Her face was flushed, her nipples appeared erect under her shirt, and her dark pubic thatch was readily apparent under her tiny bikini briefs. She was breathing deeply, and there was a thin film of perspiration on her upper lip. But she was not panicked or afraid; her dark eyes were wide and bright, and she was licking her lips. She seemed almost sexually aroused.

She looked at O'Bannon and said, "That dead asshole is my father. He's been fucking me since I was eleven. The bitch passed out on the couch is his druggie girl friend. She liked to get high and watch. Am I going to jail?"

She dropped the knife to the floor. "I'll do anything not to go to jail."

O'Bannon looked at the dead body, the woman on the couch, and then at the girl. And he made a life changing decision. "You're not going to jail. I'll take care of it."

She walked over and stood in front of O'Bannon. She reached out and began to unzip his fly. O'Bannon did not stop her. She knelt in front of him and did things that O'Bannon had only dreamed of, that his dowdy wife, Evelyn, would find unthinkable, unspeakable.

When she was finished, and O'Bannon depleted, he picked up the knife from the floor and wiped her fingerprints from the handle. He placed the knife in the hand of the comatose woman on the couch, then moved her closer to the dead body.

He said to the girl, "Here's your story..." Then O'Bannon called the Keansburg PD for backup.

O'Bannon saw her at least once a month, even after he moved on to the State Police. When she graduated from high school, he helped her enroll in the Community College of Monmouth. When she got her associate's degree he helped her with the next stage of her career. In return, she did whatever O'Bannon wanted or needed.

Now, driving south on the Garden State Parkway, he began to plan how and when he would use her again. But he had one stop to make first — Atlantic City.

The casino industry in Atlantic City was in desperate straights; casinos closing left and right, bankruptcy is in the city's future and there were no intelligent plans to try and turn things around. Despite this, however, one casino, the Golden Dream, continued to make tremendous profits. It's owner, Chairman and CEO was Murray Feldman. It was Feldman whom Martin O'Bannon was waiting to see as he stood outside the former's penthouse office on the forty-fifth floor of the casino.

After about ten minutes, Feldman's office door opened and O'Bannon saw a florid man wearing cowboy boots and a Stetson hat being roughly escorted out by a large, dark-haired man in a black, expensively tailored business suit. A voice from inside the office called out, "Please come in."

O'Bannon entered and was greeted by a dapper, slightly built but very vigorous man in his mid-seventies. He said to O'Bannon, "You know, I never knew anyone from Texas who was not an asshole. They have a remarkable consistency. How are you, Martin? It's been quite a while." He shook O'Bannon's hand.

"Over three years, Mr. Feldman. I'm well. And you are obviously prospering, sir — as always."

As they were talking, the large man returned and stood behind Feldman's desk.

Feldman nodded to the man and said, "Thank you, Gianni."

He turned back to O'Bannon. "I've been at this a lot of years. My other properties — Vegas, Aruba, Puerto Rico — are certainly more lucrative, but as an old Jersey boy, I feel obligated to keep this property functioning effectively, to the extent I can. Now, then, what can I do for you? You were, after all, very helpful to me over the years, while Gianni was working his way up."

"And you rewarded me well, sir. The truth is, I have a problem, and I need a very specialized service." O'Bannon explained his situation and his specific need.

Feldman smiled. "So mother nature and the laws of physics will settle the problem for you — permanently. It's quite clever and certainly keeps you at a distance. But that's a large area. I'm not sure you can be as certain of the outcome as would be possible by more direct and intimate means." Feldman glanced over at Gianni.

"I'll certainly keep it in mind, sir. And thank you. But for now, I have a very specific location, and the conditions are most favorable."

Feldman nodded then said to the large man, "Gianni, please check our files. We have in the past used a gentleman from Philadelphia on such matters, a Mr. Lomello. Please give his contact information to our friend Martin." He then said to O'Bannon, "You can work out the fee with your consultant. I, of course, make no financial demands, though I will not hesitate to ask you for a favor in the future."

"And I will not hesitate to deliver, sir. Thank you. It was good seeing you. Stay well — and wealthy."

The little man smiled. "That is the whole point, Martin."

***

Louis, "Louie the Torch," Lomello did not fit the usual profile of an arsonist. This was the key to his long, successful, and highly lucrative career. A 1987 study conducted by the FBI explains that the vast majority of what are referred to as "profiled" arsonists have a below normal IQ, usually between 70 and 90. (Before the term became politically incorrect, they would have been described as "mentally retarded.")

Half of all identified arsonists are under the age of eighteen; most of the other half are usually in their twenties. Anger is very often the key motivator for the arson.

None of these insights applied to Louis. What did apply was the statistic that 5% of arson is for profit.

Louis, now forty-two years old, was a Penn State engineering graduate, class of '95, who had a powerful fascination with the science of fire — and an even more powerful attraction to money. Through some 'family' connections, he came to the attention of certain individuals who, for any number of reasons, were very grateful for a building to burn down, a business to go up in flames, or a competitor or adversary to die in a fire. Louis was more than happy to oblige, for a very substantial fee. He did, however, have certain demands. Foremost among these was time to study the problem, so that he could determine such considerations as fuel, method of ignition, timing, and means of exit.

Although the timing of his contract for Martin O'Bannon was shorter than he normally preferred, only one day to prepare, the fact that Louis had been recommended to O'Bannon by Murray Feldman made all the difference. Mr. Feldman was a longtime user of Louis's services, and no doubt would be again in the future. Louis jumped at the job.

In addition to the substantial fee, what also had attracted Louis was the nature of the assignment. Most of Louis's jobs were indoors — houses, apartment buildings, factories, restaurants, etc. An outdoors job in the remotest area of New Jersey, the Pine Barrens, was professionally intriguing and challenging.

Louis arrived in Speedwell, New Jersey, the day before the scheduled job and took most of the day scouting the area, checking the weather forecast, walking through the terrain, and

172

examining the foliage. Having been born and bred in Philadelphia, Louis personally thought the Jersey Pine Barrens was a total shit hole; professionally, however, it was perfect, given the wind direction and speed, the geographic confines of the target area (which limited escape), and the abundant amounts of fuel. He was delighted.

Using the map coordinates provided by O'Bannon, Louis had determined that he would ignite the blaze in three places — two on the western side of the area, and one on the eastern side, thereby trapping the targets and precluding escape. He would use paint thinner as the ignitable liquid. This would allow for a wider and more rapid spread. Given the conditions, the targets would be quickly surrounded by the fire. Louis knew, of course, that because of the frequency of fires in the Pine Barrens, flames would easily be spotted from the fire tower on Apple Pie hill; highly skilled and experienced responders would arrive fairly quickly, though the terrain was a bitch and would slow them down.

He also knew that given the conditions, the fire would outrace the responders for the first several hours. And that would be all it would take. Arson investigators would look for and find the ignitable liquid residue when they arrived on the scene, but Louis didn't care. He would be long gone and the job would be done. Money in the bank.

***

Early the next morning Dom and Lacey reluctantly left each other's arms and set out to meet the day. Both dressed in cargo shorts, polo shirts and sneakers. They had a quick breakfast of coffee and English muffins, packed a backpack with fresh water and several power bars and set off, Abner's canoe strapped to the top of Dom's CRV. After finding the turn-off exactly as Abner described it, they portaged the canoe some two hundred yards to the put-in point.

Lacey said, "Boy, Abner was right. This is really thick back here. If the Caretaker really did or does exist, I can see how she might never be found. It still amazes me that this area is less than one hundred miles from mid-town Manhattan."

"And we haven't even gotten to the more remote spots, yet."

Dom steadied the canoe while Lacey climbed into the bow.

Then he stepped into the slowly flowing river, pushed off, climbed into the stern and they began paddling.

Although the Wading River is small and narrow — in some places only between eight and twenty feet wide — it is generally slow. But it can be a very tricky paddle. Its frequent curves and the fact that it can speed up without warning make it a challenging course. If the canoeist is not paying close attention to the water and the surrounding terrain, it's very possible to get tangled in low hanging branches, bump up against submerged debris, and even flip over, as Abner had warned.

For the first half a mile or so, the longest straightaway was less than one hundred feet, with sharp turns throughout. The slow-moving water was the color of tea, a result of tannins from the cedar trees and iron from the ground. Locals call it "cedar water." It is surprisingly clean, however, at least in the Pine Barrens.

The bottom in most places was white sand, ranging from a depth of three feet to a maximum depth of ten feet. As it was spring, the water was unusually high and tried to push them into the bank or downed logs. In many places trees with elaborately twisted trunks and branches, and thick vines and bushes hung over the river like a wild jungle canopy. The vegetation in some spots was so thick and the overhang so lush that it was almost sunless.

Dom said, "Christ, I feel like Marlow in *Heart of Darkness.*"

After a time, Dom stopped paddling and pulled out his map.

"Let's beach the canoe at the next available spot and start exploring the east side of the river on foot, like Abner said."

They found an easily accessible spot and Dom guided the canoe onto the low, sandy bank while Lacey climbed out, grabbed the bow and pulled it up higher on the beach. The beach was tiny, surrounded by trees and bushes.

Dom said, "Hey, this could be our secluded picnic spot."

"Not secluded enough for what I have in mind. Remember what Abner said about crowds. Let's check back in the early fall, when they're gone. But it really is gorgeous."

They walked along the shoreline for several yards in each direction until Dom said, "Okay, over here. There's a sand trail heading east. Let's try it."

They followed the winding, curving sand trail for several hundred yards; then the trail split — what Abner would call a "fingerboard."

Lacey said, "Which one?"

Dom looked from one trail to the other. "Let's borrow from Robert Frost; we'll take the road less traveled. Maybe that will make all the difference."

The trail Dom selected was more overgrown, narrower and seemed to have more twists and turns than even the paths they had walked so far. Dom kept looking behind him to try to memorize reference points and significant terrain features, such as there were, so they could find their way back. After nearly a quarter of a mile, they came upon a spot where the woods opened out into a small clearing. In the middle of the clearing, barely visible due to the overgrowth was a pile of old charred beams, to the side of them stood the remains of what was probably a brick fireplace and chimney.

"It's the remains of the Cloister, just like Abner said."

They walked among the haunted ruins of that night — a night of flames, screams, terror, pain and death. Lacey stood over the charred beams, feeling acutely the magnitude of the nightmare. Dom walked the perimeter of the little clearing.

"Lace, over here." He pointed to a narrow but obvious trail leading off into the woods. "This trail is heading south, parallel to the road. Remember how Abner said that Ethan Cramer would drop stuff off and the nuns would carry it back the Cloister? That means it should be going east and a bit north, towards the road. But this is going in the wrong direction. Why? I think we should check it out."

They had followed the trail for several hundred yards deeper into the wilderness when Lacey grabbed Dom by the arm and pulled him up short. She put her finger to her lips and said in a hushed voice, "Listen!"

Faintly, off in the distance, they could hear what sounded like some kind of rhythmic wailing. Dom whispered, "What's that? Is it even human?"

After a moment she said, "My God, it's keening! It's an ancient Gaelic vocal lament associated with mourning, typically in Ireland. It's traditionally sung by women, it's supposed to provide both physical and emotional release in the face of death and abject sorrow. Dom, we have to move very carefully."

They walked forward slowly until arriving at a kind of opening in the woods. Lacey nearly gasped out loud — they faced a circle of wild orchids, perhaps twenty or thirty different species. But even more stunningly, these wild orchids were carefully tended and planted over tiny patches of earth, each marked with a crude wooden cross. There had to have been over forty crosses.

Among them, tending them, keening as she went, was an old woman in torn, ragged clothes, holding a bucket filled with old gardening tools. Her hair was snow white, and she was as thin as a wisp of smoke. She was tending to the patches of earth on which the crosses stood.

Dom said softly to Lacey, "Jesus Christ, the crosses and the flowers — Lacey, they're graves, they're tiny graves. She's the Caretaker."

The old woman must have heard him, for she turned and looked at them, her eyes wide, her face fearful. Dom saw that despite her haggard, forlorn appearance, at one time she must have been beautiful.

The old woman began to rise, obviously to flee, when Lacey did an amazing thing — she began to keen the same melody as the old woman.

The woman stopped and turned back, looking at Lacey with trepidation but also with wonder. Lacey, still keening, went over to the nearest grave and knelt before it. She turned to the old woman and nodded and beckoned to her. After several minutes the old woman approached Lacey and stood next to her.

Lacey asked gently, "Who are they, Mother? Who lies beneath the orchid graves?"

In a voice hoarse from not speaking, but in what was clearly an Irish accent, the old woman said, "My babes. They are my babes — they are all of our babes. And their tormentors burn in hell."

"Mother, will you tell us their story?"

The old woman looked at Dom, who met her gaze but remained silent; then she looked back to Lacey. "Come then."

She led them through the pines to an area that was abundant

with dead leaves, fallen branches, vines, a thick carpet of ivy and lush new growth. Dom noticed that there seemed to be small mounds in several places, but they were too regularly shaped to be natural. As they got closer, Dom saw a number of earthen banks and brick-lined tunnels leading God knew where. He realized that very likely these were the ruins of an old brick factory long since swallowed up by the forest, as Duffy San Giacomo had explained.

The old woman turned again to look at them, as if deciding something. Lacey smiled at her and nodded. Then the woman climbed down into one of the tunnels and moved aside what Dom saw was a heavy wooden door, overgrown with ivy and weeds. Dom and Lacey followed her into the tunnel, bending down low as they walked several yards and into a larger open area with a dirt floor and brick walls. The space was dark, but the old woman quickly lit several candles, which provided a modicum of light. Within the space were several old wooden crates, a chair, a few tin pots and pans, several tin cups, an old bucket, and a canvas tarp over a stained, nearly rotted out mattress placed by the far wall near what appeared to be a fire pit. It occurred to Dom that she must have pilfered or scrounged these items from other abandoned buildings and houses throughout this area of the Pine Barrens.

The old woman looked hesitantly at them, but then Lacey sat down on the dirt floor and indicated that Dom do the same. The woman went and sat in the chair. She stared silently at them.

Lacey reached out and gently took the old woman's hand. She said softly, "Tell us, Mother; tell us your story."

Chapter 24

The fire caught even more quickly than Louis had anticipated; he was thrilled. The two ignitions on the west side were simple, but he had to be careful when igniting the east side, which was not far from the county highway. But here, too, luck was with him — it was midweek, early morning, hardly any traffic on the road. He had pulled his rental 4-wheel drive vehicle off the road and he was working well back into the woods.

It would be some time before the smoke was spotted from the old fire tower at Apple Pie Hill. As he always did, he resisted the temptation to stay and watch the results of his efforts. He headed back to his car and drove off, not exceeding the speed limit, his GPS giving him directions for the most expeditious way back to Philadelphia. While he was driving he called the number O'Bannon had given him.

"We're good. It's just a matter of time."

"You are a true professional, Louis. Mr. Feldman would be proud. Nice work."

Forest fires move in a kind of V-shape, like the wake of a ship. The top of the V is the head fire; the sides of the fire are the lateral fire. When the flames reach the tops of trees, as they were quickly beginning to do, it is called a crown fire. The difference between merely a blaze and an inferno is the availability of fuel — which was abundant in this part of the Pine Barrens. Louis had done his work well. The flames began quickly to move east, spurred on by the brisk winds out of the west. Flying embers advanced the fire in the direction of the wind. Add to this the backfire Louis had started on the eastern side of the target area, and all hell was ready to break loose.

***

I am Caitlin Killeen. I was but sixteen years old, just turned. My family in County Tipperary was dirt poor, nine of us there were. I was the eldest child. I was sent to America. There was a rich family would take me in, cleaning, washing, cooking. They'd

178

been from Tipperary some generations before, Ballyporeen, it was. When I came to America, they took me to their home in the place called New Jersey, to a grand house by the sea in the village of Spring Lake. The family had two children; the little girl was six years, the little boy three. Their mother was a frail, sickly woman, in bed most of the day. I bathed her and dressed her. I could see she was once beautiful, though no more. Her beauty was long since gone.

The master was a man of the law, a vigorous man, powerful and handsome in his middle years. The kind of man who needs a woman, who wants a woman, often. Soon the woman was me. He told me we could be together, we could have a life, that his missus was dying shortly. He was forceful and I believed him, wanted to believe him. Needed to believe him to make up for my sins. But then...then I became with child, his child. I told him. And he sent me away. He sent me to this place in the woods, here in the sand, among the pines. I was there for many months, five it was. He told me it was so I could be cared for, so I could be safe. He lied. There was a darkness in the pines.

There were others such as me, with child, done in by rich or powerful men, Irish men, all known to each other, they were, a kind of club. When a woman — a daughter, a servant, a mistress — became with child out of wedlock, they sent her to the Cloister. The nuns beat us and berated us, calling us whores and harlots and evil fallen women. But it was the babes who suffered most, the babes.

If one such as me gave birth to a beautiful healthy babe, it was adopted. If by chance and ill fortune the babe was not healthy, or was marked, or was of brown skin, they left them to die. The sisters left them out to die. And made us bury them, the babes, among the dead leaves and weeds and ivy.

My babe was born beautiful — but for a red mark on her cheek. The sisters said it was the mark of Satan. That she was the devil's spawn. They were going to leave her to die, like they did the others.

There was a man, brought things to the cloister in his truck. And he took away the vestments we sewed. I was one of them who met him out by the road and carried supplies and such back to the cloister house. I talked with him each time. He was sad, *said his wife was barren, she could not bear the children they wanted so much. And it pained them, though they prayed to God. And then I knew what I must do to save my babe.*

I took my babe from the filth and the squalor in which the nuns made the sickly, the marked, and the brown babes stay. I wrapped her a clean robe, the cleanest I could find. I bound it with the pin I stole from the man who despoiled me — the pin bearing the symbol of his clan, a horse with a horn and a castle.

And I spilled the lamps and set the fire from hell. I burned them all and I was glad. I ran through the woods to the house of the truck man and his barren wife and I gave them my babe, so she could be safe and with a family. I went back and watched the devils burn and was glad. But for my sins I must forever tend the graves of the babes that died, the wee ones that died by the hands of the bitch devils in their robes and their veils and their rosaries. And it was all because of him, because of Liam. It was Liam Shaughnessy done this to me.

Dom and Lacey were stunned, both by the horror the nuns of St. Keira's had perpetrated, and by the revelation that it was Brian Shaughnessy's father — a past president of the Loyal Sons of Cu Chulainn, the grandson of the founder — who had impregnated a sixteen year-old Caitlin Killeen.

Lacey was about to ask a question, when the old woman looked up sharply, sniffed the air and stood up and screamed, "Fire! My babes!"

The old woman ran to the wooden door and threw it open. Waves of smoke immediately began to fill the small space. It was so thick and filled the room so quickly that to remain inside would be to suffocate. The old woman ran out the door.

Dom and Lacey followed her — into a vision of hell. The forest around them was blazing; there was heat and smoke and the terrible roar of flames everywhere they looked. But the old woman ran between and around and through the flames towards the orchid graves, cinders and flaming branches falling all around her.

Dom and Lacey ran after her, back towards the circle of orchids. When they arrived they saw it too was an inferno, flames engulfing the graves and the orchids.

Dom said, "Lacey, the river! We have to get back to the river or we'll be trapped."

Lacey shouted, "Mother! Come with us! You'll be safe, safe."

The flames were madly consuming the abundant fuel on the forest floor and had reached the tops of the trees; it was now a crown fire and traveling at a tremendous rate.

"Mother! Come with us! Come with us!" Lacey shouted again and again.

But as much as Dom and Lacey called to her, it was as if the old woman didn't hear them — or did not care. Lacey tried to run to her, but Dom pulled her back.

"No! You'll be trapped!"

Then they both watched in horror as the old woman threw herself to her knees before the orchid graves, moaning and keening over her babes as the flames approached. And in even greater horror when the flames reached her, surrounded her, engulfed her, and finally consumed her, her mouth opening in a silent, anguished scream.

Lacey screamed and Dom grabbed her and dragged her away from the burning old woman and back down the trail towards the river.

They ran, hoping that the trails they took would lead them to the river. The flames and the smoke made visibility nearly impossible, but it was if Dom were guided by some internal GPS programmed for survival; he seemed to sense the right path. They found and ran past the ruins of the Cloister, then several hundred terrifying yards later, there it was — the river, with the canoe beached on the shore.

They slid the canoe into the river, climbed in and began to paddle southward, downstream. This part of the river was narrow, the foliage creating a tunnel of flames, burning branches, leaves and embers falling into the water all around and on top of them.

Dom shouted, "Flip the canoe! We'll get underneath it and use it as a shield!"

They capsized the canoe and ducked under water, surfacing in the space under the canoe, their hands grasping onto the canoe's thwarts. They walked along the sandy bottom, the depth changing so that at times they could walk but then would have to swim. They heard the hiss of burning leaves, and the thud of burning branches and trees as they fell into the water or on top of the canoe. From time to time Dom slipped out from under the protection of the canoe to look at the surrounding area. It was flaming and smoking and terrifying. They continued on.

They had traveled perhaps two slow, terrifying, tortuous miles when Dom again slipped out from under the canoe to check the fire's spread and location. It appeared to have made less progress in this area, and there were visible sand roads that had not yet been touched by the flames.

Then, Dom heard the blast of a car or truck horn, rhythmic and insistent coming from somewhere to the east, the highway side of the area.

"Lace, someone's signaling to us! We must be close to a road. We have to risk it and make a break for it."

"Okay, I'm with you. I love you. But I'm freaking scared to death. Let's go."

They swam out from under the protection of the canoe and over to the eastern side of the river. After climbing out of the water, they took a quick look around. The fire was less intense here, the main part of it not yet having reached this area. Again and again they heard the blast of the horn and began to run through the woods towards the sound.

Parked along a sand road in his old 4-wheel drive pick-up truck was Abner.

"Over here, Missy! Here, son! Move quick, move quick! Fire's spreading fast."

They clambered into the truck, dripping, hugging each other. Abner said, "You kids okay? Then let's get the hell out of here."

Abner took off down the sand road, jamming through the gears, finding other roads and trails that neither Dom nor Lacey even saw, making turns that didn't seem possible, plowing ahead with a fierce determination.

"We'll get there, kids. We'll get there."

The air was heavy with smoke but the core of the fire had not yet made it this far south. Eventually, they made it back to the county road.

Abner told them, "Responders been on the scene couple hours now, tankers, air drops, folks with shovels and rakes and backpacks. They'll get it under control. A fella told me it was set on purpose. Hell of a thing, hell of thing."

They made it back to Abner's and hurried inside, Dom and Lacey still sopping wet. Abner disappeared into a back room then returned with two clean, folded Army blankets; he tossed one to Dom and gently wrapped the other around Lacey. He poured them all very generous drinks of his blueberry moonshine. Dom and Lacey quickly finished off one drink then sat back with another. Lacey fought back tears as she spoke.

"Her name was Caitlin. She was only sixteen years old, Abner. He was her employer. He lied to her and used her and then, when she became pregnant, he sent her to the Cloister. When her baby was born, she knew they were going to let her baby die, just let it die, because of a red mark on the baby's face. She knew what was going to happen to her baby because she had been made to bury other babies, for five months. It must have been hell. Pure hell. And it had been going on for years."

Abner was silent, his expression grim.

Then he said, "Damndest thing I ever heard. Little babies? Them damn nuns did that to poor little babies? No wonder that sad, lost, old woman was crazy as a loon."

Dom said, "Abner, Caitlin admitted to setting the fire. She saved her own baby by giving the baby to the truck driver — Ethan Cramer. The baby had to be the one your parents wondered about all those years ago. Her name is Fiona Cramer Shane."

As they talked Abner shook his head, both in dismay and disgust. His life was simple and spare, but his values were strong and enduring. He said, "This can't stand, son. Can't let it stand. Got to do something for sure, for damn sure."

"We will, Abner, I promise you. But we need proof. If Lacey and I make an accusation about Catholic nuns abetted by the Loyal Sons of Cu Chulainn committing what amounts to serial manslaughter, we'll be going up against one of the most powerful law firms in the country — and the Diocese of Trenton. We're going to need rock solid proof. Problem is where the hell do we find it?"

Chapter 25

News of the Pine Barrens fire spread quickly via a range of news outlets, radio, broadcast TV, cable networks, the internet and social media. It sounded to Martin O'Bannon, who was back home in Morristown, that Louis Lomello had done his work well. The only troubling thing was that no mention had been made yet of any casualties, no deaths. O'Bannon told himself that since it was such a remote area, the remains of Rossi and the girl simply had not been discovered yet.

The following day, reports surfaced that there had in fact been one casualty in the Pine Barrens fire; firefighters had discovered the charred, blackened body of what they believed was an old woman. Who she was and why she was there was a total mystery.

O'Bannon was bitterly disappointed. That fucking Rossi had somehow managed to escape, along with his slut girlfriend. The kid seemed to have nine lives. But O'Bannon was disciplined enough to think it through.

Given that Rossi was still alive, there existed the possibility that he had actually learned something new in the Pine Barrens, perhaps even the truth. It was imperative, therefore, that O'Bannon learn whether he did and if so, whether he did anything with that information. That meant not killing Rossi — for the time being. It also meant finding out exactly what Rossi knew.

It was unlikely that Rossi was aware that the fire had been set to trap him. So he was still vulnerable. But he was smart and resourceful. O'Bannon decided he would once again exploit his most valued resource — at first subtly and then, if needed, more dramatically, and conclusively. But that would all come shortly. In the meantime, O'Bannon knew that Brian Shaughnessy had other work for him, what O'Bannon used to call in the old days 'wet work.' Things were getting a bit hectic, but O'Bannon was back in action, back in the game. And it felt great.

***

The morning following the fire, Dom and Lacey set out from her folks' place to try to learn more about Fiona Cramer Shane's birth and upbringing. They were headed north to the tiny town of Jenkins, along Route 563, the Greenbank-Chatsworth road.

The previous night, while he held Lacey in his arms, Dom heard her sob softly several times, as she experienced a troubled, fitful sleep. In the morning, a grim, red-eyed Lacey passed up breakfast, settling for only a cup of coffee. She was uncharacteristically silent during the first part of the drive, just looking out of the window. She did not respond to Dom's several attempts at conversation, remaining caught up in her own thoughts. They could not have been pleasant, Dom knew.

After a while, Dom reached over and gently placed his hand on her shoulder.

"This has been rough, Lace, I know."

Still looking out the window, she said, "It wasn't the fire or the possibility of dying that got me, Dom. It was the other stuff — the graves with the orchids and crosses, hearing Caitlin's story about Liam, and most of all, the babies, the babies. Fucking Shaughnessys are at the heart of this horror, from generations back. Now we learn that the guy who sent you out on this bizarre quest, is Fiona's half brother. That's probably how she got the internship. But Dom, how did she know enough to connect herself to the Shaughnessys? What led her to them in the first place?"

"I have no clue. But we absolutely need to find out. It may be the central connection to everything."

She turned to look at him. "And the nuns, Dom, the nuns. Their involvement in this breaks my heart. Dom, before I went to Monmouth University, which I loved, I went to Catholic school for twelve years — St. James Grammar School and then Red Bank Catholic High School. I was taught by lay teachers, but also by nuns. And contrary to popular belief, those sisters were supportive and nurturing and surprisingly fun."

"Like Sister Pat."

"That's exactly right. And like Sister Mary Gilbert — when I was playing girls softball, she used to take infield practice with us; she had an arm like a cannon. And then she'd hit fly balls to the outfielders.

185

"And my Dad loved being part of the Loyal Sons of Cu Chulainn Jersey Shore Chapter. He's always been so proud of the charitable work they do, and of his Irish heritage. I was proud of it, too. This whole thing has really shaken me — the seduction and abandonment of a teenage girl, nuns leaving babies to die, some kind of crazy adoption scheme assisted by the Loyal Sons. It's horrible and sickening and heartbreaking."

Her eyes were moist, but her voice was strong. "Dom, this shit has nothing to do with the Catholic Church I grew up in. Or with my proud Irish heritage. These are evil people. We have to stop them, Dom. Promise me."

"I promise, Lace. We'll get them."

After a time during which both were silent, Dom asked, "Lacey, something just occurred to me. Drawing upon your sociology background, how can someone simply give away a newborn baby to someone else? I don't mean from an emotional or moral perspective, although those are valid questions. I mean, what happens legally? It can't be that all of a sudden this baby shows up out of nowhere and the Cramers say to people, 'By the way, here's our baby Fiona'. What about a birth certificate and stuff?"

"Well, I guess they could pass it off as a home birth, especially in such a remote and unpopulated area like this. And who would be around to dispute it? Everyone at the Cloister died in the fire. And if Liam Shaughnessy, that bastard, even knew about the actual birth, he would have been unlikely to say anything.

"As far as getting a birth certificate, different states — even different counties within the same state — can have different procedures. But there are some standard requirements. A parent can go to the county seat within a year after the birth and fill out the required paperwork. It usually calls for the child's name, place of birth, date of birth, and time of birth. And then it needs a 'certifier,' someone who attended the birth."

"That's it? Jeez, Lace, it doesn't sound like much."

"Well, now that I think about it, there's actually another part to it — a thing called a 'third party statement.' In the case of a home birth, if the birth certifier is the mother or father or midwife, the filing of the birth record has to be accompanied by a statement from a physician who gave the baby care. If there was no physician involved, then you need to have a sworn, notarized statement by a third-party who was either present or had personal knowledge of the birth."

Dom considered this for several moments. Then he said, "Is it possible for us to go to the Bureau of Vital Statistics here in Burlington County and ask to see any registration for the birth of Fiona Cramer?"

Lacey shook her head. "It would be tough. We're not immediate family or relatives, so we wouldn't be allowed to see it unless we filed under the Freedom of Information Act. Approval for that could take weeks to come through."

"Shit, there must be another, faster way to get some kind of line on Fiona's birth. We have to be absolutely sure she was Caitlin's baby. And that red mark on the face is bothering me. I got a pretty good look at her at Commencement, and I didn't see any red facial mark."

"And no birthmark appears in any of the photographs of her I've seen online. It's not as if she has a birthmark like Mikhail Gorbachev. Could we be off base on this, Dom? How do we solve it?"

"More research, Lace. We're scholars. That's what we do."

Some miles later, as they approached the tiny town of Jenkins, Dom saw a sign in front of a small, green-shingled church — Jenkins Chapel. The old sign showed a red cross, an image of a bible, and included the words, "Established 1900, visitors welcome, worship services 10:45 AM, Sunday." The Pastor's name was also listed, Samuel Butterworth. Parked out front was a battered, ancient Chevrolet station wagon.

Dom jammed on the breaks, did a fast, tight U-turn and pulled into the tiny, sandy driveway. Lacey asked, "What are you doing? Why are we going to church?"

"I have an idea. Didn't Abner say that Ethan and Emma Jean Cramer were church going, God-fearing people? So, given this rural, remote area, where would they be likely to go to church? Let's give this place a shot. Maybe we'll get lucky."

The historic Jenkins Chapel is generally believed to be the smallest church in New Jersey. It was first established in 1889 on a site nearby but was moved to its present location in 1900.

Upon entering through the front door, Dom and Lacey immediately saw that the chapel did not have pews, only rows of chairs, some twenty-eight of them (sixteen on the left, twelve on the right). There was an organ up front to the right and a pulpit in the center, facing the rows of chairs. Electric candles had been placed in the white-framed windows. Lacey was struck by how spare and simple it was. Not at all like many of the larger churches and cathedrals in which she had attended Mass, with their elaborate stained glass windows and artwork, gold altar vessels, elevated pulpits.

A slender, red-haired middle-aged man who had been at the pulpit, evidently making notes for his Sunday sermon, looked up as they walked in. He wore a white shirt under a navy blue V-neck sweater and tan chinos. He gave them a wide smile.

"Welcome! For a Saturday, you two are a crowd."

"Pastor Butterworth? I'm Professor Dominic Rossi from Mount St. Benedict University. This is my colleague, Caroline Lacey. I hope we're not disturbing you."

"Not at all, Professor Rossi. But I'm Pastor Sutton. Pastor Butterworth is long retired. He now lives in a very pleasant assisted living facility over in Hammonton. I see him regularly. We leave his name on the sign to honor him for his lengthy service to the congregation. Would you two like to pray, or is there some other way I can help you?"

Lacey said, "If you have the time, Pastor, we'd just like to talk about the church and its history."

"Certainly, Ms. Lacey, it would be my pleasure." He indicated that they should have a seat and then explained about the founding of the little church back in the late nineteenth century and how it came to its present location.

He said, "We're a non-denominational church, not affiliated with any of the larger churches or congregations in the area, but we are certainly a Bible-believing congregation. Services on Sunday are equal parts prayer, reflection, and socialization." He smiled, "Folks usually bring a few baked goods, and I always have coffee and tea for the adults, and milk and fresh fruit juice for any children who attend."

Dom asked, "How large is the congregation, Pastor? Do most folks live nearby?"

188

"Yes, most folks live in either Friendship, Jenkins, or Speedwell. A few come from farther away, Shamong, Chatsworth, or even Tuckerton, but they tend to be folks who are out for a Sunday drive, see the church and get curious about us. On a good day, we may get perhaps fifteen or twenty souls. There have been times, too, when it's been only me and the Lord. But I have always found him to be good company."

Lacey smiled. "Sounds like pretty good company to me, Pastor. Are you here every day or just on Sunday?"

"From Monday through Friday, I own and operate a hardware store up in Chatsworth. I usually get to the church on Saturday morning, do whatever repairs might be needed and try to have everything set for Sunday services. As you can see, it does not really take a great deal of care or time. But I must say, I love the work. My wife, Ruth, is the organist."

Dom asked the big question, "Does the church keep any records of its activities — such as christenings, marriages, memorial services and so forth?"

"Actually, Pastor Butterworth was quite meticulous in his chronicling the activities of the church, though of course there were not all that many of them. He was also a Notary Public and people came to him for those services, too. These days, I simply enter such things on my laptop, but Pastor Butterworth wrote everything down by hand in old ledgers. Is there anything or anyone in whom you have a special interest?"

Dom decided to go for it. "Yes, sir. I'm wondering about a family named Cramer. They lived somewhere around Jenkins. I believe they would have been active in the church in the 1950s and 60s. There is a woman with the same name, an alumna, who recently received an honorary degree from Mount St. Ben's and we were wondering if she's part of that same Cramer family. If so, we're thinking of doing an expanded article in the *Mount St. Ben's Messenger*, our quarterly magazine. It would make a great story."

Pastor Sutton nodded and said, "The 1950s and 60s you say, let me rummage around in the basement a bit. Please feel free to explore in the meantime. And make yourselves at home. There is a restroom behind the altar off to the left, and a picnic table outside to the rear of the building. I'll just be a few minutes." He left them and headed down to the church basement.

Lacey looked at Dom. "Boy, you're getting really good at making up stuff. I'm going to have keep close track of you. Who knows what you'll come up with next."

"I was an English major. Fabrication comes with the territory."

As Dom walked around exploring the little church, Lacey went up to the pulpit. Resting open on it was a Bible in which a verse had been marked. It was from the Gospel of Matthew, Chapter 19: verse 13-14. In it Jesus says, "Let the little children come unto me and do not hinder them, for the kingdom of God belongs to such as these."

Lacey motioned to Dom to join her. She pointed to the verse. "I guess the Sisters of St. Keira never read this verse."

Dom read it then said, "There's a wonderful novel by the Australian writer, Morris West. It's called *The Clowns of God.* The title is a reference to children who are disabled or flawed in some way. I've always been deeply moved by the scene in which Jesus appears to the principal characters, holding a little girl who has Down's Syndrome. Jesus says,

'To you she looks imperfect — but to me she is flawless.

She will never offend me, as all of you have done.

She will never pervert or destroy the work of my Father's hands...

She is necessary to you. She will evoke in you the kindness that will keep you human...

This little one is my sign to you. Treasure her!'"

Lacey, her eyes moist, said, "We have to keep at this, Dom, whatever it takes. "

Pastor Sutton returned carrying an old clothbound ledger. "Well, this is unusual but quite interesting."

He sat down on one of the chairs and opened the ledger on his lap. Dom and Lacey took chairs on either side of him. They saw that the ledger contained scores of entries written in a fine, delicate hand. There were several columns — names, dates, and the service or occasion of the entry.

The Pastor pointed to the names of Ethan and Emma Jean Cramer; in the next column was written the name, Fiona Cramer, then "third-party birth certification and christening." The date was August 31, 1958. Pastor Butterworth had also made a note in the margin, "small strawberry birthmark, right cheek."

Pastor Sutton said, "It would appear that Pastor Butterworth not only christened your Ms. Cramer, he certified her birth, as a Notary Public. He also made a note of her birthmark, probably for purposes of identification. I suspect it was a home birth, which in those days was not at all uncommon here in the Pines. However, home births were generally attended by a midwife, though not always. I cannot imagine the Pastor was actually present at the birth. The Cramers must have gone it alone then presented the infant to Pastor Butterworth some days later.

"And look here. Pastor Butterworth also noted that he performed a memorial service for the Cramers, following their death in a fire. The service was attended only by their daughter."

"So only Ethan and Emma Jean were present at the baby's birth and only the adult daughter attended their memorial service."

"Evidently. I must conclude that the Cramers were very reclusive and not at all close with neighbors or friends. But it does seem to confirm that Fiona Cramer is the same Fiona Cramer to whom your university awarded the honorary degree. I would think that you could feel confident about going ahead with your article."

Dom and Lacey stood up and shook the Pastor's hand. Lacey said, "Thank you very much for all your time and help, Pastor Sutton. We really appreciate it. And we'll be sure to visit again."

Pastor Sutton smiled. "You both would be most welcome. And perhaps you might bring some pastries, along with your good and kind hearts."

Back on the highway heading up to Morristown, Dom and Lacey tried to put things in perspective.

Lacey said, "Okay, our Fiona is the same Fiona. And now we know how Caitlin Killeen's 'illegitimate' Shaughnessy baby legally became a Cramer."

"Pastor Butterworth must have known the baby was not Emma

Jean's, if she was a regular church-goer. He certainly would have noticed whether she was pregnant or not. But for whatever reason he went along with it."

"In a way, it's understandable, Dom. Maybe he truly believed it was for the good of the child — she would have caring parents and a stable, though poor, upbringing. So he asked no questions. But that birthmark is still an open question."

"I'm with you. That birthmark bothers me."

"So, where to next, Doc?"

Dom looked over at her. "We head to the Nursing School."

Chapter 26

In establishing pricing for prescription drugs, and by way of justifying their often immorally exorbitant costs, Big Pharma usually cites a number of statistics — for every several thousand compounds tested, only one will make it to market; it takes ten years and over eight hundred million dollars to bring a drug through the entire research, clinical trial and approval process, and then there is no guarantee that the drug will be successful; pricing considerations are based upon the advantages the new product has over existing products for the same clinical indication (i.e., a perceived advantage merits a price increase over already exorbitant prices); investors and stockholders have a right to healthy profits.

What the industry is less forthcoming about is that once approved, a drug is usually incredibly inexpensive to mass produce; then, it will have perhaps fifteen years of patent exclusivity before being able to be produced in a generic form, which costs monumentally less than the branded drug.

For example, in New York City, the cost in its heyday of a 3-month 20 mg supply of Pfizer's branded cholesterol-lowering Lipitor would have been $987; the generic version, atorvastatin, for a similar 3-month 20-mg supply would cost $67. Lipitor earned nearly $14 billion annually at its peak; Abbott's Humira is currently on track for over $10 billion annually.

Other tactics include buying the marketing rights of a smaller branded drug in an under-served therapeutic category from another company, and then jacking up the price several thousand percent. For example, in August of 2015, Turing Pharmaceuticals bought the marketing rights to a 62-year-old drug for parasitic infection and raised the cost of one pill from $13.50 to $750.

Hence, the high cost of prescription drugs.

These are not isolated examples. They are representative of the extraordinary revenue prescription drugs generate for manufacturers over a very long period time.

These numbers and considerations were at the heart of the discussion between Brian Shaughnessy and Arnold Fisher. They were having lunch in a quiet corner of the Grand Café, generally regarded as Morristown's best and most elegant restaurant.

Fisher swallowed a small bite of the excellent smoked salmon, took a sip of Chardonnay and said, "The stakes are enormous, Brian — especially for the two of us. The amounts we stand to gain, and keep on gaining, could be extraordinary. But only if we get Bill Shane elected and he follows through on his promises. Then, New Jersey will be more than 'pharma friendly'; we'll be the mecca for the entire pharmaceutical industry. Fuck California and Massachusetts. And you and I will benefit even more."

"Shane's numbers are very good — he's now leading in the polls and donations are pouring in. His family values stance will draw even more appeal. He's practically a lock. Much of this is due to help from your industry.

"But there is one minor issue. When we gathered at Fiona's, you expressed concern about the extent to which the press will go to try and uncover any controversies in Bill's or Fiona's background."

"I did. Fiona reassured me there was nothing, but I always worry about such things. None of us is as pure as the driven snow. To what are you referring?"

"The story of Fiona's upbringing is well-known and considered heroic, of course. Still, the Pine Barrens is a strange place; strange things occur there. In the unlikely event anything untoward emerges, on either Fiona or Bill, I suggest that, given the stakes, we act quickly, forcefully — and with finality — to shut it down."

Fisher looked up from his salmon at Shaughnessy. He understood the implication. "I have absolutely no hesitation in going in that direction. We will do what we must. Do you have someone with the necessary...skills and motivation?"

"I do. Martin O'Bannon, a former New Jersey State Trooper who now is a member of the Criminal Justice faculty at Mount St. Ben's and the Sergeant-at-Arms of the Loyal Sons. I would have asked him to join us, but he's handling some other business for me at the moment. He has the experience and the temperament these things require. And he enjoys this kind of work."

Fisher nodded. "Given the stakes, Brian, I agree. It is imperative that we do whatever must be done. By the way, this smoked salmon is wonderful."

**

One of the great things about being on a university campus is that there are experts in all kinds of fields all around you. On Monday morning, Dom and Lacey headed to the Nursing School to see Professor Mary Philips, Nurse Practitioner and Associate Professor of Anatomy and Physiology.

Dom had called ahead and Professor Philips was in her office waiting for them. She was a petite, attractive, blonde middle-aged woman who had served in Iraq with the US Army twelve years earlier, before joining the Nursing School faculty at Mount St. Ben's. She laughed when she saw Dom.

"Dominic Rossi, you managed to avoid my classes all those years you were a student here, and now that you're a hot-shot English professor you decide to look me up. What brings you to this side of the campus?"

It was true that Dom had avoided as many science classes as he could, out of sheer cowardice. But he often found himself working out in the gym at the same time as Professor Philips; often, they ended up playing handball or doing laps around the indoor track together. As both were ex-US Army, they had struck up a friendship.

Dom introduced Lacey and Professor Philips said, "Oh, sure! You're Ray Alexander's wunderkind. Everyone is talking about what a prize catch you are. It's a pleasure, young woman. So, what's on your mind, guys?"

Dom said, "It has to do with anatomy and physiology. Lacey and I need to know about birthmarks, specifically facial ones. Someone who recorded a baby's birth down in the Pine Barrens in the late fifties noted that there was a strawberry birthmark on the right cheek. We think it was noted for purposes of identification. Can a birthmark like that be gotten rid of?"

Professor Philips nodded. "Very often. And in the case of hemangioma, what you referred to as a strawberry birthmark, it will resolve all by itself in the vast majority of instances by the time the child is five or six, no surgery needed. Here, let's take a look."

She opened her laptop, went quickly to a dermatology site and found several examples. "Here you go. Hemangioma is a bright red, rubbery nodule of extra blood vessels in the skin. It affects maybe 2-3% of infants. It's what is known as self-involuting. That means that the skin eventually returns to its normal state, usually in just a few years.

"But when first seen by a parent, it can be very troubling. And the kids themselves need to be taught how live with it and how to explain it to other kids, or they could have a rough time emotionally until it resolves."

"Suppose a baby, say a baby girl, had developed one at birth but it resolved. Would there be any evidence when she hit adulthood?"

"Usually not much; often none at all. And if she wanted or needed to cover up any of the slight remnants, there are all kinds of specialty cosmetics available that are highly effective. What's this all about?"

Lacey and Dom explained about their visit to Pastor Sutton and the entry in the church records. They did not mention Fiona Shane or the Sisters of St. Keira.

Professor Philips said, "Assuming the hemangioma resolved fully, the interesting thing would be to learn whether it had affected the child emotionally and if any emotional issues continued into adulthood, things like self-image, socialization, how the child might — or might not — relate to others, even anger or resentment. But that's out of my league. You may want to head to the Psych Department. But feel free to keep me in the loop."

"I have one last, kind of unrelated question. How does someone go about collecting DNA, like for forensic purposes?"

"You mean like at a crime scene or something? Well, it could include things like blood, tissue, semen, saliva, hair, sweat, dandruff — a variety of evidence. The trick would be avoiding contamination in the collection. Why are you asking?"

"Oh, just an idea I was working on. Thank you so much, Mary."

Before Dom and Lacy separated to return to their respective departments, Lacey said, "Okay, so it could very easily be the case that Fiona had one of those hemangiomas Professor Philips explained, and that it cleared up by itself. But what do you think about that emotional issues stuff? Is that at all relevant?

"I think it's relevant enough that I should finally have a chat with Fiona Cramer Shane and see for myself."

"What was that business about DNA samples?"

"I'm working on an idea, for future reference."

***

The Headquarters Plaza Cinema 10 in Morristown is just off the Morristown Green, the center of town. Movie times usually tend to be around 11:30 AM, 2:30 P.M., 5:20 P.M., 7:40 P.M., and 10:00 P.M.. There is a four-level parking deck adjacent to the theatre with elevator service to the theatre lobby.

It was on level four of this deck where Martin O'Bannon had asked Edward Manning to meet him — at 3:00 p.m. precisely — at the north end of the deck. The hour was important, since O'Bannon knew that there would be very few people coming and going at that time — movies were in progress, with none set to end or begin for two hours; lunch was long past, and workers were unlikely to be going to and from work. Except for a few parked cars, the deck would be deserted.

O'Bannon arrived at the Cinema 10 and paid cash for a ticket to the 2:30 showing of some juvenile, special effects action film featuring preposterous superheroes and glamorous women in outlandish costumes. He sat through the first fifteen minutes then went back to the lobby, being sure to hang on to his ticket, and took the elevator to the fourth floor of the parking garage to await Manning.

Earlier in the day, O'Bannon had telephoned Manning to arrange the meeting. Manning had immediately asked, "Why there? Why not just come to the office on MacCulloch Avenue? And why are we meeting without Brian?"

O'Bannon said, "Frankly, Edward, this meeting is about Brian. I'm concerned about certain directions he's taking with regard to this Rebecca Glass-Dominic Rossi matter. I believe you share the same concerns. Brian's plans and methods are extreme and would be devastating to the Loyal Sons if they ever get out. We have to talk. But it's not like we can meet at the Dublin Pub or on a bench in Burnham Park. Any number of members of the

Loyal Sons might spot us. I feel strongly that we should be as discrete as possible — and as brief."

"Well, it all seems rather bizarre and cloak and dagger to me. Still, Martin, I do have serious reservations about certain matters with respect to Brian. Yes, I'll be there."

Edward Manning lived alone in an upscale condo just a few blocks off the Morristown Green. He was long divorced, a consequence of his ill-fated dalliance with a young female student years earlier. His ex-wife had remarried and his only child, now a grown woman, deigned not to visit him.

His social life revolved around attending events at the Mayo Performing Arts Center, which was conveniently nearby, attending Mass at the Assumption of the Blessed Virgin Mary parish, only two blocks away, and paying for various sexual experiences in Manhattan. Most of his day was taken up with researching and recording the history and activities of the Loyal Sons of Cu Chulainn, and meeting and corresponding with historians from other chapters, with occasional trips to visit them. Given the location of his condo, Manning could easily walk across town to meet O'Bannon at the parking garage.

When Manning arrived on the fourth floor of the garage, he spotted O'Bannon leaning against a waist-high wall on the north side of the structure, looking out at the neighborhood across the street. O'Bannon waved him over and Manning joined him at the wall. Manning did not take note of the fact that for some reason, O'Bannon was wearing thin leather gloves.

O'Bannon pointed across the way and said, "You're an historian, Edward. And Morristown has a fascinating history. Did you know that over there, what is now Martin Luther King Boulevard used to be known as Evergreen Place and before that as Water Street? The neighborhood was known as The Hollow. For a hundred years, whatever immigrant group arrived in Morristown, poor, in need of housing, seeking new lives, they each ended up down there — Italians, blacks, Latinos. Now, it's a low to moderate-income housing project. But look over there. You see along the street where there are still the old, narrow, two- and three-story tenements?"

"Why on earth are you telling me all this? I am more aware of the history of Morristown than you are. Can we please get down to business?"

O'Bannon turned to face him and withdrew a sealed business-sized envelope from his pocket. He placed it in the inside pocket of Manning's tweed blazer. "Hold onto this, Edward, and read it at your leisure."

A confused Manning said, "What is it? What's this all about, Martin?"

"For now, please look again at the tenements."

Manning sighed in clear exasperation and turned towards the wall, looking out at the housing project. As he did so, O'Bannon quickly stepped behind him, grabbed him by his lower legs and threw him out over the wall, whereupon Edward Manning fell four stories to his death right between the two dumpsters located in the service driveway of the garage — his typed suicide note still in his jacket pocket. It stated his intentions and reasons, but was unsigned, as a number of such notes are.

O'Bannon walked quickly but not too hurriedly back to the elevator and took it down to the cinema level. He returned to the action film for which he had purchased the ticket and sat through it to the end. Surprisingly, it was not too bad.

Chapter 27

On Tuesday, Dom walked into the English Department office and approached Fran Purcell's desk. Not looking up, Fran sighed and said, "Yes, Dr. Rossi, what is it now?"

"Fran, the woman we honored at Commencement, Fiona Cramer Shane, I'd like to get in touch with her. Can you please track down her contact information for me? She lives Oldwick, in Hunterdon County. The Provost's office should have it. I'd really appreciate it."

"Dr. Rossi, the whole department is completing exams, posting grades, and preparing for three Summer Sessions. I have a great deal of department-related work to do and no time for your peripheral matters."

Dom stared at her for a moment. He pointed to the sign on her desk. "That sign says, 'Administrative Assistant.' I am a full-time, tenure-track English Department faculty member in need of assistance. Your job is to provide assistance. You don't have to like it. And frankly, Ms. Purcell, I don't give a shit whether you like it or not. So, you either do what I ask or I go straight to HR and tell them you're not doing your job and your attitude sucks. Feel free to complain to them about my language. And then we'll see what transpires. In the meantime, you have ten minutes to get me the information."

She flushed and said, "Okay, fine, whatever."

After Dom returned to his office, Fran called the Provost's office. She not only got the information Dom asked for; she also informed the Provost of Dom's request.

"He's going to get in touch with Fiona Shane."

Delaney immediately informed Brian Shaughnessy of Dom's intention.

Later that day, Dom called an already alerted Fiona Shane to ask for a meeting. She was intrigued by the call. And said so to Brian Shaughnessy.

"He says it has to do with an article he's writing and he wants to interview me. I told him to meet me tomorrow for drinks at the Tewksbury Inn. I'm actually looking forward to it. But surely there is more going on."

"It's undoubtedly about Rebecca Glass and her research. That arrogant son of a bitch has become obsessed with this. He just keeps on coming. Be careful what you say, Fiona. Next week is the dinner. We want nothing unfortunate coming out beforehand. In the meantime, I'll tell O'Bannon to pull out all stops."

"I agree. With everything that's at stake, nothing and no one must get in the way of William's election, Brian. No one."

The Tewksbury Inn is a quaint former stagecoach stop built in 1800. Upon entry, there is a formal dining room to the left; an attractive space for private parties upstairs; and on the first floor to the right is the tavern room — rustic, yet warm and intimate with dark wood and a beamed ceiling. That's where Dom found Fiona Shane, seated at a table for two in a quite corner. She was sipping a glass of white wine.

"Good afternoon, Mrs. Shane. I'm Dominic Rossi. Thank you for seeing me."

Fiona silently appraised him for several seconds. Dom noted that she appeared utterly composed, almost amused, and gave off a chilly confidence.

She said, "You appear quite young to be a professor. I understand, however, that you are very accomplished. Please have a seat and order a drink. I'm having Sancerre."

Dom nodded to a waiter and ordered a scotch and soda. As he took a chair across from Fiona Shane, he noticed several things. In close proximity, she was even more attractive than she had seemed on stage at the Commencement. She exuded a kind of mature, sophisticated sexuality for which Dom was not prepared. Indeed, for being fifty-eight years old, she was stunning — slender, fair-skinned, angular cheekbones, full lips, large gray-blue eyes. There was no sign of any kind of mark on the right side of her face, though Dom could see that a touch of makeup had been carefully applied.

She wore elegantly tailored gray slacks, a matching gray cashmere sweater, with a burgundy, blue, and silver silk scarf. Pinned to the sweater above her left breast was a silver brooch in the form of a unicorn in front of a castle.

Jesus Christ, It's the same design as Shaughnessy's cufflinks!

He immediately remembered the words of Caitlin Killeen — *"I wrapped her a clean robe, the cleanest I could find, and bound it with the pin I stole from the man who despoiled me — the pin bearing the symbol of his clan, a horse with a horn and a castle."*

Fiona smiled and said, "Professor Rossi, are you ogling my left breast or my brooch?"

Dom blushed. "The brooch, it's lovely. Does it have a special significance?"

"It was a gift from my mother. Why do you ask?"

"Frankly it has to do with why I asked to meet with you. Your life story is fascinating and quite well known, of course, especially your rise in the pharmaceutical industry. But I was thinking of looking at it more from a Mount St. Ben's perspective. As an alumna, you probably receive our quarterly magazine, the *Mount St. Benedict Messenger*. In the past, I've occasionally written articles for it. I was thinking of doing one on you for our fall edition, which comes out in mid-September, as a kind of follow-up to your honorary degree. If you are okay with that idea."

Fiona considered this for a moment. Whatever else Rossi was up to, if he really was going to write an article, it might be helpful to William's campaign.

"Professor, as you undoubtedly are aware, my son will soon announce that he is running for governor, on the Republican ticket. He has an excellent chance to win. Let me be perfectly candid, I see this article as an opportunity for more exposure for William. This could be very helpful to him."

She smiled, almost flirtatiously. "And, given my connections at Mount St. Benedict, it could be very helpful to you, as your career goes forward."

Dom would throw himself in front of a train before he'd support William Shane. Nevertheless, he said, "I understand perfectly, Mrs. Shane."

"Fine. Then you may proceed with the interview."

Dom pulled a pen and a small spiral notebook from his canvas briefcase and began to ask about her childhood, her parents, and her life growing up in the Pine Barrens. He said, "I have only a limited knowledge of the area, Mrs. Shane, but given its remoteness and the scant population, it must have been a lonely childhood. Especially since you had no siblings."

"I prefer to think of it as fostering self-reliance. Solitude, hard work and struggle build character — a trait many people who live in cities and on welfare have never learned."

"How about your family life? I know about how hard your family worked. But what about them as people?"

"My parents were simple people, very much a part of the land and the woods for several generations. They were devoted to each other and very protective of me. That I would eventually go on to college was something they never would have dreamed. Unfortunately, they never saw me graduate. They both perished in a terrible fire."

Dom then asked, "Were they church-goers?"

"Indeed they were, a small church in Jenkins, very bible-centered. I found the congregation to be provincial and narrow-minded, but it was at least welcoming."

"How did you end up becoming a Catholic?"

She took a sip of wine before answering. "I received a scholarship to Holy Name High School in Tuckerton. The sisters were very good to me, and most everyone I associated with was Catholic, of course. I converted, happily, in my freshman year. Also, it was the sisters, in particular the principal, Sister Mary Agnes, who encouraged me and arranged my scholarship to Mount St. Benedict's."

Dom saw an opportunity. "Speaking of Mount St. Benedict's, how was it that a business major, with a concentration in marketing, ended up with an internship at one of the most prestigious law firms in the Northeast?"

"Internship opportunities were usually posted in the Office of Student Life and Development. There happened to be no marketing internships at the time, but I had heard about Shaughnessy and Partners. One of the Guidance Counselors explained to me that while it was not strictly in my area of concentration, they were such a prestigious firm that any connections developed there, and any recommendations I might get as a result, would be useful anywhere. I decided to give it a try. I interviewed with Liam Shaughnessy himself and got the job."

Dom saw her smile, as if at a secret memory.

"And, of course, that's where you met your future husband, Thomas Shane. I read about his tragic death. It must have been horrible for you."

She said, with absolutely no emotion, "Yes, it was. I slept through the whole ordeal. I only wish I could have helped."

"On a lighter note, what exactly attracted you to Thomas Shane? Was it love at first sight?"

Fiona's icy gray-blue eyes instantly narrowed.

"Professor Rossi, that is a very personal and inappropriate question. I suggest you change the direction of your questions, or this interview is over."

She smiled with no sincerity and asked, "Other than that, how is your drink?"

Dom knew he should back off. "The drink is excellent. Thank you."

He asked innocuous questions for another fifteen minutes, during which time Fiona had a second glass of Sancerre. She quizzed Dom about the particulars of the article and Dom tap danced around the answers. Neither trusted the other.

Finally, signaling that the interview was over, Fiona asked, "So, Professor, will I get a chance to look at the article before it is published? Just to check for accuracy."

"Absolutely, Mrs. Shane."

She nodded her approval then stood to go. "This has been a most interesting meeting, Professor. I'll leave the check to you." And she left.

Dom sat for several more minutes, finishing his drink and making additional notes. He glanced around the bar, making sure no one was paying attention. Then, he snatched up Fiona Shane's wine glass and dropped it into his canvas briefcase. He paid the check and left a generous tip. Once back in his car, he called Lacey.

"Lace, I'm on my way back to campus. I should be there in a half hour."

"How did it go?"

"That is one chilly, suspicious and guarded woman. I'll tell you all about it later. In the meantime, do me a favor. Google Irish heraldry and look up the symbolism and meaning behind a family crest or coat of arms showing a unicorn in front of a castle. I'll touch base with you as soon as I get back."

"What's going on, Dom?"

"I have a hunch about something. See you in a bit."

As he drove, he brooded on what he had learned, and what he suspected, about Fiona Shane and her mysterious connections to assorted Shaughnessys — first Liam and then Brian. Ten minutes from Mount St. Ben's, he began to suspect what the connection was — beyond Liam. And it was ugly. But it explained a lot.

He said out loud, "Oh, shit."

Once back on campus, Dom headed over to the Folklore Studies department. Lacey greeted him with a quick kiss and said, "I think I know where you're going with this. Take a look at the computer screen."

She said, "Now, here's a collection of Irish heraldic imagery and the meanings and significance attached to them. I checked the unicorn then crossed-referenced the name Shaughnessy for any connections. It turns out that the unicorn in front of a castle is associated with the Shaughnessy clan of County Tipperary. The unicorn symbolizes purity and virtue, and the castle signifies vigilance and spiritual strength — not exactly qualities I would associate with the Shaughnessy clan we're up against."

"I think it's going to get a lot worse." He told her about the interview, about Fiona's brooch and Shaughnessy's cufflinks, and reminded her of Caitlin Killeen's story about stealing the brooch from the man who defiled her.

"Here's what I think is going on. I think that Emma Jean Cramer must have told Fiona who her real mother was; as a God-fearing, church-going woman, maybe she felt morally obligated or something. And she gave Fiona the brooch that Caitlin had stolen from Liam Shaughnessy, kind of like an heirloom or a legacy. But I'm pretty sure Emma Jean had no idea of its actual significance.

"Then, when Fiona was old enough, most likely once she got to Mount St. Ben's, she researched the significance of the brooch symbolism — and found the connection to the Shaughnessy clan and traced its history, in Ireland then to America, and finally to New Jersey. That's how she was able to figure out who her real father was. So, when she learned about the internship, she went for it. I'll bet she sprung the news on old Liam at her interview. He must have nearly soiled his pants. Given who she was and what she knew, he couldn't possibly turn her away."

Lacey considered his thesis and nodded in agreement. "Okay, that ties her to Shaughnessy and Partners. But we still don't know who at the firm was the real father of William Shane."

A very uncomfortable Dom said, "I believe there is something horribly ugly about all this. You're right, we don't know for certain. But I think we can make a pretty good guess. Think about Kate Culhane's description of Brian Shaughnessy."

She appeared confused for a moment, but then said, "Oh, no. Oh my God Jesus, no. It couldn't be. That's so sick it's crazy."

Dom said, "What if Brian Shaughnessy didn't know that Liam was Fiona's father, because the old man never said anything? So Brian just does his 'cock hound' thing. But Fiona, knowing the truth, purposely lets it happen and gets pregnant. Why? She then has total power over both Shaughnessys.

"Brian, initially not knowing who Fiona really is, has to tell the old man about the pregnancy. The old man then is forced to reveal to Brian the truth about Fiona. It's potentially a disaster of unimaginable proportions. So they pressure Thomas Shane into marrying Fiona, like we originally thought.

"In the midst of all this, Liam has a stroke — he's old, his world is collapsing around him, threatening to destroy both his family and his firm. After Thomas Shane very conveniently drowns, Brian Shaughnessy takes over the firm and takes very personal care of Fiona all these years. She probably extorted him into doing it — it ensures her career advancement and she's really the one with all the power."

Lacey, her face pale, said, "That means Fiona knew Brian was her half-brother. She knew it! And she exploited it! What kind of moral sensibility must she have?"

"I don't think she has a shred of moral sensibility. She's an ice cube. She'll do whatever it takes to get what she wants. That's why she was so successful in the pharmaceutical business. Being totally amoral, she fit right in. In this case, she wanted power over the most prestigious law firm in the Northeast and a controlling relationship with a prominent, tremendously wealthy man who'd do anything she wanted."

206

"Dom, it's like Professor J said. It's conjecture, but it's consistent with what we know and has its own internal logic. But we can't prove it. All we have is a bizarre story told to us by a dead woman — who was undoubtedly crazy. So how do we get proof?"

"I'm thinking maybe two ways. First, Rebecca was a world-class scholar. Any presentation or paper would have had tons of documentation and references — and she'd keep a backup copy, someplace immediately accessible, like her house."

"So, are you going to commit a little breaking and entering?"

"Nothing so dramatic. But I do have to ask a tough lady for a big favor."

"What's the second way?"

"It goes back to something Kate said — DNA evidence — and Professor Philips' explanation of sources." He explained some of what he had in mind.

Lacey said, "Jesus, you think we can pull it off?"

"I think you and I can pull off anything. We're all over these guys."

She rolled her eyes. "Right. And next we'll work on world peace. What now?"

"Let me call that tough lady."

Chapter 28

Dom pulled out his phone and called the Office of Human Resources and asked to speak with the Senior Vice President, Helen Greenberg. She was available.

"Vice President Greenberg, it's Dom Rossi. I need a huge favor. I need contact information for Rebecca Glass's sister. She's probably listed in Rebecca's HR file."

"Dominic, information like that is confidential. Can't do it. Plus, I'm hearing some buzz that you are on Felix Delaney's shit list — he is, of course, a person of dubious credibility and a snake, but I have to maintain at least the appearance of objectivity."

"How about if I bribe you with a box of cannoli from Carlo's?"

"Be in my office in twenty minutes. I'll make coffee."
Dom told Lacey about the cannoli bribe. She said, "That's a woman after my own heart. Okay, while you meet with Vice President Greenberg, I'll hold the fort here. I have a bunch of work to do for Dr. Ray over the next few days. Let me know how it goes."

***

Helen Greenberg was a short, slender, gray-haired woman who had been at the university since the Paleolithic era. Dom had first met her when he was a freshman. She was gruff, tough, and the only Jewish employee at the university. For some reason, she thoroughly delighted in Dom.

He arrived as directed and presented Helen with her cannoli. She said, "Dominic, you're a total scoundrel. But I'm a sucker for these damn things. Let's eat."

As Helen poured their coffee, Dom opened the box and placed a cannoli on each of two paper plates Helen had set out. He said, "I met Barbara Glass Carmody at Rebecca's memorial service. She's a pretty cold fish."

"Milt and I were on vacation in the Caymans. But I certainly would have attended the service. Rebecca was a monumental pain in the ass, but she had integrity. I never got the impression she was all that close with her sister, but someone had to be listed besides Diana Bennington; hence, the sister. What are you up to?"

Dom told her about his assignment from Shaughnessy and Delaney to look into Rebecca's research for anything that might cause a problem for the university. He also told her how Delaney had told him to pull the plug, but that Dom was still trying to learn the truth. He avoided explaining about Caitlin Killeen, though he did explain about the Cloister of St. Keira, the fire, and the support the Cloister received from the Loyal Sons.

"So that's why Delaney has you on his shit list. There's something dark going on having to do with the Loyal Sons, and Delaney and Shaughnessy are afraid you'll find it. They must be in it together. And my guess is that it could ultimately end up hurting the university."

Dom nodded. "Big time."

Helen politely chewed and swallowed an obviously satisfying bite of cannoli. She followed it with a sip of coffee then said, "Dom, we in HR are expected to be pillars of discretion. I've known you since you were a seventeen-year-old freshman who could barely find his way to the men's room in the student center. So I'll be candid. I'm at the age where I can retire when I want. Suffice it to say that had Felix Delaney been appointed president of this university instead of Father Jack, like Brian Shaughnessy wanted, I'd be in a condo on Hilton Head right now, sitting by the pool sipping a Mai Tai. I'll be doing that soon enough, of course, but I wanted to stay around a bit to help Father Jack get off on the right foot. I'm old and cranky and experienced enough to be a little paranoid. My advice to you, Dom, is to watch your ass. If I can help, I will."

She handed him a computer printout with Barbara Glass Carmody's contact information. "You didn't get this from me. I don't want to know anything. But if it all works out, next time throw in a couple of Carlo's sfogliatelle, too."

Barbara Glass Carmody lived in Saratoga Springs, New York, a very wealthy, very popular resort destination north of Albany and just south of the Adirondack Mountains, about a three hour drive from Morristown. Dom decided to leave Lacey to her work and go by himself. He also thought he'd have a better chance to meet with Barbara if he were alone. He had decided not to call and risk a direct refusal but to just show up and hope he could talk his way in. He arrived in Saratoga Springs shortly after 11 on an unusually warm late-May Saturday morning.

The Carmody home was impressive — a five bedroom mansion with a three car garage on an acre and a half of well-tended lawn on Magnolia Drive, on the outskirts of the village. As he pulled into the circular driveway, Dom saw a swimming pool and cabana in the backyard whose size would have been appropriate for a country club.

He rang the doorbell; a few moments later an attractive, smiling young Latina woman in an actual maid's uniform opened the door to greet him.

"May I help you?" she said, pleasantly.

"Good morning, I'd like to speak with Barbara Carmody, please. Is she available?"

"Is she expecting you, sir?"

"Please tell her that Professor Dominic Rossi from Mount St. Benedict University is here. Thank you."

The maid appeared a bit disconcerted but nodded and walked off. Several minutes later, she returned and said, "Ms. Carmody will see you. Please come with me."

She led Dom through an immense, immaculate and extravagantly well-appointed house and out onto an expansive backyard patio overlooking the heated pool. Seated at a glass-topped, wrought iron table under a broad, striped umbrella, sipping her second Bloody Mary of the morning was Barbara Carmody.

She was wearing a mauve-colored two-piece bathing suit that left little to the imagination, a fact she was clearly aware of and obviously quite pleased with. Dom looked at the suit, and at her, and thought her delight with herself was exaggerated.

Beyond her were her two teenage daughters, even more exposed. One of the girls was doing laps in the heated pool; the other was lying on her stomach on a chaise lounge getting some sun, the top of her bikini unclasped so she could tan evenly.

Dom looked at them all and thought, *Jesus, what have I walked into?*

210

Barbara Carmody did not stand when Dom approached the table, nor did she offer him anything to drink. She merely indicated that Dom seat himself in a chair across from her. The girl on the chaise lounge looked over at him, curious.

Barbara Carmody said, "I can't imagine what you are doing here, Professor Rossi. I assume it must have something to do with Rebecca. Please explain."

"The university asked me to look into some of Rebecca's research. I've been doing so for most of the past two weeks, all over New Jersey, Maryland, and Boston. But now, to complete my assignment, I need your permission to look into whatever notes, files, or other materials Rebecca may have kept in her home."

"Professor Rossi, my sister and I lived very different lives and had very different values. Frankly, I found her sexual proclivities disgusting. And I certainly had no interest in her research. When she was teaching at SUNY Albany, only some forty minutes south, she might as well have been in Alaska, as far as I was concerned.

"But am I to understand that you want to enter her house and look around? I'm not sure how I feel about that. I'm selling the house and selling or donating whatever furniture, appliances, and decorative pieces are suitable, not that we need the money, as you can see. But your being in her house unsupervised seems inappropriate."

Dom took a gamble. "I understand your concern, Ms. Carmody. Perhaps you'd like to check my assignment with Father John Whelan, President of Mount St. Benedict University. I'm certain he'll be glad to reassure you."

She sat back and considered it, while drawing heavily on her Bloody Mary. Dom happened to glance at the girl on the chaise. Seeing him look at her, the girl, who was perhaps seventeen, turned over from her stomach onto her back.

As she did so, her bikini top fell away, fully revealing her breasts. She made no move to retrieve the top or to cover herself. She merely continued to look over at Dom and smiled. Then she slowly picked up the bikini top and casually draped it over her breasts and lay back, still smiling. The girl doing laps in the pool, the younger sister, had stopped, watched what her older sister

211

was doing, and then — giggling delightedly — lifted up the top of her own bikini and waved at him.

I'm in a fucking madhouse.

Barbara Carmody, oblivious to all of this, said, "Very well, you have my permission, Professor. But only you, alone. I want no one else in there rummaging around. Do I have your word?"

"Yes, Ms. Carmody. You have my word."

"Have you been to the house?"

"No, ma'am, I have not."

"It's a very modest Cape Cod, on Hillcrest Avenue in Morristown, number 23, up the hill next to Burnham Park. Go around the back, there are two large flowerpots on either side of the back steps. Rebecca kept a spare key underneath the pot on the right. You may use it to enter the house. Return it when you're through. We will be coming to inventory the house next week. I expect everything to be just as you found it, with nothing missing. Nothing."

Dom told her, "I assure you it will be. Thank you." He stood to go.

Barbara Carmody took off her sunglasses and looked Dom up and down. "You are an attractive young man, Professor. If you want to return the key in person, I'd look forward to it."

"Thank you, Ms. Carmody, but I'll leave it under the flowerpot. By the way, good luck with your daughters — and your family life.

The girl on the chaise called out, "Hey, I'll look for you next week!"

As Dom walked away, he recalled the famous Tolstoy quote: *"All happy families are the same. Each unhappy family is unhappy in its own way."*

***

As soon as he arrived back at his place on Wetmore Avenue late that afternoon, Dom called Lacey on her cell.

"I cannot tell you how good it is to hear your voice. It's been a bizarre day. I feel like I've crawled through a sewer and need a shower. But I got the okay to look around inside Rebecca's house."

"Can I come?"

"No. I had to give my word to Barbara Carmody that only I

would go into the place. But as soon as I finish checking it out, we should get together. We'll need to talk through what I find — or didn't find. Then we can figure out how to proceed."

"When do you figure on going over there?"

Dom checked his calendar on his cell phone and said, "Day after tomorrow. I have to start preparing for summer sessions, and I have a bunch of work to do beforehand. And I know you're busy as hell, too."

"Sounds good. How about I come to your place for lunch tomorrow and we'll formulate a strategy for how you should canvas Rebecca's house."

"Perfect. See you tomorrow."

That arranged, Dom began to add what they had learned to his schematic depicting the intersection of the elements in the puzzle. The big addition was Caitlin Killeen and her horrific story about the fire and the dead babies. Dom also included the role of Liam Shaughnessy, and its implications for the Loyal Sons, as well as for the Shaughnessy law firm and the candidacy of William Shane. And, of course, he noted the twisted relationship between Brian Shaughnessy and Fiona Cramer Shane. It was all coming together — but it all came down to finding the proof.

After updating his schematic, Dom headed over to the campus to do more work on his upcoming summer session classes. There was a surprise waiting for him when he arrived at his office — Sarah Craig.

She was standing outside of his office, leaning against the door. "This is not a social call, Dom, as pleasant as the last one was. What have you been up to?"

A suddenly wary Dom asked, "With respect to what?"

"Rebecca Glass. And that fire in the Pine Barrens, were you there?"

"That's Burlington County, why do you care about a fire down there? Isn't that out of your jurisdiction?"

"Don't be stupid. The fact that the Glass case is still open gives me room to maneuver. You told me two weeks ago that Glass had been working a lot in that area. It's just too damn coincidental. And it makes me suspicious."

"Wait a minute. I thought you'd decided Rebecca's death was a simple mugging. What does that have to do with her research in

213

the Pine Barrens?"

"Just answer me. Were you down there?"

Dom entered his office and sat down behind his desk, using the few seconds to think. Something was very wrong here.

"Yes, I was there. I was trying to retrace the route Rebecca took for the San Giacomo Engineering Company. I wanted to learn if she had discovered anything relevant or detrimental to the university."

Sarah sat in the chair across from him. Dom closely observed her body language — she was leaning forward aggressively, her hands clasped tightly to the arms of the chair, and her mouth set in a thin, tight line. She exuded hostility, aggression, and suspicion.

"What did you learn?"

"Nothing. It was a waste of time. Those woods are a maze and a mess. I wasn't in there very long either. The fire was well to the north of where I was, but I saw the smoke in the distance and got the hell out of there. I've learned enough about the Pine Barrens to know that fires occur there all the time and can spread amazingly fast. And that it's a very strange goddamn place."

Her eyes were steely. "It's also a dangerous place. New Jersey law enforcement has long known that a lot of so-called 'missing persons' are buried in there. It's unlikely their remains will ever be found. It's best if you stay away from there."

"That's very interesting about the missing persons, but I don't believe it's relevant to my situation. Anything else?"

Sarah stared at him then sat back in her chair. "How about the two guys who tried to beat you up?"

"I haven't seen or heard from them since."

"Are you going to keep after this Rebecca Glass thing?"

"I'm pretty sure it's run its course. The Provost told me I'm off the hook."

Sarah studied him. "I heard that Frank Burns fractured his ankle."

"Ankle fractures can be a bitch, I understand."

After several moments, Sarah said, "You're a nice guy, Dom. But you're a fucking boy scout. And you're in way over your head. If you're holding back on this, you could get into serious trouble. Or worse."

"Thank you for the insight. By the way, where's Mulroney?"

Sarah flushed slightly, but Dom caught it. "He's working another case. Why?"

"Just that I miss his charming presence."

She gave him a tight smile then stood to go. "Remember what I said."

Dom watched her go and thought again, *Something is very wrong here.*

Chapter 29

The following day, Dom was at home preparing lunch when Lacey knocked on his door and came roaring in. "Shit! Did you see today's *Star Ledger*?"

Not waiting for an answer, she waved the paper under his nose. "William Shane is being honored as Loyal Son of the Year by the Loyal Sons of Cu Chulainn at their annual dinner on Memorial Day — four days from now. Brian Shaughnessy is presenting the award. There will be a video presentation about Shane's career and achievements, followed by his acceptance speech. Speculation is that he'll use the occasion to kick off his gubernatorial campaign. Our girl Fiona is his campaign manager.

"And just to add to the weirdness, one of the Loyal Sons, a guy named Manning who was their Historian, evidently took a header off the upper deck of the parking lot at the Cinema 10 in Morristown. There was some kind of suicide note found on him, but the paper doesn't go into its contents. Jesus, Dom, it's like all of a sudden all matters of life and death end up involving the Shaughnessy clan and the Loyal Sons."

"Maybe he just didn't like the movie, Lace."

"Don't be a smart ass." Lacey threw the paper to the floor in disgust. Then, she said, "Okay, I get it. I'll lighten up. So, what's that you're making?"

"This is a salad with imported Spanish tuna, chickpeas, roasted red pepper, hard boiled egg, and Nicoise olives. I'm dressing it with olive oil, fresh lemon juice, and parsley. We'll put it in warm pita pockets and have it with a chilled Pinot Grigio."

"Yum."

"That's what I was thinking looking at you."

Her smile was wonderful. "In that case, lunch can wait. Let the games begin."

Later, a beaming, naked, joyous Lacey bounced out of bed and said, "Well, that'll sure work up an appetite. Put on your shorts, bucko, and let's eat."

216

Dom looked at the long, elegant, graceful lines of her body, her radiant smile, and her shining eyes; he felt a tug at his heart. In so short a time she had filled his life. Once he came back to earth he said, "Are we dressing for lunch?"

She winked at him. "Only just." She put on one of Dom's Mount St. Ben's T-shirts — it barely covered anything. Then she headed into the kitchen.

Dom served up the plates while Lacey opened the wine, and they brought their repast out onto Dom's tiny balcony overlooking Wetmore Avenue. He said, "Rebecca's place isn't far, just over by Burnham Park. Her sister told me there's a spare key around the back under a flower pot."

"What exactly are you looking for?"

"I'm hoping to at least find some notes about what she learned. The gold ring would be to stumble upon a copy of her presentation. Frank Burns told me he'd already cased the place and found nothing. That means if something actually is in the house, it's well hidden. Whether it's a paper document, a disc or a flash drive, there's just no telling. I just have to hope I get lucky."

"Dom, suppose you actually do find something, what then?"

"I guess it depends on what I find. But whatever it might be, we'll try to use it to the extent we can to expose that goddamn Shaughnessy clan."

"What do you want me to do?"

"Some scientific legwork." He went to his little study then returned with his canvas briefcase, from which he extracted a wineglass.

Lacey raised an eyebrow. "You've resorted to stealing glassware now?"

Dom said, "This is exhibit A, it has Fiona Shane's saliva on it."

"Oh, yuck!"

"It goes back to what Kate said about proof, and what Professor Philips told us about DNA samples. Here's where you come in. Remember how you told me that the Morris County DA — William Shane — comes into the Cheech several times a week? Well, for exhibit B, we need you to get Elena and Javier to swipe a fork or spoon used by William Shane the next time he has lunch at the Cheech. Place it in a plastic bag and keep it in a safe place.

"For exhibit C, I want you to call Stick. Ask him if he can swipe the razor Brian Shaughnessy uses the next time he shaves in the men's locker room at Spring Brook. If Stick wants to know what's up, it's okay to tell him."

"Shit, I might as well be picking through dumpsters. This is getting weirder all the time. I'm going to be busy for the next few days. Dr. Ray and I have a bunch of meetings with people we're hoping will contribute to the Folklore Studies program. So, I'd better get all this done today. I'll go see Elena this afternoon then call Stick when I get back and give him a heads up."

Dom said, "Great. After I check out Rebecca's, I'll give you a call. Then we'll go and collect our trash."

Lacey gave him a quick kiss and said, "Hanging out with you is an adventure."

***

The next morning, with Elena, Javier, and Stick having been given their assignments, and just before she headed over to the campus, Lacey heard a knock on her door. She opened it to find standing there a detective holding up a gold shield issued by the Office of the Prosecutor, Monmouth County, Homicide Division.

Lacey said, "Yes, Detective, how can I help you? Is anything wrong?"

"Ms. Lacey, I'm in the middle of conducting a murder investigation. The victim is Rebecca Glass. I need you to come with me and answer a few questions."

Lacey was confused. "Come with you? Where? Why?"

"Down to the Office of the Monmouth County Prosecutor, in Freehold."

"*Freehold?* I have responsibilities at Mount St. Benedict's University. I can't go off to Freehold. Can't you ask the questions here?"

"You'd best come now, Miss. Or it will get very ugly."

Lacey shrugged and grabbed her purse and smart phone. The detective escorted her to a waiting car. It did not occur to Lacey that detectives normally work in pairs.

***

Dom had been calling Lacey at the Folklore Studies Department

218

all morning, to touch base before he headed off to Rebecca's place. There was no answer. Then, he got a call from Ray Alexander.

"Have you heard from Lacey? Is she with you? We were scheduled for a meeting this morning with Professor Virginia Reed. Ginny teaches American Folk Art, and she's brilliant. We want to include some of her work in our new folklore classes. But I can't get hold of Lacey. That's not at all like her. You know she's usually a maniac for punctuality. I'm getting a little worried."

"I'm trying to track her down myself. If I do, I'll have her call you. If you talk to her first, please ask her to call me."

Now, Dom was worried. The call from Martin O'Bannon made things worse.

"Okay, Rossi, it's time to quit fucking around. You wouldn't stop, you wouldn't let it go, you had to keep at Rebecca Glass, even when you were told to back off. So now you're fucked, you and your lanky girlfriend. If you ever want to see her again, you do exactly like I tell you. No tricks, no games."

"What do you want me to do?"

O'Bannon laughed. "I want you to follow some directions. I know that's not something you're very good at, but your girlfriend's safety depends on your learning how. In fact, she's waiting for you in one of your favorite places, Rossi. You're going into the Pine Barrens."

O'Bannon gave Dom a very precise set of directions. Then he told Dom, "Be there tomorrow at noon. Alone. Or the bitch is dead."

"I'll be there, O'Bannon. But now you listen to me. I have something you want. I have proof of all the shit you and Shaughnessy and Fiona Cramer are involved in, from generations back. If it ever gets out, you're fucked — all of you. I'll trade it for Lacey."

O'Bannon had no way of knowing whether Rossi's claim was true, but he could not risk letting Rossi expose the proof, assuming he actually had it. He had to get his hands on whatever it was that Rossi was talking about. Then, they would get rid of both Rossi and the girl. It was a tricky situation. But then, O'Bannon smiled; he knew his resource was up to the task, and would relish it.

"Okay, it's a deal. The proof for the girl."

"One more thing, just so you know. If Lacey is hurt the slightest bit, if one strand of her hair is out of place, I'll rip your fucking heart out."

"Fuck you, Rossi. Noon tomorrow, you better be there."

After hanging up, Dom put his face in his hands, his bravado gone. It came at him all at once, how arrogant he'd been, how smug. Shaughnessy, Delaney, O'Bannon, Frank Burns, Fiona Shane — he was so sure he could save Rebecca's reputation, beat them all and take them down. What a fool he'd been. He had not seen things the way they really were. And now he'd put Lacey in mortal danger.

God, what have I done to that beautiful, brilliant young woman with my blindness.

He needed something powerful with which to fight back. He needed Rebecca's presentation.

***

Dom found Rebecca's modest Cape Cod style house on Hillcrest Avenue — a one car garage, small lawn, white vinyl siding, black shutters, three steps leading up to the red front door. He parked across the street and headed around to the back. The two flowerpots were there, on either side of the steps leading to the back door. Dom lifted the one on the right and retrieved the key and entered the house. With each step, his anxiety grew as he thought of Lacey and how he had threatened O'Bannon with proof Dom wasn't even sure existed. Frank Burns was a pro, and he had found nothing.

The first floor had a half-bathroom, decent-sized kitchen leading to a smallish dining room, living room, and the room Rebecca used as her office. A set of stairs led to the three bedrooms and to two full baths on the second floor. The décor was a wild mix of primitive folk art, framed concert posters of heavy metal musicians, assorted archaeological artifacts, and an eclectic assortment of personal memorabilia. The place was actually neater than Dom had expected, given how flamboyantly messy Rebecca's side of the office was at Mount St. Ben's.

In the living room on a stand of shelves was a collection of books, mostly scholarly works, though there were also a number

220

of mystery novels and assorted works by feminist and lesbian authors. He also noticed a display of several ornate and quite beautiful decorative glass sculptures.

As he thought about what faced him, his heart sank. Something as small as a flash drive or a disc could be anywhere — or nowhere. He went through the house slowly, carefully, room by room. He opened drawers and cupboards, looked in and under appliances, behind and under pieces of furniture, under rugs, examining anything that could hold something as large as a printed report or as small as a thumb drive.

He went through Rebecca's office with particular care. He examined her books, papers, printouts, desk, computer, printer, fax, furniture — and came up with a big zero. After two hours downstairs, he started on the upstairs, working in a similar manner in Rebecca's bedroom, the two other bedrooms, the two full baths, through closets and bureaus and drawers, among assorted clothing, in and under shoes. After another two hours, he'd found nothing — no sign of the proof with which he'd threatened Martin O'Bannon, the proof he hoped to use to bargain for Lacey's life.

Bitterly disappointed, Dom went back downstairs to decompress and get his thoughts together. He sat in the living room, quietly re-considering what he might have overlooked, trying not to force things, and allowing his mind to remain open to new and unexpected insights. He glanced again at the bookcase, noting once more the volumes on the shelves, each of which he had looked behind and opened.

Then, his eyes fell on the collection of glass sculptures, which was displayed on the top level of the bookshelf. He stared at it. It appeared to be genuine Murano glass, hand crafted on the famous island in the Venetian lagoon. Dom knew that it was usually very expensive, probably worth more than anything else in the house.

He continued to stare at the collection. There were several multi-colored bowls, a blue spiral cone, a glass red heart, two yellow birds, and a glass sculpture of two nude female figures embracing. He felt a sudden shock of understanding.

He said out loud, "Dear sweet Jesus — it's Moose Matson. The whole goddamn thing comes down to Moose Matson."

Dom was referring to the 1941 Abbott and Costello movie,

Hold That Ghost. It was one of Dom's favorites. He had been thrilled when Lacey had been familiar with it and could even quote bits from it.

In the film there is a famous and wildly silly bit where Lou Costello gets all confused about an old saying that the gangster Moose Matson 'always kept his money in his head.' Lou takes it literally and Bud Abbott and Joan Davis try to tell him it's just a figure of speech. There then follows a series of crazy examples of figures of speech, until a totally frustrated and exasperated Lou reaches into an old stuffed moose head on the wall of the roadhouse gambling joint that Matson owned. And sure enough, that's where he finds Matson's huge money stash.

Dom stood up and walked over to the glass collection, remembering that Rebecca had once told him, 'Dom, I keep my secrets in my heart.'

He lifted the sculpture of the red heart and turned it over. A hole had been cut out in the bottom and covered over with a piece of red felt. He removed the felt and extracted a flash drive from inside. He held it gently in his hand.

Thank you, God.

Dom raced back to Wetmore Avenue and loaded the flash drive into his computer. It contained the entire presentation that Rebecca had planned to make at the Annual Meeting of the Archaeological Association of New Jersey. The presentation itself contained photographs, copies of documents, references to Holy Innocents Orphanage and the Diocese of Trenton, maps, a brief history of the Cloister of St. Keira and photographs of the ruins — and most stunningly, a filmed interview with Caitlin Killeen, in which she told her heartbreaking story about Liam Shaughnessy, the Cloister, the fire — and the nuns leaving sick, scarred, damaged babies out to die; it also included photos of the over forty orchid-covered graves with their tiny crosses.

Dom sat for a while in stunned silence. Rebecca had once told him, "Dom, life is like archaeology. It's not just what you *find.* It's what you *learn.*"

This was why Rebecca felt she could buy a bigger home, why she could go on an extended vacation with Diana, why she could demand a promotion, a sabbatical, and research grants. She had found the means to extort everyone — the Loyal Sons,

Shaughnessy and Partners, the Diocese of Trenton, the University. And she had done so eagerly and aggressively.

If exposed, this information would rip the lid off everything and leave incredible destruction in its wake. That's why Rebecca had to be killed. But by whom? The specific orders almost certainly had come from Shaughnessy. He had the most at stake. But who exactly had carried out the hit? Burns? O'Bannon? Or was it someone of whom Dom was totally unaware?

The immediate problem for Dom was how to best use this to save Lacey. He copied the presentation electronically then began to weigh his options.

Showing the presentation to Sarah Craig would have been the most obvious way to go, but not after their last meeting. Something weird was going on with her. There was Sister Pat, but every time he'd left a message for her or talked to someone, O'Bannon and Shaughnessy had known. They must have a mole in the English Department. It had to be that goddamn Fran Purcell. Then he knew who could help — Kate Culhane.

He dropped a spare thumb drive with a copy of the presentation into a small padded envelope, and included a brief letter explaining the urgency and significance of the situation as well as his plan. He sealed the envelope and marked it "Urgent — Personal and Confidential." Then he drove to Chatham to give it to Kate.

The young man at the reception said, "Professor Rossi, you cannot continue to barge in here like this! Make a damn appointment. In any event, Ms. Culhane is in court and cannot be reached for the remainder of the day. What is your problem this time?"

Dom held up the padded envelope containing the copy of Rebecca's presentation. "This is a matter of life and death — literally life and death. Give it to Ms. Culhane the moment she returns. Tell her I said it is imperative that she looks at the contents immediately. I will call her about it as soon as I can. If I do not call within twenty-four hours, tell her I said she is to use this information as she deems appropriate."

The receptionist sighed and said, "Very well, Professor, if you insist."

Dom leaned over the desk, his face close to the receptionist's.

223

"I really do insist. And just so we are clear on this — if you don't make sure Kate gets this, I'll come for you. And if I die beforehand, I will fucking haunt you for all eternity."

Chapter 30

O'Bannon's directions led Dom to one of the most remote areas of the Pine Barrens — roughly within the township of Tabernacle, into the depths of Wharton State Forest. He left Route 206 south of the Red Lion Circle and turned onto Carranza Road, passing the landmarks O'Bannon had specified, Nixon's General Store and Russo's farm store. He continued through the bleak, empty, desolate landscape for another several miles into the forest, finally arriving at the Carranza Memorial.

In 1928, Emilio Carranza, the "Lindberg of Mexico," was on his way home from a goodwill flight from Mexico to New York, when he encountered a fierce thunderstorm and ultimately crashed and died in the Pine Barrens. An unimpressive stone monument, literally in the middle of nowhere, marks the spot of the crash.

On the second Saturday of July, the American Legion Post of Mt. Holly sponsors a weekend celebration commemorating the event, which traditionally includes visiting dignitaries from the Mexican consulates of New York and Philadelphia. The rest of the year, the site remains empty, visited only by an occasional hiker, who is usually lost, or curiosity seekers, who are usually underwhelmed since there is nothing else of the slightest interest for miles and miles around.

Dom parked in the small, deserted lot; no other vehicles were in sight. He then headed to the south side of the stone memorial. As directed, he walked one hundred fifty paces south into the thick woods until he came upon a small sand trail. He followed the trail for a quarter mile or so, the flat terrain a mix of pitch pines, scrub oak, assorted brush and vines and barren patches of sand — desolate, isolated, forgotten.

He remembered Sarah's warning about 'missing persons' actually having been buried in the Pine Barrens, their bodies never found. There was no better place in New Jersey to hide a couple of bodies. Sarah was right.

Wave after wave of foreboding began to wash over him — *something was going on here of which he was totally unaware, something twisted and evil.*

He kept walking, straight and deep into the most remote area of the Pine Barrens. After two hundred yards, as he was told to do, he stopped and looked around. And there, off to his right, some twenty yards away, he saw Lacey. She was tied to a pine tree; duct tape bound her hands and mouth, her face was bruised and puffy. Her eyes met his — he saw in them fear and anger and something else, something like a warning.

From behind a short, thick, huckleberry bush about thirty yards away, out stepped a smiling Sarah Craig. Her eyes were wide, her face flushed, she kept moistening her lips. She exuded something akin to sexual arousal. She held an automatic pistol at her side, then raised it and pointed it at Dom.

"I told you to say out of this, to stay away from here. But you wouldn't listen. Now, it's too late — for both you and your little playmate."

An astonished Dom just stared at her uncomprehending. Then came the moment of recognition, what Aristotle would term *anagnorisis* — the moment in a play when the main character makes a critical discovery. Dom saw the connection and finally understood.

"Keansburg — you grew up in Keansburg. O'Bannon was on the police force there. That's how you know him. It goes that far back. Why, Sarah? Why O'Bannon?"

"He did me a favor, when I was fifteen. It was ugly for me at home, an ugly time. My old man made me... he used to...O'Bannon helped me get out of there. We've been doing favors for each other ever since — all kinds of favors. I like doing them. And I'll be doing him another favor right here."

Another one. "So you killed Rebecca, on O'Bannon's orders."

She smiled and said with utter calm. "Let's say at his 'request.' And her dyke partner. I enjoyed it. I always enjoy doing favors for Martin. And I'm enjoying doing another. It can be hard or easy, Dom. That's all up to you. But first, where is this proof you're supposed have? I want it."

She began to walk towards him, her pistol pointed at his chest.

226

As Sarah walked closer, Dom saw a wild-eyed Lacey begin to pull and tug at her bonds, shaking her head, seeming to look towards a spot in the sand just ahead of where Sarah was walking. Dom followed her eyes — and he saw it too. Then he heard it, a soft but persistent rattle.

"Sarah, stop! Don't move! Don't step — "

"Fuck you, Dom. No games, no — "

And then she screamed.

Adult Timber rattlesnakes in the Pine Barrens can grow to be five feet long. They can strike at a distance of up to three feet. Normally, as Abner had explained, they tend to be timid and not at all aggressive — unless they are mating. These two were.

The female, some four feet long, struck Sarah on the ankle, above her leather shoes. Sarah fell to the ground; she squirmed and writhed and spun around and around, screaming and pointing her pistol at anything near her, firing wildly into the sand and brush, clutching her ankle.

Then the larger, longer male struck — and sunk his fangs into Sarah's throat, hanging on while she writhed and squirmed and tried to roll away. After several moments, his venom depleted, he slithered off into the brush.

A single bite from a Timber rattler is rarely fatal. But Sarah had been struck twice, and the combined amount of neurotoxin released into her blood stream was excessive. As the snakes slithered off, Dom ran to her and took her in his arms; he watched in horror as Sarah started seizing, gagging, her eyes rolling, her mouth salivating, her body twitching and shaking uncontrollably; a dark wet stain appeared between her legs. Her eyes met his — confused, angry, bitter, pleading.

Dom lifted her, trying to carry her back to the parking lot. "I'll get help. Just hang on, Sarah, hang on."

She shook even more violently and uttered a horrible gurgling sound; her eyes rolled back in her head, her face became contorted in agony; she became rigid, shuddered violently, then went limp. Her breathing stopped. She was utterly still.

A shaken Dom placed her on the ground and stood over her. He could not help but wonder what awful demons must have inhabited this strange, complex, disturbed woman who had shared his bed — and had come to an end like this.

227

As he looked down on her, a line from *Richard III* came to mind, *"What ugly sights of death are within mine eyes."*

Then he went to Lacey and gently began to untie her.

She said, "Oh my God, Dom. Oh my God." Once free she stood unsteadily then wrapped her arms around him and began to sob.

Dom held her close and asked, "Are you hurt?"

"No, she just punched me around some. She enjoyed it. But I'm okay. She came to my place, told me I had to go with her to Freehold to answer questions in a murder investigation, the Rebecca Glass case. I believed her.

"Then when we got to her car and I started to climb in, she hit me on the head with something then tied me up with the duct tape. When I came to, I was in the back of the Jeep, all wrapped up."

"What about when you arrived down here? What then?"

"I was conscious by then. She dragged me out of the back of the Jeep and dumped me on the ground while she wiped down the whole vehicle, whatever I had touched, wherever I had been, so there would be no trace of me having been in her car. It was then I knew what she was going to do. God, Dom, I was so scared."

He pulled her close and kissed her hair. "You're safe now, Lace, I've got you."

Lacey hugged him back then looked down at Sarah. "Is she...dead?"

"Yes. She must have been especially susceptible to the neurotoxin. Christ, what a horrible death. God help me, but somehow I can't help but feel that it's —"

"Justice. It's justice."

Dom nodded. "Lace, we have to get coldly practical now. Where's her Jeep?"

"It's back along some sand road, about a half mile away. We must have approached this place from a different direction. I'm not sure I can find it."

"We'll leave it, along with her. But I'm going to call it in."

"Call it in! Won't we be dragged into all kinds of shit trying to explain this craziness? Jesus, Dom, you know how cops are when it comes to other cops' deaths. They'll immediately see us as suspects, rattlesnake bites notwithstanding."

"Sarah was a killer and probably mentally ill. But I can't just leave her to the coyotes. I'll call it in and then we'll get the hell out of here."

"But if you make the call, the police will be able to trace your phone and learn who you are anyway."

Dom pulled out his smartphone and said, "Not necessarily. I have an idea."

He Googled "payphones in New Jersey" and learned that even in the cellphone age, there were some 6,500 payphones remaining in the state — three of which were located at the Wading Pines Campground in Chatsworth, just a few miles away.

"I'll call from a campground in Chatsworth."

He showed her the image on his smartphone screen. "Look, you can see there's a payphone right outside of the registration building. By the time the State Troopers get there, we'll be long gone."

"Okay, Dom, make the call. Then please, let's get the hell out of here and go home."

Chapter 31

Brian Shaughnessy had finished an especially enjoyable round of golf with his partners, his team having won the hundred-dollar Nassau on the final hole thanks to Shaughnessy's clutch 18-foot putt. He took some steam, showered, and was standing at the sink wrapped in a towel in the very well appointed men's locker room at Spring Brook Country Club. He was shaving.

Later, he would join his friends for some high stakes gin rummy, several glasses of single malt Scotch, then head over to Fiona's for a light meal and some vigorous sex. Life was good.

Martin O'Bannon had assured him that this Rebecca Glass-Dominic Rossi business was nearly over. Moreover, the Loyal Sons dinner was but two days away, where he would present William Shane with the Loyal Son of the Year Award, thus kicking off William's gubernatorial campaign and all but ensuring his election as governor — and Shaughnessy's own access to even more money and power.

He was feeling very pleased with himself. So much so that he did not notice that the tall young black man who occasionally served as a locker room attendant hovered nearby a bit more closely than usual as Shaughnessy went about his ablutions.

As he dressed in fresh clothes at his locker, Shaughnessy also did not notice the young black man snatch Shaughnessy's used disposable razor from the trash bin near the sink, drop it into a plastic zip lock bag and quickly head out of the locker room.

***

They made it back to Dom's, after tipping off the State Police about an abandoned vehicle somewhere near the Carranza Memorial. Lacey got cleaned up and Dom poured her a glass of wine and himself a much-needed Scotch.

As they sat with their drinks, Lacey asked, "What happens when O'Bannon and Shaughnessy find out about Craig?"

"They'll likely try to come at us again. We have to play defense. But first things first. Did you get to Stick, Elena and Javier?"

"Yeah, the day before yesterday. They told me they'd get right on it."

"Good girl. We'll set up a meet with them later today. But for now, I have a hunch about something — Sarah Craig's family problems."

Dom booted up his computer, then Googled old files from the *Asbury Park Press*. He took a guess and went back twenty years, looked up crime stories emanating from Keansburg, and then cross-referenced the surname "Craig."

"Jesus, look. Twenty years ago, a man named Gary Craig was killed by his girlfriend in the living room of his home in Keansburg. He was stabbed multiple times, a significant amount of crack cocaine was found on the coffee table in front of the sofa. They were both loaded with it. His girlfriend was found passed out with a knife in her hand. It was later determined to be the murder weapon.

"Also in the house was Craig's fifteen year-old daughter. She was ostensibly asleep in another room until awakened by the sounds of a violent argument. As a minor, her name wasn't given. But it was the daughter's testimony that sent the girlfriend away for thirty years. The first officer on the scene was Martin O'Bannon. Who knows what really happened, but my guess is that O'Bannon took care of the daughter then and ever since — Sarah Craig."

"Jesus, Dom. That was the favor she told us about."

They finished their drinks and headed out to El Chicharron. In a room that was normally reserved for private parties, they met up with Stick, Javier and Elena. Lamar was also present. They were all seated around a large, circular table working their way through a large jug of red wine and a platter of empanadas.

Javier asked, "Domingo, please explain, now that you have these things, these forks and glass and razor, what do you do with them? What do you look for?"

"Each of these things carries on it cellular material, called DNA, that a laboratory can use to determine whether the people are related and the nature of the relationship."

231

Stick said, "Shit, Dom, you just walk into some lab and ask those folks to hurry their ass up and run a bunch of high end, technical tests for you? They must got other stuff to do, man."

Dom laughed. "Good point, Stick. Tomorrow I'm going to see a big-time lawyer in Chatham and I'm hoping she has some pull with a DNA lab."

Elena nodded and said, "I see. It is the test that reveals the truth about the people. But what happens then?"

Lacey said, "We observe the connections, Elena, and we follow them wherever they lead."

Dom smiled at her. "Well said, Watson. But that leads us to another issue."

Dom explained how Shaughnessy and O'Bannon would soon figure out that Sarah Craig had failed in her attempt to get rid of both Dom and Lacey. O'Bannon would then be forced to try to do the job himself or find other means. Lacey was most at risk.

"The first place they'll look is Lacey's apartment, next will be mine, then the University, maybe even yours and Elena's, Javier. I'll be okay, but we need a place for Lacey to hole up for a day, while I work out a plan with the lawyer, Kate Culhane. Any suggestions?"

Stick was thoughtful for a bit then looked over at Lamar. "You thinking what I thinking?"

Lamar nodded. "Yeah, Granny Pearl. No one look for Lacey down the Hollow. And if they do, no one get past Granny Pearl. What you think, Lacey?"

"I'm game. But will your Granny Pearl have a problem with some total stranger barging in on her?"

Lamar smiled. "She be real pleased. You'll stick out down there. Hollow girls don't look like you. But Granny take good care you. Though she do talk a bit."

***

Martin Luther King Boulevard in Morristown leads to Manahan Village, a low to moderate-income housing project. The street used to be known as Evergreen Place; before that it was Water Street, in what was formerly — and disparagingly — called The Hollow. Most of the vestiges of that old, downtrodden area are now gone. Apartments are well maintained, comfortable, and are

232

occupied by a diverse community of mostly African-American and Latino residents.

But several two and three-story narrow tenement buildings remain, like echoes of an earlier and different era — one over a liquor store, another over a Latino grocery, a Peruvian restaurant and a Portuguese cafe. It was in a two-story tenement behind the Peruvian restaurant and across the street from the Union Baptist Church where 81-year-old Pearl Bathsheba Mickens lived, independently, contentedly, and quite feistily.

Granny Pearl had been born in the Hollow and had never lived anywhere else. She had given birth to six children, had fourteen grandchildren, and five great-grandchildren and countless nieces and nephews.

At twelve years old, her first job had been cleaning the homes of rich Irish people over in the Historic Section of Morristown; then she had spent forty-five years in the housekeeping department at Morristown Memorial Hospital. She buried two husbands, survived a gunshot wound and two heart attacks, and was currently managing quite nicely despite a touch of rheumatism.

While Dom headed to Chatham to once again barge in on Kate Culhane, Stick and Lamar brought Lacey to Granny Pearl's. They climbed the stairs of the old tenement to the second floor and knocked. Lacey saw the door opened a crack by a tiny, wizened black woman with a crown of snow white hair. Her smile was like a sunrise.

"Well my, my — aren't you a beautiful child! Though you a mite bit on the lean side, baby girl. Come in, child, come in and welcome!"

Granny Pearl looked at Stick and Lamar and said, "I suppose you boys will be wanting something to eat, like usual. Let me put the tea on."

When Granny Pearl fully opened the door, Lacey saw her replace an old Remington pump action .22 rifle in a gun rack near the front door. Then the old woman, muttering and talking, took Lacey by the hand and led her into the small, spotlessly clean kitchen.

"Child, I don't want to know how a beautiful young thing like you got mixed up with these two rapscallions, but it don't matter,

I'll keep you safe. You like milk and sugar in your tea? I got fresh baked cornbread, it my favorite, we'll have some with maple syrup, have a touch or two of Tennessee sour mash sipping whiskey help it go down smooth. And we'll chat a bit. Fontaine, Lamar, don't you boys just stand there leaving the door wide open, come in or go out. Lacey and me be just fine either way."

Lacey looked at Stick. "*Fontaine?*"

Stick said, "Don't be getting down on me now. I been fighting it all my life. Why I such a badass."

Lamar nodded his head. "Name like that, what else you expect a man to do?"

Stick said, "Granny, it just be you and Lacey have a snack. Me and Lamar got business. You call us anything happen. Lacey's man, Dom, be coming by tomorrow, slender white dude, but broad through the shoulders. Got dark hair, green eyes. You know it be him when you see this girl light up. You be okay, Lacey?"

Lacey looked at Granny Pearl muttering and puttering around the kitchen, pouring tea, slicing cornbread, humming to herself. What stories this feisty little lady must have!

She smiled at them and said, "Guys, I'm in folklore heaven."

***

An increasingly angry, frustrated Dom sat across the desk from Kate Culhane, as she held up the thumb drive containing Rebecca's presentation; she pulled no punches.

"Is it powerful? Yes. Is it heartbreaking? Yes. Are these people despicable? Certainly. Is it admissible as evidence in a court of law? Not a chance in hell."

Dom said, "They left babies out to die."

Kate then held up three plastic bags containing the wineglass, fork and razor. "And just what the hell am I supposed to do with this stuff?"

"Take it to a lab for DNA testing. It will prove that William Shane is the son of Fiona Shane and Brian Shaughnessy. With Caitlin's interview, it will be the final nail in the Shaughnessy coffin."

"Dom, listen to me. Even if a lab identifies the DNA on these items exactly the way you think, they're not admissible. You think a judge will allow a wineglass, a fork, and a razor gathered from God knows where, under totally inappropriate circumstances by totally *un*-objective *you?* Jesus, Dom, anyone who watches TV would know that. "

"I read."

An exasperated Kate said, "Dom, listen to me. We cannot make an accusation of serial manslaughter against the Cloister of St. Keira, aided and abetted by the Loyal Sons of Cu Chulainn and Shaughnessy and Partners, with the knowing complicity of the Diocese of Trenton, based on the fruit of the poisonous tree and the words of an obviously deranged old woman. The same holds for the DNA."

"They left babies out to die. They killed Rebecca and Diana. They were going to kill Lacey."

"Dom, there is not the slightest shred of physical evidence on which to make those claims. And you want me to go to the office of the Morris County DA — William Shane's office! — and talk them into filing charges?"

"Kate, you asked for proof. It's goddamn proof! Rebecca's research in its entirety — references, citations, photographs, everything. Even filmed testimony from Caitlin Killeen! And what the hell is the poisonous tree?"

Kate sighed. "The rules of evidence in a court of law are profoundly different from those of academic scholarship. That's because the stakes are infinitely greater than some pompous ass's scholarly reputation.

"As for the fruit of the poisonous tree, it's an extension of the exclusionary rule established in 1920 in the case of Silverthorne Lumber v. United States. It holds that evidence gathered with the assistance of illegally obtained information must be excluded from trial. In other words, we cannot use any of this shit that you stole! It's useless!"

Dom said nothing for nearly two minutes. His hands folded, his head down, he did not look at her.

Kate said gently, "Look, Dom, I understand what you feel — pain, outrage, anger, disgust. But my job is to be brutally honest, to tell you the truth so you can make reasonable decisions in your own best interest. What you have here, as powerful as it is to you and me, will never see the light of day in a court of law. That's just the way it is. You have to drop it."

Dom raised his eyes and looked at her. Kate Culhane considered herself a smart, tough, experienced legal professional. She was sure she had seen it all. But she had never before seen the look she saw in the eyes of Dominic Rossi. It was chilling.

His voice barely above a whisper and devoid of emotion, he said, "Fuck a court of law. I'm not dropping it. I'll take them down my way. And you're either in or you're out.

"Here's your choice, Kate — either help me, or live with yourself for letting them get away with killing babies. I hope you sleep well for the rest of your life.

"And forgive me for being a pompous academic ass, but for me this is what Aristotle calls *praxis,* motivation leading to action. I'm going to act, regardless of what the hell you do."

"I'm not sure what you're talking about. But if you're suggesting to me that you are going to do something illegal, as an officer of the court, I cannot go along with that."

Dom said with eerie calm, "I'm not suggesting that at all. But I am telling you that I am about to raise holy hell. Here's what I'm going to do, and what I need you to do..."

After Dom finished explaining, an astounded Kate said, "Dear God, Dom, you really think you can pull that off?"

"I only need about fifteen minutes. And I'll have help. Are you in?"

After several moments, Kate said, "You may not be certifiably crazy, but you are very goddamn close to being completely out of control. And, I suspect, you are capable of anything when you get your back up. However, in your own relentless, brilliant way, you have uncovered things both profound and painful. And from a purely moral perspective, you're right — I cannot let this stand.

"Okay, I will help you — to this extent. I'll take these items to a lab I work with, Techno-Gen. They'll rush it for me. I'll have the results in less than twenty-four hours, and in a format you can use for your purposes. As for the other part of it, you're on your own. And may God have mercy on both our souls."

***

A day earlier, Detective Sergeant Edward Mulroney looked upon the naked body of his partner as it lay on a slab in the morgue at the headquarters of the Burlington County Medical Examiner. The room was brutally cold, spare, white and antiseptic, the air

236

redolent of chemicals and disinfectants. Mulroney had seen a lot of corpses over the years and they'd never bothered him. But he'd never viewed one that was a partner.

Mulroney said to the Coroner, "Christ, a fucking snake bite did this?"

"Two of them, Detective. This is pre-autopsy, of course; the official results will be available in a couple of days. But unofficially, I can tell you that the bite to the throat was the one that proved fatal. The neurotoxin probably went immediately to her brain. She no doubt was highly allergic. I suspect we'll find gunpowder residue on her right hand, consistent with the shots fired most likely at the snakes, as suggested by the shell casings and snake blood evidence found in the brush. Medically, it's an easy call. The big question is what was she doing in there in the first place."

Also present was a New Jersey State Trooper, Sgt. Sally Menendez, a stocky, formidable looking Latina woman, who had worked with Mulroney now and then over the years. She had been the first Trooper to arrive on the scene, after the forest ranger had first found Craig's body.

Sally said, "Doc's right, Eddie. Why there of all places?"

Mulroney shook his head. "I'll tell you what I know, Sal, but isn't a whole hell of a lot. Let's get a coffee."

They went upstairs to the tiny cafeteria, got their coffees and sat at a table on the far side of the room where they would not be overheard.

Mulroney took a large sip of his black coffee; then he said, "Sally, you know how it is with partners. You cover for each other, stay close to each other; you'd even take a goddamn bullet for each other. But that doesn't mean you're always best friends, or even just friends. But you're fucking partners.

"Sarah was smart, tough, and relentless when it came to following through on stuff. I could always count on her. She covered my ass more than once in some very sticky situations.

"But she was like a locked room. Nothing personal ever came out, not about family or friends or even what sports teams she rooted for. And now and then, she'd just disappear. She'd always keep in touch by cell, but she'd never say what was going on.

The way partners do, I covered for her, no questions asked. I cut her some slack."

Sally asked, "But what about this Pine Barrens stuff, Eddie? I have to tell you, the place we found her? There's no more remote area in the whole state. After the anonymous call came in from the campground in Chatsworth, we spread the word. One of the State Forest Rangers, Paul Larsen from Atsion, was the guy who found her.

"I know Paul. I've worked with him. Paul Larsen could find a spitball in the Grand Canyon. He told me it took him three hours to find her body. I was there when he called the EMT guys and gave them directions to the scene. If it were anybody else but Paul, we'd still be looking for her. That's how remote it was. What the hell was she doing in there? Was it something you two were working on?"

"I'm beginning to think so."

Mulroney told Sally about the mugging of Rebecca Glass in Long Branch, and the subsequent investigation he and Sarah had conducted.

"Both of us were confident that it was a straightforward mugging. Bad luck for Professor Glass — in the wrong place at the wrong time. We found nothing at the site or in her background or history that suggested anything else. No buzz from any sources. Sarah really pressed that conclusion. I agreed. So did the DA.

"The only weird thing was that a few days after Glass's death, a colleague of hers, a smartass young English professor named Rossi, told Sarah about some paper Glass was supposed to present at an Archaeology Association meeting. Mount St. Benedict's was all in an uproar because they were afraid the possible contents might embarrass them, so they wanted him to look into it. I thought it was just academic bullshit.

"But then Rossi told Sarah that Glass had been doing a lot of research in the Pine Barrens related to the paper, that she'd gone there quite a bit. He told her he had a feeling that Glass might have found something in there. I wasn't buying it. But Sarah kept after it. She stayed in contact with this professor, even went up to Morristown to interview him. I still thought it was academic

238

bullshit. But everything kept coming back to the Pine Barrens. And Sarah wouldn't let it go."

Sally asked, "Was there anyone else Sarah talked to at Glass's college, anyone who might know more about what she or Glass was up to?"

"Yeah, when we were interviewing Glass's colleagues, we talked to a former State Trooper who Sarah knew. He's in the Criminal Justice Department there, got a real soft job. Maybe you heard of him, name is O'Bannon."

"*Martin* O'Bannon? Jesus, he has a history. And it's not good. He was a Captain, headed up the Casino Unit for a number of years. The guy was very tight with the casino people — too tight. Word was that he did special 'favors' for a guy named Murray Feldman, top dog in New Jersey gaming and a very bad guy."

"Yeah, I heard of Feldman. What else?"

"When things started to get hot for O'Bannon, he cut a deal with the State AG and took an early retirement. He had some big time law firm backing him, serious firepower. Craig knew him?"

"Yeah, pretty well, from the way they acted. What are you thinking, Sally?"

"Maybe you need to talk to this smartass young English professor again. I'm starting to see coincidences."

Mulroney looked at her. "I hate fucking coincidences."

239

Chapter 32

The two days before the Annual Dinner of the Loyal Sons of Cu Chulainn, Dom answered a knock on his door to find Detective Sergeant Edward Mulroney standing there. Mulroney did not badge him.

Dom said, "I know that in your line of work there's no such thing as a social call, so I assume this is a professional visit. Come in. Please have a seat, while I call my lawyer."

"Don't bother. This isn't professional; it's strictly personal. I figure you've heard or read about the death of Sarah Craig. I know you talked to her several times. I want to know why Sarah was in the fucking Pine Barrens. I think it was related somehow to this Rebecca Glass business, and I want you to tell me whatever you know, or even think, about what led her there. All of it is off the record, Rossi. You have my word. I just need to know."

A surprised Dom took a closer look at Mulroney. His face was slack and pale, his eyes were grim, his posture was slouched. Sarah's death was weighing heavily on him.

"Would you care for coffee or a drink, Detective?"

"Drink."

While Mulroney settled himself in a chair in the small living room, Dom brought out a bottle of Scotch and two glasses. He poured a drink for Mulroney, handed it to him, and then one for himself. There was no toast; they just drank.

Mulroney said, "A man's partner gets killed, he should do something about it. It doesn't matter what you thought of her or how you got along. She was your partner. I need to know what went down. Talk to me."

"I don't particularly trust you. So, for the record, you should understand that this has nothing to do with facts or evidence. It's just a kind of story."

"Understood. Talk to me."

"When Sarah Craig was fifteen years old, Martin O'Bannon, who was then a patrolman in her hometown, helped her get

240

through a brutally ugly and horrible situation — the murder of her father, at which she was present. The actual circumstances are cloudy as to what she actually saw, or what she did. But it's very likely that her father had been sexually abusing her. As a result of both of these traumas, she developed profound emotional and psychological problems, the kinds of problems that require years of therapy. She never got it.

"I also believe that Sarah and O'Bannon became intimate, very early on. Probably when she was fifteen. Over the years, she did favors for him, illegal favors — willingly, even eagerly. She even came to enjoy it. The favors eventually included capital crimes. Maybe it was some kind of way to validate her self-worth or maintain his approval. I don't know. But whatever and whenever he asked, she delivered — for years."

Dom could see that Mulroney's eyes were bleak, sad, sickened.

"Jesus, O'Bannon got her into that? He used her to do that, from when she was a kid?"

"Yes. But there's more to the story. O'Bannon is very heavy into a powerful and influential fraternal organization headed by a guy named Brian Shaughnessy, who has connections all over the Northeast. Rebecca Glass learned something in the Pine Barrens about the organization, something that could destroy them. They could not and cannot allow Glass's research to come to light. So O'Bannon had Sarah kill Glass and her partner, Diana Bennington. Then he told Sarah to do him another favor, in the Pine Barrens — get rid of me and a colleague of mine because we were also looking into the matter. But the snakes got in the way.

"Bottom line? I believe Martin O'Bannon essentially destroyed Sarah's life under the guise of helping her. She was likely mentally disturbed, she was certainly a killer — but she was also a victim, O'Bannon's victim. But like I said, this is just a story."

Mulroney was silent for a while. Dom thought he looked like man with no good choices, a man resigned to some kind of inevitable pain.

Mulroney put his face in his hands. "Maybe if I'd known her better...got to understand her. Maybe I could have helped..."

Dom poured more Scotch into Mulroney's glass; as he did he recalled a line from Longfellow: *"Every man has a sorrow of which the world knows not."*

Mulroney finished off the rest of his drink. He nodded his thanks, stood up, and looked at Dom.

"Rossi, you and I will never be friends. And I don't begin to understand how you fucking academic people even think or what your world is like. But you found out a hell of lot in a very short time. That's impressive. I owe you. Big time. So the story stays between you and me, always. But you should know I'm not through with this. Or with fucking Martin O'Bannon. Thanks for the drinks."

As Mulroney headed back to Freehold, he came to a decision about Martin O'Bannon. Instead of continuing to Freehold, he picked up the Garden State Parkway and drove south towards Atlantic City, where he would talk to Murray Feldman — who, as Sally Menendez had said, was a very bad guy.

***

When Martin O'Bannon learned of the death of Sarah Craig, he did not feel sadness, or responsibility, or remorse. He felt inconvenienced. And, for the first time, worried. This 'proof' Rossi had talked about, was it real? And if so, what was it?

If Sarah had killed Rossi and his girlfriend like the plan called for, the next few days would be so much easier. But now, given Sarah's fuck up, O'Bannon knew that Brian Shaughnessy would be shitting his expensively tailored pants and would demand that O'Bannon end this Rossi crap immediately — himself.

O'Bannon had no problem with that; he was in fact looking forward to it. As the saying goes, every dark cloud... The issue was where and how he could best take out Rossi and the girl.

O'Bannon had to assume that Rossi had now made the connection between him and Sarah. That meant that Rossi and the girl would expect him to come after them. They'd try to hide out somewhere. O'Bannon wasn't about to waste a shitload of time trying to figure out where. But hr also understood Rossi well enough by now to know that the fucking kid wouldn't let it go. He would try something. The trick was figuring out what and when.

242

Then O'Bannon had a hunch. And it felt perfect. The Annual Dinner of the Loyal Sons of Cu Chulainn — that smug, fucking Rossi wouldn't be able to resist it. He'd want to play in the big leagues, and that would get him dead.

***

Mid-morning on the day of the Loyal Sons' Dinner, Dom went to Granny Pearl's to pick up Lacey. Granny peered out the door at him, Lacey standing behind her. Granny recognized him from Stick's description, then put away her pump action Remington and let him in.

"My, my, look how my baby girl do light up when she see you! Just like Fontaine say. You got time for tea, child, or you got to do some business?"

Dom looked at Lacey. "Fontaine?"

Lacey said, "Don't ask."

As Dom entered, he handed a bouquet of fresh cut flowers to Granny Pearl. "Thank you, Granny Pearl, for taking such good care of Lacey. We do have some business to do now, but we'd be pleased to thank you properly on another occasion."

Granny said, "Aren't you the gentleman! Go take care your business, child, and we'll celebrate another time. And you be real good to my baby girl."

Granny gave Lacey a big hug and a kiss. "We had us a real good time, baby girl! You a good listener. I got more stories to tell, so you come back soon."

As they got into Dom's car, Lacey said, "Granny really is a genuine pearl. What a remarkable little lady! But what now, Dom? Where are we going?"

"I got us a room at the Madison Hotel, early check-in. I brought a change of clothes and some girlie things for you, plus your laptop and an extra flash drive."

Lacey looked at him. "Excuse me, but the fertilizer is hitting the ventilator, the dinner is tonight, O'Bannon and Shaughnessy are no doubt after us and want to kill us, and you got us a hotel room? I appreciate your devotion, and your passion, but don't we have other things to do?"

"We do indeed. I'll explain on the way. You're going to be a very busy girl."

As he drove, Dom told Lacey about his plans for the Dinner.

"Kate gave me the agenda. First there's an hour or so of cocktails and hors d'oeuvres, during which everyone networks and gets a little buzzed and socializes. Then the guests are called into the main dining room and sit at their assigned tables, the Chaplain offers a blessing, and the President, our pal Brian Shaughnessy, introduces everyone on the dais, a few dignitaries in the audience, and turns it over to the Vice President for more remarks. Then Shaughnessy comes back and presents the Award.

"Prior to the actual presentation and acceptance of the award, there's a several minute video celebrating the career and accomplishments of the honoree. Then, the honoree accepts the award, makes his acceptance speech, and everyone digs in to dinner and more drinks. The honoree circles the room accepting kudos and congratulations from the assembled guests. And in William Shane's case, campaigns for governor."

"But that's not how it's going to work out, is it?"

"Not even close. Here's the plan...."

Dom explained what he needed her to do. Lacey nodded and said, "Got it. I can do all that right from the room. What else?"

"I'll do my thing behind the scenes. Then we get the hell out of there before Brian Shaughnessy, Martin O'Bannon and every Loyal Son in the whole goddamn chapter come after us. I have to warn you, Lace, it could get ugly in there."

Her look was fierce. "Not much of it has been pretty so far. Remember those babies — and Rebecca and Diana. Like Abner said, this can't stand."

***

Gianni ushered Edward Mulroney into the office of Murray Feldman, who was standing at the window looking down on the famous Atlantic City boardwalk. Gianni went and stood unobtrusively to the side, watching closely.

His back to Mulroney, Feldman said, "I don't normally accept appointments on such short notice. But I am aware of your work for the Monmouth County Prosecutor's Office, Homicide Division. You have a reputation for diligence."

Then Feldman turned and looked interestedly at Mulroney. "I'm curious as to what business you believe we have to conduct."

Mulroney had seen a lot of so-called tough guys over the years and hadn't been impressed or intimidated by any of them. But this small, dapper, seventy-something year-old man looking so intensely at him was something else. This guy was the real deal.

"Mr. Feldman, I decided to reach out to you on a matter that may benefit both of us. I'll come right to the point. Next year, I will have put in twenty-five years with the cops. I'm eligible for retirement, and I'm ready for it. Frankly, sir, in my line of work, all we ever encounter is death and ugliness. I'm tired of it."

Feldman nodded. "It's understandable. Life is often like that. Where do I fit in?"

"After retirement, I'd like to get into private security consulting, in the casino industry. But I don't want to be with just any casino. Most casinos here in AC are losing money hand over fist, and they're becoming swamps. But the Golden Dream always makes money and always retains its class. That appeals to me. I'm wondering if you think there might be a place at the Golden Dream for a man with my skills and experience."

Feldman looked closely at Mulroney. "There may be. But how exactly is that to my advantage. I am, after all, not an employment agency. What can you offer?"

Mulroney leaned forward in his chair. "I've been hearing things that may be of interest to you. Word around the Prosecutor's Office is that a former State Trooper, with whom I believe you are acquainted, is coming under very close scrutiny; in fact, serious charges, capital charges, may be leveled against him.

"In an attempt to make a deal and avoid prosecution, the former Trooper has offered to reveal certain...business dealings he had with you over the years. He's promising that these business dealings will prove to be awkward for you, both personally and professionally. Basically, he's offered to throw you under the bus, Mr. Feldman."

"Are you willing to give me the name of this individual, Detective Mulroney?"

"His name is Martin O'Bannon."

Feldman glanced over at Gianni, who nodded in understanding. Feldman then said to Mulroney, "I genuinely appreciate the consideration, Detective. And upon your retirement, please feel free to contact me. A man with your skills, and insight, would be a welcome addition to our security team." They shook hands.

After Mulroney left, Feldman said, "Gianni, we have built our success on two qualities — boldness and prudence. I believe prudence in this matter requires that we preclude any potential awkwardness with regard to Martin O'Bannon."

"I'll see to it, Mr. Feldman."

Chapter 33

Since the Loyal Sons of Cu Chulainn was such a powerful and prestigious organization, an invitation to the annual dinner was considered a mark of exceptional status. Some very heavy hitters in business, industry, politics and the professions from all over the Northeast were eager to attend. Local, statewide, and even New York-based media gave the affair blanket coverage. They were all gathered at the Madison Hotel.

The elegant, Georgian-style Madison Hotel adjoins Rod's Steak and Seafood Grille, just east of Morristown in the small but well-to-do community of Convent Station. Gracious and charming, the Madison is particularly skilled at hosting private affairs, weddings, corporate meetings and social functions, and offers excellent facilities and award-winning cuisine. The Loyal Sons of Cu Chulainn had been holding their Annual Dinner there for some fifteen years. The dinner was traditionally held in the Glynallan Ballroom, which could host the Loyal Sons' three hundred-fifty members and guests comfortably and graciously.

Among its many excellent services, the Madison also offered its own audio-visual team, should they be needed. Earlier in the day, longtime and super-efficient catering manager, Richard Sweeney, received a call regarding the A-V requirements.

Dom, calling from his cell said, "Mr. Sweeney, this is Declan Moran, I'm an assistant to Loyal Sons Vice President Aidan Cavanaugh. Mr. Cavanaugh asked me to call and let you know that audio-visual support — beyond setting up the equipment in the small projection room off the Glynallan Ballroom — will not be required this year. We'll be using an outside firm called North Jersey A-V Associates, who are friends of the VP. They will have identification. I will personally be assisting them."

The ever-gracious Richard replied, "Well, that's certainly a last minute change, Mr. Moran. But it's no problem. Do you require a copy of the presentation material?"

"We are well equipped, sir, thank you,"

"Fine. If you need any help, my team will be more than happy to provide it. Otherwise, they'll just stay out of your way. Enjoy your evening."

Also taking place at the Madison that evening was a wedding reception for two hundred guests in the Conservatory, and the 25th Reunion of the Lewis Morris Preparatory School Class of 1991, one hundred of whose graduates were gathering in the Victorian Suite. And of course, there was the usual robust crowd at Rod's. Cars were pulling into and out of the parking lot, people were hurrying from one venue to another; it was a typically busy night.

Yet, despite the hundreds of guests eagerly hurrying to and from their respective venues, two very large young men in the lobby, one black, one white, could not help but stand out. Both were dressed in navy blue blazers, charcoal gray slacks, and white Oxford cloth button-down shirts adorned with maroon and blue striped ties.

Pinky Plucinski said, "'Tay, you think this knot is all right? I always have trouble with these things."

"I'm pretty sure no one's noticing the knot, Pinkster."

Dontay Robinson checked out the sign in the lobby listing the schedule and locations of the evening's events. Then he nodded to Pinky and they headed down one of the corridors.

Dontay said, "Okay, Pink, we head to the A-V control room behind the Glynallan Ballroom. Dr. Dom's meeting us there."

Prior to arriving in the Madison lobby, Dontay and Pinky had stopped in room 337, where Lacey, who was working furiously on her laptop, had prepared two plastic pin-on badges bearing photos of her two co-conspirators, a quickly designed logo, and the words, "North Jersey A-V Associates, Inc."

Lacey looked at them and said, "You two characters look about as much like A-V technicians as I look like Rihanna. Still, these badges should buy you enough time to let Dom do what he needs to do. Good luck, guys."

Dontay and Pinky made their way to the projection room serving the Glynallan Ballroom. Dom was already there, dressed similarly to the others.

"Okay, what you guys do is stand outside this door and dissuade anyone from entering. After a while, you'll probably

248

hear all kinds of ruckus coming from the ballroom. Don't worry about it. But then when I come out, we all take off. You guys head for your car, and I'll meet Lacey in the parking lot. She will have done her job and then checked out of the room. Any questions?"

Pinky said, "You mean 'dissuade' like we convince them not to come in here and bother you?"

Dom reached up and patted Pinky on the shoulder. "Pinky, you're all over this."

Dontay said, "We're cool, Doc. Sharelle's picking us up right outside Rod's. Then we're all heading back to the campus Pub. Call us and let us know how it goes."

Dom said, "If all goes as planned, you'll hear about it even before I call. Good luck guys, and thanks."

Inside the Glynallan Ballroom, guests had already arrived, the men in conservative, semi-formal attire, the few women in cocktail dresses or elegant pantsuits; Catholic clergy were in their black suits and Roman collars, and Bishop Regan of the Diocese of Trenton, was in his black cassock with purple sash and skullcap.

The officers of the Loyal Sons of Cu Chulainn were resplendent in their kilts, with Brian Boru dinner jackets and vests, sporran, kilt hose and garters, and patent leather shoes. Each officer wore the colors and trappings associated with his clan — or the closest he could come. Brian Shaughnessy, who dearly loved dressing in this manner, also wore his clan cufflinks, and pinned to his blouse was a large silver brooch boasting a unicorn in front of a castle.

The members and their guests were happily wolfing down cocktails and hors d'oeuvres, networking, gossiping, and speculating on Bill Shane's acceptance speech and his big announcement.

Among the guests, stunning in a silver gray pantsuit, her silver hair up in a bun and held by an emerald clasp, was Fiona Shane. She sipped a superb Puligny Montrachet and looked around the room, nodding and waving at the many familiar faces, chatting confidently with everyone who approached her. William was at her side. She felt more than ever that he was a lock for Governor. But she would be the real power behind the throne.

249

Martin O'Bannon was stood near one of the busy bars, a glass of Black Bush in hand, looking around the room for any signs of Rossi or the girl and any signs of trouble. O'Bannon had spoken earlier with three of the younger members of the Loyal Sons, men in their thirties, and told them also to be alert for anything unusual. He did not go into any more detail than to explain that he had heard rumors of certain elements, possibly Italian, threatening to embarrass the Loyal Sons on their big night. They were not strictly to act as security, but O'Bannon told them to be ready to step in if needed.

While Dontay and Pinky stood in front of the door to the small A-V room, Dom, who had slipped inside earlier, took stock of the equipment. It was all set up and ready to go. There was even a way to lock the door from the inside. He could keep an eye on the proceedings in the Glynallan Ballroom through the A-V room's small, tinted glass window. Still, it was risky and all a matter of timing. If Lacey let slip the dogs of war too early, everything would be blown; if she did it too late, it would have less impact. Dom sat and waited; he figured he had about fifteen minutes.

Brain Shaughnessy, surrounded by admirers and flatterers, was in a splendid mood. It was all coming together perfectly — William's acceptance speech would be covered by press from all over the northeast, his election to the governorship would be nearly a foregone conclusion, and Shaughnessy himself would reap financial rewards for years to come. Fiona would likely have less time for him, but, Shaughnessy thought, what time remained would be well spent. Fiona was sexually voracious.

The only hovering dark cloud was Rossi. Shaughnessy was annoyed that Martin O'Bannon had not fully put that issue to rest. Still, O'Bannon handled the Edward Manning situation beautifully. And he had always come through in the past. There was no reason to think he couldn't handle that little prick Rossi. But that was for later. Now, Shaughnessy would enjoy the evening and the virtual coronation of William Shane.

A somewhat anxious, yet excited Kate Culhane was nursing a vodka martini and chatting with retired Judge Robert Clark.

Judge Clark said, "You know, the older I get, the more tedious and dull these events become. They seem to have an endless sameness about them. And then I end up eating and drinking too

250

much."

Kate smiled and replied, "Perhaps tonight will be an exception, Judge."

"One can only hope, Kate, one can only hope."

Dom continued to watch from inside the A-V room as the Loyal Sons and their guests attacked the hors d'oeuvres and the drinks. Then, Loyal Sons Vice President Aidan Cavanaugh called everyone to their tables.

Once everyone was seated, Cavanaugh introduced Father Sean Gilhooley, the Chaplain of the Loyal Sons of Cu Chulainn, who gave the blessing. Father Gilhooley was born in County Roscommon but came to America at the age of fourteen months. Somehow, he managed to retain his brogue, which was more in evidence on occasions such as this. He was the pastor of an upscale parish in Morris Township and, thanks to his connection to the Loyal Sons, lived quite well for a man whose vows, in addition to celibacy and obedience, included poverty. Father Gilhooley gave the blessing, being sure to include a moment of silence in memory of the late, unfortunate Edward Manning. Following the blessing, everyone said the Pledge of Allegiance to the Flag.

Then, Cavanaugh introduced Brian Shaughnessy. The applause was loud and sustained, as Shaughnessy took to the podium.

Shaughnessy, basking in the reception, said, "Good evening everyone, and let me add my welcome to Aidan's. I must say that this wonderful annual tradition is even more auspicious tonight, graced as we are by the presence of a number of particularly notable individuals, whose lives, careers and, most importantly, whose values reflect the very best of the Irish experience in America."

Shaughnessy went on to introduce those seated on the dais — Bishop Regan; the officers of the Loyal Sons, including Sergeant-at-Arms Martin O'Bannon; a member of the Board of Freeholders of Morris County; a former Republican congressman; several previous Loyal Son of the Year Award-winners; Felix Delaney from Mount St. Benedict University; and of course Fiona Cramer Shane, whose welcome was particularly warm. Then, Shaughnessy turned to the main business of the evening, the presentation of the Loyal Son of the Year Award.

"This year's honoree, even at a relatively young age, has made impressive contributions to our community and to our heritage..."

As Shaughnessy continued to extol the virtues of William Shane, Dom's cell phone vibrated in his pocket. It was a text from Lacey. *Done. Go get 'em!*

Dom texted back, *Once more unto the breach, dear friends....*

Dom plugged the flash drive into the computer, then waited until Brian Shaughnessy said, "And now, so that we all might get to know better the life and background of our honoree, please watch the screens nearest to you."

Dom hit a button and in each of the four corners of the ballroom, large video screens slid silently down from the ceiling. Dom then hit the enter key and the screens flickered once, then a visual of an old woman appeared and a voice was heard...

"I am Caitlin Killeen. I was but sixteen years old, just turned. My family in County Tipperary was dirt poor, nine of us there were. I was the eldest child. I was sent to America..."

The Loyal Sons and guests were perplexed but also intrigued by the start of this seemingly non-traditional biographical video. While beginning with an honoree's family history, which this must be, was a frequent occurrence, this old woman looked unusually haggard and worn. Obviously, the crowd thought, it was to show William Shane's humble family background. But how did the name Killeen fit in?

Brian Shaughnessy, who had previewed and approved the original video, was utterly surprised by this version. Where had it come from? Who had created it?

"There was a rich family would take me in, cleaning, washing, cooking. They'd been from Tipperary some generations before, Ballyporeen, it was...

Shaughnessy began to experience increasing anxiety.

"When I came to America, they took me to their house in the place called New Jersey, to a grand house by the ocean in the village of Spring Lake..."

Shaughnessy turned to Aidan Cavanaugh. "What the hell is this? We didn't authorize this."

"I have no idea, Brian. It just appeared...I have no idea."

"The master was a man of the law, a vigorous man, powerful

252

and handsome in his middle years. The kind of man who needs a woman, who wants a woman, often. Soon the woman was me."

The audience began to feel unsettled, to squirm in their seats. What was this all about? Who was this woman? This was nothing like previous biographical videos. It was very discomfiting.

On the dais, Fiona Shane gazed in shock upon the woman in the video who was her biological mother. She then shot a look at Brian Shaughnessy. It clearly said, *What the fuck is going on? Do something!*

Shaughnessy leaned over to O'Bannon, "Stop this! Stop it now!"

O'Bannon jumped up from the dais and hurried over to the three men whom he had spoken with earlier. "The A-V- room, get in there and put an end to this shit. Now!'"

"But then...then I became with child, his child. I told him. And he sent me away. He sent me to this place in the woods, among the sand, among the pines."

The three men ran to the projection room but pulled up short when they were confronted with Dontay and Pinky.

Pinky, his massive arms folded across his chest, took a step towards them and said, "Excuse me, but you are dissuaded from entering the projection room."

The three just stood there and looked at each other. Then one of them, who considered himself a tough guy, took a step forward. He said, "Get the fuck..."

Pinky grabbed him by the throat and lifted him off the ground, effortlessly.

Dontay said to the guy, "You really do not want to start this, my man. My good friend here and I live for this shit. It's best that you leave — now."

Red-faced and terrified, the man nodded. Pinky lowered him the floor. The guy turned and hurried the hell out of there, the others right behind.

Back in the ballroom, guests watched the screen, both appalled and fascinated as the testimony of Caitlin Killeen continued.

"There were others such as me, with child, done in by rich or powerful men, Irish men. When a woman — a daughter, a servant, a mistress — became with child out of wedlock, they sent her to the Cloister. The nuns were cruel, beating and berating

us, calling us whores and harlots and evil fallen women. But it was the babes who suffered most, the babes."

A now-panicked Shaughnessy stood up at the dais and said, "Friends, ladies and gentlemen, this...this video is not our honoree's. I have no idea where it came from. It's all a terrible mistake! Please ignore this –"

"If one such as me gave birth to a beautiful healthy babe, it was adopted. If by chance and ill fortune the babe was not healthy, or was marked, or was of brown skin, they left them to die. The sisters left them out to die. And made us bury them, the babes, among the dead leaves and weeds and ivy."

The audience was transfixed by the video, by what they were hearing, by the horrors perpetrated on the infants. The people on the dais looked at Brian Shaughnessy not knowing how to react or what to do.

Shaughnessy started shouting, "This is a travesty! It's all lies! Lies!"

"And it was all because of him, because of Liam. It was Liam Shaughnessy done this to me."

Upon hearing this, the audience gave out a collective gasp. Assorted news media covering the dinner rushed towards Shaughnessy en masse, shoving cameras and microphones in his face and bombarding him with questions.

"Who is she, Mr. Shaughnessy?" "Is it true about your father?" "Were you aware of the nuns leaving infants to die?" "What does this have to with William Shane?" "Did Bishop Regan and the Diocese know of this?" "What's the role of the Loyal Sons?"

On and on it went. A now frantic Brian Shaughnessy pushed through the crowd and ran into men's room, where he vomited violently. Bishop Regan's personal secretary rushed to his side and very nearly lifted him out of his chair to pilot him from the room.

Martin O'Bannon struggled to get to the projection room, but there was such confusion he could not get through the crowd.

While chaos was ensuing, Dom hit the replay button then slipped out of the projection room, locking the door behind him. He said to Dontay and Pinky, "Let's move. Through the lobby then out to the parking lot. I have to stop at the front desk. Then

I'll be right behind you."

Dontay and Pinky served as downfield blockers, with Dom right behind them, as they pushed their way through the confused crowd and headed out of the ballroom, rushing down the corridors and out into the lobby. Dom hurried over to the Concierge desk and handed three manila envelopes to the young woman staffing it.

"Please be sure Mr. Brian Shaughnessy receives this. The second copy is for Ms. Fiona Shane; the third is for William Shane. It's vitally important. Thank you."

They hit the parking lot, and Sharelle immediately pulled up. Dontay and Pinky jumped into her car. Dom waited only a few seconds until Lacey pulled up in his CRV.

As he got into the car, Lacey said, "As one shepherd said to the other, let's get the flock out of here." She stepped on the gas and roared out of the Madison's parking lot.

Inside the Glynallan Ballroom, pandemonium reigned — cell phones started buzzing, texts messages were flying, guests didn't know where to look first. They were getting messages and calls about the video from seemingly everyone they ever knew. Lacey had flooded as many social media outlets as possible — YouTube, Facebook, Pinterest, Instagram, Twitter, Tumblr, whatever she could access. She had posted not only the video itself, but all of Rebecca's supporting material, as well. It was all out there, and it was generating a tsunami of response and reaction.

As for the envelopes to be given to Shaughnessy, Fiona, and William Shane, their contents were stunning.

Each envelope contained a scientific chart, whose four horizontal headings read "DNA Marker, Mother, Child, Alleged Father." The chart also had a vertical column listing "A" as Fiona Shane, "B" as William Shane, and "C" as Brian Shaughnessy; next to each name was a list of genetic markers.

A DNA test typically checks sixteen genetic markers that are highly differential between individuals. Each DNA marker contains two alleles, one inherited from the biological mother and the other from the biological father. A DNA paternity test compares the sizes of these markers between an alleged father, the mother, and the child.

Each marker is assigned a Paternity Index, a marker of how powerfully each match indicates paternity. This information is then used to generate a Combined Paternity Index (CPI), which indicates the overall probability of an individual being the biological father of the tested child.

The CPI for Brian Shaughnessy being the biological father of William Shane showed 99.9% probability that he was the father, and 0% probability that he was not.

Also included in each envelope was a typed note.

It is a wise child that knows its own father (Homer, *The Odyssey*). In this case, however, such knowledge makes for an awkward family dynamic and a fatally flawed candidate. Have a nice life.

None of this was admissible in a court of law, as Kate Culhane had explained. But as Dom told Lacey, "It'll sure shake the shit out of Shaughnessy and Fiona."

Chapter 34

Martin O'Bannon shoved and struggled and cursed his way through the crowd and out to the parking lot, where he was caught up among hundreds of people pouring out of the hotel, rushing to their cars or trying to hail a parking valet, frantically working their cell phones, gossiping animatedly in groups large and small, and trying to figure out what the hell they had just experienced.

An incensed, frustrated O'Bannon looked around frantically for Rossi, planning to beat the shit out of him when he found him and hopefully leave him for dead. Then a voice from across parking lot called out, "O'Bannon! Over here! I saw him go."

It was Gianni, Feldman's man. He was standing outside of a black Mercedes, waving to O'Bannon. "I saw him go. Come on!"

O'Bannon ran over to the Mercedes. Gianni opened the passenger door and O'Bannon climbed in.

O'Bannon asked, "What are you doing here? How the hell do you know him?"

"Mr. Feldman sent me. Told me that since that fire thing didn't work out, you might need help. Buckle up, we'll go after him."

O'Bannon hesitated then fastened his seat belt. As he was doing so, Gianni leaned across him and pointed out the passenger side window.

"Look! He came back!"

O'Bannon turned his head to look out the window. That was when Gianni grabbed him by the head and jaw and violently twisted O'Bannon's head first to the left, then to the right, then back to the left again, thereby breaking O'Bannon's neck and killing him nearly instantly. With a dead O'Bannon slumped in his seat, Gianni drove slowly and carefully out of the parking lot.

One of the things that Murray Feldman appreciated about Gianni, in addition to his unswerving loyalty and efficiency, was that Gianni had a sense of propriety. Thus, when disposing of O'Bannon's body, Gianni chose not simply to dump it in the

Madison's parking lot and further ruin everyone's evening, or on the nearby campus of the College of St. Elizabeth, where students would certainly find it disturbing. Instead, he drove several miles across Morristown to the Spring Brook Country Club.

The layout of the beautiful Spring Brook golf course boasts three consecutive par-3 holes bridging the front nine and back nine and surrounding Armstrong Pond. This challenging section is known as "the Gauntlet." On the morning following the demise of Martin O'Bannon, the groundskeepers at Spring Brook discovered a body in the left front sand trap of the par-3 tenth hole. It was near a willow tree, some thirty feet from the pin. Fortunately, no one had teed off yet, so the course was empty.

However, by the time the police arrived and began their investigation, play had been delayed considerably and was later cancelled for the day, much to the dismay and annoyance of the club's members.

As this was all taking place, Gianni was back home at the Golden Dream, reporting to a very pleased Murray Feldman, who said, "It always pays to be prudent, Gianni. Very nicely done. Thank you."

* * *

Two days later, the media frenzy that had begun the evening of the Loyal Sons Annual Dinner showed no signs of abating. Indeed, it seemed to be gathering even more momentum, as police investigating O'Bannon's murder interviewed everyone in attendance at the dinner, as well as those who had been at the other affairs held at the Madison that evening.

This together with the Caitlin Killeen video having gone viral resulted in endless news reports, speculation, and gossip regarding the Cloister of St. Keira, the activities of the Loyal Sons, Holy Innocents Orphanage, the Diocese of Trenton, and in particular the roles of Liam and Brian Shaughnessy in the debacle.

Much had transpired in two days — none of it good for the Loyal Sons or for Brian Shaughnessy, Fiona Shane or William Shane and assorted other participants. Consequently, people began to take action.

The "Partners" in Shaughnessy and Partners, absent Brian Shaughnessy, met in a private room upstairs at the Grand Café to

258

determine a way to deal with the ongoing controversy and expanding disgrace.

The most senior partner, Allan Quinn, a tall, elegantly slender man in his late fifties, said to the others, "Our futures, and our fortunes, are under direct threat. They depend on what we decide here today. To be crude but frank, this shit storm will not simply blow over. We must end it. I want to hear from each of you — I want an opinion and a suggestion. Following a general discussion, we will vote on a resolution. Then, we will act upon it."

The opinions were consistent; the resolution was unanimous: the firm as currently constituted would be dissolved; a new firm consisting of the eight Partners would be formed; each Partner would bring with him as many existing clients as possible; all Partners who currently belonged to the Loyal Sons of Cu Chulainn would immediately terminate their association with the organization; finally, Brian Shaughnessy would have no association with the new firm or with any of the partners, professionally, financially, or personally.

The new firm would be known as Solon Legal Associates, Inc., after the great Athenian lawmaker and statesman. The name would help distance the firm from any taint of scandal and disgrace wrought by their previous association with Brian Shaughnessy.

***

The Committee on Canonical Affairs and Church Governance of the United States Conference of Catholic Bishops met in emergency session to discuss the situation generally, and the impact on the Diocese of Trenton specifically. At the heart of the issue was the culpability of the Church and the Diocese in the deaths of the infants of St. Keira's. Essentially, it was a matter of 'who knew what and when did they know it?'

While there was the usual "protect the Church at all costs" mentality, it was decided that Bishop Regan had to be sacrificed and some kind of gesture should be made, public relations-wise. The Committee therefore recalled Monsignor Lawrence Mancini from his parish in Camden, and appointed him Bishop of Trenton. Bishop Regan was demoted to Monsignor and exiled to Mancini's poverty-stricken Camden parish, Our Lady of Tears.

259

***

University presidents, given their nearly unending responsibilities, are notoriously time-deprived. Father John Whelan was no exception; indeed, he proved the rule. But as busy as Father Jack was, he always found the time to say his daily Breviary, the collection of psalms, prayers, and hymns required to recite the Holy Office. It was his habit to do so while walking leisurely, and alone, around the campus pond. Everyone at Mount St. Ben's knew this was his special time and left him in peace — except, on this occasion, for Dominic Rossi.

"Father Jack, I apologize for disturbing you, but we have to talk."

Father Jack looked up from his Breviary, at first startled. "Oh, Dominic, how are you? You look troubled. What's on your mind?"

And then Dom told him the story, beginning with the charge he received from Delaney and Shaughnessy to try to track Rebecca's research protocol and learn if there were anything in her phantom paper that might prove damaging to the university; he explained about his trips to Maryland and Boston and into the Pine Barrens; he concluded with an explanation of what Rebecca had learned, and he described the contents of the Caitlin Killeen video.

He did not mention Sarah Craig by name, though he told Father Jack of the murder of Diana Bennington; nor did he reveal the incestuous relationship between Brian Shaughnessy and Fiona Cramer Shane that resulted in the birth of William Shane. He focused strictly on those matters that could have an impact on Mount St. Ben's. Then he handed a copy of Rebecca's presentation to Father Jack.

"Father, all I ask is that you take a look at this, and then decide for yourself how to proceed with respect to Mount St. Ben's."

Father Jack viewed the video that afternoon. The following day, he called together the members of the Board of Trustees of Mount St. Benedict University, absent their president, Brian Shaughnessy, and without the presence of Felix Delaney. They met in the Trustees Board Room in Old Main. Although all the Board members were prominent people in a variety of fields, this Cloister of St. Keira's business was beyond their experience.

260

Appalled and shocked, they looked to Father Jack for guidance.

Father Jack met each person's gaze and said, "The responsibility for this debacle ultimately resides with me. I saw myself as a fundraiser, a kind of glad hander. I wanted to grow the reputation and, even more, the endowment of this great university. I did not become sufficiently involved with the most important business of the university — our students and our faculty and how they operate and interact.

"As a result, Brian Shaughnessy, Martin O'Bannon and Felix Delaney took matters into their own hands, for their own purposes. This is especially true with respect to the tragic death of our colleague Rebecca Glass. What they did could have resulted in the end of Mount St. Benedict University, certainly of its reputation. I assure you, all of that changes now.

"First, effective immediately, Felix Delaney is no longer Provost of this University. It will be my pleasure to inform him, personally. Second, I urge the Board to vote to dismiss Brian Shaughnessy as President, also effective immediately. If he tries to contest it, we will fight him in the most vigorous manner possible, consistent with our university by-laws. Third, while legal matters pertaining to the death of Rebecca Glass and the possible involvement of the late Martin O'Bannon are the province of the police, the Prosecutor's Office, and the courts, we at Mount St. Benedict's will provide any assistance and answer any questions the authorities may have. It will be painful and embarrassing. But our first responsibility is to the truth. That is how we best serve our students and our university."

The Board of Trustees concurred. Brain Shaughnessy was voted out as President, unanimously.

***

On the evening of the disastrous Loyal Sons dinner, William Shane had read the contents of the envelope left at the Concierge desk. He had immediately called Marcy. She arrived within ten minutes from her apartment in nearby Florham Park to find him distraught — a most un-Bill like demeanor. He was always composed, in control. Then she read the contents of the envelope, placed her arms around him, and pulled him close.

"I'm with you, Bill, now, always, and through whatever happens. This changes things — in your life, in my life and the

261

whole damn future. But I'm with you."

The following day, Bill and Marcy went to see Fiona.

In Fiona's den, while she attacked her fourth glass of wine, a distraught, hollow-eyed Bill said, "You've killed any hope of a future for me. I'm through. I resigned my position in the Prosecutor's Office. There's no run for governor. I can't live with what you in your arrogance and selfishness have inflicted upon me, now that I see what you really are. I've been blind. My whole life is a lie!

"Brian Shaughnessy? My real father is Brian Shaughnessy? So that's why all these years he's been so close by? I always thought he was just some kind of confidant. And now I learn this! How dare you preach to me about family values! Jesus Christ, what else haven't you told me about your famous, heroic, award-winning life? What other garbage is there to discover about you and Brian Shaughnessy?"

A hard-eyed Fiona said, "You won't dare leave me. And you certainly can't go off with this...this Negro woman. Where will you go? You're nothing without me."

It was Marcy Washington who answered. "We're moving to St. Croix. I have family there. We've already registered Bill with the Supreme Court of the United States Virgin Islands. He'll be taking the Bar Exam on July 27th. My Dad has arranged for Bill to join a firm there until he can start his own practice. They welcome diverse couples in the USVI. It's a beautiful and long-standing tradition."

Fiona screamed at her son, "She's turned you against me! This black bitch has turned you against me! What happens to me? What about my needs?"

William Shane looked at her for several moments. "You've always seen to your own needs very well. But you've always been blind to the needs of others, mine included. This is payback time. Good-bye."

After they they'd left, Fiona Shane sat there, drinking her wine, facing her future. It was clear what lay ahead — derision, scorn, shame. The true nature of her relationship with Brian Shaughnessy would inevitably get out. Her career in New Jersey pharmaceuticals would be over. There was nowhere to go, no escape from what lay ahead — except, ironically, from whence she came...

***

Brian Shaughnessy — having learned of the decisions made by his partners and by Mount St. Benedict University, and having been overwhelmed by the savage nature of the media coverage surrounding the Loyal Sons dinner and the activities of the Cloister of St. Keira — sat alone at the large oak table in the ceremonial chamber of the Loyal Sons of Cu Chulainn. He was dressed in his ceremonial kilt and the accompanying trappings he usually wore on the Loyal Sons most formal occasions. He sipped from a glass of Black Bush Irish whisky and gazed upon the heraldic tapestries and wall hangings that adorned the chamber.

It had all come apart, the firm, the Loyal Sons, the university, his legacy, his life. Worse, it was not just gone; the sordid debris and detritus would haunt him as long as he lived. It was Dominic Rossi who had brought this upon him — Rossi, a young punk whom Shaughnessy had disparaged as just another arrogant, lightweight academic.

Brian Shaughnessy took another sip of the Black Bush — it was warm and sweet; it tasted of triumph, power, and success. None of which he could expect to experience ever again. All the things that had given meaning and substance to his life were gone. Soon, inevitably, his relationship to Fiona would also become known — and become a source of derision and disgust.

Brian Shaughnessy recalled the words of the Irish writer, George Bernard Shaw: *"A life spent making mistakes is not only more honorable but is more useful than a life spent doing nothing at all."* Though he tried to draw solace from them, the words provided no comfort. Honor and usefulness had no meaning for him.

Brian Shaughnessy took a last sip of his Black Bush. Then he put the barrel of the Glock 19 into his mouth and pulled the trigger. It was an ugly, messy death. But not without irony, for much of his brains and blood and assorted other gore were splattered onto the tapestry behind him — the tapestry depicting a unicorn in front of a castle.

***

Upon arriving at the Jenkins Chapel the following Saturday,

263

Pastor Sutton was perplexed to find in the chapel's driveway an abandoned black BMW 7 series sedan. After Pastor Sutton called the State Troopers, and following their quick investigation, the Troopers informed the Pastor that the owner was one Fiona Cramer Shane. There was no trace of her in or near the Chapel or in the area nearby. And none was ever found, not even by Ranger Paul Larsen, who'd been called in to lead the search. Fiona Shane had simply disappeared into the Pine Barrens, never to be seen or heard from again.

What most intrigued Pine Barrens residents and folklorists about the matter was that shortly thereafter, sightings and reports began to emerge about the return of a Pine Barrens legend, the ghost of a haggard old woman who was seen wandering through the forest, the woman known as the Caretaker.

Chapter 35

Mrs. Bonvini looked with trepidation at the tall, muscular young black man standing in her kitchen, his head shaved, his arms tattooed, his face fierce in its concentration.

She said, "Well?"

Lamar scooped up a spoonful of macaroni and cheese, hefted it, looked at it carefully, and then tasted it.

"Damn, Mrs. B, you nailed it. This is as good as my Momma's."

Mrs. Bonvini placed her hand on his arm. "Oh, thank God, Lamar, you have no idea. I've been cooking pasta my whole life but I could never get the damn macaroni and cheese right."

"It's the half milk and half cream, Mrs. B. Too much milk, it runny, too much cream, it dry. Plus, that touch of mustard powder, cayenne, and fresh nutmeg give it that deep, rich taste. And the Parmesan in the breadcrumb topping knock it out of the park. You want me to bring this batch outside now?"

Mrs. Bonvini looked out of the kitchen window at the guests assembled in her back yard, who were all happily snacking, cooking, drinking, and talking.

"Why don't you pour us some more wine. And then maybe you and I should have another little taste of the macaroni and cheese, just to be sure."

Lamar smiled and poured.

Stick was sitting at one of the picnic tables in Mrs. B's back yard, talking animatedly with Sister Patricia Schaedel, the newly appointed Provost of Mount St. Benedict University. Each was enjoying a cold can of Colt 45.

Stick said, "Mustafa? A short, stocky, black dude with a sixties style Afro, wears them old time Granny glasses, that him Sister Pat?"

"That's him, Stick. He's a professor in the music department."

Stick said, "Yeah, he come into the club now and then. Talk a bit to the regulars and the rappers. He know his stuff. How he

265

involved?"

"Earl and I are putting together a combined music and English course where we look at the interaction of music and lyrics and how each supports and reinforces the other, and how they reflect the culture of the time. Earl analyzes the music, and I analyze the lyrics, like I would do with poetry.

"We're thinking of moving from blues to country to show tunes to rock and beyond. Rap would be a big part of that. Earl and I thought you might be able to contribute, like come to a class or two and talk to the students. Give them some insight into your creative process. We received a grant, so there would be a consulting fee for you. Would you be interested?"

Stick laughed. "I be 'Professor Stick' for a couple days? Hell yes, Sister Pat, just tell me when."

Pinky Plucinski was standing over the grill, keeping tabs on the Italian sausages, burgers, and chicken. He asked, "'Tay, you think these sausages are ready?"

Dontay and Sharelle were putting place settings on the two picnic tables in Mrs. B's back yard. Sharelle had brought flowers and was arranging them on the tables while Dontay was placing the plastic cutlery and paper plates and napkins.

Dontay said, "Poke one and see what you think, Pinkster. If it's not bleeding, it's probably good."

Pinky speared a sausage with his grilling fork and placed the whole thing in his mouth. He chewed, swallowed and said, "'Tay, I'll give them another few minutes."

Earlier, Dom and Lacey called Abner and invited him to the barbecue, but Abner politely declined, saying he had never been north of the Raritan River in over seventy years and didn't want to break his lucky streak. "But son, you and Miss Lacey be sure to come on down and visit anytime, be glad to see you, sure will, be glad."

Lacey said, "I'll tell you what Abner, when we do, we want you to be our guest at the Lower Bank Tavern. We'll eat buckets of wings and drink beer. How's that sound?"

"Sounds good, Missy, real good, yup it does. I'll be seeing you real soon."

In the backyard, Kate Culhane, having brought a huge bowl of homemade potato salad and a tray of brownies, was at the makeshift bar, preparing a batch of what she described as her famous "Toreador Sangria." As Kate explained, "After two glasses you'll be shouting Ole!"

Elena and Javier were on their way over, bringing additional treats — black beans and rice, empanadas, carnitas, fried plantains — and a wealth of desserts prepared by Elena herself.

Granny Pearl was seated comfortably in one of Mrs. B's lounge chairs, sipping some Tennessee sour mash whiskey and talking to Lacey and Ray Alexander.

She said, "You know, Dr. Ray, like I told my sweet child here, I believe it was that damn river caused all the cancer down the Hollow. Black families, Italian families, everybody grew some garden in the back yards of the tenements, shared what they grew. Used water from the river to irrigate the crops. Whippany River still flow right through in the back there.

"Hundred or so years ago, an old black man fell in there drunk and drowned. They say his ghost fouled the river forever. But I think it was the damn junk yard back up the street leaking all kinds of Lord knows what-all into that poor, damn, ugly river."

Dr. Ray took notes as fast as he could write. Listening to Granny Pearl's stories and memories, Lacey got a sudden thought.

"Dr. Ray, I've got a great idea! I'm thinking of Granny Pearl and Abner — and there must be all kinds of people who have wonderful, amazing stories. What about if we develop a course called something like "Living Folklore," and we bring folks like Granny Pearl to visit the campus, or we could take students on field trips, like down to Abner's, and we could listen and film and record their stories — live. We could publish or even create filmed documentaries. There are all kinds of things we could do."

Dr. Ray jumped on it. "That's a brilliant idea! First thing Monday, let's start to work on it. We'll invite Sister Pat in on it as well. Lacey, you are a gem."

Dom was sipping a glass of Chianti, watching and listening to the numerous conversations going on around him. He smiled. It certainly was a most unusual and diverse group of people — age ranges, life experiences, educational backgrounds, personal histories — they could not have been more different.

And yet, despite their differences, all of them seemed to share a deep engagement with life, an ability to feel and experience the world they were part of on a level and with an intensity many people never could or would attain — people like Shaughnessy, O'Bannon, Fiona, and Sarah, each of whom was, like Kurtz in Conrad's *Heart of Darkness,* "hollow at the core."

As he looked at the wonderful, eclectic group surrounding him, Dom thought that perhaps it was this ability to engage and to feel deeply that enabled them to recognize each other as kindred spirits, to feel a personal connection that transcended background or race or gender or station in life. To identify, empathize and say, 'this is one of my own. This is family.'

He thought then of Anthony and Theresa. They had raised him and encouraged him to feel this way, to experience all this, to struggle and rebound and retain a sense of wonder at it all.

Dom knew it was time to introduce Lacey to his folks.

***

Several days later, with the Loyal Sons scandal still making headlines, Dom and Lacey were relaxing at Dom's place on Wetmore Avenue. To Dom's delight, and Mrs. B's resounding approval, Lacey had eagerly agreed to give up her place over the Cheech and move in with him, thus beginning the next stage of their life together.

In the early evening, Dom was in the kitchen putting together a cracker and cheese and crudité platter and had opened a bottle of wine. Lacey was on the computer arranging the details for their upcoming trip to Naples, Florida, to see their folks.

The doorbell rang and Lacey called out, "I'll get it, Dom."

She opened the door to find standing there a slender, handsome, well-dressed man, probably in his early sixties. His demeanor was friendly but uncertain.

He said, "Excuse me, young woman, but I'm looking for a Dominic Rossi. Is he available?"

Lacey looked closely at the man, looked into his eyes, and immediately understood who he was. She said to herself, "Oh, shit." But then she said to the man, "One moment please, sir. I'll get him."

Dom called out, "Lace, who's that at the door?"

Lacey hurried into the kitchen and put her hand on Dom's arm.

He asked, "What's the matter? Who is it?"

"Dom, you better brace yourself. I think this is going to be a little awkward."

Dom went to the front door and looked at the man. "Yes, can I help you?"

The man said, "My name is Peter Bartoli. I am a professor of history at Princeton University. I know this is sudden and unexpected. I apologize, but I really don't know how else to say this, other than to just say it. I am your birth father."

Dom just looked at the man for several moments, trying get some sense of recognition, trying to identify and understand what he felt.

He finally said, "Well, I guess you'd better come in."

As soon as Professor Bartoli entered, Lacey appeared with a tray on which was a bottle of Scotch and two glasses. "I'll leave you two alone, I'll — "

Dom interrupted, "No, Lace, I'd really like you to stay."

"Okay, but I'm going to get myself a glass of wine. Maybe I'll bring the jug."

Dom poured them each a Scotch. Then he picked up his glass and said to Professor Bartoli, "I don't know what is on your mind or what you want to tell me, but to borrow from Shakespeare, *'there's no legacy so rich as honesty.'*"

Professor Bartoli smiled. "*All's Well That Ends Well.* May it prove to be true."

Lacey, who was watching from the kitchen, breathed a huge sigh of relief and took a generous swallow of her wine. Then she joined them in the living room.

Bartoli said, "Your adoption was meticulously arranged, so I've always known who you are...and who you've turned out to be. Your life has been interesting and full, your accomplishments impressive. And if I understand the events of the past few weeks, it has not been without excitement and controversy. In any event, my goal today is to introduce myself and leave the door open for future contact, on any basis, if you should want that to happen. If not, I will wish you well and disappear from your life."

"Who was my mother?"

"Veronica Maggiore, a brilliant and beautiful woman. With a personality like a thunderstorm."

Bartoli went on to explain that Dom's mother was from Bologna, Italy. He said, his smile wistful, "She was fair-haired and had eyes as green as the sea, like your own. She was part of a student exchange program. I was her professor of European history.

"We became lovers; she became pregnant. I was married at the time and had more than my share of ambition. It was not possible for us to have a life together, and I'm not sure it would have worked out. Each of us was too selfish, too willful. But we wanted our child to live. So, we arranged for the adoption. We could not have been more pleased with the couple that adopted you. They loved you from the very first moment."

"What happened to my mother?"

Bartoli took another drink of his Scotch and said, with more than a touch of sadness, "She returned to Italy and became married several years later to the scion of one of Italy's great motorcar manufacturers. Tragically and ironically, she died in childbirth not long after their marriage. It is one of the great regrets of my life."

"Do I have any siblings?"

"You have a half-brother, Vincent, in Washington, DC. He's three years older than you, career military, Army Intelligence. He is a very good man, with a lovely family, a loving wife and two young daughters. "

Dom was silent, taking it all in.

Bartoli finished his drink. "So, Dominic, I do not mean to upset or disturb you. But I wanted...I needed you to know how you came to be. I will leave you now."

Bartoli looked at Lacey and said, "I can see your life is full indeed. Should you ever wish to contact me, I will always be available. If not, I will understand."

Then, Bartoli stood, shook Dom's hand and then Lacey's, and let himself out.

Lacey hugged Dom. "How are you doing, partner?"

"Shaken, but good. It was good to hear."

"What do we do now?"

"We finish making plans to visit Naples. I'm really looking forward to seeing my Mom and Dad."

Epilog

The beach at Delnor-Wiggins Pass State Park is located on a barrier island a few miles north of downtown Naples. It is one of the most pristine and inviting beaches along the southern Gulf Coast. Clean, never crowded, beautifully maintained, it is a delight. Picnic tables and grills are set back from the beach, under pines and palm trees and, blessedly, not too close together. The beach itself is wide and deep and lovely. Porpoises are a frequent sight, an estuary of the Cocohatchee River flows into the Gulf on the north end, and the sunsets are stunning.

A thoroughly relaxed, languorous Lacey was stretched out on a beach blanket next to Dom, baking in the early June sun. Her electric pink bikini, which could have fit into a shot glass, revealed the long, clean, elegant lines of her body.

She said, "If you promise not to start anything funny right here on the beach, you can put a little more suntan lotion on my back and legs, please."

Dom replied, "I'm not sure I can make that promise."

Lacey rolled over and glanced at him. "Well," she said with a smile, "in that case, I guess it's time to head back to the bungalow, sailor."

Their evening plans called for them to head back over to Anthony and Theresa's for cocktails and dinner. Lacey's parents would join them there. There was much to celebrate — and plans to make.

The day before, Dom and Lacey had flown into the airport at Ft. Myers, rented a car and headed to their tiny rental bungalow on the Cocohatchee River, only about six or so miles from each of their parents' places in Naples. Both were nervous and excited. Meeting the parents for the first time is almost universally anxiety producing.

After unpacking and settling into their bungalow, they had taken a quick shower, then went out and purchased a bottle of Veuve Clicquot champagne and headed off to Anthony and Theresa's.

Dom's folks lived in a gracious gated community, in a typically Spanish-style Florida ranch house with a beautifully maintained yard and flower gardens, a screened-in porch with a pool, and situated right on the canal.

On the way there, Dom said, "Last time, Lace, are you sure about this?"

"More than I've ever been sure about anything. Let's do it."

As soon as they pulled into the driveway, Anthony and Theresa had rushed out to greet them, all smiles and hugs and kisses.

Dom put his arm around Lacey and said, "Mom, Dad, I'd like you to meet the girl I'm going to marry."

And the celebration went on from there.

CPSIA information can be obtained
at www.ICGtesting.com
Printed in the USA
BVOW03s0225120117
473313BV00001B/72/P